Vacationland

Susan X Meagher

Vacationland

THIS TRADE PAPERBACK ORIGINAL IS PUBLISHED BY BRISK PRESS, BRIELLE, NJ 08730.

EDITED BY: CATRIONA BENNINGTON
COVER DESIGN AND LAYOUT BY: CAROLYN NORMAN AND ANN MCMAN

FIRST PRINTING: DECEMBER 2017

ISBN-13: 978-0-9987907-1-8

By Susan X Meagher

Novels

Arbor Vitae
All That Matters
Cherry Grove
Girl Meets Girl
The Lies That Bind
The Legacy
Doublecrossed
Smooth Sailing
How To Wrangle a Woman
Almost Heaven
The Crush
The Reunion
Inside Out
Out of Whack
Homecoming
The Right Time
Summer of Love
Chef's Special
Fame
Vacationland

Serial Novel

I Found My Heart In San Francisco

Awakenings: Book One
Beginnings: Book Two
Coalescence: Book Three
Disclosures: Book Four
Entwined: Book Five
Fidelity: Book Six
Getaway: Book Seven
Honesty: Book Eight
Intentions: Book Nine
Journeys: Book Ten
Karma: Book Eleven
Lifeline: Book Twelve
Monogamy: Book Thirteen
Nurture: Book Fourteen
Osmosis: Book Fifteen
Paradigm: Book Sixteen
Quandary: Book Seventeen
Renewal: Book Eighteen
Synchronicity: Book Nineteen
Trust: Book Twenty
United: Book Twenty-One

Anthologies

Undercover Tales
Outsiders

Acknowledgements

Many thanks to Sandy Thornton and Jaycie Morrison for providing feedback and advice on Dallas and Texas in general.

Gemma pointed out some inconsistencies that I never would have noticed, so I'm very thankful for her sharp eyes.

Catherine Lane's advice helped in more ways than I can count. Without a doubt, the story is significantly better due to her perceptive insights.

Dedication

To my beloved wife Carrie who is the most selfless partner a woman could hope to have. I'm incredibly lucky to have found her, and I hope I'll always merit her love.

Chapter One

THE BRIGHT, SHARP *BRRRRRING* OF the alarm clock nudged Devin Savary to toss the down comforter from her body, set her stockinged feet onto the floor, and shuffle across the burnished pine. Three steps later, she grasped the clock and silenced it. For a few seconds, the ringing continued in her ears, then an ethereal stillness settled upon the cabin.

Even though she was dressed in only a bright red union suit and thick wool socks, she wasn't cold. Spending the time, money and effort on properly insulating the cabin had been worth every cent, but a relatively warm cabin didn't make the next part of her morning routine any easier. Room temperature water was still damned cold, but she dutifully filled a basin with it, then splashed it onto her face, yelping in shock when it stung like a thousand needles. Once she caught her breath, she washed every part that was strictly mandatory for interaction with other people, then slipped into a sports bra and a fresh set of long underwear.

Now that the calendar insisted it was March, she had high hopes that the long underwear would soon be unnecessary, but since they still had three feet of snow on the ground, soon was a relative term.

Today, she chose a sky blue wool turtleneck for her middle layer, mostly because she liked the color. Having a sexy woman from Portland tell her the color made her eyes even more vivid had influenced her clothing choice more than she'd ever admit. But her outer layer was purely practical—waterproof, wind-resistant, and lightweight. And no one could accuse her of picking slate for any reason other than the fact that it didn't show dirt as much as black did.

After putting on wool socks and a headband to keep her hair from her face, she was almost ready to go. Cracking the door open, she stood in the entryway for a minute, listening for signs of life. Only the hardiest birds overwintered, and she helped them out by keeping a feeder. They were still silent this morning, but they might show up later. The sliver of pinkish orange light at the horizon bore the promise of a sunny day.

She sat on the top step, slipped her feet into her skates and laced them tight. Then she added mid-weight wool gloves, covered them with waterproof shells, and carefully descended the few stairs to stand on the ice.

With her first few strides, she concentrated on getting the kinks out of her body. Thankfully, she hadn't had to work hard this week, so the kinks were blessedly few.

Often, she towed a lightweight sled behind her, but the cabin was well stocked with pellets for the stove, food for the birds, and a few snacks for herself. Going across the ice without drag let her really air it out, and soon she was gliding across the silent lake, going as fast as she could while keeping a sharp eye out for obstacles. Even though dawn was a minute or two away, there was plenty of light to make the trip safely if you knew where you were going—and no one knew this path better than she.

With a flash, the sun peeked above the horizon, making everything sharpen and snap into soft focus. If only there were a way to freeze everything—this weather, this moment, this stillness—she'd do it in a second. Dawn on a clear day in early March was just about perfect. Cold, but not too cold. Sunny, but never hot. Quiet, but not desolate. Of course, too much perfection would be just as bad as too little. If you didn't have black flies and mosquitos and sunburn and tourists you'd never appreciate mornings like this. And Devin was appreciating the hell out of this one.

Her commute took about ten minutes, mostly because she'd loafed a little on the last stretch. This dawn was just too pretty to let it slip by unappreciated. But all good things must come to an end, and she was at the pier before she knew it. She placed her hands on the rough wood, then powered herself up until her butt was well above the planks. Twisting, she sat on the pier to remove her skates. The shower sandals she'd shoved into the waistband of her pants let her get across the street without getting her socks wet, and she quickly reached the outfitter's without sliding or slipping on the ice.

The bell over the door jangled pleasantly, then Edie's always calm, always friendly voice called out from her office, "Help yourself to whatever you want, Devin. I know you're hungry."

"No doubt," she called back.

Edie wasn't a mother-substitute, since Devin was very fond of her own very capable mother. Her boss was more like an older sister who fussed over her exactly like a mother would. Smirking to herself, Devin went over to the coffee bar and made herself a hot cocoa. It tasted so much better with steamed milk. Fresh whipped cream didn't hurt, either, and she called out, "Thanks for whipping some cream."

"Leftover from last night," Edie said. "Wish I'd been able to save a piece of pie for you, but Mike demolished it."

"Did you have Lacey and Nick and the grandkids over?"

"Uh-huh," Edie called out, clearly distracted.

Devin took the hint and let her work. Her boss spent her early mornings fussing over phone messages and deliveries, leaving her guides to fend for themselves. That was exactly how Devin preferred it. In fact, that was the main reason she only worked for Edie, rather than making herself available to multiple outfitters.

The under-counter refrigerator was a real treasure chest today, also holding some of Edie's homemade yogurt. After tossing in a little granola and a sliced banana, Devin sat at the bar and enjoyed her breakfast while reading the *Piscataquis Observer*. Other than the death of a ninety-year-old man she didn't know, and a story about local kids making the honor roll at school, there was nothing new under the sun. She assumed she'd learn more about current events if she read the *New York Times* or *Boston Herald*, but she was pretty happy deluding herself into thinking that the world was just fine. Ignorance was often blissful.

"I'm going to put all of the down coats on sale to create some space," Edie called out. "Take a look if you want to snap one up."

"Okay." She was a lightweight-layering fan, but her mom had been after her to own a proper winter coat for those times when they had a family event, like a special dinner or a wedding. Maybe this was the year. She had a few hundred bucks left in her gear allowance, and wouldn't need a single thing until fall. After finishing her yogurt, she poked around the racks, shying away from light colors that would show mud, looking up when Edie finally walked onto the retail side of the floor.

"Anything you want…half-price," she said.

"You can't make money selling coats at half-price!"

"I make plenty of money off strangers. You get the extra special employee discount."

Devin looked up and watched Edie bustle around the counter, checking the register. She was a Mainer through and through, just like Devin's people. They often teased Edie's husband for being a newcomer. Mike's folks had only been in Piscataquis County for three generations.

Edie's short, greying, sandy brown hair was still damp from her shower, her wet head a luxury people who drove to work in a big SUV could afford. If Devin tried that, she'd get frostbite of the scalp. Other than the damp hair, Edie looked like she almost always did—a sixtyish, slightly stocky, fit woman who often appeared as if she'd just heard a mildly amusing joke. Somehow, no matter how many cranky, demanding customers they had, no matter what the weather did or didn't do, Edie was always smiling a little.

"Try on that navy blue goose down," she said, pointing toward the higher-priced merchandise. "The one that goes down to your shins."

"This one?" Devin held up a navy blue coat with a fur-trimmed hood that cost more than she earned in her best week. "I don't need anything like this."

"Try it on," Edie insisted. "That's the coat all of the rich people from Boston like."

"What part of me reminds you of a rich person from Boston?"

"Try it on." Edie walked over and held the coat up, dressing Devin like she was a toddler. "Now let me see you." She took her by the shoulders and turned her, assessing her from every angle. The coat did fit nicely, coming all the way down to touch her wrists—a rarity for a woman's coat. But Devin could make do with much less—happily.

She started to wriggle out of it, but Edie stopped her. "You look great in that, kiddo. I really think you should get it."

"Not at this price. Even half of a whole lot is too much for me."

“I’ve got one in the back that has a flaw in the hood.” She slid the coat from Devin’s body and hung it back up. “It’s not a big flaw, but no one wants to pay this kind of money unless the coat’s perfect.”

“They have to take that back,” Devin said, scowling.

“They will, but they said they’d sell it to me for next to nothing. You can have it for two hundred.”

“Two hundred?” That was still an awful lot to pay for a coat. She put it on again and walked over to the full-length mirror, almost ready to bite. As she turned to look over her shoulder, the doorbell tinkled and a woman with strawberry blonde hair entered—wearing the exact same coat in black.

“Buy it,” the woman said, revealing a friendly smile. Then she used her heavily gloved hands to slap at her arms, while jumping up and down in fur-covered moon boots. “You’ll still freeze your butt off, but you’ll look good doing it.”

Given that the weatherman said it was going to top twenty-five degrees, Devin pegged the woman as an out-of-towner. Her accent, from somewhere south of the Mason-Dixon line, just made that blatantly obvious.

“You must be Sunny,” Edie said, walking over to shake her hand. “I’m glad you made it.”

“Only got lost three times,” she said, her bright grin showing she hadn’t minded.

Devin tried to discretely check the woman out while taking off the coat, which was making her sweat. Sunny had the kind of face that made you smile back, even if you weren’t in a smiling mood. Bright eyes, lots of color in her complexion, and a ton of body in that reddish blonde hair. She looked a little more substantial than some of their Boston clients did, many of whom were painfully thin, but that might have been the coat.

Devin would have bet good money that this woman hadn’t spent any time worrying about whether she could afford the luxury of a crazy expensive coat. Something about her said that she was the kind of person who just slapped her credit card down and didn’t blink when the total climbed to astronomical heights.

“Devin,” Edie said, “come over and meet one of your clients.”

Given that she'd just planned on snagging breakfast and using Edie's wifi, Devin fought against her surprise for a second or two after she'd ditched the coat. Edie never threw a trip at her without notice, but it sure seemed like she was about to do just that.

Devin extended her hand and waited while the client took off her expensive, leather-covered down mittens. When their hands met, Devin had an irrational instinct to hold on for a while. Not because the woman's hand was so soft and warm, even though it was. It was simply nice to have her hand somewhere on a pretty woman's body, even momentarily. She shook her head, trying to get that thought to leave in a hurry. Clearly it was time to get over to Portland or Bangor and hook up again. When you couldn't bear to release a woman's hand, you needed to top up your tank.

"Sunny Thompson," the woman said. Devin liked to play a game where she guessed where people were from, but she hadn't heard enough words to nail this accent yet. *Tennessee? Kentucky? Louisiana?*

"Devin Savary," she said, snapping out of her musings when Sunny's hand bumped hers and they shook.

"That's a pretty name," Sunny said. "It sounds French."

"My dad's great-grandfather was from Quebec, so I guess he was French," she said, not having much interest in her genealogical roots. "What are we doing today?" she asked, turning to Edie. "A moose safari?"

Edie gave her an overly sweet smile. The kind she used when she was trying to con Devin into something awful. "You're taking over for Matt. Come on back and I'll tell you all about the trip."

Devin tried not to glare. If there was one thing she hated, it was taking over for another guide. She'd rather walk to Canada after planning her own trip than drive clients across town without adequate prep—and Edie knew it.

The doorbell tinkled again and two men came in, filling the store with just their presence.

"What's taking so long?" the larger guy asked. He was tall and stocky and looked like a stuffed sausage in his massive dark green down coat. But it was his voice that grated like fingernails on a blackboard. Loud and harsh and loaded with… What did her mom call it? Entitlement. That was the perfect word. He acted like they should all start doing exactly what he wanted that very second.

Sunny turned and regarded him with what looked like studied patience. Kind of how Devin treated quarrelsome clients.

"We're getting organized," she said, her soft, calm voice not rising to meet his volume.

"You've been getting this set up for months!" His coat made a 'shush-shush-shush' sound as he stalked across the space to stand in front of Devin. "I'm not in the mood to wait around for the next three days. We should've been ready to go." He stuck out his hand and a huge silver-colored watch flashed in Devin's eyes. Then a meaty finger jabbed at the crystal. "You said eight, and it's eight ten."

Edie jumped in. "Edie DeLomelle," she said, extending her hand. "Sunny and I have everything planned, but your guide, Matt, has the flu. Devin's taking over for him."

"A woman?" His head turned slowly, and he spent a minute looking Devin over. She wasn't sure what criteria he used, but she could tell she didn't meet it. His gaze moved back to Edie. "I want what we paid for. You said this Matt guy was your best, and that's what I want."

"I don't think I said that," Edie maintained, still smiling. "I think I said *one* of my best. That list definitely includes Devin. She's been guiding for fifteen years."

"If a bear chases us, she's going to stop it?"

Devin replied before Edie could. "One, a bear's not going to chase us." She used the same tone of voice she had for the second-graders she'd instructed in cross-country skiing the day before. "And two, if the unthinkable happened, I could dispatch it."

"You've killed a bear?" he demanded, narrowing his eyes and staring at her without blinking.

"One every year since I turned fifteen," she said, also trying not to blink. "That's during hunting season, of course, from late August to late November. They're hibernating now. I'm guessing we won't spot our first one until mid-April."

"She really knows what she's doing?" he asked Edie. Although why he'd believe her was a mystery. She was a woman too.

"Of course she does. When my grandkids want to go camping, I send them with Devin. Only Devin," she added. "My other guides are good, but she's the one I trust with what's most precious to me."

"All right," he grumbled. "Where can I get a cup of coffee?"

"I can get you one," Edie said. "What would you like?" She moved over to the coffee bar, with the jerk right on her heels. The other guy hadn't said a peep yet, but now he walked over to Devin and extended a hand.

"Julian Gonzales," he said. "Just for the record, I don't have a problem going camping with a woman guide." He was a few years younger than the other guy, and a whole lot handsomer, with a shock of black hair that he'd combed back with some kind of gel. That made his hair gleam almost as much as his teeth, which were stunningly white against his golden skin. "Now I've just got to figure out why I'm in Maine—camping."

"We're bonding," Sunny said quietly. "We're learning how to rely on each other while we're being chased across a frozen lake by a hungry bear."

Devin let out a soft laugh. "Maybe I'm not the right person to take you, because I'm not planning on being chased by anything."

"Hank," Sunny said, adding, "that's his name, by the way. I noticed he never introduced himself."

"I probably would have learned it eventually, but that's nice to know," Devin said.

"Hank listened to some book-on-tape about people who were stranded in the wilderness. That inspired him to believe we'd be a better team if we went through some kind of ordeal." She rolled her eyes, which were just a little darker blue than Devin's. "I don't know why we had to come this far, or why we had to be cold to prove we're a team, but…"

"He's the boss," Julian finished for her. "Well, not technically, but…"

"Kinda guessed that," Devin said. "I'm going to go get our gear ready. I don't want him to throw a tantrum."

"He's the kind of guy who makes other people have tantrums," Sunny said. "All the time."

"Then I'd better get moving." Devin went into the equipment room and found a big pile of stuff Matt had already set out. She was going down her own mental checklist when Edie poked just her head inside.

"Are you going to shoot me?"

"I might," Devin grumbled. "After I take out a few bears."

Entering the room, Edie put her hand on Devin's back and gave it a brisk rub. "What was I supposed to do? They flew in from Texas, honey. He'd sue me for breach of contract if I didn't send them out."

"I know, I know," she muttered. "What's the plan?"

"Three days. Cross-country skiing, ice-fishing, and snow-shoeing."

"Three days? They don't look seem winter camping people."

"No, they don't, but that's what they want. I tried to get them to come a week earlier, when the lodges were still open, but Hank wouldn't hear of it. 'No safety nets' was his mantra."

"Great," she muttered. "Novices who don't want safety nets. Fantastic."

"Matt got fishing permits for all of them," Edie said, adding a bright smile.

"I don't like this," Devin said, looking up and meeting her eyes. "I hate having to rely on Matt's planning."

"This is a no-brainer, Dev. Really. You can easily cover seven miles today, then set up camp. Tomorrow's supposed to be nice, and you'll spend the whole day ice fishing. Then you're back home on Sunday. You've done more complex runs with ten-year-olds."

"I know that," she said quietly, "but I'd planned the trip."

Edie put her arms around Devin and gave her a very maternal hug. This was the worst part of working for someone you liked so much. It was impossible to stay mad when you thought of your boss as family.

"I'm sorry," Edie said, "but if you don't take them, I'll have to."

Devin pulled away, laughing as she did. "Well, that would be… interesting." She filled her arms with sleeping bags and started for the door. "Will you get them set up with ski boots? Hank's in a hurry."

"So I've learned," Edie said, letting out a perturbed sigh.

Sunny watched as Hank attempted to grind his finger through his phone. There didn't seem to be much point to the gesture, but that wouldn't stop him.

"Damn cell signal!" he barked before slamming the device onto his thigh. He went through two or three phones a year, so many his assistant kept a spare one in her desk.

"You're the one who wanted to be remote. You made the bed, so lie in it," Sunny said. She could see Julian's eyes widen slightly. He was a very even-tempered guy, never seeming to mind Hank's outbursts, or having the need to respond to them. He'd proven himself good at reading people, figuring out his way around Hank in an afternoon.

"This is the United States of America," Hank growled. "There shouldn't be one square inch of this country that isn't covered by screaming fast internet."

"Well, there are many inches that aren't, and you brought us to one. So put your phone away and we'll concentrate on bonding," Sunny said, chuckling at the outraged look on his face. She tossed him a pair of size thirteen boots. "See if your dainty little feet will fit into those."

That perked him up. He loved to wedge in a sexual reference wherever possible, even when no one in the group was in his target audience. "Big feet, big—"

"Big socks," she finished for him, then sat down and tried to get her own big feet into a pair of tens. Her mother often suggested she just wear the boxes, but that jibe had never struck her as funny.

Devin strode by, shower sandals slapping the wooden floor as she carried another load of stuff. Discretely, Sunny checked her out. She'd never been overly attracted to the strong, silent type, but she wasn't so set in her ways that she couldn't expand her preferences. There was nothing wrong with a tall, dark haired, broad-shouldered woman who looked like she wouldn't have to shoot a bear—she'd just wrestle one into submission.

"She's not your type," Hank said, chuckling when she turned and blinked at him.

"How do you know what my type is?"

He looked at Julian and said, "She's been after the same kind of girl since we were in law school. Brainy, drab women in pantsuits. No makeup, no jewelry, no perfume. I don't see why she doesn't just go for a guy. Same difference."

So many responses flitted through her mind it was simply too easy to pluck just one out. But she gave into the knee-jerk response and said, "So...you'd be just as happy with a pretty drag queen?"

"What?" he gulped. "Fuck, no!"

"Then explain your logic. If the only thing that matters is how stereotypically feminine a woman looks, some drag queens make bio women look like guys."

"Bio women," he groused. "They're women. You don't need to add anything."

"Right. I like women, Hank. The ones I like might not spend the better part of a week having their hair and nails done, but they're still women."

His cheeks reddened and his voice grew rougher. "I *appreciate* the fact that Angelica spends her time making herself look nice for me. That shows respect."

"I'm glad you're happy." She patted him on the leg. "See? I'm an adult who realizes your choices have nothing to do with me. Why don't you try that?"

"Maybe you should actually get—and keep—a woman. Then we'll talk."

Julian's eyes had grown comically wide. But there was nothing funny about Hank's tossed-off comment. It was either purely insensitive or insensitive and mean. Either way, she wasn't going to sit there and listen to him for another second. Getting up, she caught Devin on her way back to collect more gear. "Let me help you," Sunny said.

"I've got it," Devin said. "Why don't you have a cup of coffee?"

Sunny stayed right where she was, wounded at Devin's dismissal, even though she realized that was beyond dumb. But she was stuck, not willing to be near Hank, and not needed elsewhere. Edie must have heard the exchange, because she bustled over and took her by the arm, leading Sunny to the coffee bar.

"Wouldn't a hot cocoa be nice?" she asked as they walked the short distance. "Or maybe a cappuccino? I've got the only professional quality espresso machine within seventy-five miles, and I can make anything you can get in Texas."

Sunny cleared her mind and smiled at Edie's thoughtfulness. "Cocoa would be great."

"Did Devin give you the wifi password?" Edie asked as she started to work.

"Wifi?" Sunny's smile grew. "She didn't mention it."

While checking her mail, perversely pleased at the thought of Hank not being able to do the same, Sunny sat at the bar and thought about Hank's snarky jibe while the machine noisily warmed her milk. He could be *such* a jerk. Sometimes it seemed he went out of his way to wound people. Even though they were a fast-growing, up-and-coming firm, sometimes the money didn't make up for the bull crap. It wasn't her fault Hank's self-esteem was as easily punctured as a child's balloon.

She looked up when someone poked her in the back. Then a black stocking cap with white stripes, made by the same company who'd made her coat, dangled in front of her face. "I bought this for you," Hank said. "I don't think that hood will keep you warm enough."

"Thanks." She took the hat and stowed it in her pocket. "But I'd rather have an apology. You went out of your way to hurt my feelings, Hank, for no reason."

"Sorry," he said, dropping his chin to give her what he clearly thought was a cute half-grin. That might have worked when he was three, but his own mother had probably grown tired of it by now. "It sounded like you were making fun of Angelica."

She faced him, then spent a few seconds assessing his expression. There was a vulnerability in that childish mien that she found herself giving into again and again, unable to push her advantage. "I have never made fun of Angelica. *Never.* That's not something I'd do, and you know that."

He still wasn't able to make direct eye contact, telegraphing his hurt feelings. "Angelica spends a lot of time getting her hair and nails done, but that doesn't mean she's dumb," he muttered, still stuck on Sunny's innocuous comment.

"Do you have PMS?" she asked.

His head snapped up as his mouth opened. Luckily, he was able to tell from her expression that she was playing with him. An uncharacteristically soft laugh was a pleasant surprise, so much nicer than the braying, donkey-like guffaw he usually pulled out. "Maybe I do. Is there a term for being in a really shitty mood because your phone doesn't work?"

Edie had obviously been listening, for when she handed over the cocoa —with whipped cream, she said, "We have wifi. The password is L-a-c-e-y."

His dark eyes danced with happiness. "Sweet Jesus, why didn't you tell me that before?" He stabbed at his screen, grumbling about having had wifi turned off. Then he was gone, talking to himself as he walked over to the hiking boot display and dumped himself onto a rustic wooden bench.

"I could be wrong, but he seems like he's wound a little tightly," Edie said, her dry humor making Sunny laugh.

"You're not wrong. Why he wanted to come up here, I'll never know. But I guarantee he'll lose his mind being without his phone for three days."

"Just one day, really," Edie said. "Today's Friday, and he'll be able to use it until you take off, then he'll have it on Sunday when you return. Just one little day where he'll be off the grid."

"He's like a two-year-old," Sunny said, "and being without his security blanket is going to drive him stark-raving mad."

Chapter Two

Devin stood in the storeroom with her hands on her hips, shopping for gear. Edie had given her the all-clear to take whatever she needed, but she didn't want to take advantage of her. Ideally, she'd run back to her cabin and get her favorite boots, but Hank would have a fit at the delay. She'd normally wear hiking boots for snowshoeing, but couldn't convince herself to snag both ski boots and another pair for hiking. Even though Edie would keep half of the cost of the trip, Devin had to play fair. So she decided on a new pair of backcountry ski boots, bright red, which would look nice with her plain white skis. Just before taking off she spotted a new box of survival wrist bands and took one of them, too. Lastly, a hot pink wool buff which she pulled over her head, then checked it out in the mirror. You couldn't be warm enough around your neck, and this would let her pull it over her face if the wind picked up.

Now set, Devin made herself another cocoa to go and they all piled into the truck. Edie owned two vehicles the guides used to transport clients, a six passenger SUV, and this truck, a 4x4 with a roomy crew cab, powerful enough to roar through just about anything. One time Devin had wrapped the winch cable around a twenty inch diameter pine that had fallen across a road and dragged it out of the way like a cardboard tube. But the truck had a hundred thousand miles on it, and going over dirt roads was always a tooth-loosening joy ride. Luckily, the dirt roads were still well packed with snow, and the improved roads were completely clear.

Sunny sat in the front, leaving the back seat to the guys. While Sunny was definitely better to look at, Devin now had Hank's harsh voice right behind her head. She always carried pain relievers in the first aid kit, and was sure she was going to be the first to need one.

Partly to stop Hank's stream-of-consciousness ramblings, she raised her voice and spoke over him. "We're going to have to drive around an hour to reach the trail head."

"An hour!"

"Yeah. We're going to a remote place, into the middle of a hundred miles of wilderness. No paved roads, no houses, very few signs of human habitation."

"If it's so remote, how do we get in? I'm not walking a hundred miles," Hank grumbled.

"Logging roads." She shrugged, assuming someone would have a comment about having roads cut through wilderness. "Some people hate the industry, some couldn't survive without it, but you can't argue that the roads have made otherwise inaccessible places reachable."

She took a quick glance into the rearview mirror, glad to see that Hank's short attention span had been taken up by his phone, which she was sure was already out of the reach of Edie's wifi.

They'd barely traveled a mile, but civilization was now only visible in the rear-view mirror. The northern faces of the tall pines that lined the road were still all white, thanks to the storm that had dumped nearly a foot on them just a week ago.

Sunny must have been looking at them too. "Seems a shame to cut such beautiful trees down," she said, a wistful tone making her normally quiet voice even softer.

"They don't log around here," Devin said. "You've got to go looking for the land where the paper companies harvest from. I'm not sure about all of Maine, but no one's spoiling the view around here."

Sunny faced her, and even with just a peripheral view Devin could see her smile. "The view around here is fantastic. I honestly had no idea it would be this pretty."

"You're from…?"

"Dallas," Sunny said.

"Mmm. I've never been to Texas, but I bet this looks different."

"Texas is better," Hank decreed. "I like to look out and see what's around me. There's nothing better than standing on a mesa and looking across hundreds of miles of wide-open beauty. Who knows what's hiding behind all these trees?" Devin could see him glare at them when she snuck a look in the rear-view mirror. "It's creepy how they're everywhere you look."

"Spent much time in cold weather areas?" she asked, meeting his gaze in the mirror.

"Sure. I go to New York all the time. Boston. DC."

"But you stay in the city, right? You don't rent a car and drive to the Catskills or the Berkshires."

He let out a derisive laugh. "What would you rather do? Go out for a first-class dinner and stay in a four-star hotel, or drive to some cabin in the sticks?"

"Cabin in the sticks," Devin said without waiting a second to reflect.

"Well, then," he said, putting on a thick Texas accent he normally didn't use, "aren't you just the luckiest little filly in town?"

They'd been traveling for about an hour, and even Sunny was getting a little sick of Devin's safety lessons. Clearly, she was obsessive about making sure they took all of the proper precautions, but Hank had checked out long ago, now instructing Julian on a deal he was about to close on. He really shouldn't have been using the client's name and details of the whole thing, but Devin wasn't paying him any mind at all. She was still talking in a very precise way, repeating things she'd obviously said many times before.

"I suppose the message I want everyone to fully understand," she said, letting her head turn to fix her pale blue eyes on Sunny, "is that there's safety in numbers. No matter what, don't go off alone, and don't leave anyone behind. Bad things can happen in the wilderness, but four people can find a way over or through or around just about anything. When one person's alone...you're tossing the dice."

"I'm certainly not going to take off on my own," Sunny said. "I was in a snowstorm at a ski resort in Colorado, but that's the full extent of my cold weather experience."

"A real storm? How long were you stranded?"

Sunny was laughing by the time Devin finished the question. "More like we went inside the lodge and drank beer while we watched it come down. I thought it was an awful lot of snow, but the people who worked there didn't blink." She paused, letting Devin's laugh die down. "The beer was awfully good though."

"I like beer too," Devin said. "We brew some good ones up here."

"I don't like anything too fancy. No blueberries or chocolate for me. Just a good, crisp lager."

"I like ale, but I'm not all that particular. If I'm thirsty enough, I'll drink anything cold."

Sunny turned her head to gaze at the unbroken line of pine trees they'd been passing since they'd left the outfitter. The further they drove, the higher the blanket of snow that enveloped them. Here, many of the trees looked like they didn't have trunks at all, just graceful green branches neatly hovering in space. "Speaking of cold," she said, pointing at the landscape like it was a secret.

"It's not cold at all," Devin said, laughing softly. "We've had some wicked cold weather this year, but I think it's past now." She leaned forward to peer up at the sky through the windshield. "We got lucky today. This is the first time we've seen sun in well over a week. Pretty soon now the snow's gonna start to melt."

"Then you'll lead people on nature hikes? I can just imagine how pretty it would be here with fields of wildflowers popping up all over."

Devin let out a short laugh. "We're not known for our wildflowers. Besides, not many people want to hike during mud season, and this year's going to be a doozie. I just hope we don't get a string of really warm days, or we'll flood like crazy."

"Mud season?"

"Uh-huh. Most places have four seasons. We get five. Spring, summer, autumn, winter and mud. It's usually from mid-March to mid-May."

"The mud is...where?"

"Everywhere there's dirt. That includes an awful lot of roads up here. Hiking paths, trails... My parents' have almost a half mile of unpaved road to get to their house. When a really bad snowstorm hits, even a four wheel drive can't get down that road."

"Oh, no, not for me," Sunny said.

Devin smiled, looking a little gleeful. "When they're expecting a bad one, my parents keep their cars at a neighbor's place that's just off the paved road. Then they ski or snowshoe out to their cars to get to work."

"Then I'm glad we're here while the snow's still on the ground," Sunny said. "I've seen what rain can do to dirt roads. We've got a lot of them in Texas." She thought about that for a second. "Funny how one substance can cause different problems. We have dust storms that can scare the bejesus out of you."

"We'll have to have a competition to see which state sucks worse when it comes to dirt," Devin teased.

"Texas wins," Hank piped up. "Whatever you're talking about, Texas wins."

They were just about fifteen minutes from the trailhead, and Hank seemed to have finally finished lecturing Julian about some kind of deal. Devin was sure she'd rather shovel manure all day than work in an office, but whatever Hank was talking about sure did seem to excite him. He used his big hands when he talked, jabbing his finger in the air and making slashing motions so rough Julian almost took one in the chops.

She hadn't spoken in a while, and she cleared her throat to say, "How much experience do you all have in cross-country skiing?"

"None," Hank said.

"None," Julian agreed.

"Lots of downhill," Sunny said, "but never cross-country."

She didn't have time to count to ten, but Devin sure wanted to. Why would you specifically ask to go on a three-day cross-country trek if you had no experience?

Sunny jumped in, probably noticing Devin's unhappy expression. "We all run or hike or work out at the gym. Since we wanted to cover some ground, Edie said the easiest way to do that was on skis."

"That's true," Devin agreed. "But what if you don't like it? It's not hard to learn, but the land around here sure isn't flat."

"That's why Edie suggested snowshoes. They're our backup."

"Okay." Devin shut her mouth. They were in it now, and she couldn't very well turn the truck around based on her worry that they might have an awful time. She took a look at Hank, who'd opened his coat, showing a beer-gut hanging over his belt. If he was a runner, he needed to increase his mileage.

A short time later they pulled into the parking lot that the Appalachian Mountain Club maintained. It was a big lot, and there were only three other trucks in it. *Perfect.* They probably wouldn't see another soul.

They all got out, with the air feeling like a warm balm to Devin after their grindingly long winter. But her guests acted like they'd just fallen into a deep freeze. Camping out was going to be a real party with these babies.

"Jesus," Hank groaned. "I thought it was supposed to warm up today."

"It is warm," Devin said. "I bet it's thirty degrees."

"I do better with heat," he said. "When I played defensive tackle in college, I could get through two-a-day practices even in August and not keel over."

Devin tried to imagine Hank in a three-point stance, slightly reassured that he'd been an athlete—at one point. "I don't think you'll need to recover from too much heat up here, but once we get moving, you'll be toasty."

"Hope you're right," he said. "If it's too cold, we're going back."

Her wish for the temperature to immediately plunge wasn't granted. "Why don't I give you a quick lesson?"

Ignoring her suggestion, Hank said, "Why's this parking lot so big? I said I wanted to be out in the wilderness."

"This is plenty wild. The AMC grooms the trails, but you'll be thankful for that. Going back-country skiing is for people with a *lot* of experience."

Sunny had walked over to the luggage pickup shelter, and was now carefully reading the posted instructions. *Jesus!* The three of them were like toddlers, wandering off whenever the slightest thing caught their attention.

"There are lodges throughout the wilderness," Devin said, raising her voice so Sunny could hear.

"But we're not going to one, right?" Sunny asked, turning to face her.

"We couldn't even if we wanted to. They closed up last week. Won't reopen until summer and camping season."

As Sunny started to walk back, she said, "So you can leave your gear and have someone pick it up?"

"Uh-huh," Devin said. "You can ski or hike from lodge to lodge and have your stuff waiting for you when you arrive. Nice service," she said. "Which you could have used if you'd come a week earlier."

"No help," Hank insisted. "We're going to rely on each other. That's how you build a team."

Devin wasn't sure that was true, but she didn't have a dog in that fight. "We've got around three feet of snow on the ground," she said. "The trail's are groomed, and packed firm. As long as you stay on them, you'll be fine."

"What if we don't?" Julian asked, slyly shifting his eyes to Hank.

"You'll find out the hard way," Devin said. "We've got snowshoes for when you need to leave the trail. I'd heartily suggest using them, along with your poles. You'll sink a few inches, but you can walk in the deepest snow." They all seemed to have listened, so she started for the truck. "I'll get our skis and give you a lesson."

Hank looked at the bed of the truck, which was not exactly stuffed, but was pretty darned full. "It's going to be hard to carry all of that yourself, isn't it?"

She smirked at his not even having the decency to offer to help. "The sled I've got can handle it all. You just have to carry your own backpacks."

"Mine's heavy," he complained.

"Then you might want to dump some of the weight. Didn't Edie advise you to travel with as little as possible?"

"I thought you'd have some kind of…wheelbarrow or something."

She tried to think of how that could possibly work, quickly realizing she was wasting her time. "I've never seen a wheelbarrow that could carry a heavy load through deep snow. But if you find one, let me know."

Sunny picked up Hank's backpack, one big enough for a trek across Europe for an entire summer, and let out a groan. "What have you got in here?"

"Stuff," he said defensively, grabbing it back from her. "And I need all of it."

"You're going to have to carry it yourself," Devin said, not willing to give in. She'd wind up carrying some of their gear—she almost always did—but she didn't want to start off overloaded. That was just dumb.

"I can handle it." He put the backpack on and nearly tumbled over backwards, with Devin barely able to stop herself from laughing out loud.

"Give me a minute to get used to this," he said. "I have to drag these two on my back most of the time, so it won't be hard."

Sunny gave him a sharp look but didn't comment. Julian just looked like he didn't want any trouble. Poor guy. As if working in an office wasn't bad enough, he'd gotten stuck with a huge jerk.

After handing over skis and poles to each of them, Devin wiggled her own skis from the roof of the truck and stepped into the bindings.

"Why are your boots taller and bulkier than ours? Did Edie stick us with junk?" Hank demanded.

"Of course not. Mine are for back-country. They let me go off trail when I need to, but that's something you won't have to do." She picked up the lightweight black boots they'd chosen from the rental stock. "These weigh a lot less. You'll be glad for that as the day goes on." She tossed the proper boots to each of them, trying not to laugh when Hank bungled the handoff.

"Why don't you want these?" he persisted, glaring at her colorful boots.

She grabbed her poles and started to move across the hard-packed snow. "Every piece of gear represents a compromise. These boots paired with these skis give me maximum flexibility, but at the expense of speed. Your thinner, longer skis will let you glide along a groomed trail faster than I'll be able to go, but mine will let me blaze a trail if we need one."

"I don't question your motives," Sunny said, with her cheeks beginning to turn pink from what Devin considered really mild weather.

"Me either."

Wow. Julian was getting frisky!

Hank, seeing he was outnumbered, said, "I'm not questioning anything. I just want to know what's what."

"Let's get going on that," Devin said. "We've got seven miles to cover, so we'd better shake a leg."

⌖

Sunny trailed behind Julian as they moved around the big parking lot, practicing. It wasn't hard, not nearly as hard as sliding down a mountain on downhill skis, but she could see it would take a little time to refine her technique. Julian was doing fine, even though his stride was short. He was in good shape and would be able to lengthen and smooth out when they got going. Hank looked more like a wooden toy than a man, not bending his knees at all, and using jerky motions to propel himself. But he'd be all right, too. As he often boasted, he'd been a star football player. Maybe he'd get a burst of muscle memory and be gliding along in no time.

Devin was working like a dog, loading an amazing amount of gear in a very precise fashion onto a sled easily big enough to transport one of them. Sunny shivered when she realized that was probably its purpose. Or maybe her shivering was from the dang cold that Devin didn't seem to feel.

Finally, Devin had the sled filled, and she signaled the group. "I know I sound like a mother loading the car for a long trip, but everyone should pee if they can."

"I can," Sunny said. "Where?"

Devin tossed her head toward the trees that surrounded the parking lot. "The snow isn't deep here."

"Really? No portable toilets?"

"Not a single one," Devin said. "We can spread out to give each other some privacy." She grabbed a box she'd stowed in the door of her truck. "I've got some baby wipes if you want them. I've got a trash bag for carrying out everything we use. Just toss them in there when you're finished."

They all complied with no complaints, which must have pleased Devin. After they'd all gotten their skis back on, Devin hooked a kind of harness around herself, with shoulder straps and a wide nylon belt. "I'll bring up the rear," she said. "I'm guessing Hank wants to be in front?"

"How'd you guess?" Sunny said, laughing at the face Hank pulled. "Give me a break," she said. "The moose hiding in the woods know you have to be in charge."

"Only because neither of you are natural leaders," he sniffed. He put on a pair of dark glasses, settled his stocking cap on his balding skull, then stuck out his chin and started off, jerkily, down the groomed trail.

After they'd labored for about a half hour, Sunny looked up at the mild hill in front of them. If you'd had some momentum, you would have barely noticed it on downhill skis, but the narrow little sticks they were using might make it challenging. Devin had assured them the raised pattern on their skis would let them climb short hills, but Sunny was still a little apprehensive. Not because she was afraid of such a small incline, of course. She just didn't want to look like a klutz.

From the corner of her eye, she saw a flash, then Devin was passing them—fast. She'd left the sled behind, and was zipping through the deep, ungroomed snow like it was a slick track. Her poles were longer than theirs, and she used them with effortless efficiency, either pulling herself or pushing herself—it was impossible to tell how she was moving so fast—but she was like a scalded cat!

When she got next to Hank, she executed a kick turn, whipping around so fast that Sunny couldn't have even said which direction she'd moved. The whole maneuver took maybe a second, and she laughed when she saw Sunny's face.

"Don't you do kick turns when you ski downhill?"

"Not like that! I have to stop and think for a second, then I move kind of like a turtle."

"I've been skiing since I was three, so I don't recall learning most of this." She stuck her poles in the snow and clapped her hands together. "Ready for our first hill?"

"Let's go around it," Hank said, eyeing it suspiciously.

"That's fine if you want to add about four miles to the trip. But I guarantee you can do this," she insisted, her enthusiasm fairly infectious. "Your skis will let you zip right along. Just start up and keep going.

Stopping can make you slide down backwards, and that tends to freak people out a little."

"Would a herringbone be easier?" Sunny asked.

"Maybe," she said, nodding. "Let's see." She did that ridiculously quick kick turn again, then went to the base of the hill and turned the tips of her skis out. The hill wasn't very long, only taking her twenty full steps to get to the top. Sunny counted while she stared at her butt, which looked as hard as a rock. The amazing part was that those twenty steps took her mere seconds. It was more of a run than a climb, but after she did another insane turn, this one causing both skis to leave the ground for a moment, she came back to them, not even breathing hard. "I think it's easier to just go straight up with the classic style, but feel free to try something different."

Hank seemed very unhappy, but he started, looking a little like a cartoon from a kid's flip book—with some of the pages removed. His movements were painfully jerky and stiff, but he put his head down and made it to the top, where he paused—then fell onto his side, going down like he'd been hit by a shotgun blast.

Devin raced up the hill, reaching him so fast Sunny hadn't realized she'd moved.

Julian watched carefully, musing, "If he's hurt, I don't want to have to carry him."

"We'll come back later with a crane," Sunny agreed, chuckling. "But I really hope he's not hurt."

After she braced herself and easily pulled Hank to his feet, Devin said, "All clear. Next victim."

"I think she's staying there so she can pick us up when we fall," Julian said grimly.

"You'll be fine. Hank just let his weight shift over to one side."

"There's a lot of bourbon, beer, and barbecue in that gut," Julian said, laughing quietly. "It took a right when the rest of him didn't."

"Let that be a lesson to you," Sunny called out to his back as he started up. "Learn from your elders' mistakes."

CHAPTER THREE

THEY WERE MAKING DECENT TIME for beginners, about three miles per hour. Since they were only trying to punch through seven miles in total, Devin decided to stop early for lunch to allow them a long break to recover. The stand of trees she'd chosen had very little snow around it, allowing them to ditch their skis and not have to bother with snowshoes. She hadn't brought camp stools, so she unfolded a waterproof tarp, then lay down the thin, inflatable pads they'd lie on that night. Her three fairly happy campers sat in the sun, while she got lunch ready.

She hadn't yet used the new gadget Matt had been raving about, but it was fantastic, letting her boil two cups of water in under two minutes. Given that the whole thing, including fuel, weighed less than a pound, she was stoked.

"I've got vegetable korma, pad thai, mushroom risotto and smoked three bean chili," she said after sorting through the supplies. "Pick your poison." She slapped her hand over her mouth, then shook her head. "Bad choice of word. These are really darned good."

"How can you get risotto out of a little bag?" Hank asked.

"Freeze dried." She picked up a packet and tossed it to him. "These are locally made, and they're the best I've had. They won't rival a good home-cooked meal, but they've got more flavor and spice than anything else I've tried. And believe me, I've had them all."

"Risotto sounds good to me," Sunny said.

"Don't you have anything with meat?" Hank was frowning, having clearly expected her to shoot and roast a turkey or something.

"I brought some dried beef. That might be good in the chili."

He was shaking his head while she was still speaking. "My mom makes the best chili in Texas. There's nothing in a little bag that's going to compare."

"I'm sure you're right. But your mom's not here, so we've got to make do. How about penne with marinara sauce?"

"I guess," he sighed.

"I'll take any of them," Julian said. "They all sound good when I'm this hungry."

"I'm with you on that," Devin said. "Let's try the pad thai and the vegetable korma and see which one we like the best. Is that good for you, Julian?"

"Perfect."

She fed Hank and Sunny first, mostly because she could tell Julian wouldn't mind waiting for the second batch of water to boil. They sat on the ground, crosslegged, to have their meal. "Really good," she said, taking a bite of the pad thai.

"It is good," Julian agreed. "But I think I like the vegetable korma even better. Is this Indian?"

"I guess so," Devin said. "But I'm not very familiar with anything exotic. We don't have much of an international dining scene up here."

"You should come to Texas," Hank said, as he shoveled his penne down with lightning quick speed. "We've got everything, but our Tex-Mex is the best. World class."

"I'll check it out if I ever get down there," she said, knowing she never would.

She'd eaten faster than she normally did, and had finished while Sunny was still daintily picking at her risotto. Then her system signaled her and she grumbled to herself. Try as she might, she couldn't convince her body that noon wasn't the ideal time to get rid of solid waste. But it didn't do any good to argue. She stood up, grabbed a disposable glove, and excused herself. "I'm going to answer nature's call. I'll be gone for a few minutes, so don't worry about me."

Sunny looked up, with her fork suspended halfway to her mouth. "You're not supposed to wander off alone. You made that very clear."

"I'll be able to see you," Devin said, touched by her concern. "I just like to go well off the trail. I promise I'll be fine."

"I should go with you," Sunny said, scrambling around to get her feet under herself.

"No, really. Finish your meal. I'll come back and get you in case you have to go too." She pointed at the water bottles she'd filled with melted snow. "We're not leaving until you've each finished one of those, so drink up." Then she slipped on a pair of snowshoes and took off before Sunny could follow, since she knew from experience that an audience might stop her from going at all.

On her way back, she slowed and then stopped when she saw Hank and Julian pouring water into two more dinner packs. "Really?" she asked as she removed her disposable glove and put it with the other trash. "You know, the meals we had for lunch were each made for two people."

"Sorry," Julian said. "But I was really hungry."

"For what we're paying, we should have a chef meeting us when we stop," Hank said, obviously guilt-free. "I'm not going to go hungry."

"I brought extra meals, but only a few," she said. "Just remember we've got six meals to go." She went to the sled and counted, even though she knew exactly what she had. "I've got twenty-four packets left. No more spares." She didn't mention that she also had twelve energy bars, and a few cans of tuna, along with the dried beef. Hank was the type to gobble it all up when she had her back turned.

Devin picked one of her favorite winter sites for their campground. It was a swamp in summer, but that little depression let even a strong wind blow right over it, sometimes barely ruffling the tent flaps. She strapped on her snowshoes and tamped the snow down, making the site as level as possible.

Everyone was very compliant, doing exactly as she instructed, probably because they were all exhausted. They'd really need to sit around the fishing camp tomorrow and have a day's rest before they had to ski home.

She was working on getting the first tent set up when Hank walked up to her and crossed his arms over his chest. "I hope you've got four of those," he said, frowning at the bright green tent.

"I've got two. It might seem like it'd be better to be alone, but having two people in one small tent provides more warmth. Just breathing helps heat it up."

"So…me and Sunny and you and Julian?"

She looked up at him, puzzled. Sunny didn't look very gay, but Devin had caught a few lingering glances that made her think she might be a member of the club. But even if she was straight as a stick she definitely didn't seem like someone who would put up with Hank. But people continually surprised her, so much so that she'd stopped trying to figure them out and just went along for the ride. "Whatever you guys want is fine with me."

Hank looked over at the others and called out, "Me and Sunny in one, Julian and Devin in the other."

Julian just nodded, but Sunny's head snapped up. "The hell you say! I'm not sleeping with you."

"Well, I'm not sleeping with Julian," he sniffed.

"Grow up," Sunny said, giving him a very perturbed look. "I can guarantee Julian doesn't want to look at your hairy butt."

"I really don't," Julian agreed, nodding dramatically.

"I'll sleep with any of you," Devin said. She let out a sly laugh. "Or alone if you all want to jam in together. That would help you bond."

"You and I are sleeping together," Sunny informed Devin, with a tone that brooked no dissent. "Girls in one, boys in the other."

Hank's laugh had an evil edge to it when he said, "Two of us are bio boys as you say, but you're not very far from one, Sunny. Devin might prefer to sleep alone, since I know you'd like to get a look at her butt."

"I fear none of you," Devin said. She met Sunny's eyes, feeling a bit of sympathy for her when her cheeks got a little pinker. Working in an office would be bad enough. But working for a guy who poked you all day long wouldn't be worth any amount of money—to Devin. Clearly, she and Sunny didn't share that belief.

Sunny sat on a rolled-up sleeping bag, watching Devin put the finishing touches on their campsite. She had a really cute habit of moving her lips while she went down a list in her head. Sunny'd also seen her touching the tips of her fingers as she counted out meals and bottles of water, which was kind of charming too. But the silent checklist was cuter.

Two years earlier, Sunny had tried—hard—to date a woman who seemed to have it all. She was smart and kind and playful and darned attractive. But she'd been a flake. A serious, unapologetic flake. Always late, always losing her wallet or her keys, forgetting plans they'd made, and generally being scatterbrained. Gretchen had offered to keep an eye on Sunny's houseplants when she'd been away for two weeks, and every single one of them was dead on her return. Given that they were soaking in water, she could only assume Gretchen had come by once—probably that morning—and tried to make up for two weeks of negligence. If Gretchen hadn't been transferred to Houston, Sunny would have had to break up with her. Being the only adult in the relationship would have gotten old at some point.

Watching Devin stand there in front of the tents, hands on her hips as she carefully surveyed the layout, made it clear she was no Gretchen. Devin would no doubt water your plants, she'd also polish the leaves.

Devin's head turned a little, and their eyes locked on each other. Immediately, Sunny felt heat on her cheeks. Why did she always get caught when she was trying to check a woman out?

"I'm going to walk over to the lake. Anyone want to come along?" Even though Devin's invitation technically included all of them, she looked only at Sunny.

"I'm down for the count," Hank said. He grabbed his backpack, then stopped to pick up an inflatable pad and a sleeping bag. "I've got time for a nap, don't I?"

"Sure do," Devin said. She turned her head to catch Julian's attention. "If you want to nap, use our tent so you can have a little more space."

Sunny got up and started to walk toward the lake, then heard Devin call out from behind, "You might want a pair of these." She held up a snowshoe just in time for Sunny to step off the groomed trail and sink into snow so deep she was sitting on it.

"Need a hand here," she said, laughing at herself.

Devin buckled herself into the snowshoes, then jogged over, standing on the trail and looking down at Sunny, not even attempting to hide a big smile. "Remember what I said about staying on the trails?" She stuck her hand out, settled her grip around Sunny's wrist, then pulled hard, lifting her most of the way up. Then Devin set her feet again, grasped both of Sunny's forearms and gave another forceful pull, nearly yanking her off the ground.

Sunny brushed the dry snow from her ski pants, then stood up. "How about getting me a pair of those snowshoes. If I go myself, you'll just have to keep pulling me out."

"Happy to. Don't go away now," she said, laughing a little as she raced back to camp. It only took a couple of minutes to get the snowshoes affixed to her boots, then they started off across the fluffy snow, sinking down just a few inches.

"If I'm going anywhere difficult, I take my poles," Devin said. "But we've only got about a hundred yards to the lake, all flat."

"This is odd," Sunny said, having a hard time getting used to the lightweight but longish devices. It was harder to walk than Devin made it seem, and Sunny resigned herself to the fact that her quads would be crying for mercy by the next morning."Your snowshoes are different than mine," Sunny said, after taking another look. "Actually, everything you have is different from our stuff."

"Not really. I'm sleeping in the same tent, with the same sleeping bag. And I'm definitely eating the same food." She smiled, seeming more open and unguarded than she did when they were all together. "I've just got different snowshoes and skis." She shrugged, still grinning. "And poles. And boots."

"Yours are better," Sunny said. "But I won't tell Hank."

"They're better for *me*," she insisted. "Like these snowshoes. They're much too long for you with the tails I've got on them, but they'll let me get through any depth of snow. I don't plan on trekking through deep powder, but if I have to—I can."

"You're all about quality equipment," Sunny said. "I appreciate that."

"Nah." They walked around a small stand of trees to get their first unspoiled view of the lake. "I'm all about this." She took in a deep breath, sending out a cloud of vapor when she exhaled. "I could make do with the cheapest, most beat-up gear around, but I couldn't be happy if I was too far away from a place like this."

"It's gorgeous," Sunny breathed.

"In every season. A hundred and twenty square miles of awesomeness. Some parts, like this, are wide, some narrow, but she's a long and lovely beauty."

Sunny gazed at the lake, seeing distant, tree-covered hills in every direction, hugging a long, flat span of snow-covered ice that she couldn't even begin to measure. "Have you been all around it?"

"Uh-huh." She smiled again, her expression a lovely mix of peace and happiness. "I've explored every inch. On snowmobiles, skates, cars, trucks, canoes, sailboats, stand-up paddleboards, fishing boats, dinghies, inner tubes—"

Sunny slapped at her shoulder. "Trucks? What in the world…?"

"I don't do it much anymore, but I raced when I was a kid. In the winter," she added, chuckling. "You put some studded tires on a truck you don't mind getting dinged up and let 'er rip."

"How old a kid were you?"

"Mmm, I think I started when I was ten. As soon as I could reach the pedals, my dad let me go. My grandpa was into it too, so it was a whole family affair."

"My mother would have put her foot down if someone tried to take me ice racing," Sunny said. "Of course, they'd have had to transport me across state lines to find ice…"

"My mom knows I understand how to do things as safely as possible," Devin mused. "But I assume she'd prefer I took up some indoor hobbies."

"You don't have any indoor hobbies?"

This time her smile had a good measure of playfulness behind it. More than a hint of flirtiness too. "None I get paid for." She pointed at a spot on a distant bank and said, "If we walk out there, we'll be able to see the sun set."

"We can walk on the water? Really?"

"Really. The ice is at least three feet deep on this part of the lake." Devin took a confident first step, then settled herself and held her hand out to steady Sunny.

"I'm good," she said, now secure with her footing. "But it's darned odd to be walking on water."

"I do it every day, so it seems normal to me. In about a month, that won't be true though. There's a long period where the ice is too dangerous to walk on, but too thick to paddle through. Those in-between periods are the only times I don't like the lake. It tempts me, but won't let me in," she said, laughing at what she clearly realized was an overreaction.

"I'm not even going to ask if you're a local," Sunny said. "There's no doubt."

"Grew up in Abbot. Maine's number one town."

"Really? I haven't heard of it. What makes it number one?"

"First in the phone book," she said, chuckling, obviously having used that joke before. "It's about twenty miles south of Greenville." She blinked, then added, "That's where the outfitter is. Greenville's the big town around here."

Since Greenville was about the size of a postage stamp, Sunny spent a minute wondering how small Abbot must be. They walked a little farther, letting them get far enough away from all of the trees to gain a direct view of the setting sun.

"This is glorious!" Sunny found herself exclaiming. "I've never seen anything so pretty!"

"I know," Devin said quietly. "With the mountains in the background, all of those beautiful trees covered in snow, then this gorgeous ice..." She stuck her hands into the slash pockets of her pants and stared at the sunset with all of her attention. "Sunset and sunrise. Which one's prettier?" Sighing once again, she said, "I can't pick."

"I've got to get my phone out and take a picture." Sunny had to take off a mitten to reach it, but she finally pulled the phone from her pocket.

Devin reached for it and said, "If you stand right there, I can take a good one. It's taken me a while, but I've learned how to angle the phone to get some detail on the trees. Practice, practice," she added.

Sunny smiled for the photo, then took the camera and tugged on Devin's sleeve. "I don't want everyone to think I was all alone. Stand by me and we'll do a selfie."

Devin gamely moved to stand close, then Sunny turned the phone and took a few. She didn't have Devin's experience, so the trees were just a dark line behind them, but the sunset looked fantastic. "One more," she said, this time turning so the sun was on their faces. "We were just dark blobs on that one."

"Can't have everything," Devin said, grinning for the camera. "The sunset's nice, but I prefer photos of people when that golden light's on them. I love that light," she added, sounding like she was about to launch into a poem she'd written for it. This woman loved being outside.

The sun dipped behind the trees in seconds, and its warmth went right along with it. "Dang! It got cold in a hot second!"

"It does that," Devin agreed. "We'll have our dinner, then hunker down in our tents. We'll be warm." As they walked back, she said, "I'm guessing you haven't spent a lot of time in cold weather."

"We get some cold days. It's not odd to have sleet and freezing rain in the winter, although we lose our collective minds when that happens."

"Mmm," Devin said, adding nothing more.

"You don't think that's real cold, do you?"

"Sure it is. It's all about what you're used to. I took some people from Nunavut out not long ago. I was freezing, but they acted like they were barely cool."

"Nunavut?"

"A territory in Canada. A cold one," she added, grinning.

"So this is your full-time job?"

"Uh-huh. The only one I've ever had, and I'll keep doing it until I can't keep up."

"That's going to be a while," Sunny said, not having to pause to assess Devin's hardiness. She'd already spent enough time checking out her butt to know she had a lot of years left in her.

By six o'clock, her evening meal of vegetable korma was just a memory, but Sunny could have easily wolfed down a burger if she'd had access to one. The warm and vaguely spicy meal had taken the chill out, and as she watched Devin arrange the dried tree limbs she'd gathered for a fire, she mused that moving constantly probably aided in Devin's claim that she found the weather very temperate.

They'd all had the lecture about how easily a sparking fire could melt their synthetic clothing, so they were each covered with a woolen blanket. After Devin got the fire going, she removed her jacket, which was, to Sunny's surprise, about as thick as the rain jacket she wore on chilly days in Dallas. Then each of them exchanged first puzzled, then startled looks as she unfastened her nylon pants and whipped them off.

"You guys don't mind if I sit here in my underwear, do you?" she asked, casual as could be.

"No!" Sunny said, wincing when she realized how loud her response had been.

"It's just that I'm sweaty, and my windproof layer traps more moisture than I'd like. I always need to dry out a little before I go to bed."

"Maybe you should take the next layer off too," Hank said, clearly trying to be funny. "I don't want that synthetic to melt."

"All wool," she said, with the light from the fire highlighting her features.

Sunny knew she shouldn't stare, if for no other reason than Hank would be watching her. But she cared more about getting a good look than she did Hank's teasing. Dang! Devin was a walking, talking work of art—if you liked lean women with legs as sturdy as tree-trunks—which Sunny was finding that she did.

Hank had been right, of course. Damn his beady little perceptive eyes! She'd always gone for women who looked like professors or engineers or computer programmers. She'd never—not once—been interested in an athlete or an outdoors-woman, but her tastes were clearly changing because she was attracted to Devin. Seriously attracted to her. Attracted in a way she hadn't been in a heck of a long time.

She watched Devin hop to her feet and prowl around the campsite, checking to make sure they were all protected from flying embers, that their base layers weren't wet, that their feet were warm. Finally, she sat down on one of the inflatable pads and pulled her backpack onto her lap. "I think we deserve a treat for all the work we did today." Eyes glittering in the crackling firelight, she pulled out a sleeve of Graham crackers, four chocolate bars, and a sandwich bag full of marshmallows.

"S'mores!" Sunny yelped, unreasonably happy at the thought of toasted marshmallows melting into chocolate.

"I've had my daily chocolate, but I guess I could have some more," Hank said.

Sunny fixed him with a glare. "You brought chocolate and didn't share?"

He shrugged. "It's good for my heart. I like a seventy percent cacao with chili."

"You are such a precious little thing," Sunny said, laying it on thick. "If yuppies didn't exist you'd have had to invent them."

"You won't complain when I offer to share another thing I brought." He tossed off his blanket, with Devin leaping to her feet to grab it before it settled onto the snow. She stood there patiently, not commenting as Hank went into his tent and emerged with a bottle of his favorite whiskey.

"Well, now I know why your pack is so heavy," Sunny said. "Chocolate and whiskey."

"And pork rinds," Julian added, flinching when Hank shot him a warning glance.

"You brought pork rinds?" Sunny said. "You can't go three days without them?"

"They're my favorite snack," he sniffed. "I worked off fifty thousand calories today. I need to keep my strength up."

Just to annoy him, Sunny didn't respond. He was smart enough to know he'd burned no more than an extra thousand, so he was clearly trying to get a rise out of her. But she happily accepted the bottle and took a healthy swig. “Nice,” she said, not usually favoring hard liquor, but finding it hit the spot tonight.

Devin didn’t have any, and Julian dropped out after one modest pull, but she and Hank kept it going for a couple more rounds, with her sips matching his gulps. “That’s fine whiskey,” he said, wiping his mouth with the back of his hand, trying to look like a cowboy in an old Western.

After whittling points onto four sticks, Devin slid a couple of marshmallows onto each and they all focused on toasting their treats to perfection. It was messy, but they all got the job done, with Sunny moaning from pleasure as the warm, rich, sticky sweet goodness congealed into a few bites of perfection. “Best thing I’ve ever eaten,” she pronounced.

“I can’t argue with that,” Julian said. “I was afraid we’d just have some kind of drab energy bars. This shit’s fantastic!”

“I’m glad I had room for everything,” Devin said. “Safety equipment has to come first, but if I can manage it I always bring a treat.”

“I’m going to treat myself to some shut-eye,” Hank said. “But I guess I’d better take a leak first.”

Devin bounced up to her feet. “I’ll go with you.”

He pointed to a spot a few feet from the tents. “I’ll just go there.”

“No, no, that’s not okay,” Devin said. “You want to pee well away from the campsite. Scientists think that bears are attracted to the salt or just because it’s a unique smell, but they’re curious about human urine. We’re not going to risk it.” She paused before adding, “Even though they’re hibernating.”

“Oh, for Christ’s sake,” he grumbled. “I’ve always got to get up in the middle of the night. Are you saying I’ve got to get dressed and put on snowshoes to take a leak?”

“I brought some sturdy zipper-lock bags you can use. But you don’t want to fill one up now.” She moved over to the sled and picked up a pair of snowshoes. “Come on. It won’t take a minute. Julian? You too?”

“I guess I’d better.”

Both of the guys got up, with Hank putting up less of a fuss than Sunny expected. Devin led them over to a stand of trees, with a super bright flashlight illuminating a wide swath of snow.

While they were gone, Sunny added a few more tree limbs to the fire, feeling cold now that she had nothing to distract herself. Then she let her head drop back while she took in the magnificent show the stars were putting on. It was like being out in the middle of West Texas on a clear summer night—nothing but stars so plentiful that the sky looked like it had been painted with them.

It seemed like a half hour had passed, but the threesome finally returned, with Hank mumbling a quiet "goodnight" as he walked directly into his tent, followed by Julian, who looked like he'd rather sleep in the woods.

Devin took off her snowshoes and placed them neatly next to the entrance to their tent, then she wrapped Julian's blanket over her shoulders and tucked Hank's over her legs. Leaning over, she quietly said, "Glad to know I'm not the only one who has trouble relaxing when I know people are waiting for me."

"I was just thinking about how jealous I am of your job." Sunny tried to muffle a giggle, but wasn't successful. "Changed my mind."

"I'll admit that supervising people's private time is more pleasant in warm weather. Then I only have to warn them about snakes and things like that. Convincing people to wipe with a snowball takes all of my salesmanship skills."

Sunny swallowed nervously. "No more baby wipes?"

"I have plenty of them. I prefer snow, but I acknowledge I'm odd."

"I should go. I haven't been since the parking lot."

"We'll go before we hit the rack. You're not ready for bed yet, are you?" She checked her watch, which glowed in the dark. "It's only seven thirty."

Chuckling, Sunny said, "I could probably sleep, but I don't want to wake up at four."

"My ideal sleep schedule is nine to five, but I often wind up reading until ten or so. I still wake at five though, until daylight saving time, which takes me weeks to adjust to."

"Mmm. I can't imagine going to bed that early on a routine basis. I'm usually grabbing something to eat when you're going to bed."

"You work that late?"

"Sometimes much later than that, but not often. My usual is to stay at the office until seven. Then I swing by the gym on my way home and work out for an hour. By the time I stop and get something to eat, it's close to nine."

Chuckling, Devin said, "You'd be a big time night owl around here."

"Not really. I eat while I catch up on my favorite shows, then fall asleep in front of the television."

"No TV in my cabin," Devin said, "so I don't have that temptation."

"No TV?" Sunny exaggerated her wide-open eyes. "I can't imagine living without one!"

"Well," Devin said, grinning impishly, "I guess I could get one, but I don't have electricity, so it'd just be a hat rack."

Sunny stared at her for a moment, certain she was kidding. But when Devin simply held her gaze, she said, "I think you're teasing, but I honestly can't tell."

"I'm not teasing. I don't have running water either."

"What?" she squeaked. "How do you live? How do you stay warm? How do you…use the bathroom?"

She held up her hand and tugged on a finger as she answered each question. "Just fine, thank you. By wearing warm clothes and keeping a fire going. And…keeping myself on a schedule. If I really have to go, I have some containers I can use and dispose of. But I don't use them very often." She tapped her temple. "I've done a good job of training myself. Kinda like a housebroken dog."

"We're hardly members of the same species," Sunny said, amazed that someone around her age lived like her three times great-grandparents had. "You honestly live in a cabin?"

"I do," she said, smiling serenely.

"I know people who have cabins on a lake somewhere, but they just use them for the weekend. You know. When they're roughing it."

"I don't feel like I'm roughing it," she said, her smile so cute Sunny was tempted to lean in just a foot or so and kiss those pretty lips. "But I go to my parents' house all the time. They've got lights and refrigeration and a normal toilet and a washer and dryer and even a great big TV. I can only stand to stay a day or two, but it's nice to have little bursts of the twenty-first century."

"Do you have a car?"

"Uh-huh." Her smile grew. "I guess I could ski there in the winter, but that's a little much—even for me."

"I'm…speechless."

"I love it. No chatter, no hum from the refrigerator, no little blue lights from the electronics, no ringing phone. I'm perfectly happy in my toasty little cabin."

"So you live there alone?" She wasn't going to put on the full-scale charm offensive if Devin had some poor woman hidden in that freezing cabin out in the wilderness.

"I do. Always have."

"Always?"

"Yeah. I had a girlfriend for a few years, but we didn't live in the cabin." She let out a soft laugh. "You'd be surprised at how many people don't want to live in an unheated cabin with no electricity." She tilted her head toward Sunny. "Given that Hank outed you, I can safely ask if you've got a girlfriend."

"Isn't he a charmer?" She could talk about him without fear of being overheard, since both he and Julian were noisily sawing logs.

"I wouldn't choose him for a boss, but there aren't many people on that list." She batted her eyes, and asked the question again. "Girlfriend?"

Sunny let out a sigh. "I haven't had a live-in, committed, exclusive girlfriend since three years after I graduated from law school. And that's been a thousand years."

"I bet it's been around seven," Devin said, looking at her carefully. "Eight at the most."

"Eight's the number," Sunny agreed. "Are you always good at guessing people's ages?"

"Uh-huh. I'm pretty good." She lowered her gaze and stared at Sunny's mouth for a few seconds, giving her a *zing* that made her shiver. "But I never would have picked you as someone who wasn't lucky in love."

Sunny reached back and clapped Devin on the back. "That's where you're wrong, my friend. My luck hasn't been very good at all."

Devin stood at the edge of the copse of trees, stomping her feet to stay warm. She'd put her jacket and pants back on, but the wind had picked up a bit. Nothing severe, just a steady ten miles an hour, but it still felt like it was cutting right through her clothing. Dressing in light layers was perfect when you were moving, but it was a little short of ideal when you were standing around waiting for a woman to finish doing her business.

"Finally," Sunny said as she struggled to get her clothing in order. "There wasn't one tiny little part of me that wanted to do that, but I managed to convince my bladder it only had two choices—right now or in a tiny tent with another person two inches away. It admitted defeat and went along with the program, albeit reluctantly."

Devin turned on her flashlight and illuminated the path back to the tent. "I've got my bladder trained so well I have to remind myself to go."

"I'd be going every time I passed a bathroom if I didn't have a toilet in my apartment!"

"It's not like I never go," Devin said, chuckling. "I just make sure to go before I head home for the night."

"Speaking of night, what do I do if I have to go again? I don't think I can hit a little sandwich bag in the dark."

"I brought a cool little thing. Looks like a funnel with a short tube on the end of it. You press it against yourself and direct it wherever you want. Really handy."

Sunny gave her a blank stare. "I'll hold it. That sounds like a whole lot of trouble."

When they reached the tent, Devin bent over and unzipped the flap. "I'm going to take off my outer layer out here," she said. "I hate wrestling around with my stuff in a tiny tent."

"It is tiny," Sunny agreed, eying the space suspiciously. "I've only been in big tents. The kind where you can keep a couple of huge coolers and still have room to move around."

"This isn't that kind of tent. Go on in and I'll give you a minute to get your coat off."

Sunny started to step in, but Devin stopped her. "Step out of your boots now. Your sleeping bag's right at the opening and I know you don't want snow all over it."

"Won't they freeze?"

"I'll knock the snow off them and put them in a gear bag. Go on," she urged.

After removing her jacket, pants and sweater, Devin stood in the entryway and put their boots into gear bags, then quickly sat down and zipped the tent up. As she turned, she saw Sunny atop her mummy-style sleeping bag, coat lying across her lap, looking uncertain.

"Advice?" Devin asked.

"I'll take all you've got."

Chuckling, Devin took off her socks. "If anything's damp or wet, take it off now. For me, that's always undies and socks." She started to peel off her long underwear, finding it cute that Sunny immediately averted her gaze. Then she chucked her wet things into the corner, pulled the tights back on, and added another pair of fresh wool socks. "I normally put my undies into my sleeping bag to dry them, but Edie felt bad for not giving me more notice about the trip and snuck two nice pair into my bag. Gotta keep an eye on her or she'd give away the whole store."

"I think I'm dry. I didn't work nearly as hard as you did."

"Maybe not, but dampness isn't your friend. Did you bring extra?"

"Oh, sure. I've got plenty of clothes."

"Then I'd change." Just in case Sunny was too embarrassed to change in front of her, Devin opened her sleeping bag and slipped inside, sighing with pleasure as she rolled over, facing the wall. She bundled up her outerwear, rolling everything into a neat cylinder, which she used as a pillow. Once settled, she heard a lot of nylon swishing around, so Sunny must have been following her advice. Then a similarly pleasured sigh indicated she'd finished.

"You should have room, so take your boot bag and stuff it down by your feet. You'll be happy to have them nice and warm in the morning."

"My feet are pretty cold now. I don't want them to get any colder."

Immediately, Devin sat up, with the tent so low-slung she almost hit her head. "Unzip and kick one of your feet over here."

"Kick one of my…?"

"Give me one of your feet. Come on."

With a suspicious look on her face, Sunny raised the zipper and snuck a foot out. Davin held it in her hands, then touched the toes firmly. "Your sock's damp." She grasped the foot harder and shook it. "Did you miss the part about removing your wet socks? It was only about three minutes ago, so you can't blame your long-term memory."

"I thought they were dry."

"They are definitely not." She whipped the sock off, then briskly rubbed the foot, adding a little massage while she was at it. "It's dark, so I can't detect subtle color variations, but are your nails purple?"

Sunny craned her neck to take a look. "Yeah. I like to change up the color just to amuse myself. I've gone through about every shade they carry." She wrestled with the backpack she'd stowed near her head. "I've got some more socks."

"Toss 'em," Devin said. She took one and slipped it onto Sunny's foot. "Send the other foot over."

"I can put my own socks on, Devin. Really."

"Okay." She handed the sock back and lay down, this time facing Sunny. "Are you comfortable?"

"I will be once I finish wrestling with this dumb sock," she said, laughing.

"I offered…"

"I know you did, but you couldn't seriously want to do things like that. You're just being a really good guide."

"I didn't offer to change Hank's socks," she said, adding a playful grin.

"No, but you don't seem like someone who asks for trouble. And playing with Hank's feet would toss you into a barrel of it."

"If you're warm, you can use your coat as a pillow."

"I'm pretty good. I don't think I need to wear it." She rolled it up and jammed it against her shoulder. "Pretty nice."

"Ooo, one last thing. Your head might get cold, so I'd wear a hat."

Sunny pulled her bag close and extracted one, then pulled it down over her ears. "Don't take my picture," she said. "I know I look like heck."

She was dead wrong about that, but Devin decided not to comment. You never knew how a relative stranger would react to an innocuous comment, and when you were sleeping together it was wise to keep misunderstandings at a minimum.

They lay there for a minute, facing each other. A two-person tent was always small, but this one was smaller and sturdier than most. It was made for all seasons, so it was heavier than many backpacking models, constructed so it was low to the ground to withstand gale-force winds. Given the one thing everyone who bought a tent was concerned with was weight, the manufacturer had pared this one down to the very minimum, barely allowing two adults to lie on their sides.

The seconds ticked by, with the silence turning a little uncomfortable. Normally, Devin would flip to her other side and go right to sleep, but with Sunny facing her that felt a little rude. "Is Hank a good person to work for?" Devin asked, just trying to make a little conversation.

"In some ways, he's very good. In others, not good at all." She laughed a little, with Devin once again finding herself staring at Sunny's lips, which looked *very* kissable. "At this point, he's like a younger brother you want to strangle half the time. But you know you've got to get along, so you try to be the adult."

"He's younger?"

"Only emotionally. We're the same age."

"At least you're not really related. That's something, right?"

"Yeah. That would be worse," she agreed. Her eyes closed as she yawned, making a cute little noise. "Sleepy."

"Me too, " Devin said, already feeling her eyelids start to droop. "I usually take two people on trips, so I generally sleep alone. This is like having a slumber party."

"Yeah, I guess it is. Ready to call it a day?"

"I've been tireder, but not much. Why?" she asked, forcing her eyes open wide. "Need something?"

"I'm fine," Sunny said, her voice soft and soothing. "Sleep tight. Don't let the bedbugs bite."

"Too cold for bedbugs, but just right for a sleepy Maine guide."

CHAPTER FOUR

AFTER GETTING THE CRANKY, STIFF, slow-moving group settled with breakfast, Devin stood up to deliver yet another lecture. "I'm going to walk out and make sure the ice fishing hut's in good order. While I'm gone, I'd like all of you to stay right here—and by right here, I mean *right* here." She looked into each set of eyes, making sure they were paying attention.

"Got it," Sunny said, with Julian nodding compliantly.

"Remember what I said yesterday," Devin said, staring at Hank. "As a group, we can get through anything, but a single person wandering around is asking for trouble."

"Then why are you wandering around?" Hank asked, finally looking up. "You're not a group."

"I need to make sure conditions are right to keep you all safe. I know it seems like I'm here for my sparkling personality, but that's only partially true." She turned and pointed toward the lake. "We're going to be walking across the ice to get to the hut. Before I take you out, I'm going to check to make sure it's still thick."

"You can tell that from looking, can't you?" Hank asked.

"I wish you could, but it's tricky. The state checks the ice and posts the status, but I double-check. Just because it's two feet thick a half mile from here doesn't mean there's not a wrinkle right on our path. You can't be too careful when it comes to ice."

"Do you want me to go with you?" Sunny asked.

"Devin's probably trying to get away," Hank said, chuckling. "Every time she looks up one of us is checking out her ass."

Devin turned and pointedly shook her butt. "Knock yourselves out," she said before picking up her snowshoes. "I'll be back in a half hour, and when I return I'd really love to see you all just where you are now."

She grabbed her poles and took off, managing to get close to a jog, enjoying the cold, dry air which woke her up better than freeze dried coffee ever could. In the distance, she spotted the hut just where Edie said it would be. The hut had been located in this general area for a few years now, and was used fairly often. But you couldn't assume the people before you had neatened it up, nor that the ice hadn't suddenly gotten thinner, even though she was quite sure it hadn't.

Before stepping onto the ice she shrugged out of her coat, then draped her ice spikes around her neck. She hadn't used them the day before, since her friend Chris had been camping in the same spot just two days earlier, and had assured her the ice near the closest bank was thick and smooth. But he hadn't gone fishing, so adding a little protection was a must. There were all sorts of fancy spikes, but she'd made these from sawed off broom handles, parachute cord and nails. Spikes served only one function—to give you some purchase on the ice in case you fell in. She liked to wear hers like kids did with their mittens, under her jacket, with the handles sticking out of the sleeves. Most people didn't do it this way, but she didn't want the darned things to float away while she was freezing to death.

In all of her years, she'd only fallen in once—but once was enough. She'd been very young, five or six at the most, and her dad had yanked her right out. Just grabbed her by the back of her jacket and lifted her like she didn't weigh an ounce. Devin still remembered how frightened her mother had been once they'd gotten home. She didn't think she'd ever been hugged so hard. But it was a good lesson, and since then her respect for the uncertain nature of hard water had grown with each passing year.

Today, the ice was rock solid under her feet. The last sample from the state indicated it was as thick as it had been in January, which meant the ice-out was going to be late. It would bug the heck out of her if she couldn't get to her cabin for a month while it melted, but there was no arguing with Mother Nature.

Her fellow guides moved the hut around through the winter, depending on their preferences. Some of the super serious guys came out with sonar and spent half the morning deciding where to drag it. Then they had to use an auger to cut a new hole. To Devin, that was a huge waste of time and energy, especially for clients who just wanted to have the experience of ice fishing. So she just accepted the hut wherever it was and took her chances. Today, it was about two hundred and fifty feet from the shore, and she didn't hear a single sound save for the crunch of the packed snow under her boots. No birds, no snowmobiles, no other fishermen. It was kind of eerie, but she liked the quiet, especially after having had to be so social the day before.

The hut was pretty bare bones, placed far enough away from the next closest one so you could see, but not hear anyone. A lot of people liked to make a village, with the huts so close you could talk to your neighbor without raising your voice. That seemed like madness to Devin. There was a time to socialize and a time to fish, and in her book, there was no need for overlap.

They had a good all-weather lock on the door, and she removed the rubber cover, got the key in and opened it up. Camp stools, ice traps, a few rods and reels for people who liked to fish the old-fashioned way, fishing line, a box of jigs, some old kerosene lanterns, a hand-crank flashlight for emergencies, a few wool blankets, all of Edie's stained or worn inflatable pads, and a couple of five gallon buckets were fairly neatly arranged. Chris must have been here last. Her buddy was the tidiest guide of the bunch.

Looking down at two nasty old carpets that bracketed the hole, she shivered, then made herself do what needed to be done. Clamping her teeth onto her bottom lip, she grabbed the corner of the first carpet and shook it hard. She managed to limit her squeal to a muted one, but she had to close her eyes to accomplish even that small feat. She didn't know how many mice she'd dislodged, but she'd hear their chittering in her nightmares.

It was dumb. Embarrassingly dumb. But she dared anyone to love mice once one ran up their pant leg. Come to think of it, the mouse incident had occurred the same season she'd fallen into the lake. Must've been under a bad sign that year.

The second carpet harbored at least ten of the nasty little critters. She'd only had her eyes half-closed, letting her make a good guess at their number. Then she was finished, and she closed the door behind her as she left. That wouldn't stop the mice from sneaking back in, but they didn't like people walking around on top of them, so they'd scamper as soon as the group arrived.

Sunny turned to her right, smiling when she saw Julian jiggling his pole just like Devin suggested. It was so nice that they all had at least some experience with fishing, even though none of them had done it on the ice.

Devin suggested they use ice traps, odd-looking things that you placed over the hole that caused a flag to shoot up when a fish bit. But Hank was used to holding a pole in his hands and he wasn't to be dissuaded.

Having them all in one place with very few hazards let Devin relax, a first. She wasn't fishing, explaining that her doing so would just reduce their chances at a catch. That made sense, but Sunny could see she wanted to take the rod from Hank's hand and do it right. She'd made it clear their best chance was to move the rod back and forth and up and down in barely perceptible movements. Logically, fish were attracted to the vibration of the jig, but if Hank was trying to follow that suggestion he was doing a piss-poor job of it. His whole hand was moving, with his wrist snapping almost like he was fly-fishing. But he was concentrating, and hadn't gotten into any trouble—a good day for him. Other than an occasional loud crunch from his pork rinds, the place was silent.

"Whoa!" Hank yelped. "Got a live one here!"

"Set the hook," Devin said, jumping to her feet from her perch atop a bunch of raggedy-looking air mattresses.

"I know how to set a hook," he grumbled, before getting up and pointing the tip of the rod at the fish while balancing his weight. He was reeling in the slack while Devin was moving toward him, then he whipped the rod up over his shoulder and gave the reel a couple of cranks.

"Can you feel his weight?"

"Yup. Good size. Got a lot of fight in him." He slowly reeled him in, with Devin neither saying a word nor doing a thing. Given it was clear Hank knew what he was doing, she backed off completely. His eyes grew wide as he continued to crank, then the fish swiped his tail violently when his head breached the hole, letting Sunny see how big he was.

"Holy crap!" she yelped.

"Salmon," Devin said. "Gotta be a minimum eighteen inches at this time of year."

"He's that, easy," Hank declared.

By the time the fish was flopping around on the ice, Devin was kneeling next to it. "Sorry, Hank," she said, as she held her measuring tape out and lay the fish along it. "He's only seventeen."

"You're measuring wrong!"

Before he could complain further, she clipped the hook and slipped the fish back into the water, where Sunny watched him flip his tail hard and dart away.

"You stole my fish!"

"I saved you from a hefty fine," Devin said. "We take our fish and game regulations very seriously."

"I can afford a stupid fine," he said, steaming mad. "For a woman who makes her living off tips, you're ignoring the most important thing. Make your damn clients happy!"

She stood up and faced him, her face an impassive mask. Sunny didn't know her well, but she assumed her twitching fingers indicated she was trying to stop herself from slapping him. "It's important to me that you have fun, but it's equally important to protect our wildlife."

"You can't pay the rent with that do-gooder attitude, lady."

"I don't pay rent. Actually, if you knew how low my monthly expenses were, you'd ask *me* for a tip."

"Great. I just might do that." He went to the door of the hut, flung it open, then stalked out.

"Shit!" Sunny groaned. "He can't be out there alone."

She turned to see Devin close her eyes, probably counting to ten. Quietly, she said, "He'll be fine. The snow's only a few inches deep out on the ice, and it's grainy. He won't slip." She sighed audibly, zipped up, put on a second pair of gloves and her snowshoes, and followed him, saying, "But he might be mad enough to walk all the way back." She paused by the door. "*Please* don't leave while I'm gone." She turned and met Sunny's eyes for a brief moment. "Or fall into the hole."

"We won't move," Sunny said, hoping Hank didn't fall into one of his funks. He could be as moody as a teenager when he lost face—which he clearly had.

A few minutes passed, then Julian looked up, saying, "What's that noise?"

"I don't know. It sounds like a lawnmower or something, doesn't it?"

"No, that's not it."

They were both silent for a minute, listening as the buzzing, rumbling sound got louder. Then it stopped abruptly, replaced by voices. Sunny recognized Devin's and Hank's, but the third was novel.

A minute later the door opened and a woman in a dark green snowsuit entered. She was carrying a helmet, also dark green, with a "Maine Fish and Wildlife" decal on the front. Very no-nonsense, she had the bearing of an old-school butch—cool and calm and certain. "Morning," she said. "Devin tells me you haven't had any luck yet. Mind if I check?"

"Can we refuse?" Julian asked.

Ahh, the beauty of lawyers. No matter how mild-mannered they seemed, they all wanted to make sure they weren't being pushed around.

The woman blinked in surprise. "You're not from around here, are you."

"We're from Texas," Sunny said. "Feel free to look around."

"It's my job," the woman said. "If you're fishing, I can check to see what you've caught and whether or not you have the proper licenses."

The door opened again and Devin entered. "I've got their licenses, Jeannie." She pulled them from a plastic sleeve she'd tucked into one of the many pockets in her pants, and the officer spent a moment looking at them. Then she poked her head into the empty plastic buckets.

"Thanks for cooperating," she said, then nodded to Devin. "See you around."

"Are you going to Dee-Dee's birthday party next Sunday?" Devin asked.

"Yeah, I think so. How about you?"

"Gonna try. I don't have any trips planned, so I should be able to get there."

Sunny watched the interchange, certain these two were planning on meeting up with a group of lesbians for a party.

"If Chad can watch the baby, I'll be there early. But if he has to work, I'll have to wait until my mom gets home from Walmart."

Sunny let out a startled gasp. She'd *never* been so sure a woman was a lesbian!

"She's still working in Bangor?" Devin asked.

"Uh-huh. With any luck, she'll be there until she's ready to retire."

Devin clapped her on the shoulder as she walked out. "Hope to see you, Jeannie. Safe travels."

"You too." Then the engine started up again and Hank entered, red-faced and shivering. Sunny wished his color was from embarrassment, but she was sure it was just from the wind. She was equally sure he wouldn't be apologizing to Devin, at least not in words. That just wasn't in his nature, but she guessed he'd give her a very big tip. In his world, money made up for all forms of bad behavior.

Lake trout, roasted over an open fire, provided an amazingly satisfying meal. Thankfully, they'd each caught a couple, with Hank only mildly nursing his pride from having Julian catch the biggest fish of the day, a hefty twenty-two inch salmon. The highlight of her day was watching the look on Hank's face when Julian slipped that big fish right back into the lake. Her ears were still ringing from Hank's outraged cry, but her admiration had grown for quiet, self-confident Julian. They'd already caught enough to feed them all, and he simply didn't want to take a fish they wouldn't be able to eat.

Devin took another bite, then added a little of the penne to her fork. "Thanks for sharing," she said, catching Sunny's attention.

"I don't mind a bit. I wouldn't have caught a thing if not for your advice on how to make that jig vibrate."

"This is the best fish I've ever had," Julian said. "You got a picture of the salmon before I put it back, didn't you, Sunny?"

"I did. I'll send it to you when we get a signal."

"*This* is more what I expected on this trip," Hank said. "No girly vegetarian food."

"Come back in two months for wild turkey season," Devin said. "There's nothing girly about that."

"Shotguns?"

"You can use one. But I like a bow and arrow. It feels like you're giving the animal half a chance."

"I might just take you up on that," Hank said. "You should come down to Texas for some pronghorn hunting."

"I don't know what that is, much less how to bag one."

"Not quite an antelope, not quite like a deer," Hank said. "I've never gotten one, but my brother has. Beautiful animal."

"I think they're close to endangered," Sunny said.

"Boo-hoo," Hank said, rubbing his eyes with his fists. "They're still legal, so I'm going to keep hunting until I bring one down."

"Bet you can't hunt for moose in Texas," Devin said. "Or bear."

"If I come back, I'll get one of each," he said, not a whiff of uncertainty in his voice. "One day my entire den will have trophies mounted on the walls."

"With each of them quietly crying, 'killer, killer, killer,'" Sunny said, laughing so hard she snorted.

Devin laughed along with her, pointing to the bits of fish still on Sunny's plate. "Think that little guy jumped onto the fire of his own accord? Are the burgers you eat all cow suicides? Don't think so."

"Hey, don't get all logical on me. You know a big pronghorn head on your wall is a lot more bloodthirsty than my eating a burger."

Devin nodded. "I'll agree that it looks like the hunter enjoys the killing more than the nutrition. But I think the animal's indifferent. Either way, they're belly up."

"What's the most exotic thing you've ever killed?" Hank asked.

"I don't hunt for trophies. I just do it to keep the population in check." She shrugged, knowing her argument was a little weak. "But that assumes the fish and game people have a perfect understanding of the ecosystem, which they really don't. I guess we all have our own code about what's right and what's wrong when it comes to hunting."

"If it's legal, I'm taking it," Hank decided.

"If it's *close* to legal you're taking it," Devin reminded him, chuckling to herself at Hank's narrow-eyed glare.

It was serenely quiet as they lay in their sleeping bags, with just the dying embers of the fire making an occasional crackling sound. Sunny looked really content, with a half smile making her mouth even prettier. She and Hank had gulped down a couple of shots of his whiskey, which Devin could smell on her breath, given they were just inches from each other. It kind of reminded Devin of the last time she'd been to Portland, getting close to a sexy woman in a bar, making sure she was into it before going in for a kiss.

But kissing was off the agenda for tonight. As much as she'd like to, Devin wasn't ever going to mix business with pleasure. Besides the lack of professionalism it showed, letting herself get distracted by an alluring woman was dangerous. And she'd learned a long time ago that you couldn't be too safe when camping—especially in the winter.

She was just about to ask about Sunny's life in Dallas when a completely different set of words came out of her mouth. "When do you guys go home?"

"Not until Thursday. We've got more team-building BS planned."

"But you're staying near Greenville, right?"

"We're outside of town, but I'm not sure how far. We stayed overnight in Bangor after we flew in, so I haven't seen our cabin yet."

"Well, if you want to hang out…" She heard the words coming out of her mouth and nearly slapped herself. "Damn, that sounded stupid."

Sunny lifted herself up and rested on an arm, with Devin able to see her grin grow. "You want to go on a date?"

A date? That hadn't occurred to her, but now she was stuck. "Um, I wasn't thinking of anything formal." She cleared her throat when Sunny gave her a puzzled look. *Time to bail!* "I just thought you might be bored hanging out with Hank and Julian. I know some places where we could have a beer or two…"

"Oh, shit," Sunny said, sitting up and staring at her feet, clearly embarrassed. "I'm so sorry. I thought you were suggesting…" She let out a heavy sigh. "I hope I didn't make myself sound like a total fool."

Devin couldn't let this go on. She reached up and tugged on Sunny's sleeve. "I *was* suggesting that," she said, now more embarrassed than Sunny. There was no way in hell she'd admit to the truth—that she was simply hoping to hook up if Sunny had a free hour. She swallowed nervously, trying hard to make sure she was careful with Sunny's feelings. "I've never hit on a client before. I'm not even sure why I did it. My mouth opened and the words started to tumble out…"

Sunny lay back down, a gentle smile making her so remarkably attractive that Devin almost went for it. But that kind of impulsive behavior was so far from her norm that she was able to get hold of herself and lie there patiently, waiting.

"Don't be embarrassed," Sunny said, her voice soft and empathetic. "I can hardly tell you how nice it feels to have a woman lose control a little bit."

"That's not something I do," Devin said, "so it caught me by surprise. On every trip, getting everyone back safely is my number one priority." She let her wolfish smile emerge. "But spending some time with you is definitely my second."

"I'll have to put up with a load of teasing from Hank," she said, sounding tentative. Then she threw her head back and laughed. "But I'll bet a date with you would be worth it. Maybe you'll let me see what a rustic cabin in the woods is like, huh?"

Devin already had a picture of Sunny in her bed, and it was an image that didn't need a bit of adjustment to be absolutely perfect. "I think that's a damned good idea. But the cabin's on the lake."

"Mmm, a nice view across the lake from your cabin sounds even better."

"My cabin's *in* the lake. I've got a private island just big enough to hold it. I think you'll like it."

"I think you're right." Sunny didn't make an overt move, but she tilted her chin so Devin could reach her lips. But Devin held back. She'd let herself daydream about hooking up, but she wouldn't take a single step down that path until they were back in town—which she was *really* looking forward to. She shivered, hoping Sunny's body was the lush, curvy playground she could only imagine beneath all of the layers of down she'd been encased in. Then she sat up and dug around in her pack, finding a thin wool cap to keep her warm.

"What's that?" Sunny asked, looking at her hand.

"This?" Devin pointed at the bracelet.

"Yeah. It's cute, but it looks like it has a purpose."

She unclipped it and handed it over. "It's a present," she said.

"I wasn't—"

"I know," Devin said. "But it's white and will look better with your coat. I'll get a pink one that will match my new buff."

"You don't seem like a pink fan."

"Not usually," she admitted, "but I think it adds a little spark to my jacket."

Sunny lifted her hand, with the bracelet dangling in the air. "I still don't know what it is."

"Details, details," Devin said, chuckling. "It's called a survival bracelet, but that's overselling it. I think of it as stronger duct tape." She took the bracelet back and ran her finger along the cord. "It's made of braided ripcord. If you need to, you can unwind it and have a few feet of really tough cord to tie gear together or fix a piece of equipment. I used the last one I had to hold a snowmobile together after a client ripped off the cowling by driving it into a tree."

"Any injuries?"

"Yeah," she said. "I said I had to hold it together, didn't I?" She paused, hoping Sunny got the joke. "Oh, you mean the driver? He was fine. Almost fainted when Edie charged him for the repair, but he was being reckless." She rolled her eyes. "He'd been warned. Repeatedly."

"I like my present," Sunny said, taking it from Devin's hand. "I just clip it on?"

"Uh-huh." She reached over and helped, then flicked at the back of the clasp. "That's a little whistle. I don't need that, so I'm going to get one that has a fire starter."

"If you can find one in pink," Sunny said, smiling.

"I'm all about fashion," Devin said, settling down and re-conforming her clothes into a fluffy pillow.

"I'm really glad we came," Sunny said quietly. "I've been kind of dreading the trip, but things have turned around—dramatically."

"First time I've been happy to pick up a trip I haven't planned," Devin agreed. "Sometimes the best laid plans aren't the good ones."

Chapter Five

DEVIN LAY STILL IN HER SLEEPING bag, certain it was the middle of the night. The tent was very dark, with the wind making it shiver, fabric straining and groaning around the poles. It was a good, steady fifteen miles per hour, with gusts that might have doubled it. So much for the positive weather report. After checking her watch, she blinked in surprise to see that it was already five, her usual. Sunrise would be in an hour, and if the weather was going to turn, they'd better get the show on the road.

She started to unzip herself from her little cocoon, waking Sunny, clearly a very light sleeper.

"Hi," she said, looking as cute as a bug with her hat pulled down past her eyebrows, and her eyes blinking slowly as she tried to focus.

"Go back to sleep," Devin whispered. "It's not even dawn." She shimmied out of her sleeping bag and started to wriggle into her pants.

"Where you going? Have to pee?"

"Yeah, but that's not why I'm up." She lay on her back to get her pants fastened, then put on another pair of socks and removed her boots from the gear bag. "The weather sounds like it might turn bad. If it does, there's a shortcut we can take. But last I heard the logging companies might be taking the trees that make the shortcut worth it."

Sunny was suddenly wide awake. "How bad is the weather?" Her dark blue eyes were trained on Devin like glue.

"I don't *know* that it's bad," she admitted. "It just sounds bad. If the wind's in our faces, skiing will be tougher than I'd like."

"Oh." She hunkered down in her sleeping bag, with just her eyes and nose sticking out. "Are you worried?"

"Not worried, no. I'm just trying to make sure the trip's enjoyable."

"You can't control everything, Devin. If the weather's bad, we'll just be cold."

"We have options that can help," she said. "For the inbound trip, I normally take a trail that puts us up on a nice plateau. You get great views across a valley there."

"I like a nice view. Let'd do it."

"Hold on there. You won't be saying that if we're plodding along in the teeth of the wind. Being on that exposed plateau would suck—especially if it's storming too bad to enjoy the view."

"Okay. Can we go back the way we came?"

"Of course, but if there's a storm…" She was beginning to annoy herself with her constant planning and calculating. "If we take my normal return route, there's a long stand of trees that would give us protection for a full mile. Plus, it knocks a half mile off the trip."

"Then lets do that," she said, chuckling. "See how easy I am to talk into things?"

She smiled down at Sunny, wishing they'd met elsewhere. She'd be trying to talk herself into her sleeping bag at that very moment. "I like that you're compliant, but you'll be cursing my name if those trees have been taken. The shortcut has a biggish hill, and it could easily be icy if the wind is whipping across it." She found her headband and her gloves and stuck them in her waistband. "But if we retrace our steps, we'll be miserable if it's windy and snowing."

"I guess we should flip a coin, huh? Sounds like we'll be miserable either way."

"Not if the shortcut is still forested. That would be a much, much more comfortable trip." She shrugged. "I'd like to take a run out there to check conditions. I like to know what's up before I make a decision."

Sunny's hand snaked out of her sleeping bag, and she grasped the string on Devin's hood and gave it a tug. "You're always fussin'," she said, making her accent thick. "But that's what makes you a good guide."

"What makes me a good guide is that I'm always trying to imagine the worst thing that could possibly happen. A storm wasn't predicted, but we've had some awful ones in early March. I'm afraid trudging across a wide open landscape through a storm would be too tough for Hank. He did okay, but he's not a natural skier."

"Go on then. Make like an advance man and see what's up."

"I'll be back by six thirty. You can all stay in one spot for that long, can't you?"

"Given that we had to pull Hank out of his sleeping bag at eight yesterday, I think that's a safe bet."

"Do you have to pee? I can take you."

"Go," she said, waving her hand. "If you're not here I'll have the nerve to try your little contraption."

"Great. You'll like it." She started to slide out on her butt, but added one more warning. "I assume the guys will want to pee when they wake up, but I don't want them wandering off. Since we're leaving, it won't hurt to have a little urine near our campsite. Can you make sure they stay close?"

"Not a problem. Julian's complaint, and Hank will be sound asleep."

Devin stared at her until their eyes met. "Are you sure? I normally wouldn't worry, but Hank's like a two hundred pound toddler."

"It's fine, Devin. I can get him to behave. God knows I have to do it all day at the office."

"Better you than me," Devin said and hurried out of the tent, zipping it closed to keep out the wind that was much stronger than she'd predicted.

The strong headwind had slowed her down on the outbound run, and now she was rushing to get back by six thirty. There was no reason that was a critical time, but she liked to keep her promises—especially when guiding a group.

But even if the trip had taken longer than predicted, she was glad she'd made it. The loggers hadn't taken the trees, and once they got past the first mile of open terrain, they'd have an easier return. Hank would probably still screw her on the tip, but spending an evening with Sunny would definitely make up for that. And the faster they got home, the sooner they could see if their sparks could start a fire.

Dawn was a fuzzy, indistinct suggestion at the horizon, but the wind at her back gave her a gentle push. The problem was the thick, dark clouds that obscured the breaking day, indicating a brewing storm. She couldn't be sure they'd have a ton of snow dumped on them, but she sure wouldn't be surprised if they did. That's what you got for trusting a long-term forecast. They could use every available scientific measure, but the only reliable weather predictor she knew of was to stand outside and look around. From years of educated guesses, she thought the storm would hit them around noon. Nothing to worry about if she could gather her campers and get them on the road by nine. They'd be in the home stretch by noon, and even if the skies opened up and dumped a foot of snow on them, they'd easily make it back to the car. Driving to Greenville in a blizzard wouldn't be fun, but the truck was reliable and she'd made sure they had chains stowed away. Those could propel you along in almost any storm, slowly but surely.

She was moving along at a good pace, trying to go quickly, but not so quickly that she got sweaty and had to change clothes again. After digging her edges into a curve to wind around another copse of trees, she got down into a squat and glided down the hill, a short but steep one. The snow was fine. Not even grainy, much less icy. Hank would have no trouble climbing this one.

The wind whipped by her, whistling past her ears as she grinned like a demon. Zipping down a steep hill was a pure joy, one she'd never grown even slightly weary of.

After taking a few long strides along level ground, she realized the whistling sensation was still ringing in her ears. Devin stopped and held her breath for a second to be able to hear better. Then, like a shot, she veered off the trail and homed in on the sound, flying across a rocky patch of moguls, then climbing another hill that led her to the edge of the lake. When she hit the ice, she put her head down and hit the accelerator, skiing with abandon to reach the distress call.

Her heart pounded heavily in her chest, partly from terror, partly from exertion. She hadn't pushed herself like this in years, mainly because it was stupid and reckless to ski across a frozen lake still in deep shadows. The dark patches could easily hide logs sticking up, abandoned fishing holes, even cracks in the ice. But someone needed her, and her own safety had to suffer.

Ahead, at the very tip of the cove, near their campsite, she saw figures. One was definitely Sunny, safely on the bank. The other was…Julian.

Definitely on the ice. In lightening-quick succession, a crack like a shotgun shattered the silence, then Sunny's blood-curdling scream nearly froze her.

But Devin shook off her terror and continued to give it everything she had. Julian was on the ice, but his legs…or leg…was in the water. Her mind was racing like a greyhound, with one message repeating itself again and again. She couldn't help anyone if she fell in.

Instead of heading directly for him, she veered off, making a wide turn to jump back onto the bank and ski/run toward Sunny, who was on her knees, inches from the water. Devin jumped out of her skis as quickly as humanly possible, then stood beside Sunny while she spoke calmly to Julian. "Keep your hands in front of you," she said clearly. "If you start to slide in, put your hand over your nose and mouth. Your body will try to suck in air, but it will only get water. Do you understand me?"

"Help!" he begged, clearly panicking.

"Hank's gone!" Sunny screamed, grabbing Devin's leg in a death grip.

"He's what?" Her blood froze in her veins.

"He fell in. Julian's trying to save him!"

"I'm going to come get you," Devin said, holding his stunned, terrified gaze. "I promise I'll get you out."

She reached down, grabbed Sunny by the shoulders and yanked her to her feet. "Go get the sled. Throw everything out to make it lighter, then bring it here. And my backpack," she said, giving it her all not to panic herself. "Go!" She pushed her hard, and Sunny started to run, her snowshoes pounding across the fluffy powder.

Again, Devin turned to Julian. "I'm going to crawl out to you, but I've got to stay where I know the ice is good. Just hold on."

"Hank's under the ice! We've got to get him out!"

"I know," she said, as she stumbled across the deep snow on the bank. She could see one set of snowshoe marks on the ice, and she chose that as her path. Both men weighed more than she did, and if they made it to the hole, it was safe that far. Her heart was still slamming in her chest, but she ran right toward the hole, determined to save Julian—and then try for Hank.

She was ten feet from him when the ice cracked again, quieter this time, but just as terrifying. Julian screamed as his second snowshoe broke through the ice, almost in slow motion. Devin hurled herself to the ice in a headfirst slide, gliding across the space that separated them to reach out and grab Julian by the hair as his head dipped into the water.

She'd yanked so hard she expected to have a fist full of dark hair in her hand, but Julian's head and shoulders were safely out. They were face to face, his expression revealing the dread that must have filled him. Then he started to cough and sputter, with water spewing from his mouth as he hacked away.

Resettling her hand onto his shoulder, she spoke as calmly as she could. "You're going to gasp for breath, but that will only last a few seconds."

Just as she'd predicted, he fought for air, sucking it in like he wasn't getting any at all. Then he started to calm down, quickly becoming too calm. His gaze grew unfocused, with his dark eyes staring over her shoulder. It was clear he wasn't able to hear her, but she kept talking. "I'm going to get you out. I know you're cold, but the cold won't kill you. I promise you that."

"Devin!"

Lying on her belly desperately holding onto Julian didn't allow her to turn in Sunny's direction. "Tie one end of the red rope to a tree and throw the other end to me," Devin said.

From the corner of her eye, she could see Sunny run to the bank where the closest trees were. It seemed to take forever, but Sunny eventually called out, "I'm ready."

"Throw it!" Devin called out. "Hard as you can."

Sunny threw the rope, with the free end hitting Julian in the head. Devin held her breath, desperately hoping the ice held as she leaned even farther out and reached for it. Then she whipped off the mitten-like shells that covered her gloves, wanting to keep something dry to help herself down the line. After pulling Julian's arm toward her and kneeling on it to keep him above the water, she quickly tied a bowline, making the loop big enough to slide around his torso. Then she steeled herself and plunged her hands into the icy water. It was the most awful feeling she'd ever experienced, and in seconds her hands started to curl into balls. The pain was stunning, and she gasped just like poor Julian had. With more determination than finesse, she slipped the rope around his body, moving him around in the water like a rigid doll. Once the loop was snugged around him, she got to her feet. "We're coming out now," she said, starting to pull. If the ice had held Hank to this point, it would, with luck, hold her.

Julian was just staring—like he'd lost his ability to speak—or help.

Devin continued to tug, getting him to the edge of the jagged hole. Out of the corner of her eye, she saw Sunny take a tentative step onto the ice. "Stop!" she howled. "Go back right now. I need you on the shore. I *need* you," she insisted. That was a lie, but she couldn't save all three of them. Once she got Julian out she'd need Sunny to tend to him while she dove in for Hank. The thought of that make her guts clench. The odds of either of them coming back out were somewhere between slim and none, but she had no choice. Her duty was to bring her clients home safely—no matter what.

"Go into my backpack and find some short pieces of wood that are tied together with a cord," Devin called out, relieved to see Sunny hop to it and start throwing stuff out of the pack. She held the spikes up and started to throw them, but Devin knew they wouldn't make it.

"Go over to where I walked out and follow my path. It's safe," she said. "I promise."

Sunny was taking off before she finished speaking. It was such a relief to know she could rely on her! Devin continued to pull, keeping the tension on the rope. She knew she'd have to use some amount of force, and knew equally well that an ice cold body was a very fragile thing. Then Sunny was standing beside her. "Go back a few feet," Devin said. "I'm sure the ice is good back there." Sunny dropped the ice spikes and moved back. "Good," Devin said. "I'm going to have to work to get him out, and there's a chance I'll go in too."

An agonized cry flew from Sunny's lips.

"I'll be all right," she said, her voice showing a fuck of a lot more certainty than she felt. "If I fall in, I can use the ice spikes." She turned her head and met Sunny's terrified gaze. "Can you hold the rope and keep it taut? If I fall in, he'll go under if you don't work to keep him up."

"Yes," she said, her voice shaking hard.

"Okay. Here I go," she said, scooting to the very edge of the hole, then getting into a deep squat. She was sure it wasn't going to hold her, but somehow it did—at least for the moment. Once again she plunged her hands into the water and grabbed Julian under his arms. With all of her strength, she yanked hard and his natural buoyancy helped lift him partially out. But he was still and unyielding, not able to help in any way.

As she yanked again, she fell onto her butt, and another great crack reverberated across the lake. She tensed up, waiting for the cold to rush over her, but nothing happened. The crack was behind Julian, with another sheet of ice breaking away to dip into the water gracefully.

"Fuck," she whispered, willing her heart to slow down enough so she could work. Julian's trunk was lying across her legs, which were splayed out in front of her. It wasn't the most efficient way, but she tried to scoot backwards, hoping she had the strength to pull him along. He was almost out—then his fucking snowshoe caught. As gently as possible, she slid him off her lap, then crawled to the hole and stuck her hands into the water, barely having the dexterity to free his leg.

"God damn it," she panted, her hands aching so badly she would have believed she'd been stung by all the bees in Maine. But he was out. Frozen almost stiff. But out.

Her hands were rock hard, but she was able to peel off her wet gloves and get her shells back on. They weren't warm, but they'd at least stop the wind from making things worse. "I'm going to drag him to the bank," she said. "Do you think you can get the sled over there and help me load him?"

Without waiting to answer, Sunny took off, managing to have the sled waiting when Devin reached the bank. Then Sunny jumped into action, grabbing Julian under the arms and helping drag him close to the sled. Devin stood next to her and they wordlessly linked their hands under his back and hoisted him aboard. Devin hadn't specifically told her where to put the sled, but she'd kept it on the groomed trail that skirted the lake. Damn good instincts. Even better was her decision to bring all of the wool blankets, which she now tucked around Julian. Then another one went around Devin's arms, as a firm, clear voice said, "I'm going to pull the sled back to camp. You follow on your skis."

She found herself nodding robotically. Then she fought through her cloudy brain to say, "Hank. I have to go back."

Sunny grabbed her by the hood on her coat, nearly knocking her off her feet. "No way, Devin. We have to save Julian."

"Get him," she insisted. "Resuscitate. Training." *God damn it!* She could see the words, but couldn't get them out.

Sunny turned her, grabbed her shoulders and shook her hard. "I don't know how to resuscitate Julian. You have to do it. He's right here, Devin. We can save him." Another rough shake had her leaning close. "If you go in, I'll lose all three of you. Don't make me live with that. *Please.*"

That got in. Devin nodded, sick with the reality of her decision slamming down on her shoulders. She was *letting* Hank die. There was a chance she could save him, and she wasn't even going to try.

Sunny started to pull the sled down the path, heading back to the tents, but Devin got her wits about her and shouted, "The lodge."

"The lodge?" She nodded, clearly recalling they'd talked about it. "Is it close?"

"Not too…" It was just a hop, skip and a jump away on a normal day. Now? She had no idea.

"Will we have a better chance of saving Julian if we make it?"

"Yes," she said, certain of that.

"You're going to have to lead us," Sunny said, staring hard into her eyes. She gripped Devin's shoulder and pressed firmly. "You can do it."

It took more effort than she ever would have thought possible, but she made it back to her skis. She couldn't move very well, or ski efficiently with a blanket draped over her arms, but she had to stay as warm as she could. If she couldn't make it, Sunny didn't have the knowledge to save Julian alone.

The lodge was about a quarter mile away, hidden by the tall pines on the rise above them. She liked to camp close to shelter when possible, just in case. Now, looking up at the hill that would have normally barely registered, she gritted her teeth and forced her body to move, even though she felt like she was skiing through concrete that was beginning to set.

Sunny grunted when she started to follow, her snowshoes making soft thumps as she struggled with the sled and Julian's dead…Julian's weight. It seemed to take hours, but only five minutes had probably passed when Devin saw the beautiful building peaking out from its perch on the rise. It was the prettiest sight she'd ever seen in her life.

Now that the lodge was clearly visible, Sunny went a little faster, pulling the sled efficiently until she left the trail to tromp through deep powder. Devin struggled to keep up, finally reaching the stairs as Sunny kicked off her snowshoes and started to pull the sled up them.

"Wait," Devin gasped. "Don't jar him." It was only three steps. A two-year-old could jump up them with no problem. But carrying just some of Julian's weight took every ounce of strength Devin had. They made it, and Devin bent over and grasped her knees to catch her breath. Now they had to get into a locked building. "Wrap a blanket around your hand and break the window in the door," Devin said, knowing she didn't have the reserves to do it herself. "It's single pane."

Sunny complied without question, with glass quickly tinkling to the wooden floor. Then she used the blanket to push every shard out of the pane.

"Flip the…thing. The thing inside." *Damn!* She was losing the ability to think of the simplest words! "The thing that keeps the door closed."

Sunny stuck her hand in and turned the lock, and the door swung open. Devin swore she heard choirs of angels singing, but she was pretty sure she was just hallucinating.

Then they dragged and pushed the sled into a nook that held a pot bellied stove.

"Firewood," Devin said, seeing the neatly stacked logs that seemed miles away but were right next to the stove.

"I know how to build a fire." Sunny got to work while Devin dropped to her knees and attempted to get Julian's clothes off. His coat and gloves were easy, but she slowed down as she had to work snaps and Velcro on his snow pants. Then Sunny was at her side, quickly working to strip him of every sodden stitch. Devin scooted across the floor like a toddler to grab a bearskin rug. Once Julian was naked, she put the rug, fur side down, on his chest and tucked it around his shoulders.

Her brain was starting to work a little better, with her thoughts now clearly coming out when she spoke. "Arms and legs can warm up slowly. It's his trunk we've got to work on."

"Should I take my clothes off and lie on him?"

"No. Can't jar him any more than we already have. He'll have a heart attack if we screw this up."

"Oh, fuck," Sunny said, starting to sob. "We can't lose both of them, Devin. Promise me we won't lose Julian."

"Can't promise," she said, not willing to lie about something so important. "We'll do everything we can." She was shivering, then realized her coat and sweater and long underwear top were all drenched. She started to work on getting them off, but Sunny took over, quickly stripping her. Devin was sitting on her heels, clad only in her sports bra, which was wet from sweat. "Everything," she said. She held her arms up like a kid, and Sunny pulled it over her head.

"I'm going to go get the rest of our stuff," Sunny said, moving towards the door.

"No! I'll go."

"You're in no shape. Make sure the fire's catching."

Then she was gone, leaving a half naked Devin with a totally naked Julian, his skin blue in places, bone white in others. She put her fingers to his throat and felt a blessed pulse. Slow and weak, but regular. Leaning over him, careful not to press on his chest, she put her mouth close and blew her warmed breath into his lungs at each shallow inhalation. "Stay with me, Julian. Come on, buddy. You've got so much to live for."

Now time sped up, with Sunny back beside her in seconds, dropping Devin's backpack to the floor, then Julian's, then Hank's. "I brought everything I could," she said, panting from the trek.

"Thanks." Devin fumbled through her stuff, knowing she didn't have anything to take the place of all of her clothing. Grimly, she opened Hank's and took out all of the crap he'd brought. Whiskey, chocolate bars, cocoa packets, more pork rinds, camera lenses? At the bottom he'd added a T-shirt, a thermal shirt, and a fleece pullover. She'd never been so happy to put on clothes that didn't fit. Clothes that belonged to a man she should have never, ever left alone.

Chapter Six

JULIAN WAS SHIVERING HARD, BUT since he hadn't been doing even that earlier, Sunny took it as a good sign. His arms and legs weren't blue any longer, either, but they were pasty white and icy cold.

His head tossed from side to side, with him speaking only gibberish. Then his hands started to move as he fought to throw off the rug. But Devin gently held them still, murmuring soothing words as she simply tried to keep him from hurting himself.

Devin seemed more like herself now that the fire was crackling away and she was in warm clothes. She met Sunny's eyes and said, "I know you're going to fight me on this, but I have a dry suit. I know the odds aren't good," she said, starting to stand, "but I have to try to pull Hank out."

"No way," Sunny said. "You're not leaving here."

Her eyes widened as she took a couple of steps backward. "I have to *try*," she said, taking a wide path that would get her to the door without coming close to Sunny. But Sunny's excellent reflexes let her scoot across the wooden floor to wrap an arm around Devin's leg.

"No!" she shouted, holding on with all of her might.

"I might be able to resuscitate him!"

"Julian needs you, Devin. Now. He's alive, and we've got to keep him that way."

"He'll be fine. I think," she added softly. "The shivering, the talking. That's normal. He just needs to warm up. But Hank—"

Sunny scrambled to her feet, quickly wrapping one hand around Devin's arm, the other gripping her shoulder. "He's gone," she said, staring into her eyes. "There's nothing you can do now."

"I've got to try!" The expression on her face was somewhere between panic and terror. Sunny's heart nearly broke, but she couldn't let her go.

"Look me in the eye and tell me the odds of reviving him, even if you could get him out."

She blinked a few times, then her gaze fell to the floor. "Slim."

"I think you're lying. I think the odds are zero at this point."

"Not zero," she insisted, then quietly added, "close, but not zero."

Sunny pulled her close and hugged her rigid body. "I know you think it's your duty, but you don't have to die for him, Devin. You just don't. If anyone's to blame for his death, it's me."

Pushing away, she started to pace around the room, then stopped to glared at the broken window which was letting in a gale of fresh, cold air. "Who took off? Who abandoned you? Me!" She slapped herself hard on the chest. "I left you behind, knowing that one of you didn't listen to reason. Leaving Hank alone was like leaving a child!"

"That's not true. Hank's…Hank was a man who acted like a child. But he wasn't one. He knew he should listen to you, and to me, but he did what he wanted. He plowed through life like he was immortal…and it caught up with him." She took in a long breath. "His recklessness almost killed Julian, and it might have killed you. So yes, I feel like hell that he's dead, but you didn't cause it. He did."

"My dry suit will protect me. It *will.*"

"No." Sunny raced over to stand in front of the door, determined to stop Devin from leaving even if she had to knock her out.

Blazing blue eyes stared hard, then Devin moved back and bull-rushed her, slamming into Sunny's body hard enough to make her stumble and let out a grunt. But she hadn't moved. Devin was clearly too weak to do any real damage. "I didn't stop Hank. I didn't stop Julian. But I'm stopping you." She grabbed her by the shoulders and shook her. "You're not leaving."

"Please," she begged, too weak to overpower Sunny, but with enough raw emotion to almost weaken her resolve.

"No," she said, with her voice quivering. "It's over, and wishing it wasn't won't change that. Hank's dead." She wrapped both arms around Devin's waist, holding her tight. "He's dead," she murmured softly.

Helplessly, Devin collapsed against her, tears of rage, of futility, of helplessness flowing from her. "No," she cried as she sank to the floor. "Don't let him die."

"He's already dead. All we can do is concentrate on saving Julian."

All sorts of emotions passed through those pale blue eyes as they stared up at Sunny, then she dropped her head and softly said, "We'll save Julian." With Sunny's help, she stood, then sniffed a few times as she wiped her eyes with the sleeve of Hank's fleece. She gazed at the shirt for a few seconds, like she wasn't sure where it had come from. Then she let out a heavy sigh and moved over to Julian again. She was so exhausted that she hit the floor hard when she tried to sit, then she grasped one of his twitching hands and held it to her chest, silently crying.

Around eleven, Sunny took over sitting at Julian's side. They still concentrated on his trunk, but they'd added light blankets to his arms and legs. Not even a trace of blue remained, with his skin pretty close to its usual color. But he was still out of it mentally, not quite delirious, but very confused and disoriented.

Devin couldn't have passed a coordination test either, and she was pretty sure her IQ had fallen by a significant percentage, but she had things to do. They were going to spend the night here, since Edie wouldn't raise the alarm until nightfall. Devin had no doubt that she was a treasured member of the community, but other than sending someone out to check that her car was in the lot, they wouldn't start searching until morning. That's just how things were. You couldn't send a bunch of people out in the darkness, risking additional casualties, no matter how much you liked the missing person.

Repairing the door was the first order of business. She'd spent enough time at the lodge to have a rough idea of where the staff kept just about everything, and she poked around, finding rolls of duck tape and some papers she could use to cover the hole. When she reached the door, holding the tape in one hand and a paper instruction manual in the other, she stood there for a second, puzzled to find a pile of snow on the floor. The lodge had huge windows everywhere, but she'd not even noticed the snow coming down like crazy. *Damn!* She was slower than she thought. Thank God Sunny had stopped her from jumping into the lake. There was no way she'd have been able to keep her senses about her while diving into thirty-five degree water.

Every single time she thought about Hank, her stomach turned just like it did when she was about to be sick. She'd been guiding for fifteen years and the worst casualties her guests had ever suffered were broken bones and sprains. Even those had made her feel like crap, and she'd spent a long time going over what had happened with her fellow guides, making sure she hadn't done anything to contribute to the injuries. This one was going to take more than a little soul-searching.

What she'd give for a damn cell signal. Not only to reassure her family, but to have them reassure her. She ached from longing, so desperately wanting to hear her mother's voice that she had to stick her fist into her mouth to stop from wailing. But she couldn't do that to Sunny. She was trying to hold it together too.

The repair Devin made was a lot more haphazard than she was happy with, but it was easy and minimally effective. Then she went to check on the firewood supply, which was blessedly ample. The lodge was as green as they could make it, with composting toilets kept running by solar panels on the roof, a wood-fired sauna, and propane for cooking. No electricity, but there were plenty of kerosene lamps, along with fuel. There were some dry goods left in the kitchen, bags of beans and rice, along with some spices. But the freeze-dried meals she'd brought were better. Devin should have known how many they had left, but she was still slow and forgetful.

While walking back to the sitting room, she looked, for the first time that day, at the huge dining area. A deep sense of longing hit her, for the fun-filled meals she'd shared here, with both staff and clients. On a hunch, she went back into the kitchen and poked around until she found a couple of six-packs of beer. You could always rely on the staff to have too much beer to finish before the end of the winter season. It was plenty cold just from being in the unheated lodge, but she put one six-pack outside on the off chance that Sunny wanted one later to calm her nerves.

The sight of Julian sitting up a little, with his head resting on Sunny's lap, was enough to make her cry. Fighting the tears, she dropped to the floor to take a better look. "Hi there," she said.

His eyes were focusing again, but he blinked slowly, like it was a big effort. "Hi." His voice was weak, but it was clear he was with her. "Thanks." Devin met Sunny eyes, which were filled with tears.

"He's going to be okay," Sunny said, her voice shaking. "I'm not going to have to call his momma and tell her I let her baby boy die."

Devin nodded, not trusting her voice. One of them, probably Sunny, was going to have to make that very call to Hank's wife. Julian started to breathe heavily, and Devin argued with herself over whether to let him sleep. Hypothermia wasn't like a head injury, so it was probably okay. His body had been through an awful lot, and it was going to take a while until he got his strength back. Sleeping might help.

Sunny ran her fingers through his hair, threading them along his scalp in a soothing fashion. "Do you want to know what happened?" she asked, not looking up.

Devin wanted to leave well enough alone, but it slowly dawned on her that she'd need to give a statement to the sheriff. "I'm gonna find some paper and a pen. We should each write down everything we remember. It'll help when he have to…"

"I realize we'll have to talk to the police," Sunny said. "It's a good idea to write down what happened."

It took a while to find paper, since Devin didn't think she was strong enough to break into the simple button lock on the office doorknob. But she finally located a scoring pad they used for bridge, along with stubs of pencils. She went first, sitting by the fire in a very comfy upholstered chair. It was perverse, sitting in a nice chair in front of a roaring fire, with beautiful conifers visible right outside the big windows, while writing about a man's death.

She started at the beginning. Why she left. How she tried to make sure she returned before her clients were awake. This part was hard, but she had to be honest, so she put in the part about Sunny assuring her she could control Hank on the off chance he got up early. Once that was over, Devin could simply stick to the facts: How far she'd gone, where she'd been when she'd heard the whistle, why she'd chosen to cross the lake instead of staying on the track. Then she got into the details: how Julian was splayed across the crack, one leg in the water, how Sunny helped by fetching the rope and the ice spikes, where she'd been when Julian went under, how she'd rescued him. Lastly, and probably most important, why she'd focused only on Julian when there was a chance she could have gotten Hank out. That was the hard part, but she told the unvarnished truth. If she went in, she might not have come out. And if she hadn't been there, Sunny couldn't have saved Julian on her own. She simply didn't have the knowledge to get the job done. So Devin had, in effect, cut and run. She'd decided, in a clear-headed fashion, to get a man she thought she could save to safety, and let a man she thought was dead remain in his watery grave.

Working on the last part was hard too. Sunny had made the right call in preventing her from leaving, but she didn't go into that in her notes. None of this was Sunny's fault, and she didn't want to pin that final decision on her. The choice had been Devin's. It wasn't just the military that went by the motto "no man left behind." Every Maine guide believed in that principle, yet she'd failed to follow it.

Devin had returned to their campsite after suffering through Sunny's arguing with her for a good ten minutes. Devin was clearly a hard-headed woman when she had her mind set. But Sunny was glad she'd ultimately allowed her to go, as they now had their sleeping bags and inflatable pads that would make sleeping on the floor in front of the fire much more pleasant.

Julian was lying atop two pads, now dressed in some of his own clothing, along with some of hers. She would never again let it bother her when friends complained that she overpacked. Two sleeping bags lay atop him, and his color was finally normal, with his body not even shivering at this point.

Devin was on the floor, resting against a heavy chair as she watched him sleep. At this point Julian didn't need such close monitoring, but Devin was like a loyal dog. There was no way the poor guy was even going to be able to go to the bathroom alone until they were rescued.

Sunny had written her version of events down quickly, and was now going over it all another time, making sure she hadn't forgotten anything.

When she was confident she'd gotten everything down, she went over to sit in the chair Devin was perched in front of. Julian wasn't the only one who needed comforting. So she petted Devin's straight, dark hair just like she had Julian's, smiling to herself when her head leaned in for a little more.

"Do you want to hear my notes?"

"I guess." Devin let out a heavy sigh. "But maybe that's a bad idea. I don't want your memories to get mixed up with mine." She turned her head just a little, letting their eyes meet. "I just want to know why in the hell you were out there in the first place."

"A moose," Sunny said, feeling her stomach turn at the thought of Hank dying over something so…ordinary. She took in a breath and continued. "I heard the guys moving around, so I got dressed and went outside. They both had to pee, and I told them you'd said they could go right by the tent. That would have been that, but a moose ambled along down the trail, the one that went right to the lake."

"They move around at first light," Devin said. "I should have thought of something like that attracting him."

Sunny patted her head, then stopped trying to soothe her. Devin looked like she was made of stone, and no amount of head-rubbing was going to relieve her of her guilt.

"Hank grabbed his pack, and pulled out a full-sized professional style camera. I can't guess how much it weighed, but he obviously thought it was worth carrying. He put the strap over his shoulder, strapped on his snowshoes and took off after the damned moose."

"Did you—"

"Of course I did," she said, cutting her off. "So did Julian. We both said it wasn't safe. We both begged him not to go. We both said we'd have to go with him. But he just laughed and said we'd never forgive ourselves if we let it get away."

"Got it," Devin said. She pulled her knees up to her chest and wrapped her arms around them, compressing herself into the smallest possible package. It was clear she'd heard enough, but Sunny felt she needed to say a few more things.

"We were both yelling when he got near the lake, and that might have spooked the moose. It cut across the lake, probably to get away from us, and Hank followed. Right before the moose reached the other shore, his right rear hoof either broke through or caught on something. But I definitely saw it do a stutter step. A second later, the ice opened up and sucked Hank down before I could blink. Julian said we had to save him, but I knew we couldn't."

"An awful lot of people die trying to save someone from cold water. An awful lot," she said, shifting her gaze to Julian.

"I grabbed him by the sleeve, but he shook me off and followed the same path Hank had taken. I was screaming, but he just kept going." She took in a breath, trying unsuccessfully to banish the image that kept making her heart skip a beat. "I'm sure it took me a few seconds to remember there was a whistle on this bracelet, but when I did I blew on it until I saw you racing across the lake." She took a shuddering breath. "Then his leg broke through."

Devin reached over and gripped her leg, giving it an encouraging squeeze. "Your instincts were perfect. Really perfect."

"I should have tackled him." She started to pound on her legs with her fists, so angry with herself she was ready to scream. "I knew I should have grabbed him and held on, but I just stood there—screaming and crying."

"You can't blame yourself for that, Sunny. Really. Julian's an adult too. He decided to do something rash, but it was his right to risk his life."

She looked down on Devin, seeing the empathy in her gaze. "Would you have stopped Julian?"

"Yeah. But only because I'm trained in how to rescue someone, and I know he's not. He would have just been in the way." She nodded slowly. "Which is exactly what happened. If Julian hadn't fallen in, I could have tried to save Hank."

Once again, Sunny closed her eyes and tried to stave off the tears that kept threatening to overwhelm her. "Do you think…? Do you think he died right away? I have these horrible images of him fighting and trying to break through the ice."

"That didn't happen," Devin said, her voice low and soft. "When you fall into cold water, you have this reflex to gasp. Not just a little gasp, either. A great big gasp that usually fills your lungs with water." She shook her head mournfully. "That makes most people sink to the bottom and drown. Even if you don't sink, you start to hyperventilate. You're gone in a matter of seconds." She put her hand on Sunny's calf and gave it a reassuring pat. "He didn't suffer. I'm sure of that."

"But some people are resuscitated after being in cold water. What about them?"

"Even if he was technically alive, his system would have been so shut down that he wouldn't have been aware of what was happening."

"God, I hope you're right," she sighed. "I can't bear to think of him suffering."

"He didn't. But the people who loved him will," Devin said, once again staring at Julian, lost in her own thoughts.

By the time it was dark, Devin seemed like her old self—at least close to the self Sunny had gotten to know. She'd found some cord and had rigged up a clothesline to dry her and Julian's things, and now the lodge smelled of wet wool. Julian had been able to sit in a chair for an hour, and had eaten about half of a packet of food, but he was still very weak and listless.

Devin had quietly asked how close he was to normal, but Sunny had to be honest and admit she didn't know him well, despite sharing an office for almost five years. Julian was the kind of guy who revealed little, always sticking to business. If he had a girlfriend or a boyfriend for that matter, she had no idea. He never wanted to go out for a drink after work, and he came to their office Christmas party alone.

Those few little thoughts about work made her blood pressure start to rise. Hank's wife was high-strung and emotional, and she wasn't going to have an easy time dealing with his loss. Not that anyone should. Losing your husband when you were just…she wasn't sure of her exact age, but she thought Angelica had been a freshman at UT when Sunny and Hank had been in their third year at the law school. Losing your husband when you weren't even thirty wasn't something any woman seriously considered.

Devin had been roaming around the lodge ever since they'd finished dinner. Sunny wasn't sure if she was the kind of woman who couldn't sit still generally, or if this had upset her so much that she was trying to keep herself busy to avoid thinking of it. Her guess was that it was the latter. Devin seemed like she'd normally be pretty laid-back when she had down-time.

The front door opened, letting in a gust of cold air. "Devin?"

She appeared in the room, holding a six-pack of snow flecked beer. Sunny hadn't been thirsty, but the carton resting under Devin's arm was as attractive as an advertisement, and she found herself craving a beer.

"Yes, please," Sunny said.

"Do you want a glass?"

"Isn't the beer in glass?" she asked, re-using the quip she always pulled out when asked that question.

"It is." Devin looked at Julian, who was acting like he was reading an e-book, but he hadn't clicked a single button in the hour Sunny had been surreptitiously watching him. He was probably trying to look busy so they didn't talk to him. "I'd offer you one, Julian, but I don't think alcohol's a good idea right now," Devin said.

"That's fine," he said, looking up, a smile affixed to his face. One of the least genuine smiles in history.

"Be right back."

A minute later Devin handed Sunny a beer and kept one for herself. "I lit a fire for the sauna if you want to warm up," she said. "That would be good for you if you're in the mood, Julian."

"No thanks. I'm going to go to sleep."

Devin nodded, then said, "We both wrote down what happened this morning. For the sheriff," she added. "If you can manage, you should do the same."

"I'll have time," he said. "They won't find us for hours tomorrow, right?"

"Right. But your memories might be fresher..." She trailed off when he gave her an annoyed glance. "You'll have plenty of time." Nodding in Sunny's direction, she said, "Want to sit in the sauna?"

"Sure." She stood and tried not to sound too maternal when she said, "We'll just be over there," pointing to the blond wooden door.

"I know. Good night."

"Good night, Julian," Sunny said, forcing herself not to go to him and wrap him in a grateful hug.

When they got to the door, Devin said, "I kept the heat at a moderate level just in case Julian wanted to come in. I can crank it up if you'd like."

"Moderate's good. The stove works well, but the room's still cool. I don't want to be overheated and then try to sleep."

Devin stood there for a second, looking puzzled. "We don't have towels. Or swimsuits."

She didn't add another word, clearly waiting for Sunny to decide what to wear—or not wear.

"If it's not hot we can wear our underwear."

"That's what I'd choose," Devin said, even though Sunny guessed she'd normally strip to the skin. She seemed to be very nonchalant about nudity, given how she'd whipped her clothes off in the tent that first night.

Devin took off Hank's fleece, then both T-shirts. Her wind pants went next, then her thermal pants, leaving her in just a pair of bikinis. While she wasn't phobic about being naked, Sunny didn't like to reveal more than necessary. So she merely removed her snow pants and her fleece top before following Devin into the enclosure. She got a surprised look when Devin saw that she was still in her long underwear, but she didn't comment.

"Nice temperature," Sunny said. "It's warm, but not hot."

Devin took a long drink of her beer, crossing her legs and leaning over to rest an arm atop her thighs, clearly trying to cover up a little. "I've never had a beer while sitting in a sauna." A weak smile looked like it was trying to involve her eyes, but it couldn't quite get the job done. "I might make a habit of it."

It was strange. No doubt about that. Two women who barely knew each other, equally stunned by a man's death, now sitting in a sauna, mostly naked. Normally, Sunny would have had to work to keep herself from discreetly checking Devin's awesome body out. But all of the elements that went into her sex drive—interest, attraction, lust—had all disappeared. Looking at a very attractive, almost naked, totally available lesbian after what had happened this morning left her with as much desire as she normally felt for a strange man on the street—none.

But they were together, and it was time to make conversation, something they hadn't tried much throughout the long day. "Cute undies," she said, pointing to the bright yellow briefs with orange pinstripes. "Are those the ones Edie stuffed in your backpack?"

"Yeah," she said, her smile now a little more genuine. "I usually stick with black, but maybe I should get a little wild."

"Yeah." She sighed, dismayed at having blown the only conversational topic that had come to her.

"Um, we can talk if you want to. About anything," Devin added. "I just don't know what to say."

"I don't either." Sunny leaned over and rested her arms on her thighs. "Normally, when I lose someone, I'm surrounded by people who know me well and know the person who passed. I spend a lot of time catching up with folks I don't see very often, and that softens the whole experience." She met Devin's gaze. "We don't have that."

"No, we don't." Her gaze shifted around the room, like she was considering building a sauna for herself and wanted to get the dimensions down. "Um, you could tell me more about Hank if you want to."

"Mmm, I don't think so. Not tonight."

"Okay."

They sat in complete silence for another couple of minutes, then Sunny said, "Have you lost many people?"

"Clients?" she said, with her voice breaking.

"No, no, people in general. You know…friends, co-workers, family."

"Not many." She seemed to think for a moment. "My mom's grandparents died when I was a baby, and my dad's grandma Rose passed on when I was in kindergarten." She shrugged. "Some people from town… That's been about it."

"I guess there's a benefit to being from a small town," Sunny said, trying to joke. "Fewer people around to die."

"Dallas is a big town," Devin said soberly. "Does that mean you've lost a lot?"

"I have," she said, not having planned on having the conversation go down this particular path. "All four of my grandparents, my favorite uncle, an aunt I liked but didn't know very well, a friend from high school, and the woman I was going to spend my life with." She met Devin's eyes, seeing her mouth drop open.

"Holy smoke," she whispered. Then she was right next to Sunny on the bench, grasping her hand to hold it in both of her warm ones. "I had no idea…"

"It's not the first thing I bring up when I'm out trying to have fun."

"No, no, of course not. But…" She looked a little out of her depth, but Sunny gave her credit for not backing away. "Do you wanna talk about it? About her?"

"Um…I guess I do. I've been thinking about her all day. Maybe it would help to get some of my feelings out." She gave Devin a long look. "Sure you don't mind? I know you've had an awful day."

"I don't mind." She reached across the room and grabbed her beer, then drank about half of it in one long glug. "Didn't want that to get warm."

"Thanks for reminding me. I forgot I had one." Sunny took a few sips of her own beer, realizing she craved alcohol to help take the edge off. "Um…Morgan, Hank, a guy named Jerry and I were in a study group in law school."

"Oh, wow, I didn't know you'd known Hank that long."

She nodded. "I'm now the only survivor of that study group. Jerry died of leukemia just a couple of years after we'd graduated." She shivered with the thought of three of her classmates succumbing so early. "Anyway, Morgan knew Hank from college. They both went to Rice."

"Is that a…school?"

"Yeah. In Houston. Morgan and Hank actually tried to date for a while in college, but they were too much alike."

"They were?" The shock on Devin's face was pretty funny, especially because she probably didn't know she looked like she'd been struck mute.

"Only in a few ways. They were both very focused and hard-working and competitive. But Morgan was kind-hearted and respectful and very concerned about hurting peoples' feelings."

"Oh, that's good. That's really important in a partner."

"Yeah. But it also makes it hard for a woman who isn't one hundred percent gay. Her family was very, very conservative, very, very Baptist, and very, very much in favor of heterosexuality for all. Morgan had a hell of a time figuring out how to live her life while not hurting them."

"Mmm," Devin said, nodding. "I know a lot of people don't like having gay kids whether or not they're religious."

"The Matthews' could easily have led their own chapter of Parents and Friends of Lesbians and Gays Who We're Going to Harass Until They Change."

"That would hardly fit on a bumper sticker," Devin said, with a cute little grin finally making her look like she had earlier when they were all just having fun.

"They're awful people. I hate to think of people in stereotypes, but they fit a bad one." She let out a sigh. "Anyway, Morgan and I were attracted to each other, but she couldn't take the leap. I hung in there, though." She met Devin's gaze again. "I was too attracted to her to let go without being one hundred percent sure she could never fall for me."

"But she did," Devin said. "Right?"

"She did, but it took a long, long time for her to take the first leap. Then we were on and off, mostly off until we graduated. She took a job in Dallas, and I stayed in Austin."

"But you wanted to be together..."

"I did. But if we were going to be a couple, I wanted her to choose us. I wasn't going to follow her around for god knew how long, only to have her parents convince her to marry some poor guy."

"When did she finally come around?"

"Mmm, about a year after we graduated. But I stayed in Austin another year, just to make sure she was certain about her decision.

Eventually, we started looking for apartments. We decided to buy a condo together as a sign of our commitment."

"That's really good. I've never gotten that far with anyone," Devin said. "But I wish I had."

"It was good. We were both doing transactional law, and she finally got up the nerve to tell the partners at her firm about me. They were expanding, and they brought me in as an associate." She smiled at the thought of those early months. "It was great. She was going to tell her parents' about us soon." Her voice broke as she finished, "She loved me enough to risk losing them, even though she was terrified about it."

Then Devin's warm hand was on her knee, and Sunny leaned into her body, resting against her strong shoulder, barely registering that she was almost naked. "We lived in her apartment for about six months, then found the perfect condo in our favorite neighborhood in Dallas. We were set to close on a Friday in December." She sucked in a breath and spit out the ending. "She was killed the night before in a car accident. Black ice on the highway. Someone in the opposite direction going too fast for conditions. A little bit of a curve he didn't make." She clapped her hands together, startling Devin. "They both died. All because he was in too damn big a hurry to get home. Fifty-five mile per hour zone and he was going over sixty-five. At least that's what they think. All I know for sure is that Morgan was gone by the time the ambulance got there, probably ten minutes later."

Thankfully, Devin didn't ask any questions. Most people were off-puttingly hungry for gory details, of which Sunny knew hundreds. She'd read the police report and the coroner's finding many, many times, desperate to reassure herself that Morgan's last moments on earth hadn't been filled with terror.

"What did you do?" Devin asked tentatively.

"I couldn't stay at the firm. Being reminded of her all day, every day was too much for me. And everyone tiptoed around me in ways that just got on my nerves. Hank was going out on his own after having worked for a good-sized firm for a couple of years, and I joined him." She met Devin's eyes. "I'm glad I did. He was there for me when I was really struggling, yet he didn't treat me like I was made of glass."

"Did you buy the condo?"

"I did. But it was more than I could afford on my own—"

"Morgan didn't have life insurance? I thought most normal jobs provided that."

"Oh, she did," Sunny said, hearing the bitterness inflect her voice. "But she didn't have a will. We were going to name each other as beneficiaries on all of our work-related things, but she hadn't gotten around to it. So everything she owned went to her parents. They were *horrible* when it came out. They wouldn't let me keep so much as her favorite sweater."

"Oh, fuck." Devin let out a sigh. "I'm so sorry."

She nodded. "I shouldn't be proud of this, but I was going to sue them for Morgan's half of the purchase price. I wouldn't have done it if I hadn't known how well-fixed they were, but they were and I did."

"Did you win?" Devin asked tentatively.

"It didn't come to that. I just had to threaten a suit and they sent me a check. They didn't want her name sullied in public." She took in a breath, fighting the urge to cry. "I didn't want them to have the money that she would have spent on the condo if she'd lived. It might sound irrational, but that condo feels like a gift Morgan gave to me—something she'd really want me to have."

"I'm glad you did that," Devin said. "And I bet you're right. She would have wanted you to have it."

"I like to believe so. Green was her favorite color, so that's the color I painted the bedroom. She bought some things when we were getting ready to move. Since her parents' took them, I searched around and bought duplicates. It's kind of like she decorated the room, which gave me a lot of comfort for a long time."

"I'm very glad you did that. I know people who've lost someone and just never got it together again. That doesn't sound like you at all."

Sunny gave her what she knew was a sad-looking smile. "Don't forget, I'm still single."

Logically, they placed Julian closest to the fire. To make sure he stayed warm, Devin turned his sleeping bag so it rested lengthwise in front of the stove. Then she and Sunny lay down behind him, their feet facing the stove. Even though they were only four feet away from the heat, Devin was cold. Much colder than she ever was at home, even when her pellet stove had just about run out of fuel.

The lodge was big, large enough to serve sixty for meals, along with a huge kitchen, an office, and a large shower room. All of that space was surrounded by windows, which drained a lot of warmth out, even though Devin was sure they'd used double insulated glass. Thank God they hadn't done the same for the front door. One of the workers told her they'd left it single pane intentionally so that stranded campers could easily break in. It was nice to think of someone making the decision to let in some cold air just to help people like them.

Julian was sound asleep, with his body needing a lot of rest before he'd fully recover. But Devin could tell Sunny wasn't able to relax, even though they were facing away from each other. "Having trouble getting your brain to shut down?"

"A little," she said. "But I think it's the cold that's keeping me up. I was going to get up and put my coat on, but I didn't want to wake you."

"I'm a little chilly myself." She hesitated for just a second, but spit it out. "And sad. I know a woman my age shouldn't need her mom to give her a hug and tell her it'll be all right, but I really do."

Her nervous laugh made Sunny smile, which helped a little. "The second we get cell service I'm calling my momma. And if she surprises the hell out of me and offers to come up here and take me home, I'm not going to fight very hard to stop her." She started to unzip her bag, meeting Devin's eyes as she worked. "We can zip these together, can't we?"

"Uh-huh." She tried to hide the relief she felt. It was too embarrassing to need comfort as much as she did. "Let me." She'd done this a thousand times, and got the bags hooked together in just a minute. Sunny might have felt cold, but her body was throwing off a lot of blessedly comforting heat. Devin wasn't sure how close she wanted to get, so she held back, letting Sunny take the lead.

The seconds ticked away, with both of them giving each other quick, tentative glances. Sunny eventually scooted over until they were face to face. "Since you're taller, will you be the big spoon?" Without waiting for an answer, she rolled over onto her right side, then Devin cuddled up behind her, with their bodies touching from shoulder to knee. It was funny, but once she put her arm around Sunny's waist, she felt comforted, even though she was technically in the comforter position. It dawned on her that's how she felt most connected to people—as the one who had everything under control.

Sunny let out a satisfied sigh, then patted Devin's hand. "That helps a lot," she said softly. "Being close warms me up mentally and physically."

"Me too." She wanted to nuzzle her face into Sunny's hair, to get as close as possible. But that would have seemed weird, and she just didn't have the nerve to expose her neediness that dramatically. This was enough. They didn't know each other well, but they'd bonded—deeply—over a tragedy that neither of them could have predicted. That was enough to let her guard down and suck up all of the comfort Sunny had to offer.

Chapter Seven

DAWN HAD COME AND GONE, and now they were bored and antsy. They'd had some of Hank's cocoa for breakfast, but it hadn't gone down well. When Sunny had gotten up to dispose of the paper cups, she saw that each of them had left at least half. It just seemed too ghoulish to eat a dead man's supplies. Now all the could do was sit quietly and watch the snow fall.

Devin had estimated they'd gotten about six inches so far. The wind had been busy too, carving the landscape into new shapes and piling snow up against the door. At least that was the report from her pre-dawn reconnaissance mission. There was no reason for her to be prowling around, checking the weather, but Sunny supposed she couldn't help herself. It must have been tough to be forced to sit still and wait for rescue when she was clearly able to hop on her skis and be back in the parking lot in an hour or two. But given how things had gone the last time she'd left them alone, there wasn't a doubt in Sunny's mind that they'd all remain in the lodge even if it took a week for them to be rescued.

No one had said more than the minimum so far, and the long silences were beginning to get on Sunny's nerves.

"So… Who do you think will come for us?" she finally asked, just to break the silence.

Devin had obviously given this a lot of thought, for she answered without hesitation. "Two of Edie's regular guides will come."

"Not the police?"

"No. Not at first. The guides will have a satellite phone, and they'll call the sheriff when they find us." She was quiet for a second. "Our tracks will have been covered over, but when they see the tents are empty they'll check here before they start looking around."

Sunny let that sink in, with Devin quickly adding, "You're probably wondering why we don't all carry satellite phones."

"No, I really—"

"They're crazy expensive," she explained, clearly agitated. "And calls are about two bucks a minute. The manufacturers claim they work almost everywhere, but that's just not true. They're better than a regular cell phone, of course, but some people rely on them, and that isn't smart."

"But you think they'll work here?"

"They probably will, since we're only five or six miles off the grid. It's way out in the wilderness that they're useless. And heavy," she added. "Edie made me carry one once, and it was like lugging a brick around." She settled down, lifted her knees and draped her arms over them, making her look super casual. Like she was sitting around a campfire discussing quotidian topics with friends. "The truth is that when you're out in the wilderness you simply don't have easy access to help. If something bad happens, you've got to handle it." She looked very contemplative, and her voice dropped a little. "If a helicopter had taken off the moment Hank fell in, it couldn't have saved him."

Sunny's heart clenched with sympathy as she looked at the bereft expression on her face. Devin must have been going over scenarios ever since it happened, trying to figure out ways the outcome could have been different. But they all knew the only way things could have worked out for Hank was if Devin had been there. And that was a truth she was going to carry for the rest of her life. Hank had grossly disregarded his safety, but Devin had been gone when he'd done the dumbest thing ever. Her absence and his last careless decision had overlapped at the worst possible time.

It wasn't even nine o'clock when Devin jumped to her feet and went to the window, leaning against the glass to see just a tiny bit farther. "They're here," she said quietly.

It took another few seconds for Sunny to even hear the high-pitched engine of a snowmobile. Then they all gathered by the front door and watched a guy use a small shovel to render first the stairs, then the area in front of the door free of snow.

Devin flung the door open and grabbed the guy in a hug, holding on for a long time.

"You had us worried," he said as he removed his helmet and smiled broadly. "But I told Richie you'd obviously just had a little glitch. What was it?" he asked, with his curious gaze sliding across Sunny and Julian.

The second guy came bounding up the stairs, shaking his head. "You're the last person I ever thought I'd have to look for. Damn, Devin! We were worried sick about you."

Surprisingly, Devin pushed both of the guys outside and closed the door. She wasn't even wearing her jacket, but she stood out there for a minute, delivering the news. Both guys looked like she'd just slapped them hard in the face, then the first guy pulled her into another hug so ferocious it had to have hurt.

The door opened again, and the first guy, a big, bearded, burly fellow, stood in the entryway, helmet in hand, staring at the floor. "I'm sorry for your loss," he said, almost mumbling.

"Yeah," the other guy added, also not able to look up and meet her eyes. "Sorry."

"Thanks," Sunny said. "We're ready to head home. How are we going to do that?"

Devin was in the room now, but she'd moved far away, leaning against the back wall like she wanted to disappear. Then she stood up tall and cleared her throat. "I think we need to stay until the sheriff gets here."

"Julian has to get to a doctor," Sunny said. "And I want to be with him." Devin started to open her mouth, but Sunny kept going. "I understand you need to stay, but we can give statements later, once we're sure Julian's all right."

"You're right." Turning to the first guy, Devin said, "You brought a satellite, right?"

"Yeah. It's on the sled. Be right back."

Devin went over to where she'd placed her outer layer of clothing to dry. When she picked up her jacket, she handed it to Julian. "My stuff should fit you. You can put it on under your own. Every layer helps."

"You need it," he said, pushing it back toward her. "You'll freeze."

"I've got an insulated dry suit somewhere around here. That'll keep me warm in any weather."

“We brought two sets of insulated coveralls,” the guy with sandy-colored hair said. “You should keep your stuff, Dev. Your dry suit doesn’t breathe.”

“All right,” she said, looking a little defeated. It was clear she felt more in control if she was doing something for her clients, but she was out of options at this point.

The first guy came back in and quietly said, “I called. They’ll be here in about two hours.”

“Two hours!” Sunny yelped. “Did you tell them this was an emergency?”

“A death in the woods is always an emergency,” he said. “Without a helicopter, two hours is as fast as they can make it.” He looked a little tentative, then said, “If one of you can drive a snowmobile, I can stay here with Devin.”

“That’s not a good idea,” Devin said. “I want both of you guys to be with them in case anything happens.”

“I’ve driven a snowmobile a few times,” Sunny said. “I’m sure I can handle it.”

Devin shook her head firmly. “You’re right about Julian. He should be seen by a doctor, but Richie and Chris should both be with you. I’ll be fine, even if I have to stay over another night.”

“Why would you have to do that?” Sunny asked.

“Well, the sheriff won’t get here until close to noon, then we’ll have to go to the site. They won’t leave until they’re sure they’ve done everything they can to…” She swallowed, obviously finding it hard to speak about Hank as a thing. “Recover the body. By the time we’re finished, it’ll be close to dark.”

“I’ll come back,” the first guy said.

“You don’t have to, Chris. I’ve overnighted in much less hospitable conditions. I don’t want you driving all over creation just to hang out.”

He looked like he was going to argue, but finally nodded. “All right. But I’m leaving my snowmobile at the parking lot. You ski over and get it while you’re waiting for the sheriff. Then I won’t worry about you so much.”

"I will." She put her arms around him and held on for so long Sunny was a little stunned. They were so obviously fond of each other she thought they might have been lovers, but he gave off a brotherly vibe, looking like he was going to cry as he stood there, rubbing her back and speaking quietly into her ear.

"Are you sure you're going to be all right?" Sunny heard him ask.

"Yeah. Will you call my mom and dad when you get back? You don't have to tell them what happened, just say I got delayed and won't be home until tomorrow."

He nodded, but even though Sunny didn't know him from Adam, she could tell he was lying. He was going to tell Devin's parents the whole story, making it just a little bit easier on her. "I've got to call Lori first. She's a nervous wreck."

"Sorry I worried you guys. Couldn't be helped."

"I know." He hugged her again, then moved toward the door, catching Sunny's gaze. "We brought a little sled, so you can bring your gear back if you want."

"I can take everything," Devin said. "Don't waste your time packing up."

Sunny and Julian spent just a couple of minutes getting their backpacks ready. Then Devin helped them into the very well-used insulated coveralls the guys had brought and walked them down the stairs. Sunny had the instinct to hug her, but thought that might have looked odd, so she just got on the back of a snowmobile and waved as they took off. Devin stood there, all alone on the landing, with the blowing snow creating a vague cloud around her body. Her posture was erect, chin held high, but Sunny nearly broke down in tears at the desolation that shone in her haunted eyes.

Devin had everything from their camp neatly loaded onto the sled attached to the back of the snowmobile by the time the deputy roared up on his powerful machine. There were just three deputies assigned to cover the whole area, and she knew all of them by sight. She'd gone to high school with Rich, and knew Kenny from various bars around the county.

Luckily, this was the third guy, the one she'd never spoken to. It was best to keep this strictly professional so no one could say she got let off easily because she knew the guy.

She'd put on her dry suit, just to add some insulation for the trip on the snowmobile, but she hated wearing it, thinking it made her look like she was trying to impersonate a superhero, with all sorts of silver inset panels on the skin-tight garment that added nothing but silliness to the thing. But she'd left it on, thinking she might need it when they went down to the lake.

She stepped onto the landing, then went down the stairs to meet him. "Devin Savary," she said, extending her hand to shake. "Do you want me to take you to the spot where my client fell in?"

"No, thanks. The Warden Service is going to conduct the search. They're equipped for it." He nodded toward the lodge. "Let's go inside and you can tell me what happened."

She turned and went back up the stairs, eager to get out of the dry suit immediately. It was bad enough looking like Ironwoman when you had a good reason. But looking like a kid in a Halloween costume while a deputy was taking your statement was just weird.

Devin and Deputy Hardin spent a very unpleasant two hours together, going over every detail of that horrible morning. She drew a map of the scene, taxing her very poor drawing skills, then another of the route she'd taken to check on the shortcut. He added them, along with her handwritten recollections from the day before into a weatherproof case he carried.

It seemed like he was trying to trip her up, or make her change her story, but she supposed that was just his job. Finally, when she was sure he couldn't possibly have any other questions, he posed the worst one. "Don't you wish you could go back and change a few things?"

Her head dropped for a minute, then she forced herself to look him in the eye and tell the truth. "I think I'll wish that a few times a day for the rest of my life."

There was a sobering level of sympathy in his eyes when he said, "I killed a kid—a child—in Afghanistan. He was trying to take our tank out, and I was one hundred percent justified." He nodded slowly. "He was about nine, and a perfect image of the look on his face when he fell is etched in my brain." His shoulders rose in a shrug. "I saw it all the time at first, but not very often now." His big hand settled on her shoulder. "This wasn't your fault, Devin. Some people are bound and determined to find trouble."

"I know," she said, swallowing around the lump in her throat. "And those are exactly the ones you should never, ever leave alone."

The search team had to cut a hole in the ice to dive in. Funny how one cold night could seal the ice right back up. There were six divers working in teams, two at a time. After a team surfaced, they'd go to a portable warming hut they'd set up and stay there, waiting for their turn again. These were people who did this all winter long, rarely having what anyone would think of as a good day at the office. But as long as Maine had icy lakes, people would fall into them, and very few would come out alive.

They called it a day at four, giving them enough time to get back to their trucks and get home. But they'd be back tomorrow, and the day after and the day after that. If the weather held, they'd stay until they found him, ignoring the cost and the futility of the entire exercise. But if it started to get warm, they'd move on to their next reclamation effort and come back when they could use a boat. If he didn't come to the surface, it was because he or his clothing was stuck on something. One way or the other, he'd be found eventually. Just about everyone was.

Devin got on Chris's snowmobile and followed them back to the parking lot, even though she really wanted to put her skis on and be alone for a while. When they reached the lot, she bit at her lip, trying not to cry, but she failed miserably. Chris and Lori, her dearest friends, were in their truck with the engine running, waiting for her.

By the time she got her helmet off they had her wrapped in a group hug, with the guys from the Warden Service murmuring their goodbyes as they locked up their snowmobiles, got into their trucks, and took off.

"You poor thing," Lori said, repeatedly kissing Devin's cheeks.

"I'm not lying on the bottom of the lake," she grumbled. "My client's the one you should feel sorry for." She wiped at her tears, finding them frozen.

"I didn't know him," Lori said. "I know you, and I know how responsible you feel for your clients."

"I screwed up," Devin whimpered, burying her face against Chris's broad shoulder. "I screwed up so bad."

It took a half hour to dig her truck out from the drifts that had buried it up to the wheel wells, but the three of them worked until she could get the chains on. Then they secured the snowmobile in its trailer, and were ready to go. But Lori insisted on riding with her. What were you supposed to do when you craved alone time like a drug, but your dear friend wanted to be with you? You sucked it up and let her. No question.

Luckily, Lori was such a good friend, and so used to living with an equally fastidious guide, that she didn't press for information. Instead, she talked about her kids, Caleb and Brody, almost making Devin smile at the little guys' exploits.

The drive didn't seem to take as long as it usually did, thanks to Lori's distracting her, but when they pulled up in front of Edie's, Devin's heart froze in her chest when she spied her dad's truck. "Did you tell him to come?" she asked, twitching her head in the direction of the silver truck.

"I tried to talk them out of it." She patted Devin's leg. "I convinced your mom not to go all the way out with us, so I was partially successful."

"Thanks for that. I'd just rather talk about this in private—"

Her door flew open and her mom was pulling on her before she had the truck turned off. Devin unbuckled and slid out, almost stepping on her mom's feet. "I'm all right," she said. Then her dad was there, grabbing the little of her that her mom didn't have hold of. Then Edie joined in, making Devin feel awfully good—but very, very raw. This was too much emotion for her to handle at one time, but the cold night helped her out. They had to go inside so they didn't freeze. Edie called her husband Mike and told him to hurry over, and soon the whole store was filled with all of the other guides and a few of their girlfriends. Lori's mom brought the boys over and they ran around the store with such joy that the mood in the place lightened up a bit. Finally, Richie showed up with a couple of cases of beer and they had what seemed to Devin like a happy wake. It was nice to know how many of your friends loved you. Really nice. But she wished they'd just have mentioned it the next time they saw her around.

She'd had more beer than she should have, given that her stomach was completely empty. There was no way she should, or could drive back to Abbot, and no way her mom would let her go to her cabin alone.

Devin walked over to Edie and said, "Have you spoken to Sunny?"

"Right before you got here. She's back at Lakeside."

"Lakeside? All the way up there?"

"That's what she said, Dev."

"Is Julian in the hospital?"

"No," she said, smiling. "Mike drove him to Bangor."

"He's gone?" Devin was sure her mouth was hanging open.

"Uh-huh. The doctors gave him the all clear and he got a seat on the New York flight. He said he won't have any trouble finding a connection to Dallas." She gripped Devin's arm and nodded. "He needed to get home."

"What about the sheriff?"

"They took Julian's statement when he was at the hospital. He didn't have much to say, though. Other than the fact that you saved his life." She hugged her again, really hard. "You did, Devin. I know you feel responsible for Hank, but you got Julian out. Most people wouldn't have."

"Most wouldn't have let a guy with the self-control of a toddler get into trouble in the first place. If Hank hadn't fallen in, I wouldn't have had to rescue Julian." She pulled away and stood up tall. "Do you have a contact number for Hank's wife? I need to call her."

"You can't," Edie said, flinching at the heated look Devin gave her. "Word got over to Jackson, and he told me in no uncertain terms that neither of us should contact his survivors."

"What in the hell does this have to do with your attorney? Hank's wife deserves to know what happened."

"Sunny can call her, Dev. She was there too."

Devin closed her eyes, taking a few deep breaths. "I don't like that. That's the coward's way out."

"Please don't," Edie said, her eyes filling with tears. "I could lose the business if she sues us and wins a big judgment. Anything you admit to…"

Devin shook her head, trying to get that distressing thought to leave her head. "I need to see Sunny. I don't want her to be alone."

"You're not driving…"

"Of course I'm not. But I need you to back me up. My mom's not going to want to let me go, but I have to, Edie. I really have to." Her brain wasn't working at its full capacity, but she finally thought to ask, "Why didn't Sunny go home with Julian?"

"She said she wasn't ready to leave, but I think she wanted to make sure you were okay."

"She's a nice person," Devin said. "And she deserved a fun trip, not this mess."

It took forever to submit to crushing hugs from her fellow guides and gentle kisses from everyone else, but Devin was finally, thankfully, back in her own car. She was in the passenger seat, but it was still nice. Her dad was driving, with her mom following behind as they drove all the way past Rockwood, a good half hour north. Devin couldn't figure out why the group had chosen to be so far away, but the lodge and cabins at that part of the lake were pretty, if a little rustic for city people.

Her dad was usually just as quiet as she was, sometimes a little more, but he talked a lot on the drive. Mostly he tried to reassure her, the same way everyone at Edie's had. But those obviously sincere efforts hadn't gone down well. She knew what she'd done, she knew what she should have done, and she knew what she hadn't done. No one could convince her that she couldn't have prevented Hank from going onto the ice, so no one could convince her it wasn't her fault that he had. Her dad must have realized his comments weren't making a dent, because he gave her a look as they were crawling along the very long private road that led to Lakeside and said, "You know how much your mom and I love you, right?"

“Of course I do.” She reached over and gave him a playful punch to the shoulder, one of the ways they showed affection. It didn’t look like a loving gesture, but they’d been doing it since she was tiny, and it had the same impact as a hug or a kiss. Maybe more.

“Well, I just want to tell you…in words…how glad we are that you’re not in the lake with that guy. I know you, Buddy, and I know you would have been in there if you hadn’t been focused on saving the other one.”

“I would have,” she admitted, “but I would have done it safely.”

“You can’t be safe enough.” He gave her a quick look. “We both know seasoned guys who’ve gone in and didn’t live to tell the tale.”

“I know, Dad. Being on the ice is dangerous, even when you know what you’re doing.”

“Right. That’s why I feel nothing but relief to have you here with me.” He clapped her on the leg, slapping her so hard her skin tingled. “I feel bad for the guy who died, but he was an idiot who forced my baby to risk her life. Fact is, you can’t stop some people from competing for the Darwin Awards.”

As a high school science teacher, her dad had always enjoying joking about the awards. It was one of their ongoing things, both of them agreeing that some people really did improve the gene pool by removing themselves from it. She’d never stopped to consider how even the most reckless people left a big hole when they departed—no matter how dumb or ill-considered their exit strategy.

CHAPTER EIGHT

SHE HADN'T BEEN ABLE TO call, but Devin was pretty sure Sunny would be at the lodge. There were few places to go in winter, with even the closest restaurants a long drive away. But even if there were great nightspots right next door, Sunny wouldn't want to be out tonight.

After they pulled up in front of the office/owner's cabin, Devin jumped out and went to her dad's truck to kiss her mom goodbye.

"Thanks for driving all the way up here," Devin said.

"I'd go to the moon for you, and you know it."

"Yeah, I do," she said, a little embarrassed at how emotional she felt. "I'm still thankful though."

"Do you have everything?"

"Yeah. I'll just grab the stuff I bought." She ran around to the passenger side of the truck and took out two bags. "I'll be home tomorrow."

Her mom got out and hugged her hard, then her dad handed her the keys, bending to kiss her cheek. "Take care of yourself, Buddy."

"I will. See you."

As they started to drive away, their headlamps cut across the property, landing on a pretty woman with reddish blonde hair who'd poked her head out of her cabin. Devin put her backpack over one shoulder, then hustled over to her, carrying all of the stuff she'd brought. "I thought you might need some dinner," she said, hoping Sunny didn't feel like she was being stalked.

"Get in here." She grabbed her by the sleeve and tugged, pulling her into the surprisingly large cabin.

"Nice," she said, looking around. "I've never actually been inside one of these."

"But you've been up here?"

"Uh-huh. I've picked clients up here quite a few times." She made herself smile, even though she was nervous and edgy. "No one's ever invited me in."

"Well, I didn't technically invite you," she said, trying to tease, but still looking a little stiff, "but I'm really glad you're here."

"Me too. Have you eaten?"

"I had some lunch at the hospital." She made a face. "The freeze-dried stuff we had was better."

"How about a grilled ham and cheese sandwich? I brought everything to make them."

"Sounds great."

Devin started to walk to the kitchen, but Sunny gripped the sleeve of her jacket, pulling her to a stop. "Thanks for coming," she said, offering a very faint smile. "I didn't want to be alone tonight."

There was way too much emotion in the room, so Devin nodded and continued the short walk. It was a tiny kitchen, with a sink and a two burner camp stove the full extent of the appliances. "No electricity, huh?" Devin asked.

"Hard to believe I chose this on purpose. I thought the best way to get away was to really get away." She shrugged, clearly melancholy. "I didn't realize I'd be all alone."

"You're not," Devin said, trying to amp up her enthusiasm. "You hired a full-service guide. I not only lead you around, I follow you home and cook you dinner." Just to keep the conversation going, she said, "Is this a three-bedroom place?"

"Uh-huh. I could easily see coming up here with a couple of kids and going hiking and kayaking in the summer. It's really wholesome."

"It is. This is one place your kids can't spend their whole vacation playing a video game." She laughed a little. "Well, they can start out doing that, but then they'd run out of juice."

"Having only a lantern makes me feel like Abe Lincoln. Didn't he do his homework on a slate tablet in front of a fire?"

"Probably. But then so did most people. We've only had electricity for a blink of an eye."

She got the one frying pan heated up, then melted some butter in it and carefully placed the sandwiches she'd made in the pan, listening to the satisfying sizzle. "I don't cook much, since I don't have a heating source in my cabin, so this is kinda fun."

Sunny walked past on her way to snoop inside the grocery bags. "Ahh. You brought some beer. Want one?"

"I've had quiet a few already," she admitted. "So many my parents wouldn't let me drive."

"I was going to ask why I heard so many car doors opening and closing." She walked by again, stopping to place her hand gently against Devin's back. "I bet they were worried about you."

"They were." She flipped the sandwiches over, pleased that she'd gotten them a nice golden brown. "Did you call your parents?"

"My mom. She called my sisters so I could get to the call I really didn't want to make."

Devin continued to stare at the pan, not wanting to see Sunny's expression when she revealed how her talk with Hank's wife had gone. "Wanna talk about it?"

"No. But I'd like to make it clear I'd prefer to never make another one of those calls."

Devin nodded, not having anything to add to that. "Just about ready," she said. "Can you find us a couple of plates?"

"Right here." Sunny placed them on the tiny counter, no more than eighteen inches of it.

Devin slid the sandwiches onto the plates, managing not to drop either of them onto the floor. "Grab a seat. I'll serve you."

The main room held a love seat and two upholstered chairs, along with a wooden coffee table, tiny tables by the chairs, and a good-sized wood-burning stove that was throwing off plenty of heat to keep the main room toasty warm.

After ripping open a bag of chips and adding some to each plate, Devin delivered the sandwich to Sunny, who accepted it with a smile. "Health food," she said, looking up and meeting Devin's eyes.

Devin dropped to the other chair and settled the plate on her lap. "Do you normally eat healthy food?"

She took a big bite, then nodded. "When I can. Sometimes I get stuck at the office and have to eat junk, but it's not my preference." As she wiped her mouth with a paper napkin she added, "All bets are off when I'm on vacation, though. This is really good, by the way. A well made grilled sandwich is definitely one of my indulgences."

"I eat pretty well normally, but it's crazy when I'm at my parents' house. My mom's a nurse and thinks she's going to live forever if she avoids sugar and processed flour." She tossed a chip into her mouth. "All four of my grandparents are alive, and none of them have heart trouble or diabetes or high blood pressure. I figure I've been dealt a good hand."

"That can all change in a second, can't it?" Sunny snapped her mouth closed, then reached over and gripped Devin's arm. "I didn't mean for that to come out that way. Damn," she muttered. "I'm just seeing the dark side today. I can't get past it."

"It's only been a day," Devin reminded her. "I don't think you get over losing an old friend just because another page comes off the calendar."

"No, no, I know that's true."

They put their heads down and finished their dinner, with Devin wishing for possibly the first time in her life that there was a TV squawking away in the background. Even the hum of the refrigerator would have been nice. But the only sounds were when Sunny put a potato chip in her mouth, and she even stopped doing that, probably because the crunch was too loud for her own ears.

Despite not wanting to hear herself swallow, Devin got up and grabbed a beer, standing by the sink to drink half of it. She'd only eaten half of her sandwich, but that was plenty. She honestly didn't want the food to sop up the alcohol, needing every drop of it to calm her jangled nerves.

"Not hungry?" Sunny asked when she returned and sat down.

"Not very. I normally eat really early."

Sunny put her plate down, with a decent portion of her sandwich also remaining. "Wish I had a TV," she said, pouting a little. "It seemed like such a good idea to be off the grid. Now I want a TV and internet and movie streaming and anything else that might distract me." She threaded her fingers through her hair and ruffled it, leaving it a mess when she dropped her hands to her lap. "Was it like this all the time before people had electricity?"

"Only when there was something really upsetting that no one wanted to talk about." She let a slight smile show. "That's just my guess, of course. I don't have a single fact to support that belief."

Sunny's gaze lingered on the beer bottle that Devin had just drained. "I don't want to have to worry about you driving home after you've been drinking. Maybe—"

"I was planning on staying." She shifted her focus, trying to look in Sunny's general direction, but not directly at her, just in case she shot down the idea. "But if you want me to shove off, I can get a ride home."

"You want to stay? Really?"

Devin allowed their eyes to meet. "I really do. I know I'm not very good company, but I don't want to be alone. I thought maybe that was true for you."

"It is," she said, clearly relieved. "It really is. I was dreading being in this big place all by myself."

"Why'd you stay?" Devin asked gently. "You could have gone home with Julian."

"I know." She swallowed the last of her beer and purposefully set the empty on the little table next to her. "I guess… I think I wanted to delay the inevitable, you know?"

"Which inevitable?"

"Having to see my family, and Hank's wife, and our co-workers. I thought I could get away with claiming I was staying to oversee things. Like I was somehow going to help with the recovery effort." She met Devin's eyes, with what looked like fear reflected back at her. "I want to hide out here until I feel like I can bear it."

"When were you supposed to leave?"

"Thursday."

"Then why don't you just keep your original reservation? That'll give you three full days to let this sink in." She swallowed nervously. "I'll stay right by your side if you want me to."

"God, I'd love that," she murmured. "But I have to go back. I've got a staff that's going to need some reassurances."

"How about one day?" Devin said. "Just one day to give you a chance to breathe a little."

Sunny looked like she was going to refuse, then she nodded once. "One day. That's not what I need, but it'll help." She took a deep breath, then said, "Then we'll both get back to business."

"I'm not going to be ready in a day," Devin said. "I'm certain of that."

"Then you'll take a little time to get back to normal. You'll know when the time is right."

Devin nodded, not allowing herself to say the truth; that she couldn't imagine ever working as a guide again.

Sunny didn't wear a watch, and her phone was long dead, so she had no idea what time it was when she said, "I guess I'll get ready for bed."

Devin seemed surprised, but she nodded agreeably. "Go right ahead. I'm sure we'll both feel better if we get some sleep."

After brushing her teeth and putting on some flannel pajamas, Sunny came out of the bathroom. Devin was standing in the middle of the room, holding her backpack in her hand. She seemed profoundly indecisive, just standing there staring blankly at the bedroom doors, two on one side of the short hallway, one on the other.

"You can use whichever bedroom you like," Sunny said. "I don't have a preference."

"Um…" Devin grasped her backpack to her chest, with her gaze shifting between the rooms. "I thought you might get cold again," she finally said, her voice remarkably soft. "There's no heat in the bedrooms…"

Sunny stuck her arm out and grasped the hand that rose to meet her own. As soon as their fingers touched, a shiver of relief ran through her. Clearly, she needed comfort as much as Devin in. "Come on. We'll use the big bed."

"Sure?" She seemed a little hesitant.

"I never would have gotten to sleep last night without having you close. Why mess with success?"

She finally showed a hint of a smile. "Which side do you like?"

"I…" She stared at the bed in the faint glow from the lantern. "I don't care. You?"

"I don't either. Living alone means you don't need to know things like that."

"Then you take the side closer to the door. You've had more to drink than I have, so you'll have to get up to pee."

"I'm trained," she said, revealing a crooked smile. "I hardly ever get up."

"Well," Sunny said, pulling the wool blanket and fluffy comforter down and sliding between the sheets, "if you have to, you're set."

Devin quickly took off her sweater and pants, leaving her in her long underwear. It took until that moment for Sunny to notice she was wearing her own clothes again. Thank God her stuff had dried. Seeing Hank's roomy fleece hanging off her body had been a constant reminder of his absence.

Devin got into bed and started trying to get her sports bra off without first removing her top. "This isn't as easy as it looks," she grumbled.

Sunny waited until she was settled, then scooted close. "Will you hold me?" she asked, with her voice breaking. "I'm so damn lonely."

"Yeah." Devin put her arm around Sunny's shoulders, then kissed the top of her head when she snuggled close. "I'm lonely too."

She patted her side and burrowed into her body. "This is good," she sighed. "Much, much better."

"Feel free to wake me if I snore."

"Do you?"

"No one's ever said I do, but it's been a while since I've been with someone who was around long enough to complain."

"No complaints," Sunny said. "This is all good."

CHAPTER NINE

EVEN THOUGH SHE'D SLEPT WITH a decent number of relative strangers in the last few years, when she woke an uneasy feeling washed over Devin —embarrassment or some kind of discomfort she couldn't name. Her arm was tucked around Sunny's waist, and a few chilled fingers barely touched her hand. She'd been far more intimate with people she'd known far less, which made it even stranger that this little bit of contact was making her feel so weird.

Stealthily, she extracted her hand from Sunny's body, waited a few seconds to make sure she didn't wake, then rolled onto her side and slipped out of bed, pausing to tuck the covers around Sunny to keep her warm.

Shivering from the cold, Devin tiptoed into the living area to stoke the fire, which had burned down to nothing during the night. She should have gone home to get more clothing before driving up the night before, but she hadn't, and was now stuck with only her long underwear, a sweater, and her outer layer, which was better suited to snowshoeing than it was to keeping warm in an icy cabin.

After she was satisfied with the fire, she took two wool throws and wrapped one around her shoulders and the other around her waist. Nearly hobbling, she went into the bath and took care of business, then came back into the living area and sat close to the stove.

A long time later, Sunny walked up behind her, making her start.

"Hi," Devin said, turning to look at Sunny's sleepy face and squinty eyes. "You don't look like you're quite awake."

Sunny patted her shoulder then moved to sit next to her on the sofa. "Willing to share your warmth?"

"Oh, sure." She pulled the throw from her legs and placed it over both of them. "The fire's really throwing off some heat."

Sunny bumped her with her shoulder. "Bet it wasn't when you got up. Thanks."

"I'm used to getting up in the cold. I don't like it," she admitted, "but I'm used to it."

"Do you have any plans for today? And if you do, can I tag along?"

Devin scooted around so they were facing each other. "I'm going to be right next to you until you leave Maine. I mean that."

"Thanks," Sunny said quietly, with a hint of color rising to her cheeks. "I'm not usually so needy…"

"You don't have to explain," Devin said. "I could hardly stop myself from jumping on that snowmobile and taking off with you guys yesterday. That was a long two hours."

Sunny pulled her hand from the blanket and gripped Devin's arm. "I'm sorry we had to leave. I was just worried about Julian and—"

"You did the right thing. I'm just letting you know that you're not alone. We're both pretty fragile."

"Yeah. That's what we are. Fragile." Surprisingly, she scooted down and let her head lie on Devin's leg. "But I feel better now." Her head tilted up a little. "You?"

"Yeah. I feel better." Devin wanted to run her fingers through Sunny's messy hair, desperate to touch her as much as she'd allow. The closer they were, the less alone she felt. But she couldn't push it. She'd let Sunny decide how close to be. Luckily, she didn't seem to be embarrassed of her feelings, something Devin would work on if she had any sense.

The owners of the resort bustled around the office in their cabin, going out of their way to make sure Sunny was able to use their satellite internet connection. Janice was pleasingly plump, to use a term Sunny's grandmother had favored, with a good ash blonde dye job. She seemed a little anxious, but maybe that was because she'd learned of Hank's death and wasn't sure what to say.

Sunny looked up when the door opened and Devin stood there, looking sheepish.

"Good morning," she said, extending her hand when Janice approached the door. "Devin Savary. I don't think we've met, but I've picked up clients from here over the years."

"Janice Greene," she said. "It's good to meet you, Devin. Edie talks about you like you're the best guide in all of Maine."

Sunny winced when she saw the stricken look on Devin's face. *Damn.* It was going to take her a long time to get over this.

"Yeah, well, I think the world of Edie, too." She turned her head to give Sunny a quick smile, then met Janice's gaze again. "Do you mind if I use your internet when Sunny's finished? I told my parents I'd keep in touch."

"Of course," she said, giving her a quick pat on the back. "You two stay as long as you like. We'll do anything we can to help," she said, looking like she was about to cry. "Anything at all."

As Janice walked away from the desk, Devin moved to sit on the corner of it. "I guess she heard the news," she said, sounding painfully bruised. "I think I'm gonna have to get used to that. The whole county will be talking about this."

Sunny finished the email she'd been working on, then stood. Leaning over, she whispered into Devin's ear. "That's true. But then something else will happen and that'll be the thing everyone's talking about. Bad news doesn't last long. Trust me. Once everyone in my office had offered condolences about Morgan, her name was only brought up in business matters."

"Right," Devin said. "I know you've had more experience with this kind of thing than I have. I'll take any tips you've got to spare."

Nodding, Sunny gave her a pat on the shoulder. "I'll go get my wallet and we can grab breakfast."

"I'll just be a minute."

Sunny went back to the cabin to get her things and lock up. When she returned, Devin was typing away quickly. "My mom's not happy with me," she said. "I thought I could just leave her an e-mail, but she must've been sitting right at the computer. We're essentially texting."

"What's wrong?" Sunny stood next to her, but went out of her way to not snoop.

Devin let out a sigh. "She wants to see me. She thinks I'm in bad shape."

"Are you?" Sunny asked gently.

"No more than normal for having something like this happen." She shrugged. "I think. How the heck do I know? I've never let a client die."

Sunny put her hand on Devin's shoulder and squeezed. "Maybe you should go home. Your mom knows you better than anyone, right?"

"How about dinner?" Devin asked, looking up and fixing Sunny with her pale blue eyes.

"Dinner?"

"Yeah. At my parents' house. My mom can interrogate me for a while, and we can get a decent meal."

"I'd love to. If your mom doesn't mind, of course. Maybe she'd rather have you alone."

"She'd love to cook for us. That's one of her favorite ways to show she cares." She tapped a few keys then waited a minute. "We're on. Anything you don't eat?"

"Not much. Rattlesnake?"

Devin smiled and typed a bit more. "I can guarantee we won't be having rattlesnake." She logged out and stood. "But right now I'm hungry enough to try it."

They went to one of the only local places that was open year-round, which was, fortuitously, Devin's favorite spot in the area. She had a passing acquaintance with their server, and if the woman had heard about Hank's death, she didn't let on, prattling about local gossip like everything was absolutely normal.

After they'd eaten three times more than Devin ever consumed for breakfast, they got back into her car. "Would you mind if I ran over to my grandparents' house? I've got to take care of some things over there."

"Of course not."

"Great. It shouldn't take me too long. Then we can do whatever you want—as long as we've got whatever it is." She shrugged. "We don't have a lot of choices at this time of year."

"There's more going on in the summer?"

"No," she said, chuckling softly. "But you can sit outside if the bugs aren't too bad. That just about doubles your entertainment options."

◆

A while later, Sunny threw a stick into the woods, waiting for a pair of elderly dogs to mildly wrestle over it and return it to her. The "thwack" pause "thump" pause "crack" of firewood being split and tossed into a pile was lulling her into a very zen-like state.

Devin was working her butt off, but she clearly had more energy than any two women Sunny had ever met. It must have been impossible to keep her in a chair when she was a kid.

Sunny turned when she heard footsteps crunching the snow. Devin's grandmother, a spry, fairly sober sort, was carrying two mugs, and she offered one to Sunny. The woman didn't look much like Devin, but she was tall for a woman her age, with short, straight white hair and a sharp, alert aspect to her pale eyes. It was kind of funny, standing there in a huge down parka, hat, scarf and fur covered boots while an octogenarian stood next to her in only a red plaid shirt, khaki pants and short boots.

"Thanks," Sunny said, sniffing the cocoa before taking a sip. "Delicious." She twitched her head in Devin's direction. "She's going to be jealous."

"She won't even notice. When Devin gets her mind around something, everything else fades away."

"She splits that wood like a robot."

"The girl doesn't do anything halfway. Never has. Even as a little thing she'd sit on the floor and concentrate on her blocks like she was a certified engineer. I could cook an entire meal and not hear a peep out of her."

"She's such a nice person," Sunny said, feeling herself tearing up. "It just kills me that she feels so guilty about what happened."

"It'll take time, but she'll be all right." She took a sip of her cocoa, then spoke again, sounding nothing but pragmatic. "She hasn't had many bumps or bruises up to this point, but you can't get very far in life and not have your share."

"That's true," Sunny agreed. "I just wish she didn't blame herself. That's got to make it harder."

"No doubt." The older woman let a quick smile show. "But what kind of awful person wouldn't feel guilty? This will take a bite out of her, but she'll learn from it." She nodded sagely. "I just hope this doesn't put her off her job. She's as good a guide as Maine's ever had."

It was almost dark when they got back to Devin's parents' home. The front door opened moments after their headlights brushed across the house, and a pair of dogs gamboled across the lawn, nearly doing somersaults to show their excitement. They surrounded Devin, jumping and whining for her attention.

"You can't say they're not enthusiastic," Sunny said as she caught a look at Devin slamming her eyes shut in embarrassment.

"I should have trained them better, but it's tough when three people are in charge."

The dogs raced back and forth between them and the front door, managing the round trip three times during the moments it took the humans to walk the same distance. A tall, lean, man with a little gray sprinkled through his otherwise dark brown hair pulled Devin into a long hug. He smiled over his daughter's shoulder and extended a hand.

"Mark Savary," he said. "Peggy and I are very glad you were able to come, Sunny."

Mark was kind of awesome looking. Like the kind of guy they used to sell trucks or Viagra. A sturdy, strong, regular guy with strong features and kind eyes. "It's nice to meet you," she said, smiling at Devin who just half-turned, remaining in her father's embrace.

"Sunny's been a good sport," Devin said. "She let me spend most of the day with Gram and Gramps, making sure they have enough wood to last them until warm weather eventually comes."

"I was going to do that," he said, rapping on the top of her head as he finally let her go.

"I saw it on your 'to-do' list last time I was over and thought I should help out if I could. That's the deal, Dad." As she entered the house, she bent and unlaced her boots, then kicked them off. "I'm home and I'm hungry," she called out.

A nice-looking woman, probably in her late fifties or early sixties emerged from the kitchen. She had some of Devin's features, but was a little shorter, very thin, and lacked Devin's rangy muscles. Her hair was lighter than her daughter's, probably dyed, a nice pale brown that might have had a little blonde in it when she was in the sun. "It's so good to meet you, Sunny," she said, walking over to enfold her in a hug. "Thanks for keeping an eye on this one." She let go, then reached around to swat Devin on the butt, laughing when her daughter grabbed the spot and let out an outraged squawk. "Convince me that hurt," she said, trying to get in another smack.

"It didn't," Devin admitted, "but you never know when you might wind up and give me a good one."

"I *should* give you a good one. I'm still miffed that you were going to shrug us off by email." She met Sunny's gaze. "I'm glad you two are spending time together, but I need to hear her voice. She can get awfully mopey."

"I don't get mopey," Devin said. "I just like to be alone more than you do."

"Because you like to mope," Peggy insisted. Now she wrapped her arms around Devin and gave her a gentle, loving hug. "I've been so worried about you," she murmured, just loud enough for Sunny to hear. That tender expression hit Sunny like a blow. If she'd added up all of the times her own mother had tended to her in such a gentle fashion it wouldn't have come close to the care Peggy was lavishing on her daughter at that single moment. Some people were just cut out to be good parents, and it certainly looked like the Savarys were two of that group. Devin was a lucky, lucky woman—despite the events of the last few days.

They were back at the cabin by eight, with the people of rural Maine obviously not staying out until the wee hours. Sunny got ready for bed, then went into the bedroom where she found Devin, lying on her back.

"Hi," she said, looking remarkably cute. She'd taken a shower and had changed into a new set of clothes at her parents' house, and had brought some pajamas along. Now she was wearing a pale blue long-sleeved shirt with the black outline of a moose on it. Her hair was splayed out against the white pillowcase, and Sunny was struck with a longing to slide into bed next to her, take her in her arms and kiss the dickens out of her. But that was out of the question. She hadn't gotten any sexual vibes from Devin since that first night, and would have been turned off if she had. There weren't any vibes on her side, either, but she still wanted to kiss her. Maybe she just needed extra closeness, or maybe she needed to take her mind off the constant thoughts of Hank, but she was just going to have to suck it up. She'd once again get into bed and cuddle with her, having to satisfy herself with compassion and understanding and true empathy—not a bad trade off.

The next morning, Sunny stood at the check-in counter at Bangor Airport, Devin at her side. They hadn't spoken much on the drive, and she was certain Peggy's characterization of Devin as sometimes being mopey was true. She simply didn't have the usual spark in her eyes or a quick, witty reply to Sunny's observations. Of course, Sunny was a long way from chipper, too. Having to go home and face her co-workers, family and friends was stupendously unappealing. She loved many of them, and liked all of them, but she simply didn't want to talk about Hank's death with anyone. Most of all, she dreaded having to sit with Hank's wife and explain the whole thing. She'd do it, and do it by tomorrow night—but the list of things she'd rather do was very, very long.

She handed her ticket to the agent and waited for her boarding pass. As her bags slid noisily down the conveyer belt, she thought of just a few days earlier, when those same bags had been on the conveyer in Dallas, and she'd been filled with anticipation of this great adventure. What a difference a few days made.

Devin put her arm around her shoulders as they walked to the security line. There were about ten people waiting to go through, and Devin pulled her off to the side. "Are you going to be okay?" she asked gently.

Sunny could only nod. She was sure her voice would break if she tried to speak.

"Will you call me when you land?"

"Yeah."

"I'm going to…" She cleared her throat, and when she spoke again her voice was high and shaky. "I'm going to miss you."

"Me too." Their eyes met as she bit at her lips. This was crazy! They'd been through a trauma together, but that didn't mean they were more than supportive survivors. She had to start thinking rationally. They'd stay in touch for a short time, then drift away when their normal lives took over once again.

Devin moved a little closer, so close that Sunny could see how long and dark her lashes were. "I don't think I'll be able to sleep without having you close."

"It's not going to be easy." She let out a sigh. "I wish you were coming with me. If I knew you'd be there at the end of the day, I might be able to get through this."

Her eyes opened wide. "If you'd asked, I'd be sitting next to you on the plane. Do you want me to go buy a ticket?"

"No, no," she said, touched by how sincere Devin seemed. "I can't ask you to drop everything to babysit me. It's just the next few days that'll be tough. I'll be back to normal soon."

"Sure?" She turned her head to gaze at the ticketing area. "I'm not joking—at all."

"I'm sure. You go back to work, and I'll go back to work, and we'll… we'll get through this."

Devin's pretty blue eyes blinked slowly a few times, then she cleared her throat and almost whispered, "How long does it take until you're not thinking about the person every minute?"

The question hit her like a blow. Devin was as tough as nails, but she'd clearly never had to struggle with this kind of emotional pain. Sunny ached for her, knowing how overpowering it could be. "Um, it takes a while," she admitted. "But then it starts to lift. You'll still have some awful moments, but you'll have fewer of them, and they come less frequently." She tried to smile, but knew her expression betrayed her sorrow. "Talking about it helps, but mostly you just have to let time pass."

"Okay," she said, letting out a soft sigh. "I wish you were going to be here. Talking with you has kind of let me keep it together."

"Me too," Sunny said, fighting the overwhelming urge to cry.

"I'm going to miss you. A lot." Then Devin's warm hand slid across her cheek to settle in her hair. As Devin's face grew closer, Sunny closed her eyes. Then their lips met, gently, but with a spark of heat that zipped down her body to land in the pit of her stomach. She pressed into Devin's soft mouth, wishing they could stay just like that for days, touching each other with a tender intimacy that she needed more than she could say.

But the soft lips moved away. Then the hand once again brushed across her cheek in a lingering, gentle touch. The last thing she felt were the tips of Devin's fingers, soft as an angel's, leaving a hint of warmth on her skin. Then she was gone, loping across the wide, slick floor to disappear through the soundless, distant doors.

Chapter Ten

On Monday morning, Devin walked up the stairs of the outfitter's just as Edie was entering.

"What's got you over here at this time of day?" she said, looking up sharply when Devin's foot hit the first step.

Devin removed a bag from Edie's grip, helping her get everything inside as the door quietly closed. "I'm taking off on a little hike and I need to buy a couple of things."

"Hike?" Edie set everything on the counter by the register, then peeled off her gloves, giving Devin the fish-eye the whole time. "What kind of hike?"

"Just a hike." She was consciously trying to be cool, but knew her tactic wouldn't be very effective. Edie could have been a bomb-sniffing dog in another life. "I thought I'd wander around while there's still some snow on the ground."

Edie's dark eyes narrowed as she slipped her coat off and draped it over the counter. "There's a lot of snow, but you know it's getting muddy in the sunny spots. I think you've missed your window of opportunity, Devin. It'd be safer it you waited until May."

"I'm sure that's true," she said, moving behind the counter to look at the good stuff—the high-priced electronics. Picking up the beacon she'd been thinking about, she said, "What did this little beauty set you back?"

"Four hundred and we're good."

"No dice." She peered at the device, pressing various buttons. "I want to see the invoice."

Edie sighed heavily. "Four fifty, all right?"

"Done. Let me fill up on some of those good freeze dried meals and I'll get out of your hair." She went into the supply room where Edie kept boxes of the stuff, but she had a shadow, almost able to feel her boss breathing down her back.

"Why do you want an avalanche beacon? You must be going somewhere truly awful."

Devin let out a laugh. "Not awful at all. I'm just giving into my mom's understandable fears."

Edie grasped her by the shoulder and held her still. "What do you mean 'understandable?' Are you going somewhere prone to avalanches?"

"No, but I just let a guy die. Why wouldn't my mom think I can't take care of myself?"

Now both of Edie's hands were on her shoulders, pressing hard. "Your mom doesn't, in any way, think you can't take care of yourself—or others. If she said anything even close to that, she was talking with her heart, not her head."

"She didn't say that in so many words," Devin admitted. "But she really threw a fit when I said I was going to hike the Maine portion of the Trail."

"That's nearly three hundred miles!"

Devin put her head down and started poking through boxes to find the meals she liked the best. "I know how far it is. I couldn't get her to calm down until I agreed to just do the hundred mile wilderness portion and finish up on Mt. Katahdin."

"You know as well as I do that you're not supposed to be on the trail until mid-May." Edie grabbed her arm and shook it. "They don't have that rule just to be spoil-sports. It's too dangerous at this time of year, and you'll be all alone. If you fall and break something it could take a day to find you!"

"It wouldn't kill me to lie on the ground for a day." She filled her arms with the meals and went back out to the counter. Then she counted everything and started to scan the meals in, ignoring Edie's heated gaze that she was certain was aimed at the back of her head. After scanning the beacon, she whistled softly. "I've never spent that much here at once. Good thing you'll take a check."

"I don't like this," Edie said, her voice low and slow. "I don't like it one bit."

"I'm all set," Devin said, turning to meet her eyes. "I'm signing up for a service that lets me hit a button and send an 'a-ok' message once a day. Plus, this thing has GPS. Both you and my mom can keep track of me."

Edie moved over to block Devin's exit from behind the counter. Now when she spoke her tone was more empathic. "Why are you going, honey? Is it just too hard to be here…waiting?"

Devin nodded, then filled her backpack with the meals and beacon. "I don't want to be around when they find him. I know that's the coward's way, but I just don't have the guts."

When Edie's arms wrapped around her and held her close, Devin had to fight not to cry. She managed, but it was damned hard. "You're one of the bravest people I've ever met. But if you need to be out, I understand. So get out there and tromp around in the snow until you're ready to get back to work. There's an awful lot of people who want to get a peek at a moose, and you're my most reliable finder."

Edie knew that a moose safari was Devin's least favorite job. Moose just didn't like to be seen for the most part, and she hated wasting the gas and the time and energy to try to guess where they were going to be. "I can't wait," she said, leaning in to give Edie a kiss on the cheek. "Tell Mike that even though I won't be back in time for the first day of open-water fishing, he'd better leave some rainbow trout for me."

"That's weeks from now, Dev," Edie said, staring at her soberly.

"I know. I'm going to keep walking until I feel better. If I get to Katahdin and still don't feel right, I'm gonna keep on going. I might wind up in New Brunswick, so I'm packing my passport."

"Please take care of yourself," Edie said, grasping her in a fierce hug. "I love you. You know that, right?"

"I do," Devin nodded soberly. "And I love you too. I promise I'll be as careful as I can be."

"Are you taking a weapon?"

She walked to the front door and stood there for a minute. "I don't want to, just because of the weight." She shrugged. "We'll see if I've got any room in my pack. I'll have a knife, one way or the other."

"I'd feel better if you had a gun."

Devin stood at the door and gave her a smile. "You don't think I can outrun an angry bear?"

Edie clearly didn't want to smile back, but she couldn't help herself. "No, I don't, but you're hard-headed enough to try."

The next morning, Chris's truck pulled up in front of the house. Devin flicked the porch light to show she'd heard him, then girded her loins to say goodbye to her mom.

They were right by the front door, and Devin was starting to think she'd have to forcefully pry her mom's arms from her waist. But she was finally released as her mom stepped back to peer into her eyes. "Are you one hundred percent certain you're in the right frame of mind for this trip?"

"I swear I'm fine," Devin said, with the other hundred times she'd sworn the same thing obviously not having much punch.

"Have you ever, and I do mean ever, thought about hurting yourself?" Gentle hands cupped her chin, with her mother's eyes piercing hers with an alarming amount of heat.

"Not once, Mom. I swear. I want to get away, but only for a little while. I fully intend to see my hundredth birthday."

"I want you at *my* hundredth birthday party, sweetheart. Without you..." She sucked in a breath, her famous self-control keeping the tears from her eyes. "You mean the world to me."

"I know, Mom. And I promise I'll be home when I'm feeling back to normal. I'll ping you every night when I make camp, okay?"

"All right." She held up the note Devin had given her. "And I'll text Lori and Sunny after I hear from you." She gripped her cheek and pinched it hard. "You'll have a lot of angry women on your hands if you miss a day."

"I won't miss a day. Promise."

When she opened the door, she saw Chris had already loaded the skis and poles she'd left outside.

"Morning, Peggy," he said. "Looks like a good day to start a trek."

"Did you have a hand in talking her into this?"

Chris held his hands up. "Lori asked me the same thing! Why do you two think I can talk Devin into or out of anything?"

"You're just like she is, with extra testosterone," Peggy said, laughing a little. "You strong, silent types drive me nuts!"

"Then you should have married a weakling who won't shut up," Devin joked, giving her mom one last kiss on the cheek. "I'll ping you tonight, Mom. I'll probably be so close you can throw a rock and hit me, but I promise I'll check in."

"Be safe. But most of all, do what you need to do, baby. I trust you."

Chris grunted when he picked up her pack. "You've got to be nuts," he said quietly after her mom had closed the door. "Are you carrying a full-sized mattress in here?"

"No," she grumbled as she climbed into his truck. "But my mom insisted I take more clothes than I need, along with a first-aid kit complex enough to let me set up a field hospital. My dad made me take two compasses, two water purifiers, and enough fuel for my camp stove to last a year. Edie guilt-tripped me into taking a gun, along with enough ammunition to slay everything I encounter that's larger than a field mouse. Lastly, my gram gave me a jar of peach preserves. A Mason jar," she stressed. "You can't refuse your grandmother, even when you don't have anything to put preserves on. I guess I'll eat it for dessert—today," she added. "I'll probably make myself sick, but I can't afford to carry the extra weight."

"Nothing from your other grandmother?"

"Cash," she said, grinning. "I didn't argue with her about that. I can always use an extra fifty bucks."

He tugged on the stocking cap she wore, pulling it down over her eyes. "You are such a spoiled little princess. I swear you've got all of Piscataquis County wrapped around your little finger."

She just shrugged, a little embarrassed by what a big deal everyone had made over her going on what was, from her perspective, a simple hike. But it was early spring, and the weather was always chancy at this time of year. Plus, she'd just let a guy die…

Chris interrupted her musings. "We've got an hour drive ahead of us. Tell me what you've packed, and I'll tell you what you can leave in the truck. The last thing I want is for you to hurt your back from lugging too much stuff."

"Finally," she sighed. "The voice of reason."

The drop off point was only an hour from Greenville, but the trail would take her almost exactly a hundred and fifty miles to Mt. Katahdin, the highest point in the state, the terminus of the Appalachian Trail. Devin was planning on making that her stopping point, but she was determined to keep going if her head wasn't back on straight by the time she got there. She was planning on covering only five miles a day—a very modest goal. But she had every intention of taking it very, very easy. If she covered five miles a day, she'd be at the top of the mountain in thirty days—which seemed about right to her. Other than conquering the Northern Forest Canoe Trail after she'd graduated from high school, the longest she'd been out on her own was two weeks. So it was past time to strike out for a good, long while.

Neither she nor Chris had a need to keep a conversation going, so it had been about an hour since he'd spoken. But they were getting close to the drop off point and he obviously had some items on his list.

"Have you talked to Sunny or the other guy since they've been back in Texas?" he asked, trying to sound casual.

"Yeah. Well, not Julian. He sent me a nice email, thanking me for pulling him out, though."

"Sunny's doing okay?"

"Mmm. Not especially. It's fallen to her to call all of Hank's clients and tell them what happened. I guess that's taking up most of her time." She shrugged. "And she's going to have to go to the funeral." She closed her eyes and rubbed them with her fists. "*I* should have gone, both to support Sunny and Julian and to pay my respects to Hank's widow, but Edie made me promise I wouldn't. Thinking about not being there is driving me fucking nuts."

"Why can't you go?"

"Edie's lawyer thinks I might upset Hank's widow. I guess he assumes I'll talk to her, and that anything I admitted to could be used against us."

"Fuck," he grumbled. "Who invented lawyers?"

"Sunny's a lawyer, and she's a nice person."

"Yeah." He let a few seconds pass. "No way you could go down there and help her, huh? Like after the funeral."

She turned slowly and stared at the side of his face. "Doing what? I could paint the office and maybe rewire it if it wasn't too complex, but that's about all I could offer." She slapped his shoulder. "What's wrong with you?"

"Nothing." He let the cab fall into silence for a minute, then added, "I just thought you might… I don't know. Lori said you told her she was gay, and I thought you might…like her."

"I do like her," she said without hesitation. "I like her a lot. But I can't help her get her law office in order, and she can't help me right now. We've both got things we've got to get through, and we've got to do them alone."

After yet another round of solemn promises to be safe and alert, Devin watched Chris turn around and exit the empty parking lot. Then she clicked the toes of her boots into her bindings and started to ski. Her pack was still ridiculously overfilled, close to fifty pounds, but it would get just a hair lighter every day. With any luck, so would her mood.

Chapter Eleven

SUNNY SAT IN THE PARKING LOT, gripping the steering wheel so hard her fingers ached. She'd had some tough weeks, some *very* tough weeks. But the one that had just crawled along at glacial speed had, without a doubt, been the worst of her life. Shaking her head, she decided that was a mark she definitely hadn't tried to top.

It had been horrible to show up at the office, trying to hold it together while every member of the firm had been crying helplessly. Then having to call client after client, going into detail when pressed, glossing over the sickening facts when it became clear a client truly only wanted to know who was going to finish up his deal. Heartless bastards.

Now, sitting in the parking lot of Melendez Home for Funerals, she was fairly certain she simply couldn't get out of the car. It was just too much, and she had too few emotional reserves to call on. But she had to go. She *had* to. Angry with herself for not specifically arranging to wait for her best friend, she felt trickles of sweat start to slide down her back. They'd gotten an unexpected heat wave, with temperatures topping out at eighty degrees, hot for early March. She couldn't sit in the car unless she left the engine running, and that would only attract attention.

Summoning whatever strength she possessed, Sunny got out of the car, taking a breath of the warm, dry, spring breeze. Ahead of her, she spotted a big SUV that disgorged five of their law school classmates. *Oh, god.* She was going to have to personally speak to at least a hundred people. And every single one of them was going to ask, with their eyes, if not their mouths, what in the hell had happened. How had a healthy, vigorous, Dallas native wound up dead in an icy lake? Even though she'd witnessed every moment, she still didn't know what to say. There was no explanation that made sense.

Feeling like she was on the verge of entering a lion's den, Sunny reached the entry door and pulled it open, finding a sober-looking man in a black suit standing just inside. "Can I help you?" he asked, his voice professionally empathetic.

"Perry," she said, trying to keep it simple.

"Down this hall to the left." He showed a quick, sedate smile. "Mr. Perry must have been very well-loved."

She nodded, unable to comment, then walked as quickly as her shaking legs would allow. The guy hadn't been exaggerating. There were so many people in the hallway there was no way to get into the room. She recognized a few faces and forced herself to head for them. Then it was just shake hands, hug, nod, and feel completely numb as she was absorbed into the throng. She wasn't even trying to get into the room, but she was propelled along as people recognized her. By the time she broached the entryway, there was a small opening, then she saw the casket, blessedly closed, but massive, terrifying, permanent. Her heart was racing, and she was sure she was as pale as a sheet. Then she saw her. Angelica. Sitting on a sofa just a few feet away from the coffin, crying hysterically as Hank's brother and an older woman tried to calm her down. She was gasping for breath, moaning, as everyone nearby tried not to look in her direction.

Tingles started in Sunny's head, then some static sounded in her ears. Just as she was about to close her eyes, a pair of arms settled around her waist, supporting her. "We're getting out of here," Callie murmured. "Just hold onto me. I've got you."

Another arm slid around her from the other side, and she turned to see Teresa, with a grim, determined expression on her face. "Excuse us," Teresa said, her clear, firm voice making people scatter. Every person they passed turned to look at her, with sympathy etching their expressions. She knew she should have been embarrassed to not be brave enough to get through a wake, but she wasn't. She simply wasn't brave enough, or strong enough to stay in there another moment.

The sun hit her in the face, and she blinked rapidly, before holding a hand up to protect her eyes. "Gotta catch my breath," she whispered, her voice not strong enough to project.

Two benches flanked the entryway, and her friends guided her to one. But people were still entering, every single one of them trying, and failing, to avoid staring. "I can't…"

Callie stood in front of her and pulled her to her feet. "Our car," she said. "Teresa, will you bring it around?"

Without comment, she took off, her high heels tapping on the asphalt as she raced away. Slowly, they walked toward the lot, with Callie gently rubbing Sunny's sweating back. "We've got you," she soothed. "It'll be all right."

"No, it won't," Sunny whimpered. "Hank will still be dead. And it'll still be my fault that he is."

⁂

They found a dark bar just a couple of blocks away, and after gulping down a glass of water and taking a few sips of bourbon, Sunny began to feel more like herself again. "It was too much like Morgan's…"

"Why didn't you wait for us?" Callie asked again, clearly frustrated. "I told you we'd be there by two thirty."

"I don't know," she moaned. "I… I think I wanted to force myself to do it on my own. I thought I could get through it. But when I saw Angelica…" She let out a shaky sigh. "I was right there just a few years ago. Exactly in her position. Of course, I wasn't recognized as anything other than Morgan's *friend,* but I know how she feels, damnit. I know just how she feels."

⁂

It took an hour, but by four Sunny was confident she could go back. Both Callie and Teresa had tried to argue her out of it, but she just couldn't brush this off. Hank had been her classmate, her friend, her partner. She owed him a lot, but more than that, she had to pay her respects to Angelica. She'd never forgive herself if she chickened out.

With Callie and Teresa flanking her, she made another attempt, getting down the hallway, which was significantly less crowded now. There was still a big crowd in the viewing room, but Angelica was no longer actively sobbing. She looked like she'd been beaten, with red, swollen eyes, blotchy cheeks, and running mascara, but she was upright.

Then she looked up and met Sunny's eyes. It took her just a second, then her voice rang out, clear and strong. "Why didn't you stop him?" Then she collapsed into tears again, with Hank's brother lifting a hand to wave Sunny away.

In a flash, she was being hustled out of the room again, now more stunned than anything. "Jesus Christ!" Callie grumbled. "If she wanted someone to grow old with, why didn't she marry a guy who didn't chase every shiny object that flashed in front of him? The whole world should have been watching out for him? What the absolute fuck?" she said at full voice as the poor guy at the door opened it wide, clearly hoping they left quickly.

"I don't blame her," Sunny said once they were outside once again. "I really don't."

"I do," Callie fumed. "I blame her for making a bad situation worse."

"No, no," Sunny said, cupping her cheek and looking into her stormy eyes. "If the family of the guy who killed Morgan had been at her wake, I would have caused a scene. I know I would have."

Callie grasped her shoulders and gave her a quick shake. "You. Did. Not. Kill. Hank," she said, emphasizing each word crisply. "Hank did something stupid, and you weren't able to stop him. Can't you see how different that is?"

"No," she said, closing her eyes. "I really can't. Angelica and I both lost someone we'd pledged our lives to, and there was a person who could have prevented their deaths—but didn't. That's all Angelica can think of right now, and I have nothing but sympathy for her. She just wants to turn back time." She wiped at the tears that raced down her cheeks. "So do I."

CHAPTER TWELVE

AFTER THREE SOLID WEEKS OF easy, slow progress, Devin still hadn't laid eyes on another person. That was exactly what she'd hoped for when she'd had the idea, and it turned out to be just what she'd needed. She was enjoying her time alone so much that she slightly resented having to check in every night. Being truly cut off from the world would have been ideal. But she loved her family and couldn't bear the thought of making their lives worse so hers could be marginally better.

Today would be a good test of her beacon. She was nearly at a peak—a tall one. Nowhere near as high as Katahdin, but a good one nonetheless. She loved clambering up the side of a mountain, exposing her body to the wind and the sun to reach the summit. It always felt like she'd really accomplished something, even though she was only able to stand up there and look down on where she'd just come from. It was kind of silly when you thought of it, but a big part of the fun of hiking.

The summit had lost all of its snow from the sun beating down on it for the last couple of weeks, and it actually felt like spring when she started to climb. That was a very good sign.

It was slow going, with ice in every crevasse and snow packed deep on shaded boulders. But eventually she stood on the summit and gazed down at the majesty of Maine. There couldn't be a prettier place on earth. It just wasn't possible to combine the beautiful pines, the undulating topography, the clear streams, and crystalline lakes in a format that could beat this.

The wind was really whipping, as it seemed to on every peak. But she had to keep this image in her head, to really enjoy it. The last half of a mile had been a real bitch, making her doubt her ability to continue a few times. But she'd kept her head down and forced herself to put one foot in front of the other and keep going, no matter how much it hurt. Her legs shook, her back ached, her shoulders felt like knives were embedded in them, but none of that pained her as much as her lungs, which pleaded for air. But she'd made it, relatively unscathed, and now she sank to the ground, removed her pack, and rested her elbows on her knees, just taking in the beauty.

By the time she was ready to leave, the sun had started to descend, and she knew she had to get a move on. She was going down on the shady side of the mountain, and the snow would be an issue. She grabbed a tube of some sickly sweet orange gel that gave her an energy boost and started to walk down, never her favorite part of a hill. About a third of the way down the snow began to reappear in spots, then it evened out and in another hundred feet it was February again. It was almost dark when she reached the base, and she'd had to struggle through shin-high snow for the last bit. But putting on her skis wouldn't have helped much at all. When the snow was beginning to melt like this, you spent as much time taking them off as putting them on, and that just seemed like a waste of effort.

It was too dark to keep going, so she started searching for the perfect spot to set up camp. There was a slight clearing ahead, and she made for it, then stopped abruptly when she spotted something odd. There, just off the trail, were the last few inches of a moose's antlers. Her curiosity got the better of her, and she moved closer, using the moon for additional light. Of course she had a flashlight, her dad wouldn't have let her go to the garage without one of those, but she didn't really need it. There was plenty of light left to figure this out… She got closer, then released her pack and let it slide off her arms. She carried a lightweight aluminum avalanche shovel, and she took it from the pack and started to dig the snow out from around the antler.

In all her years, she'd never come across one. This one was probably going to be impossible to carry, but she was already thinking of ways to strap it next to her skis when her shovel hit something hard. Moving back a step to get some force behind her, she kept digging, finally revealing the top of a skull and a lifeless, frozen eye staring at nothing.

Yelping, she jumped back and gawped at the moose, clearly intact. Not only had she never come across a spent antler, she'd also never seen a moose carcass—frozen or dead in any other way. Given how many moose Maine had, and how often she was in their habitat, it had always puzzled her that she hadn't stumbled upon one. But moose were solitary, wary animals, and she figured most went deep into the woods when they were ill, seeking the solitude they seemed to need to survive.

She was wasting the little light she had left, but she couldn't stop. Another fifteen minutes of hard digging had the body mostly exposed. He was a young bull, no more than three or four years old. He'd died before he dropped his antlers, or he was so young that he'd held onto them. Some two or three year old yearlings held them until spring. But these antlers were developed enough to make Devin pretty sure he was nearing the prime of his life.

Now that she had him pretty well uncovered, she found her flashlight and looked him over carefully. At first glance, there was nothing wrong with him. He didn't have a mark on him and there was no blood staining even the deepest snow. She couldn't see all of his legs clearly, but the ones on his left side looked perfectly fine. He'd been well fed, with even his fur full and uniform in color. His belly wasn't distended, nor were there any other signs that he'd been in any form of distress. In all, he was a gorgeous creature, dead for no reason she could see.

The snow would melt in the next month or so, letting other creatures send this guy into another realm. But she felt an inexplicable need to cover him up again, to give him a proper, albeit temporary, grave. It took less time to cover than uncover, then she had to rush to get to the clearing and set up her camp. But first she pinged her mom, already feeling guilty for waiting so long.

For the rest of the evening, Devin reflected on the moose, the image in her head making her unaccountably anxious. Slowly, the picture gained focus and she began to settle down. There was one concrete fact that bound all of us, human and animal, together. We would all die. You could do everything right and die young, or do everything wrong and live to a ripe old age. The truth was there was only so much control any of us had over our longevity, and the only way to make our limited time count was to enjoy every minute you had.

Leaning against a tree, looking up at the stunningly clear sky, so filled with stars it was impossible to find an empty space, Devin tried to remind herself that so far she'd lived her life in exactly that fashion. This was nothing new, nothing earth-shattering, but it soothed her fragile psyche.

Thoughts of Hank filled her head and slowly came into focus. She'd done the right thing that morning. It hadn't worked out for Hank, but that didn't mean she'd screwed up. She'd treated a fully-functioning man like an adult, and he'd acted like an impulsive child. That wasn't her fault. Checking out the alternate route that morning was exactly what a good guide should have done. Hank's actions didn't change that fact. She'd done her job, and he'd followed his destiny.

Just like the moose, Hank had been culled from the herd far too young. There was no explaining it. Some animals just didn't reach their potential.

Devin picked up the beacon and looked at the dim lights that appeared when she touched a button. All of a sudden, she didn't mind being tethered to her family. In fact, she was damned glad she had the thing. If she fell in the woods, someone would come and set her back on her feet before she froze to death. That wasn't much, but it was incredibly comforting as she peered up at the sky and tried to figure out her place in the vast, unexplainable universe.

The weather didn't know how to read the calendar. The first day of April shouldn't have been cold enough to freeze your eyelashes, or windy enough to create tears that hardened as they fell. The snow fell so hard and so heavy that it created white stripes on her thighs as she squatted to pee.

The unrelenting wind had disturbed her sleep so badly that she eyed the tent as she got her clothes in order. No one was watching the clock, so she gave into temptation and marched right back to her cozy little tent. If it cleared up, she could try for the summit later, but it wasn't going to clear up. She knew the weather around Mt. Katahdin well enough to know that.

Once inside, she wrapped her sleeping bag around her shoulders and picked up her beacon. She wasn't sure her mom would understand the message, but she sent an "a-ok" ping, hoping that would make it clear that today was going to be a rest day.

In fact, she needed one. This last week had been harder than the first three put together, with a nearly constant bracing wind, almost always blowing directly into her face, and lots of short, steep climbs that sapped the energy right out of her. One day it had rained until she thought Noah would float by. Then the next day snow showers had annoyed the heck out of her as she ascended a difficult technical part of the trail. She gave herself points for getting up and over a bunch of slick, icy boulders, but she'd only show a select few the photos she'd taken. Her mother would wring her neck to know she'd even tried the climb in those treacherous conditions.

The best news was that she'd eaten most of the weight she'd started off with. In fact, her pack was so light it was like not even wearing one. She pulled out some dirty clothes and folded them into a pillow shape, then lay down with the sleeping bag draped over herself. That was good enough for a nap. A nice, long nap on a cold, snowy spring day.

The only thing she wished she had was her e-reader. Books let her jump into someone else's life for a few hours, lives she'd never be able to live. Lori made fun of her for reading romance novels, but she didn't have a bit of shame about indulging in a pastime she found so rewarding. So soothing. Her own romantic life had been pretty dismal, and it gave her a boost to see how other people did it. Of course, their lives were more glamorous or more exciting than hers would ever be, and the problems the characters had were usually few, and very specific. But it was always satisfying to read about the couple overcoming whatever those issues were, and she always believed they'd live happy days together.

Her thoughts strayed to the moose again, unable to let go of the similarities she felt with those creatures. They were clearly less interested in being intimate or connected to their kind than she was, but she couldn't deny that she was more on the moose side of the closeness scale.

She sat up and wrapped her arms around her knees, hugging herself tightly. Why was that? She knew she'd be a good partner, but she hadn't found anyone who wanted her as she *was*. And she'd never met a woman who made her want to change. Not even a little, if she was going to be completely honest. But she wanted it, damn it. She wanted someone to do more than mate with when she was in heat. She just needed someone who understood her moosiness, and didn't try to make her into something else. *That* was going to be a challenge. Women were unaccountably attached to electricity and running water. They didn't know what they were missing.

The next day she labored up Mt. Katahdin, a tough climb in any weather. It had been over a year since she'd climbed it, and there was no question that today was going to be rougher than her last trek. A solid month of hiking and climbing and skiing had taken a lot out of her, even though she'd gone slowly. To distract herself and try not to think of the sprained muscle in her side, she thought of the future—her future.

She loved Maine as much as anyone could, but she'd never been anywhere else. What if Maine was the ugliest state in the whole country? She laughed at that. There was no way in hell that was true. But she'd never spent any significant time in a big city, or seen a desert, or a prairie. Maybe a cactus would turn out to be her favorite plant, an armadillo her favorite animal. She thought about that for a while, acknowledging that everything she'd thought of could be found in a single state. A state where a pretty woman with a kind heart might be amenable to a visitor.

A gust of wind hit her from the side, making her knees buckle. The sharp granite bit into her skin, but she stayed put until her heart rate slowed enough to let her get her feet under herself.

Crouching low on that unforgiving hill, digging into the rock with her fingertips, she had a moment where her life flashed before her eyes.

Holy fuck!

Her heart started to race again as she let herself imagine the sensation of the fall. Would she have any regrets? What would her last thought be?

Devin tried to clear her mind and center herself again. Still shaky, she got into a crouch to keep the wind from knocking her over and took a few tentative steps. After a minute of second-guessing herself over each step, she started to climb with more confidence. By the time she'd flushed the near fall from her head, she'd made a decision. She was going to Texas. It simply felt like the right place to be at the moment, and Sunny seemed like the right person to be with. She couldn't have stated why she was sure of that, but she truly was.

An hour later, she stood at the peak. Her phone was down to five percent, just enough to let her blow the rest of the battery on some snaps of the breathtaking view. Clouds were hovering a thousand feet below her, with the sun rising up through them, making the whole horizon look like a huge mound of orange and red and yellow cotton candy. She tilted her gaze to stare at the bright blue skies above her. Maybe the prettiest blue she'd ever seen. The whole trip had been worth it. Worth every step. She was feeling like herself again. Exactly like she'd felt a month earlier. Now it was time to be around people again. If she was lucky, one particular person who'd captured her imagination would feel the same.

Chapter Thirteen

DEVIN SAT AT THE COUNTER of a diner in the first true town near the base of the mountain. It wasn't much of a town, but it had everything she needed—a place to eat and stay out of the rain. She still had a week's worth of mushroom risotto and penne with spicy sauce in her pack, but it would be a long time before she could work up an appetite for either. Living on the same four entrees for a month had reminded her of how much she loved food. Now, as she sat in an otherwise empty diner and wolfed down a plate of meat loaf, mashed potatoes, and broccoli, she savored every bite. She was trying to keep up her end of a conversation with the woman behind the counter, but not talking for a month had either rusted her vocal chords, or she'd simply forgotten how to make small talk.

"Are you doing a thru-hike?" the woman asked. She was in her sixties, at least, and had probably been standing behind a counter her whole life. She had that stoop-shouldered, yet muscular look a lot of long-term servers had. Her name tag read "Greta," but Devin didn't like to call people by their names if they hadn't been properly introduced.

"No, ma'am. I just did a section. From Caratunk to the summit. That's only about a hundred and fifty miles."

"That's enough," she said, nodding. "Are you supposed to be out there this time of year?"

Greta was playing with her. Everyone who lived close to the trail knew exactly when the season started.

"It's frowned on," she admitted. "But I like being out by myself. I sure did miss real food, though." She popped a forkful of broccoli into her mouth. "Especially fresh vegetables."

"Where's home?"

"Not far. Abbot."

"Don't think I know it."

"It's at the south end of Piscataquis County."

"That's a long walk. You hitching?"

"No, ma'am. I've had enough adventure for a while. My friend's coming to pick me up. She should be here pretty soon if your clock's right."

"It's close to right." She pushed herself away from the counter and went into the kitchen, returning a minute later with a small bowl of cooked carrots. "You look like you could use a little more. Did you start off skinny?"

"Not too. I didn't realize I'd lost weight until this morning when I put a bra on for the first time in a month." She laughed at the way that sounded. "That might be more information than you wanted to hear."

"I've heard worse," she said, chuckling. "We serve alcohol, you know."

"Right," Devin nodded. "I know how that can go."

Greta's head lifted and her eyes narrowed as they followed something outside. "Either I've finally got another customer, or your friend's here."

Devin turned on her stool and felt a huge grin cover her face. "My friend's here!" She dashed for the door, opening it to pull Lori in and wrap her in a hug. "Missed you," she murmured, shocked by how clearly she could smell every bit of her. Shampoo, face soap, deodorant, detergent and softener on her clothes. Even a bit of Bowzer, Chris's dog, on her coat. Being away from everything artificial sharpened your senses in ways that always amazed her.

Lori squeezed her hard, then pushed her away to take a good, long look. "Did you forget to take food?" She gripped her chin and tilted her head left and right. "Damn, your cheekbones are sticking out like a model's."

"My mom will kill me," she said, wincing. "Maybe I should stay with you for a week and let you fatten me up."

"Then your mom will kill me. She called me at five this morning, you know, double checking to make sure I hadn't forgotten to come." She rolled her eyes. "That's after she called last night to tell me you were camped at the base of the mountain."

"She was probably checking my GPS ten times a day."

"I checked five, but I don't love you quite as much as she does." She grabbed Devin once more and placed a flurry of kisses on both cheeks. "That's not true. I easily love you as much as your own mother."

“Let her eat her vegetables,” Greta said. “She’ll blow away in that wind.”

Lori looked up, clearly surprised at Greta’s attempt at supervising.

“Hungry?” Devin asked. “I’m spending the money Grandma Savary gave me. Order anything. It’s on me.”

“I guess I could have a bite. What do you recommend?” Lori asked Greta.

“The meatloaf’s good. But just about everything is good enough.”

“I have to cook dinner when I get home, so I’ll stick with something light.” Her smile grew brighter. “A chocolate malt with chocolate ice cream’s light, isn’t it?”

“As a feather,” Greta said, heading over to the malt machine to whip one up.

⁂

They’d only gone a short way when Lori clapped Devin on the leg and said, “Got news. The rescue team pulled Hank out just a couple of days after you left. His camera strap had caught on the branch of a tree on the bottom of the lake.”

“The bottom?” she asked, swallowing at the sick feeling that had settled in her gut.

“Yeah,” she said soberly. “He must have sunk like a stone. You *never* could have gotten him out.”

“Fuck,” she grumbled. “Do you know more?”

“Not much. His wife waited until he was found to have the funeral. Sunny sent your mom the notice from the paper.”

“I’ve got to call her,” Devin said. “But she’s probably at work, having to do two jobs.”

“Yeah. Your mom said things have been tough for her.”

“And unfair. I got to run off and clear my mind, while Sunny’s working like a dog.” She let out a sigh. “Life can be so unfair.”

⁂

They weren’t far from Greenville when Devin said, “Are you in a rush?”

Lori made a show of checking her watch. “Um, given that I left the house five hours ago, not much of one. Why?”

"Your mom's got the kids?"

"Yes, Devin," she said, with exaggerated patience. "I'm going to wait until Brody's six to leave him in charge. Now are you going to spit out what's on your tiny little mind?"

"Will you drive me down to Dover? And wait for me?" She paused, thinking, "Shouldn't take too long. Maybe an hour if they can take me right away."

Lori reached over and grasped her ear, giving it a good twist.

"Ahh!" Devin swatted her hand away. "You don't have to hurt me!"

"Explain yourself or your nipple's next."

"You wouldn't..." Then she thought about it. Lori hadn't given her a tittie twister since grade school, but she wasn't above using force when Devin frustrated her. "I charged up my phone while I was waiting, and found what looks like a good tattoo place in Dover. I'm getting one."

"You are?" She turned briefly and stared, open-mouthed. "You're the only person I know under fifty who doesn't have one. Why now?"

Devin leaned across the seat and grasped Lori's arm. With her thumb, she traced the words printed on her wrist in a curly script. "Same reason you have the boys' names. When something means a lot to you, you want it to mark your body, as well as your soul."

When Lori pulled up in front of the house, she gave her horn a honk, leaned out when Peggy opened the door, and shouted over the dogs' wild barking, "I tried to talk her out of it."

Devin watched her mother scamper across the lawn, headed for her like a guided missile. In seconds, she was wrapped in a stranglehold, arms pinned to her sides. "What did you do?" Peggy demanded, shaking Devin playfully.

Then her dad was next to her, and when he put his hand on her shoulder, she winced in pain. "Not the shoulder!"

"You hurt yourself!" Her mother let go, then started to feel around the joint. "Did you fall?"

Wriggling away, Devin pulled her gear out, then walked over to the driver's side and kissed Lori goodbye. "Thanks for nothing, tattletale."

"What did you do?" Peggy demanded. "I knew I shouldn't have let you two have the day together. You're always up to something."

"See you!" Lori called out, waving as she peeled out of the drive, sending gravel flying.

"Can we go inside?" Devin begged. "Please?"

"Are you hurt?" Peggy asked, her patience clearly at its end.

"I'm not," Devin said. "But I got a tattoo to commemorate what has been a really meaningful experience."

Her mom's face scrunched up into an unhappy frown. "Oh, Devin. Why did you get one now? I thought you were old enough to have gotten past that silliness." She put her hand on her arm and started to lead her into the house. "How did you lose so much weight, honey? You're skin and bones."

"I'm not skin and bones," she said as they entered the house with the dogs racing around, proudly bringing their toys to drop at her feet. "I'm lean. Like a greyhound," she said, squatting down the let the dogs like her face.

When she stood, her mom poked at her waist, then pulled her sweater up and tried to grab some skin. "Good lord! You look like you did when you were fourteen. All legs and muscle."

"I'll put that on my on-line dating profile. 'Lonely woman, all legs and muscle…'"

"Let's see the tattoo," her father said. "If you're going to mark up the skin we gave you, the least you can do is show it to us."

Shrugging, she yanked off her sweater and clutched it to her chest.

Her mom delicately traced the image, being careful to stay away from the actual sore spots. The sterile plastic wrap that covered the image crinkled from the pressure of her finger. "It's nice," Peggy said. "Not too busy."

"Just an outline?" her dad said. "Are you going to have it filled in later?"

"Nope. I'm done. The guy who did it convinced me to keep it simple."

"You know how to care for it, don't you?" Peggy asked. "You don't want to get an infection. That's like a burn, you know."

“That’s why it hurts,” Devin agreed, chuckling. “Any chance of some food? I’ll take anything but penne with spicy marinara sauce or mushroom risotto. If I never see those two things again, it’ll be too soon.”

“Go take a shower and put on your pajamas,” Peggy said, swatting her on the seat. “I missed the heck out of you, but you smell like… I don’t even know what you smell like,” she admitted, chuckling.

“Back in a few,” Devin said, heading down the hallway to her room. As she peeled off her clothes, she twisted around to check out her shoulder. The tattoo was bigger than she’d wanted, but the guy had been right. If you were going to do an outline of a moose head, you had to do it big enough to really see it. That poor dead buck wouldn’t know or understand that an image of him now rested on a woman’s skin. But she’d know. And she’d keep the lesson he taught her close to her heart. You only had so much control over the outcome, but you had plenty of opportunities to create the life you wanted. You just had to get off your duff and make it happen.

After gobbling down more food than she should have, Devin excused herself for the night. As soon as she was in her room, she dialed a number and waited, impatiently, for the call to be picked up.

“Devin?”

“Hi,” she sighed, so relieved to hear Sunny’s voice she could have cried. “I’m finally home.”

“God, I was worried about you,” Sunny said. “*So* worried.”

Soberly, Devin said, “I really didn’t want to upset so many people, but I had to get away. That’s just how I am, Sunny. When I’ve got to think, I have to be alone. Really alone.” She cleared her throat and gathered up her nerve to say, “My mom told me how often the two of you talked. Thanks for doing that. I think it really helped her to be able to chat with someone who wasn’t used to my tricks. Did she complain about me every time you spoke?”

“Of course not. And, just so you know, even though I’m glad it helped, I didn’t call her to be nice. I kept in touch because I was kind of losing it. Talking to your mom calmed me down a little.”

“I’m sorry,” she said quietly. “I just had to…”

"I know. Your mom explained you've always been like this. But you're the only person *I* can vent to, and I really needed someone to unload on a few times in the last month."

"Like when they found Hank's body?"

She was silent for a few seconds, then quietly said, "Yeah. I could have used you then."

"How about now?"

"Sure," she sighed. "Talking to you will help."

"Today's Wednesday, right?"

"Yeah, I think it is. I'm so busy, days pass without my noticing, but I think it is."

"I'll be in Dallas on Friday. There's a morning flight to New York, and I can get to Dallas from there."

"Really?" She was silent for a few seconds. "You're really going to come down here?"

"I am. If you want me to, that is.

"Oh, I do," Sunny said. "I need someone to talk to, Devin. I really do."

"So do I," Devin said, even though she hadn't really had that instinct until about three minutes earlier. It had taken a while to develop, but now that she felt it, she would have taken off right that minute if there had been a way.

Early on Friday morning, Devin dragged her biggest gear bag out to her mom's car. The weather had finally agreed that it was April, and she was surprised at how happy she was that she didn't have to wear gloves. That was all she wanted from spring. No gloves. Well, no snow boots was a nice thing, too.

Her mom came out of the house, hurriedly locking the door. "I can't believe you're taking such a big bag! Are you *moving* to Texas?"

"The odds of that are pretty slim," she said, smiling at her mom. "But I booked an open ticket, and I promised to stay until Sunny feels better so…"

They got into the car and Devin looked over when her mom slapped her thigh.

"I'm proud of you. I'm sure this is hard, but being a good friend requires sacrifices."

Devin ducked her head and nodded. "I try to be a good friend, but I'll admit I'm looking forward to getting away again. Even though I'll be where Hank lived, I'll be further away from where he died."

"I think you'll be able to let go of some of this misplaced guilt down there, sweetheart." She patted her leg again, this time keeping her touch soft and gentle.

"I let go of most of that out on the trail, Mom. I'm sad, but I feel much less guilty." She tentatively touched her shoulder. "I had an encounter with a moose that helped me work that out."

"An encounter…?"

"He was dead," Devin said. "It's kind of a long story. But I've really let go of a lot of the guilt. Promise."

"I'm so glad to hear that," Peggy sighed. "I hope you can help Sunny let go of some of hers. She's very fond of you, you know. Maybe you'll… who knows?"

"Yeah," she said, nodding. "I like her too. When I was out on the trail I'd decided I was going to visit her."

"Really?" Her eyebrows hiked up. "You? Going out of your way to see a woman? Should I reserve the church hall for a June wedding?"

"Yeah. Do that," Devin said, smirking. "I'm sure Sunny wants to quit her successful law practice to live in my cabin." She turned to face her mom, trying to keep a straight face. "You don't think she'll mind that I don't have a bathroom, do you?"

Chuckling, Peggy said, "She'd be a lucky girl to land you. Using Edie's bathroom after a quick skate or paddle across the lake is a sacrifice any smart woman would make."

⁂

Devin sat in the middle seat of a row near the back of the plane, nervously chewing gum to keep her ears from getting stuffy. The fact that ears got stuffy was one of the only things she knew about flying, courtesy of her grandmother. Both sets of grandparents had taken winter vacations to Florida, so they were old hands at this. But this was Devin's first time, and she was more nervous than she thought she'd be. Given that she'd only been back in civilization for two days, jamming herself into a metal tube with a whole lot of people and being ordered around like she was a toddler wasn't going down easy.

When they backed away from the gate to taxi down a long runway, her stomach tumbled around like a tennis shoe in a dryer. Finally, they were off, zooming up through the clouds to bank and shudder a little, with a strange, high-pitched whine that set her teeth on edge, but which no one else seemed to notice. In fact, no one seemed to notice anything. Was she the only person who knew they were flying through the air at a ridiculous rate of speed?

She was holding onto the armrests with such force that her fingers began to cramp, then the plane leveled off and she let out a sigh of relief, only to jerk sharply when a bell sounded. But that must have meant it was okay to use the bathroom, because the woman next to her got up and squeezed past.

The plane got relatively quiet then, and she was able to relax slightly. Proud of herself for not having screamed out loud, nor broken into tears, she released her hold on the armrests. *Not bad at all,* she thought until the plane jerked and seemed to drop a few feet. Again, she didn't exactly scream, but the muffled whimper she let out compelled a sweet-faced older woman across the aisle to reach over and pat her arm. She wanted to give her an "OK" sign, but there was no way she was going to release her grip on those armrests. That might have been the only thing keeping them in the air.

Once, when she was in high school, Devin's class had gone to Boston to walk the Freedom Trail and generally run a little wild. Since that day, she hadn't been in a crowd as large as the one she was in now. And this was just the airport. Given that it wasn't likely most Dallasites were at the airport at that moment, how big must the city have been?

In her mind, Dallas was kind of a cowboy town, with ranches and rodeos and snakeskin boots and ten-gallon hats and lots of barbecue. She didn't know anyone who'd ever been there, save for Sunny, of course, and she'd never had the slightest urge to visit. But here she was in this massive building, and she was supposed to find one pretty woman with reddish-blonde hair. She might have had more luck finding a pig in a poke, and she didn't even know what a poke was.

Her phone chimed and she pulled it from her pocket to read the incoming text. "Look for a guy who's holding a sign with your name on it." She blinked at the message, confused. Then she looked up and saw a gaggle of guys standing behind a rope line, all of them holding sheets of paper with names printed on them. Oddly, there was one with her last name, printed in a big, bold font.

She approached the guy and nodded. "I think you're here for me."

"Devin?" he asked.

"Yep."

"Do you have your bags?"

"Right here," she said, giving the gear bag a kick.

"Follow me." He picked up the ungainly bag like it was empty, then strode quickly along the shiny stone floor. Her phone chimed again and she took another look.

"The driver has my address. I left a key with the doorman. Call me when you get there!"

Devin slid the phone back into her pocket. This was not what she'd expected, but apparently you had to be on your toes once you hit the Lone Star state.

The key slid into the lock, and Devin pushed the door open. She'd been on elevators before—a few times when she'd stayed in a hotel in Portland—but she'd never, ever ridden an elevator to get to someone's house. The apartment was surprisingly cool and very quiet, with heavy curtains covering the windows. She put her bag down and went to a window, flinging open the curtains to see—another building! Craning her neck, she saw that the building across the street was a few stories taller than Sunny's. It had to have been some kind of office building—unless people in Dallas wore shirts and ties when they were sitting around their apartments.

She sank into a nice, comfy chair located in a corner of the room and stared out at the buildings that surrounded her. Never had she felt more like an ant in one of those little glass farms she'd had when she was young. There were people everywhere. Up, down, and sideways. How could you live like this? Her mind was spinning when her phone chimed again.

"I see you in my apartment."

Of course she did! Everyone in Dallas could see right inside! Then Devin recalled that Sunny had asked her to put an app on her phone that would track her.

She punched Sunny's number and tried to get her bearings while it rang. Then a warm, soothing voice said, "How'd it go?"

"I'm alive, so it went pretty well," she said, realizing she meant that literally. If you survived, you'd had a good flight.

"I'm *so* sorry I couldn't get away, but I truly couldn't. When it became clear the closing I was at would go longer than expected, I tried to get one of my sisters to fetch you, but I struck out there too. You didn't have any trouble, did you?"

"No, not at all. I tried to give the driver money, but he must have taken pity on me when he realized I was from another world."

"Oh, shit! I paid with the app. It didn't dawn on me that you don't have car services and wouldn't know that."

"We have *two* car services," Devin said, laughing at herself. "Both Roger Olson and Pete Draper will drive you anywhere you need to go. But I'm pretty sure they don't know what apps are. They usually just want you to take them to breakfast or something as payment."

"You get settled in," Sunny said. "The dresser in the guest room is empty, so you can put your things away. Are you hungry? I have some leftovers in the fridge."

"I could eat," she said. "I'll take a peek."

"You can use the computer in the guest room if you want."

"No need. I brought a book."

"It's a nice day. If you want to sit outside, you might need to dust off the chairs. I haven't been out there in a while."

"Outside?"

"Yeah. I have a little balcony."

"Where…?" Walking to the far end of the room, she opened the drapes to reveal a small table and four chairs. "Got it," she said.

"Relax and enjoy yourself, okay? I'll race right home the minute I can get out of here. I promise I won't be later than seven."

Devin took a look at her phone. It was just noon. "Okay. I'll be waiting."

Sunny's voice dropped into a different register. A warmer, even friendlier one. "I'm so glad you're here, Devin. Really, really glad."

"Me too. See you soon." Then she hung up and went to see what was for lunch. The kitchen was big and modern and looked like it had been created on one of those home shows her mom liked—the ones where the team raced to finish the kitchen on a deadline. This one looked like the builder had just pulled away minutes earlier, with not a speck of dirt or grease anywhere. Sunny was either amazingly neat, or she didn't cook.

Inside the huge refrigerator was a good selection of condiments, four beers, two bottles of wine, and a container of some kind of soup. Sunny didn't cook.

Devin found a spoon and stuck it into the container, then took a bite of what turned out to be…chili? Damn, after eating it every third or fourth day on her hike, she was sure she'd never eat it again. But this was different. Even though it had the flavor of chili, it was mostly chunks of meat, with no beans at all. It would have been better warm, but she wasn't in the mood to figure out the microwave. She was still in wilderness mode, not yet used to everything being like she'd prefer. It always took a while to get back in the habit of requiring your food to be hot and your bed to be comfortable.

After gulping down the cold chili, Devin hunted around in the kitchen until she found some all-purpose spray cleaner, then grabbed a few paper towels and headed for the balcony. Once she'd gotten the door open, she stood there and assessed the space. The architect must have wanted to technically have outdoor space, while making it as indoor-like as possible. The balcony was only about eight feet square, brick walls on both sides, poured concrete floor and roof. The apartment was oriented so it would have only gotten direct sun in the morning, and this little space was so covered up, with a brick wall almost to her waist, that she bet it wasn't even very bright then. But Sunny had been right. It was a nice day, and she decided to clean off a chair and enjoy it.

Everything was a little small, probably four fifths normal size. But the diminutive space probably couldn't handle full-sized chairs. Especially not with a nice bicycle stashed against a wall.

After removing a lot of gritty dust from both the table and the chairs, Devin sat down and tried to experience the neighborhood in much the same way she did a new hiking trail. But it wasn't so easy to open your senses when you were mostly enclosed in brick. Still, she was warm, which was awfully nice after their extended winter.

Looking down the street, she decided that term didn't really fit. This had to be a boulevard or a parkway or something to indicate its size. The street was wide, but no cars were parked along it. Actually, there was very little traffic, given the highway-sized proportions of the road.

Sunny's apartment building couldn't have been the only one in the area, but the other buildings looked much more like office buildings than places to live. And they all looked so new! Like the whole shiny neighborhood had just been laid down in the last few years.

Devin stood, then went to the opening and leaned out, peering up and down the curving street. Big, glass-walled office buildings took up half of the space, with smaller, no less impressive ones made of steel or concrete filling in the other spots. Some of the buildings had restaurants on the ground floor, with a nearby one wafting off the scent of something delicious being grilled. Well, *that* wasn't what you wanted to smell when you were still kind of hungry.

Sitting outside when you couldn't see or feel the sun wasn't all that exciting, so Devin went back inside and kicked off her shoes, then closed the drapes so the people in the offices couldn't look at her, and plopped down on a very comfortable sofa. She dug the book she'd been reading from her bag, getting right back into the tale of a pair of lesbians who should obviously be together, but were too mixed up to realize it.

When she got to the first sex scene, she skipped it entirely, then let the book drop to her lap. Reading a good sex scene usually got her in the mood, and the last thing she needed was to let her hormones convince her to make a play for Sunny. This was *not* the right time for that kind of nonsense. Unlike the women in the book, her belief wasn't some silly plot device to keep a couple apart for a hundred pages. Both she and Sunny were off their games, with the ground shifting precariously beneath them in nearly every way. Adding the complication of a physical relationship was just plain dumb. But she *really* wished things were different. Even though she hadn't been in a relationship for seventeen years, there was something reassuring at the thought of having something close to that with Sunny. Just having someone who'd listen to your fears would be awfully nice.

Now antsy, she got up and wandered around the apartment, looking only at the things that were openly on display—and only in the living room. She hated to have anyone snoop around her personal stuff, so she never did it to others.

The apartment was pretty darned nice. It wasn't huge, but it was plenty big for two people—so long as they didn't mind a bunch of strangers in cubicles across the way staring at them. The furniture was top-quality stuff, current, but not weirdly modern. It was exactly the kind of stuff you saw on TV shows that featured women like Sunny. Professionals who lived in major cities who had expensive, tasteful apartments. The kinds of places where everything looked like it had been carefully chosen.

Sunny had the usual collection of photos from trips she'd been on lying around, and Devin recognized some of the landmarks. Either Sunny had a lot of friends, or she went through a lot of friends. Devin bet it was the former. Sunny seemed like the kind of woman who'd stick with a group of people through thick and thin.

Looking carefully, Devin saw five of the same faces appear in multiple photos, and she decided a bookish-looking woman with a pretty face, warm smile, and wire-rimmed glasses had to have been Morgan. In the largest photo, centered on a shelf, she stood behind a grinning Sunny, with her hands draped over her shoulders, gently holding her. They weren't kissing or touching in any other way, but there was something about their familiarity with each other that suggested they were lovers.

Devin picked up the photo and looked at it for a long time, trying to get a feel for what they'd meant to each other. She gave up after a while, finding it impossible to learn anything about a relationship from a few photos.

Just as she was heading back to the sofa, a picture of a younger Sunny caught her eye. Devin grabbed the frame and dropped to the sofa to examine the image, mesmerized in a second.

Sunny was wearing a tiny white top with "Texas" printed across it. Her rust-colored skirt, if you could call it that, barely covered her underwear, which you could plainly see since she was jumping into the air with her legs kicked out wide. Big rust and white pom-poms were held way above her head, and her smile was enough to weaken your knees—if you were still standing after getting a look at those stupendous legs.

Devin had *never* been attracted to the kind of woman who'd choose to be a cheerleader, always finding her interests pointed toward people like herself—women who had little interest in team sports at all, much less cheering other people while they played them. But there was something so absolutely compelling in that sexy smile and athletic pose that she found her preferences taking a big turnaround in the blink of an eye.

CHAPTER FOURTEEN

AT SUNNY'S SUGGESTION, DEVIN HAD brought clothes for spring and summer, and she spent some time putting all of the stuff away in the guest bedroom. It was a nice space, with a big bed decorated with bright, summery colors and a whole bunch of pillows. A glass topped desk in the corner held a large computer monitor and a printer, with piles of folders filling all of the available space.

The apartment had gotten a little warm, and Devin took a look outside by parting the curtains, only to have the sun hit her right in the face. No wonder there were curtains on the windows! Squinting, she realized the sun was behind her and was only reflecting off the glass-walled office building across the street. It was probably nearly as hot as if it had come directly into the apartment, though. The air conditioning bill must have been crazy!

She went into the attached bath, set up all of her toiletries, then decided to take a shower. Normally, she stopped shaving her legs in the fall, and didn't start up again until summer. But it was summer in Dallas, even though it was still April, so she spent a very long time rendering them bare and smooth. After she'd finished, she put on some athletic shorts and a tank top. It felt odd to have so little clothing on in the spring, but it had been amazingly warm out, and the apartment was getting hot even through the thick curtains.

Back to the sofa, this time lying on her side with the book resting on a throw pillow. A nap wasn't out of the question. Devin laughed at herself. She never napped at home, but she was drowsy and lazy after doing absolutely nothing all day. No wonder people complained about travel. It was exhausting.

The click of a door opening woke her from a light doze and she got to her feet in a second.

"I'm home," Sunny's cheery voice called out.

Like the dogs did when she entered the house, Devin raced to the foyer and stopped abruptly when her bare feet hit the tile.

Sunny looked like one of those detectives on that show Devin tried to get over to her parents' to watch. The one where the women ran around like crazy, but always looked pretty and polished and composed, even when wrestling with a suspect. Her hair looked like it had been freshly cut, just ticking the collar of a blue and green print blouse tailored to fit very snugly. A navy suit created out of fabric made to caress her body showed off every sexy curve. Devin's brain tried to understand why they were close to the same height, then she noticed the shoes. They weren't exactly *high* heels, but they added a couple of inches, equalizing them almost perfectly. Then Sunny dropped her black leather briefcase and let her purse slide off her other arm to land on the floor.

They were about two feet from each other and it became clear that neither knew what to do next. Other than smile stupidly, that is. Then Sunny's arms lifted and Devin moved forward to have them settle around her body. The sigh that flowed past her ear made the hairs on the back of her neck stand on end. It felt so damned good to have Sunny's warm, curvy body enveloping her own that she was tempted to burrow against her and stay there all day.

As Sunny's arms slid down to release her, Devin moved back a couple of inches. Their faces were close, and she made the mistake of staring at pink, pouty lips, so easily reached. Without giving herself time to think, she let her arms wrap tightly around Sunny, who smiled when she closed her eyes and tilted her head back, just waiting to be kissed.

The urge to merge with her hit Devin like a ton of bricks. In a second, Sunny's body was pressing hard against her own, then she realized she'd pushed her against the door. Their lips touched, tentatively at first, then boldly, with Devin rubbing against her, unable to get enough. Sunny's hands roamed over her body, sending chills up and down her spine as they slid under her roomy tank top to caress her bare back.

The sexy sighs that rumbled through Sunny's chest made Devin kiss her hungrily, needing more of her in every way. Her hands went to thread through that golden-red hair to hold her still. Then she really went for it, kissing her so thoroughly Sunny slumped against her, like she'd lost control of her muscles. But that only lasted for a moment. Then, in a burst of strength, Sunny was propelling her backward, their mouths still locked together. Devin's calves hit the sofa, then she was sprawled across it with Sunny lying on top of her, continuing to kiss her like she was intent on devouring her.

It had been a long time since a woman had claimed her so possessively, and Devin relished the feeling. She loved variety, and having a woman take charge so assertively was a very welcome change.

Mouths still merged, Sunny fought to wrestle with her jacket, then threw it aside by snapping her arm out roughly. Now her heated body rested heavily atop Devin, trapping her deliciously. Still they kissed, nearly in a frenzy, with soft, satisfied sounds continuing to pour from Sunny.

A tiny voice of sanity bit at Devin's conscience and she pulled away to murmur, "We shouldn't."

Sunny's head lifted, then her long lashes blinked slowly as she fought to focus. "I know," she whispered, then went right back to kissing the stuffing out of Devin.

Relieved of the responsibility to be a careful adult, she reached down and pulled that attractive shirt from Sunny's slacks. Then a hand reached under her top to grasp and squeeze her breast. She purred like a kitten, growling, "Do that. More."

Both hands got in on the action, and she fought to slip under Sunny's print shirt, but it was too form-fitting to allow for that kind of play. But Sunny was eminently flexible, not to mention responsive, and she dipped her head and peeled the shirt off like she was skinning a banana. Devin couldn't imagine that Sunny had planned on their doing this, so she must have regularly worn a sexy, lacy bra. *Good.* Devin had never been with a woman who wore anything sexier than a sports bra, and she was into it. *Really* into it.

Her hands went to Sunny's breasts and squeezed them just like her own had been, but that was clearly too much. A quiet whimper made Devin calm down and treat her much more gently. "Better?" she murmured as she licked a wet stripe up Sunny's sweet-smelling neck to latch onto an earlobe and nibble.

"Mmm-hmm," she purred, with her eyes now closed and a pleased smile curling her lips. "Just right."

Devin had a very sharp picture of Sunny that she'd carried around in her head for the last month. But that picture and this reality weren't even close. In her mind, Sunny was a little fleshy, maybe fifteen or twenty pounds over her ideal weight. Kind of like the sexy women from an earlier era, when women jiggled when they walked. But under all of that relatively pale skin Sunny was built like a rock—muscular and solid, not chubby in the least. Luckily, the curves those muscles carved into her body worked on Devin just the same as the supple flesh she'd been fantasizing about. She was hot for her. *Smoking* hot.

Their lips merged again, with Sunny's tongue driving Devin crazy for what seemed like a very long time. As they continued to get more heated, Sunny's thigh slowly pressed forward until it was wedged between Devin's legs. She growled again as her body took over and started to grind. She couldn't recall the last time a woman had her so turned on that she started to hump her leg, but it was suddenly the best idea she'd ever had.

Her breast was gripped in that almost-too-much hold, her lips were being kissed like they were made of nectar, and her sex was furiously rubbing against Sunny's muscular leg. Devin gripped her shoulders, cleared her mind of every sensation but the pressure against her clit, then closed her eyes and held on tight. Only vaguely aware of Sunny's labored breathing, her overheated body, and the sexy scents that wafted off her skin, Devin concentrated, thrusting hard until she felt her body begin to pulse. A few more rough thrusts and she cried out, grasping Sunny's body tight as a flash of golden light filled her vision before growing fuzzy, then fading. As her eyes opened, she let out a whoosh of air. "God damn," she breathed. "I'm moving to Texas if that's how you do it down here."

Sunny's sweet face hovered right above her, eyes sparkling. "Show me how you do it in Maine."

She was far too ashamed to ever admit it, but Devin loved to show off in bed. She grasped Sunny by the hips and used her core to flip her over, trying not to wince when that sore muscle in her side complained. Then she looked down into Sunny's pretty eyes and chuckled. "We're usually under some blankets, but I think I can handle it."

"Kiss me," Sunny said, closing her eyes as her hands laced behind Devin's neck and pulled her down.

She slowed down now and took her time, determined to ramp Sunny's excitement back up slowly. This was *way* too much fun to rush. While they kissed, Devin insinuated her hand between their bodies, managing to get Sunny's slacks open. She clearly wanted to rush things along, for she lifted her hips the second the zipper slid down.

Smirking, Devin eased them off her body and tossed them aside, leaving her in her undies, a state she wanted to keep her in for as long as possible.

"I want to feel your skin," Sunny murmured.

Devin whipped off her tank top and lay back down, letting their bellies rest against one another as she felt the heat between her legs start to build again. "You're so damn sexy," she whispered, gripping Sunny in a fierce embrace and squeezing her tight. "And I'm *so* glad I'm here."

Those gorgeous blue eyes opened wide, and Devin saw just a hint of moisture build in them. "I've missed you," she whispered. "It was so hard not being able to talk."

"I'm here now. And I'll stay for as long as you want."

Sunny put her hands on her cheeks and looked deeply into her eyes, making Devin feel like she could drown in those fathomless blue depths. "Be careful what you promise," she said, with more than a hint of sadness showing. "You're the only person I feel..." She let out a heavy sigh. "Right with. Do you know what I mean?"

"I do. I really do." Then she bent her head and kissed Sunny's trembling lips, letting her mouth speak for her heart, this time without words.

Devin lay on her back on the leather sofa, with Sunny on her side, cuddled up against her. They were both completely naked, both exhausted.

It had to have been late, at least for Devin, who'd not only lost an hour from the time change, she'd gotten up at four.

They hadn't eaten, and her belly was not only empty, but rumbling. Still, she had no desire to get up. She was throbbing from her last orgasm, with her legs twitching involuntarily every minute or two.

"We should move," Sunny murmured, so tired her words lacked any semblance of crispness.

"Don't wanna."

"Air conditioner…" she said, not bothering to finish the sentence.

Devin reached behind her and freed a soft throw from the back of the sofa, then managed to spread it out over much of Sunny's body. She sighed in response and settled even more firmly against Devin, losing what little muscular strength she'd maintained.

"Sleep," Devin whispered, bending her head to kiss Sunny's hair.

"I haven't slept since I left Maine," she mumbled, breaking Devin's heart. She'd meant every single word she'd said earlier. As long as Sunny needed her, she would stay deep in the heart of Texas.

Sunny struggled to wake, finally blinking her eyes to find her head resting on Devin's lap. "What…?"

"Hi," Devin said, looking down, eyes bright.

Sunny stared at her for a minute, puzzled to find Devin stark naked, holding a book in her hand.

"How'd I wind up here?"

"Well…" She shifted a little and put her book down. "I obviously wake up a lot earlier than you do, so I lay there for a long time, then started to try to extricate myself. Eventually, I discovered that you sleep like you're in a coma."

"Only when I'm really, really tired—"

"I'm not complaining," Devin interrupted. "It worked out fine. I got up, made myself some tea, realized that you've got nothing to eat but the condiments I found yesterday, then came back here and decided to finish up my book." She waved it in front of Sunny's face.

"What kind of book is this?" she asked, grasping it and giving the cover, a photo of two women's interlaced hands, a long look.

"Take a guess." Devin took the book back and thwacked it against Sunny's leg. "But I've got to say, our evening was hotter than the sex scenes in here. These were all 'fade to black,' and I hate that. If you're going to get me all revved up, show me some skin."

Of all of the mornings she'd imagined when she'd learned Devin was going to visit, lying naked on the sofa, talking about books was not even on the radar. But Devin seemed so remarkably comfortable just chatting, that it was starting to feel at least semi-normal. "I used to be a voracious reader, but that's just a memory. Now I'm lucky to read the front page of the newspaper."

Devin looked down upon her, with Sunny touched by the compassion that showed in her eyes. "Let's see if we can change that, huh? If you don't have any free time, you can't recharge your batteries."

"I know." She clutched the throw to her body, then realized she'd be leaving Devin stark naked if she took it with her. "Um…I know this is silly, but I'm embarrassed to get up."

Devin reached down and carefully tucked the blanket around her body. "Then wrap yourself up. I'm fine."

"Of course *you* don't mind being naked. You look like an ad for a gym." She scooted to the edge of the sofa and stood, feeling like an idiot standing there with a short wool blanket wrapped around half of her body.

"There's not a part of you that isn't pretty," Devin said, letting her eyes slowly move down Sunny's body. "And I think I saw every inch last night." Her grin grew wider. "No, I'm sure of it. It took a while, but I saw it all."

Sunny dropped down to sit next to her. It was too weird to look her right in the eye, so she leaned against her as she spoke. "You've…okay with that? You don't regret getting carried away?"

"Do you?" she gasped, turning her whole body to stare.

"No, not at all. I'm just kind of… It's odd to sleep with someone and then have to face them the next morning. Once the magic's over, it's strange."

Devin snaked an arm around her and gave her a hug. "Then let's make sure the magic isn't over. Wanna take a shower with me?"

Sunny sat up and forced herself to look her right in the eye. Devin's expression was utterly guileless, as innocent as a child's. "Are you always this cool and calm after you have sex with someone for the first time?"

"Uh-huh." She stood and grasped Sunny's hand to pull her up too. "I never fool around unintentionally, so if I meant to do it, what's there to be embarrassed about?"

"I don't know," she said, feeling more confused by the second. "I thought it was normal to be embarrassed."

"Nope. Not normal at all. *This* is normal. We go about our business."

Now she was facing Devin, having to look up a little to maintain eye contact. "That's it?"

"I think so. Since I've seen every part of your body, it's time to start learning other things. Like how hot you like your shower, and where you like to eat breakfast—since it sure isn't here!"

"I kind of like this," Sunny said, even though she kept the throw securely tucked around herself as they walked toward her bathroom. "This is going to be different, but I guess it's time I changed things up. Well past time, as a matter of fact."

The shower in Sunny's room was definitely the biggest one Devin had ever seen. All glass, with no tub at all. Nozzles shot water at you not just from above, but from right in front of your chest. Dirt would have to really go out of its way to remain after you were pummeled by all of this water.

Devin had the soap in her hands, and after she'd worked up a lather, she started to wash Sunny's body, really taking her time to explore her. She hadn't had the opportunity to do that kind of thing—to leisurely take a look around—for an awfully long time. When you were only with a woman for a day or two you didn't waste time getting familiar. But it wasn't going to be like that with Sunny. No matter what eventually happened between them, this was *not* a one-night stand.

It was hard to concentrate on the overall picture, since Devin was so attracted to her an ache started to build between her legs as her slippery hands explored. But she pushed those thoughts aside and really tried to just be in the moment.

There was some facial cleanser on the shelf in the nook that held soaps, and she put some on her fingertips and started to massage it into Sunny's skin.

Now that she was carefully looking at her in the bright light of day, she could see how exhausted she was. Her skin didn't have the fresh, healthy hue it had in March, and Devin was sure the dark circles under her eyes were a new development.

When she tickled under Sunny's chin with the soap, her hand was quickly pushed away.

"Watch it. You'll get lost in my double chins."

"What?" Her hand fell to her side as Devin stared blankly. "There's just one chin here." She bent and placed a kiss on the pale skin. "It's a cute one, but it's all alone."

When Devin stood again, she expected a smile or even a laugh, but Sunny's body shivered for a second, then she broke down in tears. Devin enveloped her in a hug, pressing Sunny's cheek against her chest as she pivoted to shield her from the spray. "Tell me what's wrong," she soothed.

"Everything. Just everything." She sucked in a breath and let it out, then took in another, obviously trying to calm herself. "This has been the worst month of my entire life." When she looked up, Devin was astounded by the amount of pain she saw in her eyes. "Quite a feat when you know my partner was killed by an inattentive driver before either of us had turned thirty."

Realizing this story was going to take a while to tell, Devin turned off the water and dried Sunny before using the towel to quickly blot herself. Then she found a robe on the back of the door and wrapped her in it before tucking a dry towel around her own waist. A few seconds later found them on Sunny's bed, with Devin holding her in her arms while she gently stroked her soft skin. "Tell me everything," she soothed. "Start anywhere you want."

"You *know*," Sunny murmured. "It's obvious what's wrong. Having to talk about Hank all day long, explaining how he died to clients, other lawyers, vendors, the UPS delivery woman. Every damn day someone comes in or calls, and I have to go into it again. It's never ending," she said, shivering again.

"I'm so sorry," Devin whispered. "That must be torture."

"It's awful. And I have to handle all of his work. We didn't do the same kinds of things—purposefully. I did the things I was good at, and so did he. That made for a good team, but now I'm the quarterback *and* the wide receiver. And I can't throw the goddamn ball!"

"I didn't think," Devin said. "I knew you'd have to do that, but…"

"I can't sleep," Sunny continued. "Every night I wake up at two or three and I'm up for hours. So I'm fighting to hold the office together while I'm totally sleep-deprived. I'm not exercising. I'm blowing up from eating nothing but junk." She tilted her head so their eyes met. "I'm about to drown in—" She pulled away and got to her feet, stumbling a little. "God damn it! I can't even complain without being hit in the face with his death. I'm not about to drown. *Hank* drowned."

Devin got up and approached her gently, then wrapped her in her arms again. "I can't fix this, but I can help. We'll make sure you get some exercise and eat right. And we'll talk about this all you want. If you get some of this out it might not disturb your sleep as much."

Sunny looked up at her, such an innocent, child-like expression on her face that Devin almost cried. "I slept through the night last night. Jammed up against the cushions of a sofa, with you almost on top of me—I slept."

"I did too," Devin said, holding her close and breathing in her clean scent. "We're going to help each other heal, Sunny. No matter how long it takes, I'm not leaving here until we're both better."

"Promise?" she asked, her voice shaking.

"On my honor. With me gone for a while, the fish population of Maine will explode. It'll be good for tourism."

A short burst of air and a little grunt was the biggest laugh she could pull out of Sunny, but it was a start.

"I promise that we're going to get better," Devin repeated. "Together."

CHAPTER FIFTEEN

DEVIN WAS DRESSED AND READY to go when Sunny emerged from her room, wearing a sea-foam green tank top, khaki shorts, and flip-flops.

"Are you really hot-blooded?" Devin looked down at her own jeans and long-sleeved T-shirt. "I was trying to decide which jacket to wear."

Sunny raised an eyebrow. "It's supposed to hit eighty-five today. You might want to rethink that."

"Eighty-five! The weather app on my phone said it was only going to get to *twenty*-five." She took the phone out and shook her head when she looked at the screen. "It's set for home." Looking at Sunny, she muttered, "Damn, a sixty degree difference is going to take some getting used to."

"It was seventy-five yesterday, Devin. Didn't that register?"

"It did. I just thought yesterday was unseasonably warm, or that today was going to be unseasonably cold." Heading back to the dresser to find her summer clothes, she added, "Why'd you tell me to bring things for cooler weather? Once it's over sixty, I'm in shorts."

"Then you'll be in shorts," Sunny said, chuckling softly. "It can be below sixty in April, but it's sure not common."

"This is going to take some getting used to," Devin said, more sure of that fact with every minute that passed.

⌖

Devin walked out of the guest room in some baggy khaki shorts and a sky blue tank top. The top was big too, purposefully, like the kind some women wore to the gym to barely cover a sports bra.

"Is this okay?" she asked, pulling on the shirt.

"Fine with me," Sunny said, able to see her black bra when she lifted her arm. "I can't see enough of you to satisfy myself."

"I have every type of winter clothing you can imagine, but just a few things for summer. It only lasts eight to ten weeks, and I'm in or on the water most of the time..."

Sunny went to her and playfully tugged on her shorts. "Did you borrow these from a much larger woman?"

"I lost weight," she admitted. "I don't have a scale, so I don't know how much, but at least a size. Maybe two." She pulled the shirt up. "Without this belt, they'd be around my ankles. I should have tried stuff on before I packed. I could have borrowed something from my mom."

"Let me buy you a couple of things. You spent so much to come down here, the least I can do is make sure your clothes don't fall off you."

Devin gave her a darling smile. "I can afford a new pair of shorts. I just hate to buy anything right now, since I'm sure I'll put the weight back on. I've hovered around the same number since high school."

"Lucky girl," Sunny said, stepping back to take a look at Devin in the morning light.

When they'd been in Maine, she hadn't thought to ask how old Devin was. With her remarkable stamina, endless energy, and youthful complexion, Sunny had been sure she was in her mid-twenties. Now she saw that she'd been wrong. They had to have roughly been contemporaries.

The sexual charge that had ignited the moment they'd laid eyes on each other must have blinded her to a lot of details. Hiking for a month had clearly left Devin's face exposed to wind and cold and a lot of sun. It was actually kind of funny to see how tan her face was compared to the rest of her skin. When you added that wind-burn to her almost concave belly and sinewy muscle, she looked like she'd been out on the range too long during a harsh winter. A winter where supplies had been few. Sunny put her hand to her shoulder. "Come on, cowgirl." Devin flinched a little, and Sunny let her fingers move to touch some…plastic? Turning her, she gasped. "Did you have this yesterday?"

"Uh, yeah," Devin said, chuckling. "Do you think I got up before dawn to find a tattoo parlor?"

"Let me see," Sunny said, pulling her roomy top aside. "A moose," she said, charmed by the broad outline of an impressive head. "It's nice, Devin. Simple."

"I'm still getting used to it," she admitted. "I'd never wanted one before, but I was out on the trail, and decided a moose was my spirit animal."

When Sunny pulled back to look at her face, Devin was grinning. "I don't really go in for that kind of thing, but I had an encounter with a frozen moose that made me let go of some of my guilt. I slapped this guy on my back to remind me of that moment." She swallowed, with her throat moving slightly. "It was important."

Sunny wasn't sure if they were only supposed to touch when they were actually having sex, but she couldn't help herself. She slid her arms around Devin's body, rewarded by an equally enthusiastic hug in return. "I'm glad you let go a little bit. You're blameless," she murmured. "Completely blameless."

They'd done nothing more energetic than walk around the neighborhood, but Devin was about ready for a nap after lunch. The very warm weather was draining, especially mixed with the blazing hot sun. Maine got some hot weather too, but you could always go into the woods or jump into a lake and be shivering, no matter how hot it got. Her part of Maine didn't have much concrete or reflective glass, either, making Dallas feel much, much warmer than a similar temperature back home. But she wasn't about to ask for a break. If Sunny was perking along, window shopping and explaining all about the history of her neighborhood, Devin wasn't going to wimp out.

"So you've lived in Dallas all your life?" she asked.

"Except for college and law school. My daddy was born here, but my momma's from Texarkana."

"Is that far? I'm pretty weak on Texas geography."

"Everything's far in Texas," she said, showing that playful smile that Devin found herself more and more attracted to. "She moved to Dallas after high school and got a job working for the same oil company my daddy did. I'm not sure what each of them did at the time, but they got married pretty quickly and had me." She let out a sly laugh. "I'm not certain that's the real timeline, though. I think I might have been on the way before they ran to the justice of the peace."

"That wouldn't happen now. I've had friends whose kids were attendants in the wedding. People don't seem to do things in order like they did just a generation ago." Devin stopped to look in a housewares store display window, wondering what kind of people outfitted their patio with nine hundred dollar wooden lounge chairs and two hundred dollar lemonade pitchers. "What does your dad do now?"

"Now?" Sunny shrugged. "I'm not even sure he's still working, but if he is, he's probably in sales. That's what he's best at." Her expression changed, and she sounded dismissive when she added, "He's got the gift of gab."

"You're not sure if he's working?" Devin stared at her for a second. "Does he live around here?"

"Last I heard, he was in Dubai, but that's been years."

"I *know* that's far," Devin said, offering a tentative smile.

"It is." She nodded, while gazing at that perfect patio. The one just waiting for a very wealthy family to stretch out on those pretty chairs. "I haven't seen him since..." Her brow furrowed for a few seconds. "The summer before I entered seventh grade."

Devin knew to tread lightly when it came to parents, but that merited some digging. "Was it his choice to leave?"

"It sure wasn't mine." She was still vaguely looking at the window display, but it was clear her gaze wasn't focused. "I came home from school one day to find my mother throwing all of his stuff onto the porch." Her gaze moved up to land on Devin. "She'd always had a temper, but it had never been like this. She told me..." She took in a slow breath. "Well, I don't need to repeat what she said. But she made it clear my dad wasn't ever going to step inside that house again. He didn't."

Devin grasped her forearm, staring at her. "What happened?"

"He..." She looked down at the sidewalk, then her eyelids fluttered closed. "He'd been having an affair with one of my mom's friends. She got pregnant..."

"Oh, shit."

"Yeah," she agreed, nodding solemnly. "It was an 'oh, shit' kind of day. He must have come by during the night to get his things, or my mom burned them in the street." Shrugging, she added, "I wouldn't put it past her."

"So he just took off?"

"Pretty much. Janet, that was the woman's name, had a son a little older than me. There was a big custody battle, which the father won, almost unheard of at the time. I guess my dad and Janet didn't want to stick around here and have everyone gossip about them. They left behind her son and his three daughters, and took their new baby to Houston to start over."

"You said 'was.' The marriage didn't last?"

"It did not. After a few years, he took off for this fantastic opportunity in Dubai. When he stopped calling home or sending money, Janet divorced him." Shrugging again, she added, "I heard that from Janet's son. We went to the same high school. After he graduated, my source for information dried up."

"But he's your dad," Devin said gently. "Don't you want to know what happened? Maybe he had a good reason—" She stopped herself. "I'm sorry. That was a stupid thing to say. There's no reason good enough to abandon your kids."

"I would tend to agree. My youngest sister doesn't even remember what he looks like." Her expression turned a little dreamy when she said, "I thought he was the handsomest, smartest dad in the whole world. But I also thought we were a happy family, so my view was clearly skewed."

"That's so screwed up. It must be awful to lose a parent for any reason, but to have one just take off..."

"It wasn't good." She looked up at Devin with what was clearly a forced smile and said, "I keep hoping I'll find out he struck it rich in the oil business and feels so bad about leaving that he sends each of us a few million bucks."

Devin could see the pain in her eyes, and found herself asking the question, even though she knew the answer. "That wouldn't make up for his leaving, would it?"

"Not even close," Sunny agreed, turning away from the picture-perfect patio to stride back out into the blistering Texas sun.

✦

She wasn't sure what words she'd used to convince Devin to let her buy her some dressy clothes, but whatever they were, they'd worked. Sunny held up another outfit for Devin to try, this one unstructured. "I don't think they make clothes for a woman your height with a waist this small," she said, then caught herself and started to chuckle. "That was a dumb thing to say. You look just like a runway model, but I think their stuff is held on with pins."

"I'm happy to wear my jeans," Devin said. "My belt will hold them up…"

"Let's try this one. If it doesn't work, we'll go casual."

"Hope it doesn't work," Devin said, smiling that cute little impish grin.

"I appreciate that you're willing to get dressed up for this dinner. I really do."

Devin gave her a little shrug. "You're not asking me to jump through flaming hoops, Sunny. We're going to a birthday party for your close friend. I understand that you want me to fit in."

"You *will*," she said, realizing she'd stressed the word a little too much.

Devin's smile showed she didn't have any worries about that. "I can hold my own just about anywhere," she said. "With people, that is. I'm still shaking from that flight. I'm definitely more moose than eagle."

Sunny hadn't said anything, but Devin could tell she was nervous. She seemed like a good driver, but as she approached a big hotel, she paused to turn into the circular drive for valet parking. Devin pointed at a couple across the street getting into their car. "There's one you can nap for free."

"Right. But those people in front of me might be leaving too." She put her hand up to shade her eyes. "Should I wait?"

"Take the one on the east side of the street." When Sunny gave her a puzzled look, Devin pointed. "Right there."

"How on earth would I know that's the east side of the street?" Sunny said, putting on her blinker to show she was going to turn and nab the spot.

Devin waited for her to laugh, but she didn't. "Just look at the sun," she said, worried she was treating her like a child. "It sets in the west, right?"

Blinking for a second, Sunny nodded. "Um…sure."

"Well, since it's afternoon, the way it's sinking is west, so the opposite is east, right?"

"East it is," she said, completing the U-turn. The look on her face showed she was slightly embarrassed not to know something so basic to daily life, but she was nowhere near as embarrassed as she should have been! How disconnected did you have to be from the natural world to not know how to tell which direction you were heading?

She gazed at Sunny's profile as she quickly and efficiently backed the car into the fairly tight spot. The camera she had on the bumper gave her an awful lot of help, but she still did a very neat job. So she could throw her car into a tight u-turn and parallel park, but she didn't know where the damn sun set! What kind of craziness was that?

Devin had been amazingly compliant in allowing Sunny to buy her an outfit, but she was sure expensive restaurants in four-star hotels were out of her usual experience. She was learning, however, that Devin wasn't afraid of trying something new, even something out of her comfort zone.

The restaurant, although crazily expensive, wasn't stuffy or serious. That was a big plus, but Sunny was desperate for Devin to like her friends—and vice versa.

She waved as they entered and caught sight of Teresa and Callie, the birthday girl, flanked by Linda and Lauren, all looking up with anticipatory smiles.

"As usual," Sunny said, going first to kiss Callie, not just her oldest, but her dearest friend, "you look great!"

"So do you," Callie said quietly, holding on tightly. "You look much better than you did last week. More like your old self."

"Trying hard." She put her hand on Devin's shoulder. "Everybody, this is Devin Savary. Devin, meet Callie and Teresa and Linda and Lauren."

"Good to meet you all," Devin said, shaking each extended hand. "Thanks for inviting me to tag along. I know it can be awkward when long time friends have a newcomer pop in."

"We're *very* happy to meet you," Callie said, "after hearing about you for a solid month." She graced her with her luminous smile. "The way

Sunny talks about you, I thought you'd be wearing a red cape." Her laugh was always infectious, and Devin joined right in. "I don't know what I'm talking about," Callie admitted. "Does Super Woman wear a red cape?"

"I have no idea," Devin said, "but I'm not very unique where I'm from. I'm just another Maine guide."

The server walked over and she and Devin ordered drinks. Then Teresa leaned forward and said, "Sunny told us you're a guide, but I don't know what that means."

"Oh, yeah, I guess most places don't have a program like we do in Maine." She nodded, looking so cute and serious. "You take courses and gain work experience to learn the trade, then you're tested and licensed. I'm a master guide in recreation, hunting and fishing." She shrugged. "I've considered being tested in sea-kayaking, but I don't have the required hours. Where I live is a long way from the ocean."

"So you have to have a license to take people on a trip?"

"Oh, gosh, no. But most people prefer to hire an experienced guide. Luckily," she added, giving Teresa a charming grin.

Sunny was watching her avidly, enormously pleased that she didn't seem intimidated to be with a CPA, two attorneys, a senior VP for a big bank, or a professor from SMU. Devin was as proud of her profession as any of them were, and she'd probably logged more hours than any of them had—for a lot less money.

Devin had been a little antsy about dinner. Not that she was intimidated by people with fancy jobs. Most of her clients had money and were professionals. Otherwise they couldn't afford to come to Maine and hire her. But she wanted to fit in with Sunny's friends—especially this crowd, her inner circle. Thankfully, they all seemed like nice people. You couldn't make much headway when people were jerks. But Sunny just didn't seem like the kind of woman who'd welcome jerks into her life. She might be related to a few, though. Devin would have to learn more about her immediate family before she made up her mind, but so far they didn't sound promising.

Sunny was engaging in an intense discussion with Lauren, and Callie leaned over to speak quietly. "Are you planning on staying long?"

"I told Sunny I'd stay until she was..." She shut her mouth, not sure how frank Sunny had been with her friends. ""Um, until I'm ready to go back to work." She shrugged. "I'm a long way from taking clients out again."

Callie nodded sympathetically. "I can't imagine. But I knew Hank, so I can't say I was surprised when I heard he'd done something so foolhardy. He was the kind of guy who raced through life without paying attention to any warning signs."

"Maybe so," Devin said, "but you have to take people as you find them."

With a soothing tone, Callie lowered her voice and said, "You did your job. Accidents happen." More loudly, she added, "Don't let this take you off the path you've chosen for yourself. You don't want to be like Julian."

"Julian? What about Julian?"

In a second, Sunny's hand was on Devin's arm, but her gaze was directed at Callie. "We haven't talked about that yet."

Callie looked like she was going to snap off a sharp comment, but she took a breath and said, "I know I should have more sympathy, but you don't walk away from your job with no notice. That's just not right."

"He quit?" Devin stared at Sunny blankly.

"He did," Callie said. "Now Sunny's doing the work of three people while Julian's at home, fielding offers from other firms."

"He said he couldn't stand to come back and be reminded of Hank," Sunny said. "I can hardly blame him for doing something I've done, Callie. Come on now, give him a break."

"You did no such thing. After Morgan died, you stayed on until they could replace you. And she was your lover, not just your boss. There's no comparison!"

"Whether there is or not, he's gone. And I'd rather have him gone than feel like I was holding him hostage. A guy who doesn't want to be there makes it hard on everyone."

"But he had relationships with the clients! He was on the verge of being made partner."

"I know that. But I'm doing fine with the temp I've got. She's a very quick learner."

"She's working until ten or eleven every night," Callie said, giving Sunny a fierce scowl. "I'm about to quit my job and go over there and pull her out of the fire."

"I'd jump in if I knew anything about a law office," Devin said. "But if the walls don't need painting, I'd be no help at all."

Once they were back in the apartment, Devin kicked off her sandals and started to unbutton her blouse, continuing to chat. "I hate to have you spend so much money on dinner," she said, "but I appreciated it at least a hundred dollars worth." A sly grin peeked out. "A hundred dollars of *your* money, that is. If I have to spend more than ten bucks on dinner, I'm always tempted to steal the silverware just to make sure I get my money's worth."

"I'm glad you enjoyed it," Sunny said, watching her unstructured slacks pool at her feet before she bent and picked them up.

"So?" Devin inclined her head toward the hall. "What's your pleasure? Sleep alone?" Her grin grew, taking on a sexy vibe. "Or together?"

"Um, I haven't thought about it." In fact, she'd thought of nothing else on the ride home, with thoughts of how to convince Devin into joining her in bed tumbling around in her head on a continuous loop.

In her usual straightforward fashion, Devin walked over until she was right in front of Sunny. Her big blue eyes blinked slowly, making her appear a little vulnerable. "If you don't have a preference, I'd like to sleep together."

"I have a preference," she said, smiling up at Devin. "Being with you last night gave me the best rest I've had since March the second."

"Then let's do it," Devin said, moving aside so Sunny could lead.

She started down the hall, with Devin saying, "Why don't we just assume we'll sleep together? Is that cool?"

"Very cool," Sunny said.

"We don't have to have sex," Devin added, "but it usually relaxes me. I think that's part of the reason I slept so well last night."

That was so like Devin. Pragmatic and direct. Sunny was smiling to herself when she reached out and grabbed the doorframe of her bedroom, holding on like there was a forcefield she couldn't cross. Devin nearly bumped into her, but she didn't say a word. Stuck, unable to move or speak, Sunny could feel her body start to shake, certain she would start crying. Then Devin grasped her hand and tugged her into the guest bedroom. Patiently, with a darling smile barely curling her lips, she started to undress Sunny, speaking softly as she did. "You look really nice in this shirt," she said. As the garment fell from her shoulders, Devin added, "But even better out of it."

Immensely thankful that they didn't have to talk about her visceral reaction to entering the bedroom she unreasonably thought of as hers and Morgan's, Sunny let out a breath as she focused only on Devin's calming voice and her warm, gentle hands. She hadn't specifically agreed to sleep together for the duration of Devin's visit, but she honestly couldn't think of a single reason to sleep alone when the alternate choice was to cuddle up with her new human security blanket.

CHAPTER SIXTEEN

ON SUNDAY MORNING, DEVIN LAY on her back, with Sunny pressed up against her side. It was chilly in the apartment, with cold air blowing over their bodies, making her pull the sheet up to her shoulders. If it was her apartment, she'd have the windows open, or if air conditioning was required, she'd kick the thermostat up enough so it was barely cool. But Sunny's comfort level clearly required Arctic-like conditions.

Sunny stirred, smacked her lips together, then asked in a sleepy voice, "Are you awake?"

"Uh-huh. Want to get up?" She turned and put her hand on Sunny's belly, giving it a tender pat. "Or would you rather sleep a little longer while I go out and buy some things to make breakfast?"

"Here?" she asked, still sounding hazy.

"Yeah," Devin said, chuckling. "You've got a big room on the north side of the apartment that you probably haven't entered. It's called a kitchen."

"How can I know where the north side of the apartment is?" she murmured. "I can't see the sun."

Devin smiled at that. Being able to take a little teasing was mandatory in her book. She gave Sunny a kiss on the cheek, then got up and pulled on her clothes from the day before. "Go back to sleep. I'll be back in a few."

"I'm arguing," she said, then flipped onto her side and was asleep before Devin could get her shoes laced.

Devin wasn't sure how the grocery store had ripe melons in April, but given how much they cost, the store might have built their own micro-climate to turn a summer fruit into a springtime one. But she'd decided to purchase some good, healthy breakfast food for Sunny, damn the expense. She worked too hard, slept too little, and had far too much stress in her life. Eating well couldn't counteract all of that, but eating poorly could make it worse.

The shower was running when she returned, and she quickly sliced up the fruit and added a small bowl of plain yogurt for some protein. Some people didn't like the plain stuff, but Sunny could pop some blackberries into it if she needed flavoring.

By the time Devin had filled a tray with their food, Sunny was out of the shower, singing softly to herself as she bustled around in her bedroom. Devin entered, making her jump.

"I didn't hear you come back!" She clutched a towel to her chest, eyes wide with alarm.

"I'm pretty quiet, but even if I wasn't, you were in the shower when I got here. Nice grocery store," she said, placing the tray on the bed. "For billionaires. Want to eat in here? This room's the brightest one at this time of day."

"Sure. Let me get dressed."

"Not too," Devin said, adding what she hoped was a sexy grin. "I thought we could spend a little longer in bed." She caught the puzzled look Sunny gave her and added, "If you want to, that is."

With a quick nod, Sunny walked into her huge closet, returning a few seconds later in navy gym shorts and a powder blue tank top.

"You're probably overdressed for the weather," Devin said. "It's gonna be a scorcher."

"I swear it's not usually this steamy at this time of year. It's supposed to cool down by tomorrow, then you'll get to see what spring's really like in Texas."

Devin smiled up at her, then took a plate and started piling fruit onto it. "Hope so. I'd have to get up well before dawn to go for a run in this heat."

After taking some of everything, Sunny stacked some pillows into a mound and leaned against them at the head of the bed. "This is a nice treat. I love having breakfast in bed, and it's so much nicer than ordering in."

Devin was sure her mouth had dropped open. "You order breakfast to be delivered?"

"I don't have a cook so…yeah." She took a bite of pineapple and nodded enthusiastically. "Fantastic! This isn't canned, is it?"

"Heck, no. They were so ripe, I could smell them when I walked into the store. I felt like I was in Hawaii."

"Have you been?"

Devin stared at her for a minute. "How would I get from Maine to Hawaii without being on an airplane?"

"Ahh!" She started to laugh. "I think I might need a little more sleep. My circuits aren't firing."

"I think that's just what you need. You look awfully pretty," she said, trying to make sure she framed her comment properly. "But tired. You need all the rest you can get to help yourself recover."

"It's tough," Sunny said, taking a bite of yogurt and making a face. "Mmm. I was expecting vanilla."

"Got any? I can add a few drops if you want."

Chuckling, she shook her head. "I don't consider vanilla a condiment, so I don't have any."

"Add some blackberries. That'll help." Devin watched her place a single berry atop the yogurt and try again, but it was clear she wasn't happy with the taste.

"Do you mind?" Devin took the bowl from her, tossed a handful of berries on top, then pressed the spoon into them, squeezing the juice out and dying the pristine white yogurt a pale purple. Then she added a few chunks of pineapple. "You'll like it better now."

Sunny took another bite, this time looking pretty pleased. "Big improvement. I usually don't eat yogurt, since the kind I like is full of sugar and calories, but I might be able to adapt to this."

"I like some protein first thing in the morning, so it's one of my favorites." Devin finished up by eating some slices of a super sweet orange. "Damn, your fruit is so much better than ours at this time of year."

Sunny had gotten most of her yogurt down, and she dabbed around her mouth with the paper towel Devin had provided. "Delicious. You can make breakfast for me any time."

"Ready for a nap?"

Standing, Sunny picked up the tray and put it on a spring green chair that sat at an angle near the corner of the room. Then she moved back to sit next to Devin. "Um, can we talk about what's going on here?"

"Absolutely." Devin sat up straight and gazed directly into Sunny's eyes. "What's going on?"

Sunny blinked a few times. "You don't know?"

"Not really. I mean..." She stared a little harder. "What are you getting at?"

Sunny's index finger flipped back and forth between her body and Devin's. "What's going on with us."

"In terms of what?" She took Sunny's hand in her own and pressed it to her chest. "I thought you wanted me to stay for a while."

"I do! But..." She gently disentangled her hand from Devin's grip, stood, and moved over to stand by the window and gaze out. The view was nice there, looking towards a decent number of trees, with only shorter buildings littering the view. "I enjoyed the hell out of what we did on Friday night, but I thought you were coming to give me some emotional support. I'm still kind of amazed that we ended up in bed."

"We didn't technically end up in bed. We couldn't make it that far."

"Right!" Sunny nodded forcefully. "I didn't expect that, and now I'm wondering what it all means."

Devin walked over to put her arms around Sunny's waist. She was clearly troubled, even upset, but Devin couldn't guess why. "I'm not sure what you mean. Are you asking if I regret that we had sex?"

"You don't, do you?" She whirled around, eyes so wide they would have made Devin laugh if this wasn't so serious.

"Hell, no. I've never regretted having sex, and if I was going to start, I wouldn't start with you." She looked shy or tentative or something in that neighborhood, but Devin had no idea why. "Tell me what's on your mind. I kind of thought that agreeing to sleep together meant..." She moved her hands to let them settle onto Sunny's shoulders, maintaining eye contact. "Act like you're in court. Just tell me the facts."

"I'm a real estate lawyer. The only court I've been in was mock court in school," she said, shaking her head, "but I know what you mean." She pulled away to pace back and forth in front of the window, with her hands jammed into her armpits. Devin didn't know her well enough to read her, but she seemed like a tiger in a cage, anxious and trapped. "What does this mean for the future? Do you want to be…what? Girlfriends? Or did you just have an irresistible urge?"

"I like you," she said, knowing that sounded pathetically weak. "I saw you and…" She shrugged, knowing she should say more, but not having a lot to add. "Um, I don't put a lot of prior thought into a lot of things I do. If it seems right, I jump in. Maybe you're different that way."

"I'm definitely different. I usually think long and hard before I have sex with someone." She blinked up at Devin, then spit out the question that was probably making her so nervous. "Do we have a future?"

She hadn't thought they'd be having this kind of discussion on her second morning in Dallas, but the last thing she wanted to do was lead Sunny on. "I haven't been in a relationship since I was twenty. I don't generally think that way." From the puzzled look on her face, Devin could see that Sunny didn't get her point. "I don't think about relationships. I just…" Frustrated, she asked, "You know what I'm good at?"

"So far, going down on me," she said, with what looked like a reluctant smile making her eyes twinkle. "You're awesome, as a matter of fact."

The cutest grin settled onto Sunny's face when she talked about sex. She seemed a little tentative at discussing things like that so bluntly, but Devin could tell she was also getting a charge out of it. Sunny might have been one of those women who thought she should behave in a certain, proper way, but really wanted to be a little more daring. "Besides that," she said, laughing along with her. She thought for a few seconds, trying to make sure she got this right. "I'm best at paying attention to how I feel in the moment rather than thinking about the future. And today, I feel really good that I'm here, with you. Safer, too. I've had two nights of no bad dreams or waking up in the middle of the night. I like that."

"And that's…" Anyone could see that she was struggling, but Devin wanted to make sure they had things straight between them. "Is having sex part of what makes you feel good?"

"Yeah. Sex is part of what makes me feel close to a woman, but if you don't feel the same…"

"No, no, I guess I do," she said, but there was a hint of uncertainty in her tone. "This just isn't how I usually do things. I generally wait to make sure we're both intent on having a long-term relationship before I go any further."

"Then we'll do that," Devin said decisively. "We'll just pull back and treat each other like we did in Maine."

A sultry smile curled the corners of Sunny's lips. "Maine was cold, and we were both in shock. But now…" She shrugged. "It's kind of silly to act like strangers after what happened on Friday. I mean, we had fun, right?"

"I sure did. And if you weren't having fun, you are a master at faking it." Devin grasped the hem of Sunny's top and pulled it over her head. "You've got too much fabric hiding this beautiful body from my very appreciative eyes." The shorts got the same treatment, allowing them to fall to the floor and pool around her feet. "Now you're perfect."

A seductive smile settled onto Sunny's pouty lips, then her voice purred low and rough, "Let's get after it." After linking her hands behind Devin's neck, she pulled her down for a long, gentle kiss, with hints of pineapple and blackberry and honeydew making Sunny's lips taste like candy. For the first serious discussion about relationships she'd had in many, many years, this hadn't gone badly at all. Maybe avoiding these kinds of talks like the plague had been a waste of precious time.

Devin waited until eight to call, even though she knew Lori had been up for hours. But mornings were a busy time at her house, and Devin wanted to make sure they could talk and not be interrupted. After dialing, she sat on the comfy chair by the window in Sunny's room, idly trying to figure out how to get to a bunch of trees in the distance without being run over by the traffic that rolled down every street between where she stood and where she wanted to be.

"Hi there," she said when Lori answered.

"It's about time! I can't believe you've let me sit here biting my nails for three whole days!"

"I've been busy," Devin said. "I can hardly pick up the phone when I'm lying in bed with a pretty woman, can I?"

There was a significant silence, then Lori said, "You did what?"

"I was surprised myself," Devin said, a notable understatement. "But we started ripping each other's clothes off before she got past the front door on Friday evening. Then we did basically the same thing all day yesterday. I haven't had so much sex in so little time since I was in my twenties." She laughed, thinking of how long that had been. "And it didn't happen very often even then."

"Tell me everything," Lori demanded.

"I know you don't mean that. Let's just say that I haven't been this attracted to a woman in forever. Sunny's smart, sensitive, kind-hearted, close to her family, and absolutely acrobatic in bed." She let out a laugh. "Too much info?"

"I'm not some naive child, Devin. Just because I don't sleep with women doesn't mean I can't imagine what it's like. It's not rocket science."

"Yes, it is!" She laughed, always ready to tease Lori about anything lesbian related. "And Sunny should win the Nobel Prize in…whatever rocket scientists win prizes for."

"Your dad would know, but don't tell him why you're asking. I guarantee he won't want to know what you've been up to."

"You've got that right. But I'm going to call and talk to him anyway."

"Hey! Don't think you're going to cheap out on me and hang up. I want information. How surprised were you to find out Sunny's as much of a strumpet as you are?"

"She's not a strumpet." She paused for a second. "Neither am I, if I'm right about what a strumpet is. Don't be all sex negative on me. Just because you're with the first guy you slept with doesn't mean everyone has to do the same."

"You know I'm teasing you," Lori said, gentling her voice. "We always joke around about things. What's up? Are we going to have to Skype so you can see my face?"

"Maybe." A morsel of guilt had been floating around in her head, and she decided to share it. "Um, to be honest, Sunny's more like you than me."

"In what way?"

"In the sex way. She didn't tell me how many women she's been with, but I got the impression it's not many. She said she always waits until she's in a long-term relationship."

Lori didn't say a word for a few seconds, with Devin easily able to picture her expression. Slightly puzzled, already fighting her instinct to lecture. "Um, how are you planning on coming home soon if you're jumping into a long-term relationship?"

"I'm not. Getting into a relationship, that is. I think I made it clear that I'm looking at this as a day by day thing. At least I hope I did."

"Devin," Lori said, her tone already in lecture mode. "What's gotten into you? She's so shaky that you rushed down there to help her through a tough time. How does that translate to her needing more fucking? Especially after she told you she needs a commitment you're not going to give her?"

"Before," Devin said, wincing. "We had sex before she told me that. We had sex before she took her jacket off, Lori. It was like in a movie!"

With a long-suffering sigh, Lori said, "So you had sex, then she told you she needed a commitment, and you apologized for misreading her and backed off. Right?"

"I offered to. I swear I did. But she said we might as well keep going, and I wasn't about to argue with her. I *like* her," she insisted.

"You've been *liking* women for almost twenty years, Dev. And I know you've hurt, or at least seriously disappointed, some of them. *Please* don't do that to Sunny."

"I'm being honest with her. I swear I am. I told her I don't do any long-term planning when it comes to things I like."

"That's not true," Lori said firmly. "You decided a long time ago that you don't want a relationship. Day by day implies you're open to sticking around if things work out—and you're not. Unless you've changed completely in a weekend and now know you were made to live in a big city."

"*That's* not gonna happen. I can't even describe what it's like here."

"Try," she said, the frustration leaving her voice, now replaced with curiosity. "I need to have an image of you down there."

"I don't know what to say about it," Devin said, truly at a loss. "It's big, for sure. And dry. And green, but not naturally."

"What?"

"You can tell all of the tiny little patches of grass get their water from a sprinkler system."

"Ahh."

"Yeah. It feels like it might be dry more often than not. And it's flat." She thought for a minute. "Busy. Congested in some neighborhoods, but not this one. And it smells funny."

"Funny how?"

"Not sure," she said, trying to conjure the scent of the place in her mind. "Smells I'm completely unfamiliar with. Some kind of plant or the kind of grass they have, I guess. I went by some flower yesterday that smelled like grape soda."

"What?"

"It's different here. Really different. But it's not bad. I'm just… surprised all day long. Sunny lives in a neighborhood that's full of office buildings and expensive restaurants. They've got these big, wide sidewalks, but no one's ever on them. It's like a ghost town, but the buildings are full of people."

"Is it like Portland?"

"Not in the least."

"Boston?"

"Nope. Boston's old and historic. Everything seems new here. And if there are tourists, they're not in this neighborhood. I haven't seen people walking around with guidebooks or anything."

"Do you like it at all? It sounds awful."

"I haven't investigated enough to know if I like it."

"Get out of bed and look around!"

Lori was back to her usual teasing—thankfully. "Sunny insisted that I drive her to work this morning. It wasn't far—probably five miles, but I could've run and gotten there faster than we did in her SUV."

"She has an SUV? Does she have a bunch of kids you haven't told me about? God knows I'd never drive one if mine wasn't filled with the boys and all of their stuff."

"Maybe it's not an SUV. It's new, and German, and it rides like a luxury car, but it's bigger and taller than a sedan."

"That's a crossover. They're popular—with yuppies."

"I think I can safely say that Sunny's a yuppie. She's got what has to be an expensive apartment, a fancy car, she shops at a fancy grocery store that would make your weekly food budget run out by Tuesday, and each couple tossed in three hundred bucks for dinner on Saturday night."

"She's a yuppie," Lori said soberly. "No doubt."

"She's also got a nice bike on her balcony, and that's what I'm driving from here on out. I thought I was going to be killed fifty times when I drove home! My hands were shaking so hard I almost couldn't get the car into the space in her garage."

"She has a garage? I thought she lived in an apartment building."

"She does. A tall one, with an office building across the street that's even taller. Right now I'm looking at some guys throwing little foam basketballs into a trash can."

"You can see them from her apartment?"

"Hell, yes! They're not fifty yards from here, Lori. It's weird!"

"Send me a picture. Right now. I've gotta see this for myself."

"Soon as I hang up I'll text you one."

"But even though you're up in the clouds, with traffic that makes your hands shake, and plants that smell like grape soda—you're staying?"

"Yeah." She cleared her throat and made herself say it, even though she hated to reveal her vulnerability, even to Lori. "I feel more like myself when we're together. The walls were closing in on me just a day after I got back from my hike. It's better here."

"Then don't even think about coming home, even though it'll kill me to have you gone for long."

"I know. It will me too, but…"

"Do what you need, Devin. You've always been good at that."

"I'll try. I'm still off my game, but I think I'll get back to normal faster by being away. At least, I hope so."

"I do too. Have some fun, but be kind. Think about what she needs too, okay?"

"I will. Promise."

"But don't stay a minute longer than you have to. Even though the snow's melting fast, the kids are still mostly in the house. Without you to divert them for a few hours a couple of times a week, I might lose my friggin' mind."

"I'll be home," she said, smiling at the thought of her little buddies. "You keep those rug rats out of trouble until I get back. As soon as I do, I'll take them to my cabin for a whole weekend so you and Chris can have some grown-up time."

"Don't taunt me! You can't get my hopes up like that and not follow through."

"As soon as Sunny and I are both feeling better, I'll be home. I miss it and you so much it's not even funny."

Once she'd talked to Lori, Devin felt a little more grounded, a little more like everything was normal. It wasn't…not by a long shot, but having that home connection let her put on the only decent clothes she owned, lace up her black running shoes, and take the elevator down to the lobby. She had a good internet signal, and she knew where the bus stop was, so it was just a matter of following directions, something she could do in her sleep.

It was warm out, but the heat didn't bother her until she'd had to stand on the corner for over fifteen minutes. The bus schedule clearly wasn't to be taken literally.

The first part of her trip only took about twenty minutes. She disembarked and started up again, walking nearly two miles, if the map on her phone was correct. By the time she got to the right street, sweat was running down her cheeks, only partly from the heat. Nerves had a heck of a lot to do with it, but focusing on that wasn't going to get the job done. She'd brought some tissues, and she used them to blot her face and her hands, then she shoved them into the pocket of her black slacks and walked up the front sidewalk of a pale beige stucco home. It was awfully big, but seemed about average for the neighborhood. She wasn't sure if this was a particularly nice area, but the lawns were all manicured, and she hadn't seen even a single old car parked in the driveways.

She took a look at herself in the rear view mirror of a German car in the drive, adjusted her white shirt, and hiked up her slacks. Her belt was on the last notch, but it wasn't really getting the job done. After shaking her hands out to bleed off some tension, she rang the bell and stood up tall, trying to project confidence.

The door opened just a few inches, and a woman's voice said, "I'm sorry, but I'm not interested in changing my religion."

The door started to close, giving Devin just a second to say, "I'm Devin Savary. I'm the guide who was with your husband—"

The door opened wide, and a frazzled-looking younger woman stared at her. Devin stared back, seeing a lot of blonde hair, pinned up haphazardly in a pile on the top of her head, a surprising amount of eye makeup, and bright pink lips. The woman wore a thin, white terrycloth robe, with her substantial breasts straining the fabric.

"*You're* the woman? The actual woman? You're not some clerk from the insurance company?"

"No, ma'am," she said, shaking her head. "I'm the actual woman."

She gathered up her robe and held it together at her throat. "What are you doing here?"

"I wanted to talk to you," Devin said. "It didn't seem right to call, and I thought a letter would be too formal." She swallowed nervously. "I thought you might have some questions, so this seemed like the thing to do."

"I'm going out…" She cast a quick look behind her.

"I can come back another day. When would you like to meet?"

The woman leaned close to the screen, peering over Devin's shoulder. "Where's your car?"

"I took a bus."

"There's no bus close to here."

"I know. I had to walk a couple of miles after the bus. I came from Uptown."

"Uptown?" She looked like she wanted to call the authorities, but she relented and opened the screen door. "Come in. If you went that far out of your way to come today, I guess I can be a little late." As Devin crossed the threshold, the woman held out her hand after arranging her robe again. "Angelica Perry," she said.

They shook, and Devin repeated her name, just in case it wasn't already etched in Angelica's mind as the enemy.

"Have a seat. I'll get you a glass of water."

"I'm all right," she protested, but Angelica was gone. Not hearing a single sound coming from what should have been the kitchen, Devin scanned the room. The house was even bigger than it had looked from the front. The room she was in had to be twenty by thirty, and it was decorated like an older person lived there. Not an elderly person. Just someone who'd been working for twenty years or so. She didn't have any way of characterizing the place other than that. It simply looked like a house for a fifty year old couple.

Angelica hustled back in, now wearing a pair of jeans and a pale blue sweater. Her hair had been combed just enough to pull it back into a ponytail, making her look even younger. She handed Devin a glass, kept one for herself, and sat down in a dark red plaid covered chair. "Tell me why you're here."

"I don't know what you know, and I thought you might have questions. Plus, I wanted to offer my condolences. I'm really sorry your husband died." She looked down at the floor when she heard Angelica let out a sharp gasp and start to cry. "I'd do just about anything to change what happened," she continued, raising her voice a little. "But I know that's a wish that can't happen."

"Why did you let him go?" Angelica moaned, grabbing a tissue from a box right on a heavy, dark wood side table.

Devin cleared her throat, just about to burst into tears herself. Watching a woman who couldn't control her grief made her shake with sympathy. But she reminded herself of Edie's lawyer's edict, and tried to sidestep the question. "I didn't let him go, Angelica. He just went. I swear I would have gone in after him, but I had to pull Julian out of the water first. By the time I got him on solid ground, Hank had been in for at least ten minutes. No one comes out alive after that long."

"You should have been there. If Sunny and Julian were too afraid to stop him, you could have."

Still staring at the floor, Devin said, "I can see why you'd think that. But that's just not how it was. Hank had an accident. It wasn't anyone's fault. Awful things happen every day, and his luck didn't hold up that day."

Angelica took a deep, shaky breath. "You don't think he was stupid?"

Devin's head shot up. "Stupid?"

With her head shaking roughly, she repeated herself. "Do you think he was stupid for walking on the ice?"

"No," Devin said softly, seeing she needed to hear this—whether it was true or not. "He was curious. That's all. He saw a beautiful creature, and he wanted to take a picture of it." She paused, trying to think of any kind of compliment she could add. "I was only with him for two days, but I could see the childlike enthusiasm he had. He was just unlucky, Angelica. The ice should have held him. He found the one spot that had thinned out early. Sometimes a branch or a log will create a little wrinkle…" Angelica was looking at her like she'd been going on too long, so she stopped. "Hank wasn't stupid, and anyone who says he was doesn't know what they're talking about. Ice is inherently dangerous. I've known people who've fallen in who've lived by that lake their whole lives. The last thing I'd call any of them is stupid."

Angelica nodded, now fully in control again. "Thank you. People have been saying some really cruel things."

"Some people are really cruel," Devin agreed.

"They are." She was quiet for a moment, then she said, "Do you really know people who've fallen in and lived?"

"I do. Several of them."

Peering at Devin with intense focus, Angelica said, "Have they told you what it's like?"

"One did," she said quietly. "He said he didn't have time to even think. He gulped in some water, and the next thing he knew he was lying on the ice, receiving CPR."

"He wasn't terrified?" she asked quietly.

"No. He said there wasn't time. He was surprised, but then he was unconscious. The cold takes people fast. It's much worse for their loved ones than them."

"It's been horrible," she moaned, starting to cry again. Devin hesitated just a second, then got to her knees and scooted over to wrap her arms around Anjelica, holding her gently. She didn't speak. Didn't have a word to say that would help. But it just seemed right to at least offer some comfort.

"Thank you," she finally sniffed. "That helps a little. I've had so many nightmares about him fighting and trying to claw his way through the ice."

"That didn't happen," Devin said quietly. "I *promise* you that didn't happen. He sank like a stone. Peacefully."

Angelica nodded a few times, then started to pull away. Devin got to her feet quickly and stood there, undecided about what to do next.

When Angelica stood also, she started for the front door. "I appreciate that you came," she said, turning to look at Devin. "I don't know what I'm going to do next. Everyone wants me to sue."

Devin just shrugged. She didn't think Angelica was asking for her opinion.

"He was too young to die," she continued. "I've got bills…"

Devin walked for the door. When she got there, she said, "I'm not here to talk about that. You'll do what you think is right." She met Angelica's eyes again. "I just want you to know how sorry I am. If you have any other questions I can answer, you can call me. Want my number?"

"I don't think I'd better," she said quietly. "My attorney might not like that."

"Attorneys don't like people to talk like people," Devin said, sparing a slight smile. "But sometimes you have to do what's right." She nodded briskly. "Talking to you was right, no matter what."

"Thank you," Angelica said.

Devin opened the door and stepped outside. "I wish we'd met under better circumstances."

"I do too," she agreed. "I've met a lot of people in the last month that I'd rather not have."

"Take care of yourself," Devin said. "I know it will take a very long time to feel like yourself again, but you'll get there."

With a wry laugh, Angelica said, "You have no idea how many people have told me that because I'm young and pretty, I'll find another husband right away."

"Those are people you should avoid," Devin said. "Stick with the ones who know people aren't replaceable."

"Thanks," Angelica said, sounding wistful. "I think I'd like you if I'd met you another way."

"That would have been nice," Devin agreed, nodding goodbye as she walked back down the sidewalk, heading for the bus.

Sunny slipped her key into the lock and paused at the door, with the slight hope that Devin would greet her the way she had on Friday night. But then her nose started to twitch, and she followed the scent, finding the most improbable thing happening in her kitchen—heat was being applied to food!

Devin looked up and grinned, and in a second Sunny's wish for another roll on the sofa was back. Then she saw all of the never-used pots and pans resting on the counter, as well as spices and herbs and onions lying there, and decided to tamp down her frisky libido and pay attention to the trouble Devin had clearly gone to.

"What in the world are you doing?" she teased. "Someone's going to call the fire department, since this is definitely the first time any complex food scent has leaked from my apartment door."

"Get used to it." Devin wiped her hands and walked around the pass-through to take Sunny into her arms and give her a gentle kiss. "You need healthy meals and more sleep, and I'm going to make sure you get both while I'm here." She tapped her on the nose with a finger. "Thanks for taking a car service home. I was not looking forward to driving again. Especially alone."

"But you have to, Devin. You can't be stuck here all day with no transportation. You'll go stir-crazy."

"No, I won't." She let go and went back to the stove. After sticking a spoon into a pan, she grasped the salt shaker and added a little. "We've got about fifteen minutes until dinner's ready. Want a drink?"

"Are you going to tell me what we're having? I can't guess, but it smells great."

"You'll see." She put her hands on Sunny's shoulders and turned her toward the hall. "Let's go take this suit off you."

They went into the bedroom together, then Devin sat in the center of the bed and pulled her legs up so she was sitting with her elbows on her knees, like a kid watching her mom get ready for an evening out. While Sunny went into her closet to hang up her jacket she said, "Did you use the pool?"

"Didn't have time."

She put her slacks on a hangar, then came back into the bedroom. "Did it take all day to cook?"

Devin laughed. "Just an hour. But I didn't get home until five, so I had to hustle."

Staring at her, Sunny said, "What am I missing? You dropped me off at seven thirty this morning."

"Well, after I got home, I had to regroup to get my hands to stop shaking." Her laugh was remarkably infectious, and Sunny found herself joining in. "I swear I saw more cars today than I have in the last two or three years—combined."

"Aww." Sunny sat next to her and draped an arm across her shoulders. "You told me you were a good driver."

"I am. I'm just not psychic, so I don't know what all of the crazy people are going to do. People were honking and swearing at me when I refused to go over the speed limit."

"If you won't drive over the limit, you'd better stay off the Central Expressway," Sunny said, chuckling. "You'll be squished like a skeeter on someone's windshield."

"I don't normally drive slow, but I had to keep listening to my phone for directions. I would have missed my exit if I'd kept up with the speed-demons."

"You'll get used to it. In a week, you'll be zooming around like everyone else."

"Not gonna happen. I'll walk, ride a bike, or take a bus. I did all three of those today, as a matter of fact." Her expression grew serious, and she said, "But I accomplished both of my objectives."

"Going to let me in on them?"

She nodded. "You won't like the first one."

Sunny could feel her heart start to beat faster. "Are you going back already?"

"No! I told you I'm staying until you're feeling better, and are able to sleep through the night. I didn't just say that, Sunny. I *meant* it."

Sunny sat next to her on the bed, placing a hand on her knee. "Sorry. I'm pretty jumpy these days."

"I know," Devin soothed. "Um, I ignored the advice of Edie's attorney, and went to see Angelica."

Sunny was looking down at Devin before she realized she'd leapt to her feet. "You what?"

Appearing a little sheepish, Devin said, "I know it wasn't smart, but it's wrong to just let a woman wonder about what happened. She had questions that I was able to answer. It was the right thing to do."

"Oh, Devin," she sighed, sinking down to sit beside her again. "Everything you said can be used against you. Everything!"

"I don't care," she said, an obstinate look covering her face. "If I did something wrong, I should be punished. But I don't think I did. I also don't think I said anything Angelica can use against me. But if she does…" She shrugged, like that was a minor issue.

"We can talk about this later." She let out a weary sigh. "I just hope this doesn't come back to bite you on the ass."

"If it does, it does. I can live with that."

"All right," Sunny said, clearly unable to change history at this point. "What else did you accomplish?"

"Well, I cleaned off your bike, filled the tires with air, and set out. It took me a while, but I'm gainfully employed."

Once again, Sunny leapt to her feet and stared down at Devin. "You got a job? Already?"

"Uh-huh. I start tomorrow."

"Devin! I want you to have time to relax and get your bearings again. You don't need to work."

"I do," she said, pursing her lips and nodding. "I can't just sit around. Can't do it."

Sunny stood there for a minute, quickly realizing that Devin wasn't going to be talked out of this. "Tell me about this job." She went over to her dresser to find something to sleep in.

"I'm going to be on the opening crew at that fancy espresso place we went to this morning. Fair Trade."

"That's almost at my office! You *have* to drive to get there. You have to!"

"No, I don't. I can be there in twenty minutes if I crank it." She jumped up and went to the guest room, returning with a black T-shirt with the large company logo across the back, a smaller one over the breast. "I can wear my khaki shorts, but I might have to get suspenders. I think I'm going to have to cave in and buy a smaller size until I get back to my normal weight."

Sunny stared at her for a second. "You really want to ride a bike across town to make coffee?"

"I do," she said soberly.

Putting her hands on Devin's waist, she gazed at her for a few moments, trying to keep her anxiety at bay. "I'm worried about you riding a bike through traffic. You're afraid to drive, Devin. Now think of how little protection you'll have on a bike."

"I'll be at work before there's any traffic at all. I start at five thirty."

"Oh, good lord!" She walked over to poke through her dresser again.

"This is ideal," Devin insisted, clearly believing her own fantasy. "They only want me until eleven, so I can ride home when traffic is still light."

"Five thirty until eleven is full time?"

"Not even close, but that's their standard schedule. I assume they want to make sure they don't have to pay overtime or have to put me on their insurance plan."

Sunny slipped on an old, soft T-shirt and went over to hold Devin in a loose embrace. "This is really what you want?"

"Uh-huh," she said, looking touchingly sincere. "I thought it was the best of the four jobs I was offered."

"Four!" Sunny slapped at her with the flats of her hands. "Are you pulling my leg?"

"Why would I do that?"

Damn! Her earnestness was going to take some time to get used to. When she was talking about work, her sense of humor disappeared.

"I started off in Uptown, then worked my way out, trying to stick to the places you said you liked." She held up her hand and ticked off the jobs on her fingers. "I could have stocked shelves at your fancy grocery store, but they wanted me to work from ten p.m to six a.m. I was tempted, but worried it would interfere with our time together, so I nixed that."

"What else?"

"That French bistro you like wanted me to scrub the floors and clean the bathrooms, but that was after closing too. The dry cleaner you go to offered the afternoon shift, but they wanted to pay next to nothing. Same thing for the gourmet deli where we bought those delicious brownies." She narrowed her eyes, clearly annoyed. "They've got a lot of nerve charging four bucks a piece for those, then trying to get by with paying their counter help a pittance."

"Damn, Devin, you were busier than a one-armed paper-hanger."

She blinked, looking blank. "A what?"

"A really busy person."

"I like to be busy," she said. "After I'd been to all of the places you like in Uptown, I decided to head out to the coffee place we went to this morning. With all of those office buildings around there, I figured they'd have a brisk morning business."

When a timer started to beep, Sunny took her hand and led her back into the living room. "And you made dinner on top of all of that."

"Sure did," she said, going back into the kitchen to taste her creation one last time. "Two or three more minutes." She started to pull out plates, then paused, looking reflective. "People say it's hard to find work, but I've never in my life had a problem, and that includes when I was living in a town with fewer than fifteen businesses."

"That's because you're willing to do things they usually hire undocumented workers for," Sunny said, trying to make sure she didn't sound like she was chiding her. "I don't know anyone who'd clean a restaurant."

"Why not?" She pulled some silverware out of the drawer and placed it by the plates. "Work's work."

"I guess it is," Sunny agreed, wondering how her friends would react to having Devin hand them their dry cleaning or make sandwiches for them at the deli. Then she took another look at that contented grin and decided she didn't give a good god-damn what anyone else thought. She just wanted Devin to be happy.

When Devin emerged from the guest bathroom the next morning, she got into her shorts and T-shirt, then went to investigate when she heard the other shower running. After knocking, she opened the bathroom door. "Morning," she said, raising the volume so Sunny could hear her.

"Hi."

"Um…what are you doing up? You didn't leave for work until seven yesterday."

"As long as you're up at the ass-crack of dawn, I might as well get up with you and work out before I go to the office."

"Nice," Devin said, really pleased that Sunny wasn't complaining about her alarm going off at four forty-five. "Can I make you breakfast?"

"I'll get something after my spin class." She turned off the water and pulled her towel from where she'd draped it over the glass. "Actually, I'll come by Fair Trade and see if you know how to make an iced coffee."

"I don't, but I'll learn. Need help drying your back?" Devin was trying to use a sexy voice, but thought it just sounded silly.

"Ha! I fell for that line on Sunday, which is why we didn't leave the house until dark. You'd better just give me a kiss and go start filling the locals up with caffeine."

Devin opened the door a crack and stuck her head inside. Sunny's warm, wet lips made her wish they could play around like they had on Sunday, but she wasn't about to be late on her first day. "See you soon," she said, grasping the edge of the towel and rubbing it over Sunny's golden red hair. "Dinner will be ready at six."

"Is that a subtle hint not to linger at the office?"

"Nope." Devin leaned in and kissed her one last time. "But I've got to get to bed by nine, and I need time for my food to digest. If you're not home when I'm ready to eat, I'll warm up your meal when you get home. No pressure."

"You're the only person who has ever said that to me," Sunny said, chuckling. "I could get used to that."

◆

While sitting in her car, stuck in an utter standstill, Sunny pressed a button on the center console and said, "Call Callie." After a pause, the phone dialed itself and rang twice.

"I'm stuck in traffic," Callie said when she picked up. "You?"

"The same. I'm no more than a mile from work, but I haven't moved for a minute or two."

Callie yawned loudly. "To be honest, I don't mind traffic if you're available to talk. What's going on?"

"Want to play a game?"

"Um…sure."

"Okay. Guess what I did seven times this weekend?"

"Seven times." Callie was quiet for a minute, then said, "I can't guess. From what you've told me about Devin, you might have gone on seven hikes or shot seven cows."

"You don't shoot cows!" She laughed at Callie's total lack of connection to anything outdoors. "And we didn't technically hike, but I climbed all over her like she was a human jungle gym."

"What?" Callie shouted. "You had sex with that delicious-looking woman? Damn it, Sunny, you know I love Teresa to death, but I was fantasizing about Devin in the dirtiest terms imaginable the other night!" She stopped abruptly, then said, "I can't believe I just said that about your girlfriend. She *is* your girlfriend, right?"

"Not technically," Sunny admitted. "I thought she was just here to lend me some moral support, but then we started having sex. Things got even stranger when she got up on Sunday and went to the store, then made breakfast and served it to me in bed."

"No!"

"Indeed she did. And when I got home last night, dinner was waiting for me. Home made dinner," she stressed.

"God damn it! A woman with a body like that can cook?"

"She can. But the weirdest thing, the thing that's really got me puzzled, is that she got a job."

"What do you mean she got a job? She's been in town for thirty seconds."

"To be precise," Sunny said, still amazed by this fact, "she turned down four jobs before accepting one at Fair Trade. She hopped on my bike and rode over there at five o'clock this morning, then made me a perfect iced coffee." She jiggled the cup so Callie could hear the ice shaking around.

"What in the holy hell are you talking about? A fitness model blows into town on Friday, and on Tuesday morning she's your barista as well as your cook and sex partner."

"I think my luck is turning," Sunny said, smiling contentedly. "Exactly one hundred and eighty degrees."

Sunny didn't reach the front door until seven thirty, but no one could say she hadn't tried. She entered quietly, expecting to find Devin in the living room. But the room was cool, quiet and empty. The scent of something tasty lingered, getting more faint as she walked down the hall. Devin was in the guest bedroom, leaning close to the computer screen, oblivious.

"Hi," Sunny said quietly, making Devin nearly levitate.

"Shit!" She whirled around in her chair. "How did you sneak up on me like that? If you'd been a bear, I'd be dinner."

Sunny started to lean in and give her a kiss, but pulled back at the last second. If Devin liked to take it one day at a time, it was probably smart to not push being casually affectionate. Since she'd never had a 'friend with benefits,' and wasn't at all sure what the rules were. "I'm no bear, but I'd love dinner. Is it in the oven?"

"Yeah. Let me save this and I'll get your plate while you change clothes."

"What are you working on? You were awfully intent when I came in."

"Just a flyer." She got up and slid by Sunny, leaving her to read the text.

Handywoman

All Forms Of Home Repair and Maintenance

Top-Quality Work

References Readily Available

A stock image of a woman in coveralls marched around the frame of the page, giving it a playful look. Sunny was still staring at it when Devin came back into the room, bearing dinner on a tray.

"Like it?" she asked. "I know it's amateurish, but I don't think people expect a flashy ad."

"What in the heck is this for? Was one day of making coffee enough?"

A cute smile covered Devin's face. "Take off that nice blouse. You don't want pasta sauce on it."

Sunny shucked her suit, and started to unbutton her blouse as she walked back to her own room. "You can talk while I walk," she called back.

"I'll wait. My mom hated me yelling in the house. It must have made an impression."

It took just a minute for Sunny to put on a T-shirt and jeans, then she was back in the guest room, unable to pull her attention from the flyer. "I'm starving, but the damn flyer has me fixated."

Devin pressed on her shoulders, making Sunny settle into the desk chair. Then a tray was placed in front of her, bearing a chicken breast covered in mozzarella cheese and thick tomato sauce. "Eat," Devin said. "It's awesome, if I do say so myself."

Even though her curiosity about the flyer was unanswered, she dug in and took a big bite. "Ooo," she groaned. "You've found my Achilles' heel. What kind of tomato sauce is this? It's perfect."

"I made it. Actually, since I had all afternoon, I made a lot of it and froze most of it." She leaned over Sunny and moved the cursor around by manipulating the mouse. "Do you think I should add anything? People back home would want to know exactly what your skills were, but I thought I might be able to wing it here to figure out what people are willing to pay for."

Playfully poking Devin with her fork, Sunny said, "Will you please tell me why you want to be a handy-woman?"

"Because I'm free from eleven until five. I'm not going to sit in this apartment and twiddle my thumbs until you get home. I'd go nuts."

"But…"

"But what?" Devin turned her again, so they were now facing each other. "Does it bother you that I want to stay busy?"

"No, of course not. I just don't know anyone who'd mind a lot of free time."

Devin stood up and put her hands on her hips, looking absolutely puzzled, like Sunny was using an unfamiliar language. "Your friends didn't seem lazy."

"Far from it." She took in a breath, bound and determined to tell Devin a little of her history, while shoving in a few anecdotes about her family. But the breath departed in a slow stream, along with her intention. "I guess I'm just thinking of myself. I'd love a few afternoons off."

"No way you can make that happen, huh?" Devin asked, leaning close to gaze into Sunny's eyes.

"No way. Things are getting worse, not better."

Devin sat on the bed and put her hands on her bare knees. "I've got just under two hours until bed. I'd like to hear all about it."

Taking another bite of the chicken, Sunny chewed thoughtfully, thinking of how to explain all of the stress that had only gotten worse.

"Um, I've been arguing with Angelica. That's one reason I was so flustered when you said you'd gone to see her."

"Arguing?" Devin's eyebrows shot up.

"Pretty much. We don't see eye to eye on a lot of things. At this point, I think she's going to dissolve the partnership."

"She can do that?"

Sunny continued to eat, having been so busy she'd skipped lunch and was now famished. She held up a finger as she chewed, then swallowed and spoke again. "When I joined him, Hank only had an associate and a paralegal who did everything from answer the phone to help draft contracts. He was swamped, and needed help badly. I knew he'd run roughshod over me if I let him, so we negotiated forever, but finally agreed to a partnership. He had fifty-one percent and I had forty-nine. That meant he won every argument, but we generally agreed."

"I thought Julian was a partner."

"No," she said, chewing quickly and swallowing. "We were going to make him one, but hadn't finalized things when Hank died."

"So Angelica can do what she wants?"

"Essentially. Either of us had the ability to dissolve the agreement, so I knew that was a possibility… I just didn't think she'd do it." She took in a long breath and leaned back in her chair, fatigued from thinking about it. "She could sit at home and get fifty-one percent of the profits for doing nothing, but I think she's going to try to sell the firm to a larger one."

"You can buy and sell law firms?"

"Uh-huh. I'm not sure how much she'll get, or if the purchaser will want to keep me around, so things are definitely up in the air."

"Um…" Devin was staring at the carpet, then her gaze slowly moved up until it landed on Sunny's face. "Do you think she'll sue me?"

"I don't know," Sunny said quietly. She waited until Devin looked at her again to add, "I sure hope not. I've already warned her that I'd testify for the defense, which would ruin her case."

"Thanks." Devin just sat there for a moment, like she wasn't sure what she should do. She finally got up and put her hand on Sunny's shoulder. "It makes me feel so much better to know you don't think I'm responsible."

"You aren't," Sunny said, her voice rising in tone and volume. "No one could get me to say otherwise."

Devin's gentle touch caressed the side of Sunny's face and she leaned into it, feeling her racing heart slow its beat. There was something so damned reassuring about Devin. Just being close to her made Sunny feel that things would eventually be fine, no matter how unlikely that seemed at the moment.

"I'm sorry things are so stressful for you." She squatted down until they were eye to eye. "Is there anything I can do? Anything at all?"

Despite her intention to let Devin set the tone, Sunny couldn't resist her pull. She placed her plate on the desk and wrapped her arms around Devin's body. In just a minute or so, she felt their breathing sync up. "This helps," she said quietly.

"It helps me too. The closer we are, the better I feel."

Sunny pulled away and gazed at her lovely face. "We could lie down and get even closer."

With a half-grin, Devin said, "You'll get indigestion if you lie down so soon after eating dinner."

"Then you lie down and I'll sit up. Like on the floor at the foot of the bed." She started to slide her hand under Devin's t-shirt and explore every sinfully well-defined muscle. "I'll let my meal digest while I have dessert," she purred.

Devin got to her feet and extended a hand. "I'll clean the kitchen tomorrow. We've got plans tonight. Big, big plans."

CHAPTER SEVENTEEN

ON SATURDAY MORNING, DEVIN FOLLOWED her normal schedule, getting up at 4:45. She wandered around the apartment for a while, then decided to clean the house as a substitute for her morning bike ride. She worked hard and fast, spending a lot of time making the windows sparkle. But having the place neat and clean must have meant a lot to Sunny, since the apartment looked like she'd just moved in, with absolutely no clutter, despite her having been there for a while.

After making sure all of the photos on the entertainment center were arranged the way they had been, Devin sharpened her ears, thinking she might have heard Sunny's voice. Tiptoeing down the hallway, she smiled when a soft, "Devin?" echoed from the guest room.

"Hi," she said, poking her head in to see Sunny lying on her side, with her curvy, sexy body draped over Devin's pillow, which was pressed against her chest.

"Are you up?"

"Way up," she said, laughing a little as she entered the room and sat on the edge of the bed. Sunny looked so pretty, lying there like she'd been posed by a photographer who was going for "scorching hot." Devin's hand went to her hip, then delicately touched her, feeling her engine start to rev as soon as their skin met. She wasn't sure which of Sunny's many attractive parts turned her on the most, but it didn't really matter. They all worked together to get the job done.

She leaned over and kissed Sunny's sleep-warmed cheek. "I've been cleaning the house. I don't want you to spend your weekends doing that kind of thing."

Clearly puzzled, Sunny said, "I don't clean my own house. Someone comes in every Monday."

"Fuck!" Devin started to laugh. "I've been breaking my neck getting your windows clean. You mean to tell me someone's going to do that all again two days from now?"

"Neat-Nicks doesn't do windows. I have to hire a different service for that." She lifted herself up and rested against a braced arm. "Hiring window cleaners was on my to-do list, so you didn't waste your time." Then she cupped Devin's face with her hands and kissed her gently. "Thank you."

"Can you cancel your regular service for the week? I've got the place friggin' spotless."

"I'll have them do deep cleaning, like the oven and the refrigerator."

"No offense, but they don't do a great job. They don't even take the cushions off the sofa to vacuum. There's all sorts of dirt and crumbs under there."

"You vacuumed? I slept through that?"

"No," she said, chuckling. "I wasn't going to wake you up with a noisy motor flying around the house. I just got everything ready to go."

"What time is it?" Sunny asked, leaning around Devin's body to see the clock. "Oh, god! You let me sleep half the day away."

"Not half." Devin grasped her and maneuvered her so her torso was draped over Devin's legs. With the tip of her finger, she trailed across the dark-tinted skin under Sunny's eyes. "If it means you've got to sleep all weekend, we're going to make sure you're rested."

"Are you this nice to everyone?" Sunny batted her eyes, looking even sexier. "You'd be awfully busy if you provided this kind of service to all of your clients."

"Very, very few. You haven't seen me cleaning Julian's house, have you?"

"You're partial to girls?"

"I'm partial to you." She picked Sunny up a little, then bent and kissed her tenderly, suckling on her lower lip for a few seconds. "Really partial."

Sunny linked her hands behind Devin's neck, pulling her down until they were lying face to face. "You look very tired," she said, tickling around her ear until Devin started to squirm. "I think you need a nap."

"I'm not tired. I've only been up for six hours." She flipped Sunny onto her back, then got to her hands and knees and loomed over her. "I'm a great big ball of energy. Wanna see?"

"Yeah. I really want to see that," she said, with her smile beaming brightly. "Want me to take a shower?"

"We'll take one together after we play for a while."

The phone rang, and Sunny made a sour face before rolling over to grasp it. "Hi, Momma."

All of the playful, lighthearted affect she'd just shown was gone in a matter of seconds. Sunny hadn't spoken of her mom much, but given the look on her face, their relationship wasn't filled with joy.

"No, I don't have anything planned. I guess we could do that." She put her hand over the speaker and said, "Are you willing to have dinner with my mom?"

"Of course. I'd like to meet her."

"Okay," Sunny said, after nodding a few times. "Sure. I can do that. Text me the list."

A little frown settled onto her expressive face, then she sighed and nodded again. "All right. I'll make reservations, but we'll probably have to go early or late. That's a very popular spot."

She shimmied up to sit with her back against the headboard, clearly trying to get off the phone. "Just text me what you want, Momma. I'll do it. Okay. Okay. I will. No, I will. Okay. I'll let you know when our reservation is. See you later."

After clicking off, she tossed the phone to the bedside table. "We've been summoned. Sure you don't mind?"

"Not a bit. If we go somewhere fancy, I can wear the clothes you bought me last weekend. But you've gotta let me pay this time."

Her expression turned troubled, but she tossed her head and used her hands to swipe her hair away from her face. "Let me get this organized. I just need a second."

Then she was on the phone again, typing quickly. "I've got an app that lets me make reservations…" She looked up. "Five thirty or nine."

"Given that I go to bed at nine, I vote for five thirty." Devin smiled, but she wasn't kidding. She needed to stay on a schedule to be at her best.

"Got it. We can skip lunch."

Devin waited for her to finish tapping in her info, then put the phone down again. "It's almost noon and you haven't had breakfast yet, so lunch is probably a good thing to skip." She took Sunny in her arms and cuddled her mostly bare body. "Sure you don't want a little breakfast?"

"I guess I should." She pulled away and headed for the bathroom. "Just give me a second."

As soon as she'd gone, her phone chirped. "Want me to answer?" Devin called out.

"That's my text ring," Sunny said. "Is it from my mom?"

Devin picked it up and looked at the display. "Yeah," she said. She wasn't usually a snoop, but her eyes scanned the long list.

Detergent (unscented)

Fabric softener (unscented)

Dishwashing liquid

Toilet paper (4 ply)

Paper towels (2 ply)

Olive oil (extra virgin—Italian)

Balsamic vinegar (From Modena—not US)

White wine (two bottles)

Rose (two bottles)

Red wine (one bottle)

(Make sure the wine is rated 95 or above on Wine Spectator)

Scotch (Single malt)

Letty Pryne lipstick—Ice red (No substitutes!)

Matching nail polish.

That was it. No "please," no "thank you." Devin stared at the phone for a minute, wondering what she'd do if her own mother sent her a long list of things to buy. She'd hop to it, of course. The difference was her mother would only ask if she was physically unable to leave the house. And then she wouldn't need the lipstick or the nail polish, would she?

Devin wasn't particularly happy to have Sunny buy her more dressy clothes, but once she reminded herself they were purely for Sunny's enjoyment, she was able to let go of her unease. Yuppies sure did like to spend money, and if spending her hard earned money made Sunny happy —why give her a hard time?

The outfit for Callie's birthday dinner had been on the sexy side. This one, a thin pair of tapered black slacks and a black and white print top, fit more closely. Devin wasn't sure what message she was supposed to be sending, but Sunny was dressed similarly—although she filled her clothes out a lot better. Sunny was also wearing makeup, something she would have had to use a shotgun to get Devin to do. She must have realized that, since she didn't even propose it. But she did offer to give Devin's hair a little bounce by using her curling iron. Her automatic response was to refuse, but Sunny looked so hopeful she let her play with her hair until she seemed happy. Nervous, but happy.

That's just how she seemed now, but the nerves were getting worse. They were pushing a shopping cart around a huge grocery store in Plano, a place Devin had never heard of. They'd found everything on the list, except for the lipstick and nail polish, which was going to require another stop.

After plunking down over two hundred dollars for the stuff, they set off again, going to another strip-mall, this one even nicer than the last. "I'll just be a minute," Sunny said. "You can wait in the car if you'd like."

"Okay. I won't be much help in a beauty supply store anyway," she said, laughing a little at the mere thought. As soon as Sunny exited, Devin called Lori, impatiently waiting for her to answer.

"Busy?" she asked.

"I'm making dinner, but I can talk. What's up?"

"Oh, shit. I keep forgetting I'm an hour behind you."

"I don't. But I'm smarter than you are, so that's what I'd expect." She let out an evil laugh, one that nearly made Devin tear up. She missed her so damned much!

"I'm sitting in a hot parking lot, waiting for Sunny to buy makeup for her mom. That's after we went to the grocery store and spent two hundred bucks buying her fancy wine and liquor and vinegar that had to be from a certain spot in Italy."

"Is she…disabled?"

"Don't think so. But I guess she could be. I suppose I'll find out."

"Um, if you don't mind my asking, why are you meeting her mom?"

"'Cause she asked me to."

"Um…" Devin could hear the background noise change, then Lori's voice got clearer and louder. She'd probably gone into the bathroom, the only spot she had any privacy. "Are you going specifically to meet Sunny's mom, or are you just tagging along?"

"Mmm, good question. Let me think. Um, her mom called and asked to go out to dinner, and she included me. I guess she did that because I'm a guest, but…" She took in a breath and spit it out. "I have no idea what Sunny's told people about me, you know? Everyone might assume I'm her girlfriend."

"Only one thing matters," Lori said quietly. "Does she?"

"I haven't said a single word that would give her that idea. Not one. I'm only here to help her get back to normal."

"Does she know that? Have you said those words?"

"Those exact words? Maybe not. But I made it really clear that we're taking this one day at a time. Isn't that clear enough?"

"No. It's not, Devin. You've got to be as clear as a stream."

"All right," she sighed. "I will if I have to." She thought for a second, then added, "Is it weird that Sunny bought me more nice clothes so I'd look acceptable?"

"Yes," Lori said firmly. "You don't do that for a casual visitor." Clearly irritated, she added, "Why'd you let her do that? You argue every time I try to buy you a donut."

"I want the damn donut, Lori. But I don't want some silly black and white outfit that makes me look like somebody else. I'll never wear this stuff again, and it cost a lot!"

"You could wear it to a funeral. Black's always appropriate."

"Yeah. I just have to make sure whoever dies does it on a hot, sticky day in August. Even then I'd look like an idiot showing up in a tight top and shiny pants that fit like a second skin."

"Pictures. Now," Lori demanded.

"Give me a second. Sunny's coming back, so we'll do a selfie. Gotta go." She jumped out of the car and caught up with Sunny while she was still on the sidewalk. "Will you pose for a selfie with me? I want to show my friend back home my new clothes."

Looking utterly charmed, Sunny stopped and put her little bag onto the ground. They were standing under the colonnade, so they were in shade, and Devin started to fuss with her phone, getting the angle right.

"We don't have any pictures of us together, do we?" Sunny asked.

"I guess not." She thought for a second. "Wait. We do. We took one at sunset on the lake. Remember?"

"Oh, damn, that was a nice day."

She looked so happy thinking about that day—the day before everything changed. They stood close and both smiled while Devin held her arm out as far as she could get it. As they walked back to the car, she looked at the snaps and knew, right then, that they needed to clear things up. In the picture, Sunny was beaming at her exactly the way you looked at your girlfriend.

Once a guard had raised a security gate to let them into a intensely landscaped development, they drove around curving streets, passing what looked to Devin like pods of four condos or townhouses. Each unit faced a different direction, but other than that, they were identical. Creepily identical.

Sunny slowed, then parked in a driveway in front of one of the units, but how she knew which one was the right one was something Devin was going to have to study. When they got out, Devin grabbed the heaviest of the bags, then followed Sunny up the sidewalk toward the front door.

The whole complex looked like it had been neatly set down by people who also made doll houses, with everything exactly the same. Recently planted trees, shrubs, and flowers filled a big square planter in the center of each front yard, each of which you could mow in under three minutes. While the plantings were pretty, each one had the same skinny tree, the same purple and gold flowers, and the same little evergreens. Sunny marched up to the forest green door, the same color as every other door in the whole complex, and knocked. As they waited, with Sunny staring at the door with a completely blank expression, Devin mused about how long it would take her to lose her mind if every single house in her neighborhood was identical. She guessed an hour, but obviously some people liked uniformity.

The door was locked, and Sunny must not have had a key, for they stood in the hot afternoon sun for a while. When the door finally swung open, Devin was greeted by a face from the future—if Sunny started spending a whole lot of time trying to look like she was going to be photographed for a magazine. Perfect hair, perfect makeup, perfect jewelry. There was no way this woman had gotten ready in less than two hours, and that was only if she'd rushed. Devin normally wouldn't have had a reference point for that, but she'd spent the whole morning with Lori before her wedding, and had witnessed how long it took to look like you hadn't gone to much trouble to look wonderful.

Devin was flat-footed, and at a serious loss for words. While she routinely dealt with rich people, they were on her turf and were planning on doing something outdoors. This woman looked like her preferred exercise was drinking martinis in expensive hotel lobbies, while flirting with equally wealthy men.

"Hello there," the woman said, extending her remarkably soft hand to grasp Devin's and tug on it to draw her into the house. "You must be Devin."

"Yes, ma'am, I am. Thanks for inviting me tonight."

"I've been waiting for Sunny to invite me to her place, but since that's not going to happen I had to take the bull by the horns." She still hadn't looked at Sunny, which was beginning to feel very weird. Her blue-gray eyes roved up and down Devin's body, only managing to increase her discomfort. "I'm Winona, by the way. I suppose Sunny would have gotten around to introducing us, but I don't want to be late for our reservation."

She placed her hand on Devin's arm and led her to the kitchen, where she was clearly supposed to put the purchases. "Did you have any trouble finding the couple little things I needed?" she asked, finally acknowledging Sunny's presence.

"Everything you asked for," Sunny said.

Devin wasn't sure how long it had been since they'd seen each other, but she got a hug and a kiss every single time she walked through the door at her parents' house, not just a sidelong glance.

Winona tossed her hair, its golden color lighter and brighter than Sunny's. The color was probably artificial, but it looked fantastic. The only other significant physical difference between mother and daughter was that Winona's shoulders and arms were covered in freckles, while Sunny's relatively pale skin was flawless. "Let me get my purse so we can get this show on the road. We'll have time for a drink at the bar if we hurry. Will you drive, Sunny?"

"Sure." She still had her keys in her hand, as if she'd expected a quick turnaround.

"Your house is lovely," Devin said. It really was, which was a relief. She'd have lied if she'd had to, but she preferred to be able to give an honest compliment.

"Oh, thank you. I suppose it's nice enough," Winona said. She finally gave Sunny her full attention. "We made a good choice on this one, didn't we? It's doubled in value since we bought it. Just two bedrooms and two baths, but I manage."

"Do you live…alone?"

"Uh-huh." She scanned the counter, like she was reminding herself to take everything vital. "But I need an office. I have an awful lot of paperwork, and I'm forced to keep it in the guest bedroom." She took Devin by the arm again and said, "Want to take a peek?"

"Um…sure." They went on a quick tour of the immaculate house. It was fancier than Sunny's place, with more art on the walls and more things strategically placed on tables and bookcases. The furniture was nicer in some ways, but it was fancier too, which Devin didn't care for. You could take all the velvet and silk in the world and haul it to a dump and she wouldn't have minded a bit. Except for underwear, as she'd recently discovered. When it was on Sunny's body, it took on a new, very welcome significance.

Devin only knew about houses based on watching home renovation shows at her parents', but she could tell this place was fitted out with all of the latest and greatest. "I love your tile," she said when they paused in the master bathroom. "It looks like a waterfall."

Winona gave Sunny a superior smile. "I told you it was worth the extra money. You can't cut corners when you're choosing fixtures."

Sunny just shrugged, then led the way to the front door. "We'd better get going if you want to have a drink."

"I'm a girl who loves a good drink," Winona said.

After a short drive, they pulled up to a place with valet parking attendants racing around like mad. As they walked into the serene, luxurious entryway, Devin decided her part of Maine, and this part of Texas were very different animals. She'd thought the restaurant they'd gone the previous Saturday night had been a special occasion place in honor of Callie's birthday, but this spot was even ritzier. If this was the kind of place people in cities routinely went to, she was truly in a whole new world.

They lingered in the opulent, quiet bar for a long time, with her mother going on about the decorating. While she was very knowledgeable about the kinds of wood they'd used, who'd designed the lighting, and where the carpets came from, Devin couldn't possibly have heard of any of the businesses or architects or designers she'd mentioned. But Sunny knew her mother said what she wanted to say, not much caring if it was something you wanted to hear.

After they'd finished their second round, a hostess started to lead them to their table. But Devin asked to be shown where the rest room was, and she peeled away. Sunny knew it was coming, but even she was surprised by how fast the comments started. The pretty woman in a sleek black sheath was still pushing their chairs in when Winona said, "Is that really the best you can do? That girl looks like she should be working in the kitchen, not sitting with us."

"She looks great," Sunny said, angry with herself for going to the trouble of buying Devin a new outfit. There was no way she'd ever get her mother's approval of a new girlfriend, and trying for it just made her feel stupid. "I think she's remarkably pretty."

"Pretty?" Winona accepted the napkin the hostess handed her and placed it onto her lap. "She *might* be attractive if she wore some makeup and jewelry, but even that would be a stretch. Why, she's as plain as a tin pail! It's such a waste to be thin and have a nice body, but not try to show it off." She blew out a frustrated breath. "I will *never* understand why you can't find a woman who fits in with us."

"With us?" Sunny tried to swallow the anger that threatened to engulf her, but she wasn't very successful. "Devin has two professional parents who own a nice house on a big piece of land. Twenty years ago, all four of *us* were living in a stiflingly hot two bedroom apartment, and you were struggling just to feed us!" She spotted Devin crossing the room, looking pretty as a picture to Sunny's appreciative eyes. "If you compare our families, she's the classy one."

"It's not what you have," Winona whispered hotly, "it's what you look like you have, and she looks like an overgrown Camp Fire Girl—which she is!"

As Devin sank into her chair, Sunny watched her mother's expression slide into a warm smile. A smile as fake as the day was long.

Devin was beginning to regret asking Winona what she did for a living, for she was finding out—in detail.

"So people hire you to organize their closets?" she asked, sure she hadn't gotten that right.

"No, no, that's not even close to what I do. I organize people's *lives.* My clients couldn't organize a two-float parade without me, much less their complex lives."

Devin took a look to her right, seeing Sunny distractedly playing with her salad. "I think I'm missing something," she said. "I'm sure we don't have anything like this in central Maine."

Sunny looked up. “You don’t.” Then she sat up straighter in her chair and said, “Momma—”

“*Please* call me Winona in public. Everyone in this restaurant is a potential client, and I want to look like I’m working.”

Shrugging, Sunny continued. “Winona caters to people who like being told what to do. There are a lot of them,” she added. “Mostly very wealthy women with a few kids and lots of social obligations. They get overwhelmed and hire someone to make decisions.”

“About what?” Devin asked, still thoroughly confused.

“Winona’s like hatchet woman for people who don’t want to be the bad guy.”

Waving her hand in front of her own face while keeping her expression blank, Devin said, “Nothing. Not a word of that made sense.”

Sunny squinted at her for a few moments, then tried again. “Winona might tell a woman to throw most of her kids’ toys away. Then she’ll force them to store the few treasures they’re allowed to keep into a nicely decorated wooden box with the kid’s name on it. That means all of their sports uniforms, trophies…”

“Why would anyone want a participation trophy?” Winona interrupted, making a sour face. “If you win a significant trophy, by all means put it in a place of honor. Build a little shrine to it. But these people are hoarding meaningless junk.”

“And this is why you won’t find the first picture I ever drew,” Sunny said. “Or my report cards or photos of my first gymnastics class.”

“It was clear you weren’t going to be Georgia O’Keefe or Olga Korbut,” Winona said, dismissively. “Who wants that junk?”

Devin didn’t say a word. She just thought of the little plaster cast of her handprint that her parents had been playfully swiping from each other for over thirty years. What would it have felt like to have both of them trying to get rid of it?

On the ride home, Sunny was as quiet as a mouse. She didn’t look angry or even annoyed. Maybe she was just drained from spending over four hundred bucks on a dinner she sure didn’t seem to enjoy.

Devin had been dead set in her plan to speak about their relationship, but now wasn't the time—for sure.

The highway was amazingly crowded for a Saturday night, and Sunny had to concentrate to avoid being run over or sideswiped. Everyone was in such a damn hurry! And where were they all going? It seemed like everyone on one side of town wanted to get to the other, and vice versa. Why not just pick a side and stay there?

They reached the building's garage, then walked through the nearly silent space with the clicking of their heels against the concrete the only sound. They had to switch elevators to reach the set that went to the apartments, and Devin watched as Sunny did as always—stop to talk to whomever was on duty. It didn't even matter if the person was particularly nice. She did it because *she* was. She really was, Devin decided as the elevator climbed to her floor.

Without comment, Sunny went into her room to get ready for bed, and Devin did the same. Then they met in the guest bedroom, with Sunny falling to the bed like she'd been hit with a stun-gun. "Tired," she sighed.

Devin scooted over so she was pressed against her shoulder and hip. "Did I tell you how pretty you looked tonight?"

Sunny turned slightly, then shook her head. "You were too busy fussing with your new clothes." Playfully, she gave her a poke to the belly. "Have you ever worn anything other than jeans?"

"Shorts," she said, chuckling. "You've seen 'em." She let her fingers trail down Sunny's cheek, glad she'd taken off the makeup she'd worn. She was so much prettier when her eyes weren't all fake looking with mascara and shadow and liner. "I'm sorry I didn't take the time to tell you how nice you looked. You're an extraordinarily pretty woman, you know."

"I did not know that," she said, laughing a little as she made her accent stronger. Devin loved it when she did that. It was almost like she was singing when she really put it on thick.

"Well, you are. It was pretty cool to walk into that fancy place with such a pretty woman on my arm."

"I wasn't on your arm," Sunny said, reaching over to tug on her nose. "And I can guarantee no one took a second look at me."

"I did," Devin said soberly. "I took a second and a third and a fourth look. If your mom hadn't been there, I wouldn't have looked away for a second."

"You're as crazy as a jay-bird, but I'm not going to argue with you. If you think I'm pretty, it's settled."

"Then it's settled." She scooted closer, waiting for Sunny to tuck an arm around her, which she did. "But that's not why I like you."

"No?"

"No," she said, trying hard to make sure Sunny got the message. "I like you because you're such a nice person. You tease and you poke a little fun at people who deserve it, but you're kind. I love people with kind hearts."

"Aww," Sunny purred, giving Devin a squeeze. "That's nice of you to say."

"I'm not just saying it. I mean it." She touched her chin, making her turn her head so they were gazing into each other's eyes. "I'm really glad we met, Sunny. The circumstances suck, but that's been the only bad thing about knowing you."

"I feel the same," she said, with her eyes filling with tears. "I'm awfully glad we met." Her hand roamed up and down Devin's side, tickling her skin as those cool fingers slid under her tank top.

They had to have the talk. But they were mostly naked and lying close to each other in a soft, comfy bed, with icy air blowing over them. Sunny's sexy body was warm and pliant and clearly willing. Why resist something that obviously made them both feel good? As Sunny carefully tilted Devin's head and slipped her tongue inside her mouth, she sighed with pleasure. They were both willing. Very willing.

Devin carefully closed the bedroom door, tiptoed out of the apartment, passed the semi-sleeping doorman, and started to walk around the deserted streets of Uptown. It was just six, but it was seven at home, and she knew the Carters would not only be up, they'd have finished breakfast.

Lori answered on the first ring. "Thank me," she demanded without preamble.

"For…?"

"For not letting Chris make a copy of that picture of you and Sunny. He wanted to blow it up and give it to everyone you know just to prove you could be a model if you ever got tired of being a guide."

"Right," she said, laughing. "He wants to make fun of me for the rest of my life."

"That too," Lori agreed, "but I could tell he was thinking dirty thoughts about you, Dev. He might deny it, but he wanted a bite of some Savary last night."

"No offense, but eww! I mean, if I had to be with a guy, he'd be a good one, but I don't have to, so I never will."

"How'd your talk go? Is Sunny upset?"

"We had sex," Devin said glumly. "Good sex. Really good sex, as a matter of fact, but I'm mad at myself for caving in so easily. It's just really hard when you've had such a long dry spell…"

"What the hell? Is there something more here? Do you like this woman enough to be in a relationship?"

"If she lived in Maine? Yes. Definitely yes. But she doesn't, Lori, and let's be honest—she's never going to."

"You never know…"

"Sometimes you do. Sunny's got a fancy apartment, and a fancy car, and she pays most of the mortgage on her mom's apartment, which is even nicer, as well as bigger. I bet she spends in a month what I do in a year."

"That wouldn't be too hard. You're a skinflint."

"I am not! But I don't waste money like Sunny does. If my mom craved a nice apartment, and I had the money to get her one, I'd buy it, but I'd move in with her. But I bet Sunny would take a nosedive off this building if she had to do that."

"You didn't like her mom?"

"Not much. I mean, she'd be okay if you were just talking to her at the grocery store, but she's not my type. I don't think she's Sunny's type either, but we didn't really talk about it."

"Because you were having sex."

"Pretty much."

"What time is it there?"

"Six fifteen. Why?"

"By eight, I want you to make it clear to Sunny that you're going home as soon as she's able to be alone. No excuses!"

"Can I make it noon? She sleeps an awful lot."

"Fine. Send me a text to let me know you've done it. If I don't hear from you by one, I'm coming down there to do it myself."

Devin started to laugh, finding it odd that her laughter bounced back at her off the empty buildings. "That would be something, wouldn't it?"

"It's going to be a reality if you don't gut it up and do it. Now!"

Even though she'd been in Dallas for ten days, Devin hadn't yet investigated the neighborhood very thoroughly. The one thing she'd noticed, and was now confirming, was that you couldn't get a hearty breakfast before seven, with the place Sunny liked not even opening until ten. *Ten!*

Frustrated and hungry, she finally went to the closest branch of the omnipresent coffee chain and had one of their breakfast sandwiches. There was nothing technically wrong with an English muffin, an egg, and a little ham, but having it come out shoved haphazardly into a paper wrapper just felt so damned cold. Talking to a friendly waitress started the day off right, even if the food wasn't the best. It was the interaction you were paying for.

On the way home, she dawdled, wishing she could find any sign of nature to settle her nerves. There *had* to be some around. But she sure hadn't seen any. Twice a day she traveled the length of the Katy Trail, a very nicely landscaped bike path that let her cut across town for a couple of miles. She'd also stopped at every park she'd seen, and, on the recommendation of a co-worker, had taken a spring nature walk in the Botanic Garden. But none of that was nature, a fact she'd been unable to convince anyone of. Nature was the stuff no one was in charge of. The glacial lakes, craggy mountains, and wild waves crashing against the rocks along the Maine coast were nature, and she hadn't seen even a hint of it in ten days. That was, by far, the longest she'd ever gone without it, and she was just about at her wit's end.

It was sunny, and warm, with a fresh, cool breeze blowing through Uptown, but she was as glum as she ever got as she slid her key into the lock, surprised to hear Sunny's voice.

"I really wasn't planning on babysitting today, Tiffany. Why don't you see if Momma can watch him?"

She looked up and waved when Devin entered, then patted the seat next to her on the sofa.

"What do you mean, you're already on the way? It's not even seven thirty!"

Closing her eyes, she let her head fall back onto the sofa. "That's really not playing fair. You're putting Ashton in the middle here, and he's too young for that kind of thing."

Like it weighed a thousand pounds, she slowly lifted her head and gazed blankly at Devin for a moment. "What choice do I have? How long is this world changing round of golf going to take you?" She was quiet for a second, then yelped, "How long? I'm supposed to watch Ashton all day? Great. Just great. Thanks for the notice," she groused, then hit the "end" button and let her phone fall to the sofa. "Do you like kids?"

"Sure. Well, some kids." She sat next to Sunny, clearly able to see how unhappy she was at the prospect of babysitting. "How old is the kid?"

"Nine. He's my only nephew, and I love him, but he can be…" Sighing, she got up and headed for her bedroom. "You'll see."

Ashton was a jerk. A nine-year-old jerk, but a jerk just the same. Devin often had to deal with spoiled kids, but she'd never managed to enjoy the experience. This one had obviously been raised to believe the sun rose and set at his whim, but you could tell his self-confidence was as thin as a sheet of paper. While she had some sympathy for kids raised so poorly, she just didn't like being around the little weasels.

They'd been at the rooftop pool since nine, when it opened. Devin hadn't known it existed before today, but that was no great loss. Although it was a very nice pool for an apartment building, going from three feet to nine, it was too short to allow for serious swimming. Still, it would be nice to dive in after a hot bike ride.

Young Ashton also loved to dive right in, but he was a terrible swimmer. He repeatedly and purposefully ignored his aunt's advice to stay in the shallow end, risking his own life, and annoying the hell out of Devin.

Sunny had gone to retrieve him ten times, with Devin dragging him back to safety at least that many. Each time she'd gone, he'd fought her, flailing his arms and legs to "accidentally" kick or punch her while claiming he was swimming. Given that he didn't do the same thing when Sunny went, he was clearly sending a message. Once she'd gotten it, she decided to give him one back. On her next lifesaving turn, she swam to him and grasped his flailing hands. "It's time for a lesson, pal. You need to learn how to tread water if you're going to keep doing this."

"I know how to swim."

"No, you don't. If you did, we wouldn't have to keep coming to get you."

"Aunt Sunny! Tell her I know how to swim!" he yelled, his shrill voice making her ears ring.

"He knows a little," Sunny called back.

"Fine. Swim to your aunt," Devin said, dropping his hands.

The kid started to slap at the water like he was swatting a swarm of flies, then gasped and swallowed enough water to make him start coughing. In a second, Sunny was next to him, wrapping the little jerk in a protective hug. He put on a big show, crying and acting like a two-year-old, with Sunny playing right into his game. "Devin! How could you!"

"He's fine," she insisted. She stared at Sunny until she looked up. "I want to help him learn to protect himself. If he's in a pool, he should know how to survive."

"He takes lessons," Sunny said, clearly defensive.

"If your sister pays for the lessons, she's wasting her money. A kid his age can easily learn to tread water. He just needs a little patience."

"Let's just go back to the shallow end and play football." She stroked the kid's attractive face and he nuzzled against her like a puppy. "Do you want to play football, Ashton?"

"Yeah," he sobbed, soaking Sunny for all of the sympathy he could.

"Come on. We'll play with you."

Devin rolled her eyes as Sunny towed the kid back to the shallow end. He sat on the steps for a minute to get himself together after his horrible ordeal, then stared at Devin with a cold gaze. "Who are you?"

"I introduced you," Sunny said. "This is my friend Devin. She's from Maine."

"Is she your girlfriend?" he demanded.

Devin blinked at that. She was surprised, but kinda pleased the kid knew his aunt's sexual orientation. But she wasn't as pleased when Sunny skirted the question.

"Devin's a nature guide," she said, trying to sound excited by this revelation. "She's seen bears and moose."

"I have too," he insisted. "I've seen every kind of animal. Even dinosaurs."

"Not many dinosaurs in Maine these days," Devin said. "I can't remember the last one I saw."

"They're extinct!" He stared at his aunt. "Tell her."

"I think she was teasing you, Ashton." She put on a big, fake-looking smile. "Devin loves to tease people. Kind of like you do. Like when you took my phone and wallet out of my purse the last time I visited your house. Remember how funny you thought that was?"

He started to laugh, his near-death experience now forgotten. "That was *so* funny! You had to come all the way back to get them."

"Yeah, that was hilarious," Sunny said. "And I couldn't even call to see if you had them. It would have been even funnier if I'd run out of gas or had an accident." She met Devin's gaze and rolled her eyes.

Ashton didn't bite at the diversionary tactic. He could obviously stick with a topic if it truly interested him. Aiming his dark eyes at Devin, he said, "You wouldn't come all this way if you didn't want something from her."

That wasn't a sentence a nine-year-old would come up with on his own. Clearly, he was repeating something he'd heard at home.

But Sunny didn't take the lead. She swam after the foam football that had begun to float away, leaving Devin to figure out how to respond.

The kid kept going, asking directly, "Is she your girlfriend?"

With the ball in her court, she went for it. "We're not girlfriends, Ashton," she said, not allowing her gaze to travel back to Sunny, lest she lose her nerve. "I like her a lot, though."

"Then why aren't you her girlfriend?" he persisted. "Aren't you gay?"

"Yeah, I sure am."

"So's she."

He said that in such an accusatory tone, Devin had to laugh. "Yeah, I know. But just because you really like a woman doesn't mean you're her girlfriend. Your aunt and I are very good friends, but we're not able to be girlfriends."

"Why?"

Devin shot a look at Sunny, who was listening as intently as Ashton was. This was the coward's way out, but Devin took it anyway. "Well, we live really far apart. Your aunt wants to be here so she's close to you and the rest of your family. Plus, she's got a great job. The same thing's true for me, but my job and my family are in Maine. When it's time for me to get back to work, I'll have to leave." Now she met Sunny's gaze directly, which was wary. "But I wish she lived closer to me. If she did, I'd do anything in my power to convince her to be my girlfriend. She'd be a perfect one."

That wary gaze morphed into a bright smile, a smile that said she felt the same.

Success!

The kid glared at Devin for another second, then grabbed the foam football and winged it right at her. Luckily, her reflexes were good, and she grabbed it before it smacked her in the face. "Keep trying," she said, determined not to show he was annoying the hell out of her. "If you concentrate and put some effort into it, you'll be able to clock me."

There was a changing room near the pool, and Ashton ran in to use the bathroom. Devin watched him run on the slick tile, knowing Sunny was wasting her breath when she cautioned him.

"Nice kid," Devin said, trying her best to sound sincere.

"He's going through a tough phase," Sunny said, looking a little embarrassed. "He was a doll when he was a baby, but ever since Eric's ex-wife moved to Houston…"

"You haven't talked about your sisters much," Devin said, not saying the whole truth. Sunny hadn't talked about them at *all.* "I don't know the story."

"I haven't told you?"

"Maybe I forgot. What's the deal?"

Sunny started to speak, keeping her voice low. "Tiffany's husband has two girls with his first wife. They used to live close by, so visitation wasn't an issue. But they moved to Houston four years ago, and Eric has to go down there every other week to see them."

"Every other week?" Devin's brows rose in surprise.

"It was a *very* contentious divorce, and the move just added more drama. Now that they have the visitation schedule worked out, he feels like he has to honor it." She sighed as she resettled her rust-colored baseball cap onto her head. "The girls are getting to the age where they're not really interested in being with their dad every other weekend, but he's going to keep going until they opt out."

"Can't they come here once in a while?"

Ashton blew out of the door, hooting as he ran for the pool, jumping into the water that Devin was sure was too deep for him.

Sunny rolled her eyes as she started to swim for him. "*No one* wants that," she said, giving Devin a meaningful look. None of Devin's close friends had blended families, but one of her pals from high school had been obsessed by her father's other family, always concerned with how much of his time, interest, and money the new kids got. The girl had basically kept a scorecard, toting up plusses and minuses. The whole thing seemed exhausting to Devin, but if your dad was gone every other weekend, maybe it made perfect sense to keep a tally.

Even Ashton was water-logged by noon, then he started begging for his favorite lunch. Sunny knew she only had herself to blame, since she gave in every single time, but he usually quieted down when he got his way.

"Do you mind going out for burgers?" she asked Devin.

Devin gave her a puzzled look. "You mean get into the car and drive for burgers?"

"Yeah. The place Ashton likes is about fifteen minutes away."

Devin shrugged, but it was clear she wasn't happy. "It seems silly to get in the car when there's every kind of food within walking distance, but…" She let her gaze follow Ashton, who was running up and down the hall, still in his dripping swimsuit, which he'd refused to remove.

"Thanks," Sunny said. "Ashton! Let's get going. There's always a line at this time of day."

The day had really heated up, with a lot of humidity in the air. A storm was clearly brewing, but not a drop of rain had fallen in over a week. They all piled into the car, but Ashton, in his wet suit, forbade the use of the air conditioner. Sunny wasn't about to comment on the firm set of Devin's jaw, nor was she going to get into another squabble with Ashton. Instead, she popped the sunroof, allowing air, albeit hot and sticky air, into the car.

Her prediction had been accurate. There was a line full of cranky people, all wanting their burgers right then. Devin walked over to the counter and came back with a sheet showing all of the options along with detailed nutritional information. "I think I'll have the apple cranberry salad with grilled chicken," she said, after perusing it like it was the Rosetta stone.

"Have a burger," Sunny teased, giving her a bump with her shoulder.

"No thanks. I'm crazy for burgers, but when I'm hot I like something lighter."

"Bites!" Ashton piped up. "Nine bites and fries. And a malt." He started to poke Sunny in the leg. "You get that too."

"I was thinking about a burger…"

"Bites! Get bites!"

At this point, all she wanted was for Ashton to quiet down. She would have eaten pig's feet if that's what it took. "Okay," she said quietly. "We'll share chicken bites."

"You too," he said, elbowing Devin in the back. "Everyone has to get chicken bites."

She looked at him for a few moments, then shook her head. "I don't like chicken bites. You get what you want, and I'll get what I want. The freedom of choice is what makes America great." She revealed a cute smile that relieved a lot of the anxiety that had been building in Sunny's gut.

But Ashton wasn't smiling. There was no earthly reason for everyone to have to eat the same thing, but once he got on a topic it was darned hard to get him off it. "Everyone has to have the chicken bites," he insisted, raising his voice.

"Nope." Devin stuck her hands in the back pockets of her shorts and rocked back on her heels. "Not gonna happen. You go your way, I'll go mine."

He grabbed Sunny by the arm, hard enough to leave a bruise. "Make her!" Now he was flat-out yelling, making every other person in line look at Sunny like she was failing as a mother. Her instinct was to proclaim they shared only a portion of DNA, but didn't think that would buy her any sympathy. If only Devin wasn't being such a jerk about this! She was as hardheaded as Ashton.

Leaning close, Sunny whispered, "Will you act like you're going to have the damn chicken? I'll still buy you a salad. He won't notice once he gets his food."

Devin leaned back and stared at her for a second, then said, "I'm honestly not very hungry. I'll just have the imaginary chicken bites."

"Thank the good lord," Sunny murmured, hoping her prediction was correct and Ashton didn't notice that Devin wasn't eating. She wasn't sure what Devin would do if he kept pushing her, and she didn't want to find out.

Tiffany and her husband Eric were running late, which seemed to irritate the hell out of Sunny. Given that she was usually so accommodating, this must have been a common occurrence.

They'd been watching cartoons for hours, and Devin was sorely tempted to get on the bike and go for a ride—anything to get away from Ashton's demands and Sunny's need to placate him. But she couldn't just walk out. Everyone had some pain-in-the-butt relatives, and you had to put up with other people's so they'd put up with yours. Her dad's brother's second wife was a mean-spirited, spiteful woman who Devin swore could make the grass die just from walking across it, but she expected her friends to treat her Aunt Martina with respect. Now she had to suck it up and do the same with Ashton.

"We could go back to the pool," Devin suggested.

Sunny's eyes got wide as Ashton ran for the front door, ready to go.

"My sister will kill me if he's in his wet swimsuit when she gets here," Sunny whispered, obviously flustered.

"Then she should have been on time." Devin got up and went to the guest room to put her suit on, while listening to the delightful sound of the kid opening and slamming the door while he waited. Such a little charmer!

As the sun set and it got cooler, Ashton calmed down and demanded less attention. Or maybe all of the carbohydrates he'd gulped down had finally gotten to him. He was playing with a raft, content to push it while kicking. He wasn't kicking very efficiently, but the raft kept him afloat, Devin's only concern at this point.

It was eight o'clock, and they'd had the kid for twelve hours. While Devin didn't play golf, she knew a round didn't take more than four or five hours—tops. Instead of asking what kind of nerve Tiffany had for dumping the kid on them for the entire day, she said, "What does you sister do for a living?"

"She's in marketing," she said. "Right now she's working for a corporation that runs some high-end restaurants. I guess she's trying to impress them, so she's working crazy hours. Same for Eric, actually. They're never home in time for dinner."

"Who watches Ashton?"

"A neighbor has a home-based day care and she watches him until Tiff gets home." She made a face. "He's one of four kids the woman watches, two of them infants, and the other one a toddler. Needless to say, he hates it."

"I would too," Devin said, watching the kid talk to himself, keeping up both ends of the conversation, something he probably had to do a lot.

"Yeah. I wish I could help more, but I just can't get over there at three in the afternoon to pick him up from school."

"Are they good parents?" Devin asked, starting to feel a little sympathy for the pint-sized jerk.

"Mmm, that's hard to say." She seemed to be thinking about the question carefully. "Tiff always seems like she's fighting for Eric's attention, trying to impress him. I think Ashton plays second fiddle when Eric's home, then Tiffany lets him do whatever he wants to make up for it when they're alone."

"Nice," Devin said. "That should set him on a good course." She slid off the coping and swam over to where Ashton was playing, hoping to engage him a little. He certainly hadn't earned her efforts, but it sure sounded like he'd been left to his own devices when it came to learning how to be a social animal.

⌖

The doorman announced a visitor at nine o'clock, Devin's bedtime. She'd been thinking of whether she was going to get up and head for the guest room, but Tiffany saved her from abandoning Sunny.

When Sunny went to answer the door, only Tiffany appeared. She looked a little like Sunny, and a little like their mom, but you wouldn't have been surprised if someone told you they were friends rather than sisters. There was something missing. Something Devin couldn't put her finger on. Tiffany was about Sunny's size, and had her coloring, but she just didn't have "it," the special something that made Sunny so attractive.

Given that Tiffany had let Ashton come upstairs on his own, she must not have been sure he'd be as compliant about returning, requiring her to actually get out of the car.

She strode across the floor, with her hand extended. "Tiffany Berrinson," she said, giving Devin's hand a hard shake. "Devin?"

"That's me," she said, nodding. "Nice to meet you. Did you and your husband have a good match?"

"Oh, Eric is such a good golfer I spend most of my time just watching him. You know how it is when someone's an expert at something? It's fascinating."

"I've never played golf," Devin said. "I'm told we have some nice courses, but there aren't any close to me."

"You're from New Hamp—"

"Maine," Devin said. "Central Maine. Far from most places anyone has heard of."

"Well, maybe Sunny can take you golfing while you're here. How long are you staying?"

"I'm not sure. Things are kind of up in the air for me."

"She's going home," Ashton announced. "She's not here to mooch off Aunt Sunny."

"Kids," she said, chuckling as she grabbed him and pulled him close, subtly covering his mouth with her hand. "Is your swimsuit wet?" Her gaze landed on Sunny, so hot it might have burned her.

"Devin said I could go after dinner," he said, ratting her out without a moment's hesitation.

"We were bored," Devin agreed, ignoring the signals Sunny was sending from behind Tiffany's back.

Sighing wearily, Tiffany turned to Sunny and said, "We're going to have to take some of your towels. He'll freeze in the car."

If he was her kid, that suit would have been off the minute they'd returned to the apartment, or he'd face the consequences. But he wasn't hers, so Devin zipped her lips and kept them that way.

After Sunny ran to fetch towels, Tiffany herded the kid toward the door. "Your daddy's going to be upset that we're taking so long. You know he hates to wait."

When Sunny returned, she thrust the towels out and grabbed the door handle. "Drive safe," she said, kissing her sister on the cheek and Ashton on the top of the head.

Ashton didn't respond, not turning around to even wave. Given that Devin was used to kids that age hugging her and making a big deal about saying goodbye—kids she'd just known for an hour or two—she found herself unable to even comment. As soon as they were past the door, Sunny closed it and leaned against it. "There's no better way to convince yourself not to have kids than to spend the day with one."

Thinking of all of the fun days she'd had with kids, her instinct was to defend them as a class. But she wasn't going to argue with Sunny, who clearly had a point of view earned from experience. Actually, it probably wasn't a good idea to press any of her opinions about loaded topics. When you were just passing through, you didn't really have a dog in the fight.

After they'd both gotten ready for bed, they met in the guest room bed. Sunny cuddled up to Devin's body, completely quiet for a minute. Finally, she said, "Did you have an awful day?"

"No, but I would have rather spent it alone with you." She kissed her cheek and threaded her fingers through her hair, having found a head rub was a surefire way to relax her. "I just hate to have you running around all day when you need time to recharge your engines."

"Yeah, I do," she allowed.

"You probably don't even feel like we had a weekend, with all of the socializing we did."

"I guess." She rolled onto her side and let out a sigh. "But you can't say no to family."

Devin begged to differ. But she did her differing where it was most appreciated. In her head.

Chapter Eighteen

DEVIN HAD LIVED THROUGH SOME hot days. Days when the heat and humidity made her feel like every ounce of her energy had drained from her body by noon. But this kind of heat was a different thing. It was the first day of June, a time when she could reliably leave the house without a jacket at home. But here, in Dallas, she was tempted to go to a barbershop and get a buzz cut. When your hair was the only additional thing you could take off and not risk arrest—you were damned hot.

She was sitting under a pretty little multi-trunked tree covered with large spikes of blue blossoms. The woman who'd hired her to cut the grass was friendly and knew exactly how she wanted things done, but she didn't know what the tree was called. That wasn't uncommon. The people she'd worked for so far didn't know the first thing about the plants in their yard —other than they didn't want to take care of them on their own. But that was good for business. Very good for business, as a matter of fact. She'd raised her hourly rate until the calls declined to a manageable number, but she still had more work than she could possibly get to. If she had any sense, she'd quit the coffee shop, but she was afraid working ten hours a day in this heat would kill her.

She removed her phone from her pocket and took a few photos of the tree, determined to learn the proper names and suggested care practices of the local plants. You sounded more like a real landscaper if you knew what the hell you were talking about.

The sliding door opened and a pair of yappy little dogs burst from it. In a second they were on her, licking the sweat from her legs like she was the tastiest thing they'd ever encountered.

"Jasmin! Ariel!"

Melody followed along after the dogs, bearing a pitcher that started to sweat by the time she'd walked twenty feet. Devin was vaguely cognizant that Melody was drop-dead beautiful, but it was the huge glass of ice sitting on the tray that truly captured her attention.

A substantial minority of women in Dallas had blonde hair, a fact Devin hadn't been able to make sense of. She didn't hear many Scandinavian surnames, and most of the women weren't particularly fair, but dying your hair blonde was a whole lot more common than she was used to. Melody was one of their number, with long blonde hair and tanned skin, all wrapped up in a gym-toned body. Devin took a quick look as Melody walked toward her, noting breasts that seemed larger and firmer than the original models. That set her thoughts rambling, making her wonder if the men of Dallas demanded their women be blonde, and fit, and large-breasted, or if the women had decided that all on their own. The rich people of Dallas, that is. They were the only ones who seemed to play that game.

"I brought you some lemonade," Melody said. "My housekeeper makes it from scratch."

Melody had just the tiniest bit of a Texas accent, but every once in a while a word crept out that made Devin think she'd worked on losing a much stronger one. Why you'd want to do that puzzled her, but she'd noticed it a lot, particularly with women. Yet one more thing she'd never understand.

"Thanks," Devin said, accepting the glass and nearly draining it. "Hot," she added, thinking that about covered it. "I don't charge for my breaks, in case you're wondering." She held up her phone and showed Melody the screen. "I use a timer and stop it when I can't go on another second." She laughed a little, showing she was teasing.

"I'm not worried about that. I can tell you're honest." She turned and took a look at the back of her house, a huge edifice of tan colored stucco, with balconies off every bedroom and a massive, vine-bedecked structure looming over the patio. "Do you see that strip of grass between the pool and the patio?"

"Uh-huh." Devin got to her feet and faced the house.

"When we get a big storm, water pools up there. Last year, we got three inches of rain in an hour, and water got into the house. Our builder told us we needed a French drain, whatever that is," she said, laughing softly. "But we haven't been able to find anyone who'll do it."

Devin had taken off her ball cap to let the sweat cool her, but she put it back on and walked over to the area. It was a narrow space, maybe three feet wide, and hard as a rock. "What's the problem? This looks like a pretty straightforward job to me."

"It's too narrow to use machines, and no one reliable wants to do it by hand. I was going to ask Esperanza to go down to the home center and see if any of the day laborers would do it, but I'd much rather have someone who speaks English." She paused briefly. "Not that I have anything against Spanish speakers. I just want to be able to ask for what I want and not have to have an interpreter."

"Mmm." Devin nodded, then got down on her knees, took her pen knife from the back pocket of her cargo shorts, and jammed it into the dirt. "I can do it, but you're going to have to water the hell out of this area so I can get a shovel into it." She looked up at Melody, who was blocking the torrid sun, giving her a saintly halo effect. "I mean a lot of water. You might need to water for an hour or two every day for a week for the water to get down to where I need it."

"Will you do that? Neither of us has time."

Devin shrugged. "I'll do anything you want. But I'll have to charge for travel time, too. You're at the edge of my range." She laughed, acknowledging she was probably the only bicycle-riding landscaper in the Metroplex.

"Let me have Esperanza come get you. Where exactly do you live?"

"Uptown."

She blinked, clearly puzzled. "Uptown? In Dallas?"

"Uh-huh."

"That's miles from here!"

"I know. Believe me, I know. But since I've been doing your friend Christie's yard, I'm happy to take other jobs around here. It saves a little wear and tear on the engine if I can do two or three jobs on the same day." She slapped at her thighs, which had gotten darker than they'd ever been.

"Can you give me a quote on the drain? I know it will be a lot of work, but it'll be worth it in the long run. Having water come under the doors once was too much."

"Sure. I'll have to plot out the whole thing to get the drainage right. We'll need clean gravel and a four-inch perforated pipe." She crossed her arms over her chest and tried to recall exactly how she'd done the drain at her grandparents' home. "We'll use some landscaping fabric to keep the dirt from clogging the pipe. Of course, we'll have to have someplace to put the topsoil I have to get rid of." She looked around the yard, searching for any place she could dump it. "I hate to have to cart it away, but I think we'll have to."

"Whatever you think," Melody said. "You're the boss." She gave her a luminous smile, the kind of smile Devin used to have to drive all the way to Portland to get. But she wasn't looking for those kinds of seductive smiles any longer. Sunny easily fulfilled all of her bedroom needs.

Sunny reached the bedroom before Devin, and she was just settling down when she looked up and saw her crossing the room. "Damn," she said, not having been aware she was talking out loud.

"Damn what?" Devin whipped off her tank top, and tossed it onto a chair. Gone was the harsh, wind-burned tan from April, now replaced by a burnished bronze hue that covered everything her swimsuit didn't expose. She'd gained weight too, making her look younger and fitter and healthier. Sunny's heart clutched for a second, thinking of the Devin she'd met on that fateful day in March. She looked exactly like that again, but with a glowing tan.

After meeting Sunny's gaze, Devin moved toward the bed. She had such an effortlessly sexy way of gliding across a room. Graceful and strong and purposeful. There was nothing about Devin that was mannish to Sunny's eyes, but she reminded her of a guy she'd dated in college, a swimmer. They'd both had the confident stride of an athlete, with every muscle ready to work at a moment's notice. A sexy ball of energy, poised and coiled.

"Sorry," Sunny said, embarrassed at being caught. "I just catch a look at you sometimes and can't stop myself from leering."

Devin slipped into the bed and laced her hands behind her head, making her modest but nicely shaped breasts stand up tall. That was a super-sexy move too, but Sunny was pretty sure she didn't intend for it to be.

"You make it sound like you shouldn't leer."

"Well, it's kind of... I don't know. Do you feel objectified?"

She turned and gave her a hungry look, like she was about to take a big bite. "If that means you look at me and think dirty thoughts—feel free." She moved an arm to snug it up under Sunny's neck, then tumbled her close just by bending her arm. "I do that to you," she purred into her ear. "All the time." Little kisses along her jawline made goosebumps break out. "I did it tonight when you came in the door. That dress you had on was probably supposed to be business-like, but it was super-sexy."

"I don't want to look sexy at work!"

"You look sexy everywhere," Devin murmured, increasing the force and the range of her kisses. "You're the sexiest woman I've ever shared a bed with."

"I am?" Every time Devin said something like that it caught her by surprise. She hadn't slept with very many women, but none of them had seemed overwhelmed by her looks or her sex appeal.

"Hell, yes. No doubt. By the time the front door's open, I'm ready to get down to business." Her laugh was quiet and low. "That's why I keep nudging you into bed earlier. One of these days I'm going to have you in here ten minutes after you get home. You can eat a sandwich while I start at your feet and work my way up."

Sunny laughed at the playful look on her face, but there was a serious aspect to her expression that touched her heart. Devin was the most beguiling combination of sober and silly that Sunny'd ever the pleasure of knowing. A shiver ran up her spine, as it often did when she looked into those enchanting blue eyes. If only they had more than tragedy and sex to bind them, she would have done anything in the world to convince Devin to give them a chance as a couple. But Devin had been one hundred percent consistent—she was going home the moment Sunny released her. She flinched when she had to face the fact that Devin would have to bring it up sooner or later. They couldn't *both* act like she was in Dallas because she wanted to be. But Sunny wasn't going to voluntarily send the woman away who'd made her life so much better. Only a fool would do that, and she was nobody's fool.

Riding a bike in a torrential downpour wasn't a heck of a lot of fun. It was even less pleasant when you'd just wasted a ten mile ride to tend to someone's lawn, only to be rained out. It hadn't been coming down very hard when she'd been there, and she knew that most people would have fired up the mower and cut the grass anyway, but Devin wasn't about to do a poor job just for her own convenience. Sometimes she wished she could, though. Life would be easier if you didn't have a conscience.

Her phone buzzed in her pocket, and she wanted to let it go. But only a few people ever called her, and all of them were important. It was tough to see through the pelting rain, but she spotted a bus stop in the distance and raced for it. The phone stopped ringing on the way, and she unzipped the protective baggie she carried it in and looked at the message on the screen. "Call Sunny," she said, and the phone did her bidding.

"Hi, there," Sunny said. "Am I catching you at a good time?"

"If you're trying to see if I've drowned, you called at the perfect time. I haven't," she added, "but it's nip and tuck."

"It's raining there?"

Devin held the phone up, getting it close to the narrow metal roof of the bus enclosure. "Hear that?"

"It sounds like someone's hammering!"

"It sure does. I'm just glad I'm heading home. The storm's going to pass me in a few minutes. What's up? It's not like you to call at this time of day."

"Is it safe to be out in a storm? Do you see any lightning?"

"Not yet." She let out a laugh. "Are you trying to keep me on the phone until I do?"

"No!" she yipped. "Go home. Right now."

"Sunny, you called for a reason. Spit it out."

She let out a sigh, the kind of sound she made when she was frustrated. "It's nothing big. My little sister called and needs me to go over there. I just wanted to let you know I'd be late to supper."

Devin smiled at the way she'd put that. When she talked about her family, she almost always let some southern inflection or phrase color her speech. "Is there anything I can help with?" Despite having been in Texas for over two months, this elusive sister hadn't been sighted, which was truly odd.

"Where are you?"

"About a mile from home."

"Oh, no, she's all the way down in Oak Cliff. I'll go."

"It's only two in the afternoon, Sunny. I can get just about anywhere and still have time to get home and make that lobster mac and cheese you've been craving."

"Oh, God," she growled. "I'd forgotten that's what we're having." She took in a breath audible enough for Devin to hear. "Are you sure you don't mind? I'm embarrassed to tell you what she needs."

"Then text it to me. Do me a favor and look up how to ride to her place, will you? I'll turn around and head south. Later."

Devin pedaled like a banshee, trying to get to wherever she was going before she was sucked into a drainage culvert by a river of runoff. She spotted a grocery store up ahead and went for it, deeply appreciative that a number of shopping centers had colonnades to protect you from the sun, since they also did a fantastic job of keeping you out of the rain.

Brittany lived just few blocks from a major thoroughfare, so finding her neighborhood was no problem. It took nearly an hour, though, since Devin had to be careful to avoid water-filled potholes and inattentive drivers. Finally, she reached the neighborhood, one filled with small bungalows. It was a neat little area, kind of cheery despite the gray skies that were now just spitting out a light drizzle. As she rode along, looking for the proper house number, Devin's thoughts went to Lori, thinking that she'd love to live in a place like this, with other families and tons of kids for her pair to play with. But Lori was as firmly planted in Maine as Devin was. Texas was not in her future.

When she reached the house Devin shook like a dog, trying to fling her wet hair from her face, then pressed the bell. When she realized it hadn't rung, she knocked. A minute later, a younger version of Sunny opened the door.

"Are you Devin?"

Assessing her for a second, Devin decided this sister also didn't have the appeal of the original Thompson sibling. But you couldn't say she wasn't cute. Or sexy. Actually, it was obvious Brittany put a lot of effort into looking sexy, a tactic which had never appealed to Devin. You either had it or you didn't, and trying to amp it up was just kinda sad.

"Yeah," she said, "Brittany?"

"That's me. Come on in," she said, opening the door wide.

Devin stepped inside and took a quick look around. The living room was on the small side, dominated by a big tv and a pair of recliners, but there were some big boxes in the corner, with smaller ones lying on top of them. There were no pictures on the walls, but the room was painted a girly lilac, making it look like pastel-loving college guys had decorated it. Sunny had spoken of this sister so infrequently that Devin wasn't sure how old she was, but she looked to be around thirty. Maybe a little younger. Devin also didn't know what she did for a living, but whatever it was didn't require her to be in attendance on a Wednesday afternoon.

"Your sister said your cable's gone out?"

"Yeah. I called the company and they said it was working fine. I guess they can tell if the signal's getting to the house, but that's all I know." She tossed her hair over her shoulder, while batting her pale blue eyes, a move she'd probably unconsciously mastered to make her look helpless. It worked, but Devin couldn't imagine wanting to look like you didn't know how to take care of yourself.

"Well, I'm no specialist, but I know a little bit. Do you know where the line comes into the house?"

Brittany laughed, like she'd asked her to solve complex math problems without a calculator. "How would I know that?"

"I'll look outside," Devin said, grumbling to herself. As she walked out into the clearing afternoon, she considered how a woman could manage to own a home, yet have no idea of how the utilities came into the building.

It wasn't hard to find the entry point, which was the attic. Of course it was. Devin went back inside, finding Brittany sitting on a recliner staring at the nonworking television set. She looked up expectantly, as if she'd expected Devin to not only have found the problem, but fixed it.

"Do you know how to get into the attic?"

"The attic?" Brittany blinked slowly as her head tilted to the right. "There's an attic?"

Realizing she'd have to figure things out for herself, Devin walked into the hallway, seeing the usual framing around a rectangular access panel in the ceiling. "Got a ladder?" she called out.

Brittany walked into the hall and stared up at the spot, clearly surprised it had been hiding there. "I've got a chair."

"Great. Can you get it?"

Brittany returned in a minute with a kitchen chair, a not very sturdy looking metal-legged model with red leatherette upholstery. Devin had seen recreations of these in stores around Dallas, but this looked like an original. She wasn't crazy about standing on a sixty-year-old chair, but she wanted to get this over with quickly. "Will you hold it for me? I don't want it to slide."

"Sure." Brittany was pretty adept at holding a chair steady, but it was quite a few inches short of what Devin needed. So she had Brittany get her a broom, then used it to pop the panel up and push it out of the way.

"I'm gonna jump, so hold it steady," she instructed. She was damned glad she'd split so much wood during the winter, because doing a pull-up into an attic from a wobbly base was at the very end of her physical abilities. Grunting and cursing under her breath, she pulled hard, then settled onto one of the joists, her arms shaking from fatigue. "I guess I should have asked for a flashlight before I got up here."

"I might have one," Brittany said, scurrying away.

The place was dark as pitch, filled with very old-school insulation, pink fiberglass that didn't have a paper cover on it. The attic was only a few feet high in the center of the roofline, significantly less at the eaves. Devin wasn't afraid of dark or narrow spaces, but she already itched at the thought of crawling over that exposed insulation wearing only shorts and a T-shirt, with every exposed inch of skin still dripping wet.

Brittany returned and held the flashlight up, with Devin leaning over to grab it. Then it was just the usual game of finding where the line came in and following it. In a matter of moments her skin was itching like she'd been rubbed with sandpaper, but she found the wire—which had been chewed through. Now she really itched. Only rodents did that kind of thing, and she hated rodents more than she'd admit to anyone on earth. After shimmying back across the space, she grabbed onto the edges of the opening and lowered herself to the chair, then jumped to the floor.

"Good news and bad news."

"Um, I like good news," Brittany said. The sun was starting to peek out, entering the bedroom windows behind her and illuminating her hair, which was much redder than Sunny's. Devin decided that Brittany had a nice face, not as nice as Sunny's, but open and friendly, not at all like Tiffany's posed smile and artificial laugh.

"I think I can fix your problem. A hardware store should have everything I need."

"Great!"

She started to head back to her recliner, but Devin stopped her. "I've never been to this neighborhood, and I rode here on my bike." She waited for a response, but Brittany just stared at her blankly. She didn't look like she was unwilling to help, just that she wasn't aware she should.

"I'm going to write down exactly what I need, and you're going to go to the store while I sit down and have a glass of water. Unless you have beer," she added. "That'd be even better."

Brittany blinked at her slowly, then nodded. "Are you sure I can do it? I've never been to a hardware store."

"It's a perfect day to start," Devin said, then went into the kitchen to look for something to write on. She had a feeling Brittany couldn't be trusted to remember what to buy without an explicit note.

"She has rats?" Sunny said, shivering noticeably when Devin recounted the highlights of her afternoon.

"She does. But she doesn't know that, since she only wanted the good news. At some point, you should tell her to hire an exterminator."

"I'll call in the morning." Sunny put her arms around Devin from behind and held her close, leaning into her like she often did. It was like having a warm, soft blanket tossed over your shoulders, and Devin found she liked the sensation an awful lot.

"She can't handle that on her own? She seems a little less busy than you are, given that she was sitting around the house on a Wednesday afternoon, doing nothing."

Sunny let go, then opened the oven door and let out a sensual purr. "Good God, that looks delicious. Handy-woman and gourmet cook. That might not be a common combination, but it's my favorite now that I know it exists."

"Did you change the subject on purpose?" Devin grasped the back pocket of her shorts and turned her around. Then she put her hands on Sunny's shoulders and gazed into her eyes. "Shouldn't you let your sister take care of herself?"

"Sure. That's exactly what I should do. But she won't, and I'll have to clean up an even bigger mess later on." She kissed Devin's cheek and went to get out plates for their dinner.

"Does she have a job?"

"At the moment? She's surveying her options. But she has plenty of training. After she got her associate's degree, I put her through a paralegal program, but the work bored her. So I sent her to learn dog-grooming, since she's always been a dog nut. That was a no-go too. Apparently, she likes playing with dogs, not grooming them." She tapped at her chin for a moment. "Lastly, she's a licensed physical therapy assistant, but she discovered many of the people who need PT are in pain, and that freaks her out."

"Does she have a…boyfriend? Girlfriend?"

"She didn't the last time I checked, but you can probably tell we don't hang out much." She shrugged amiably. "She mostly calls when she needs something."

"You don't spend any time together?"

"Not really," she said, looking away. "I tried when she was younger, but she's into a few bands she follows…"

"Follows? What does that mean?"

"Oh, you know, she'll spend a week or two following one of her favorite bands across Texas. Local bands," she added. "She and her friends are…" She shrugged again. "They really seem to enjoy doing that."

"Doesn't it take money to do that?" Devin asked, trying not to sound like she was being a scold.

"Little bit," Sunny agreed, not commenting further.

Devin watched her set the table, carefully lining up the silverware just so. She had more questions, but the big ones had already been answered. Sunny was the family ATM, help-line, delivery service and babysitter. And not one of the people who took her money or her time offered a damn thing in return.

Chapter Nineteen

Since the year she'd graduated from law school, a group of anywhere from six to twenty of Sunny's friends got together and rented one or several houseboats on Lake Travis during June. This year they'd planned on a group of nine, with Devin's addition making it a nice even ten, all couples.

The rental period was from Friday to Sunday, and, as always, Devin was up before Sunny, who was still trying to get all of her parts moving in the same direction.

"Coffee?" she mumbled as her feet hit the floor.

"On its way," Devin called out from one of the other rooms.

She had such an exquisite sense of hearing Sunny was fairly sure she'd be able to hear a whisper, but she didn't push her luck. Instead, she relished the beauty of being able to croak out a plea and have a nice, fresh cup of Joe delivered. Since Devin was now a connoisseur of well made coffee, she'd convinced Sunny to buy a burr grinder and a French press. Now just hearing the grinder start to whir made Sunny's taste buds perk up, readying themselves for the first taste of Devin's perfectly made brew.

It would take a few minutes for the whole process to reach completion, so she got into the shower and shaved her legs. As she turned off the water, the shower door opened and she was met by a pair of tender lips, followed by a steaming cup of coffee made from beans hand-picked in Ethiopia—or wherever this latest batch came from. Devin was always experimenting, certain she'd find the perfect bean if she let her tastebuds travel the world. "Good?" she asked, one eyebrow raised in question.

"Delicious. Really, really good."

"Sulawesi," Devin said, grinning. "I couldn't find it on a map, but I think it's a keeper."

"How are you still single?" Sunny asked for the hundredth time. "You cook, you clean, you're tidy, you don't snore, and you're absolutely fantastic in bed."

She shrugged, the way she always did when she was complimented. Devin wasn't particularly humble, but she didn't seem to think she was anything extra special—which she undoubtedly was. "You don't understand how remote my cabin is. Or how much alone time I need. Not many people want a girlfriend who takes off for weeks at a time just to wander around in the woods."

"Their loss." Sunny took the towel Devin handed her and started to dry off. "I could tell them what they're missing, but that would be against my own best interests."

"I'll put you down as a reference if I ever need one." Then, with a little grin, she left the room, probably to clean the kitchen and leave it as neat as a pin. No one had ever been less in need of a reference. Devin could just show that smile and have women throwing their house keys at her. So why was she single? There was one, simple, irrefutable answer. She wanted to be.

Sunny pointed the car in the direction of Austin, thinking that the vehicle might have the way memorized by now. If she hadn't agreed to return to Dallas for Morgan, she would have happily lived in the state capital for the rest of her life. The city simply fit her better than Dallas, in nearly every way. It was a little smaller, even though it had grown more than Sunny was happy with, more intimate, friendlier, more laid back, and had better food. If she could have a do-over, she would have returned to Austin after Morgan's death. But she'd been back in Dallas for less than a year, she had the condo, and the offer from Hank was too good to pass up. Having Callie close by was a significant factor too, and was probably the main one in convincing her to stay all this time. But now that things were all going to be up in the air again, she might be tempted to return to where her heart belonged—in Hill Country.

Turning her head, she spied Devin gazing out the window with a great deal of interest. That was Devin's default mode. She was a person who paid a lot of attention to everything she encountered.

Devin must have sensed she was being looked at, for she turned and said, "Will it take long to get out of town?"

"Mmm, to be honest, we never really get out of town on this drive. It'll be all highway, usually with a lot of traffic."

Devin gazed at her for a few seconds, then said, "Does that ever bother you?"

"What? Traffic?"

She stared out of her window for a minute, then quietly said, "All of it. So many people. So little solitude."

"You're not getting enough of that, are you?" Sunny asked, gritting her teeth while she waited for the answer.

Devin turned her head again, with her pale eyes searching Sunny's for a few seconds. "I haven't gotten any. There isn't any to be had."

"Sure there is." She laughed nervously. "I'm sure you're all alone on the bike trail on your way to work in the morning. Heck, I bet you're alone on the way home too. Not many people are riding bikes when it's over ninety."

Nodding, Devin said, "It's not uncommon for me to be alone on the bike trail." She took in a long breath and let it out audibly, continuing to stare out the window. "But that's not solitude."

Sunny didn't want to do it, but she had to ask. "Are you unhappy?"

A huge sigh of relief left Sunny's lungs when Devin turned back to her and smiled. "Of course not. I've really enjoyed spending all of this time with you." She reached over and put her hand, which was very warm and had developed calluses at the base of each finger, onto Sunny's thigh. "I'm stoked about being out on a big lake all weekend. I love water to death."

"Me too. If I lived in Austin, I'd get a boat for sure."

"Canoe," Devin said quietly, turning again to stare out at the steady stream of cars. "A canoe's the way to travel on water."

Sunny normally only had the time and the opportunity to see her friends on Saturday night. That seemed like a very small amount of time to get all of your socializing in, but no one had time to get together for dinner during the week, with all of her friends working hard and not living particularly close by.

They'd been to Callie and Teresa's home, a big, rambling place about a half hour north of Sunny's, several times, as well as to Linda and Lauren's home near SMU, but that was it. It wasn't uncommon for Sunny to mention an invitation to a party or a movie or a play, but she turned almost all of them down. Devin got the impression that she used to do a lot more, but now guarded her time at home pretty zealously, which made sense. If they didn't have Sundays to chill, they wouldn't have hardly any time alone.

They didn't head into Austin proper, bearing west onto a state road well before town. The last bit of the trip reminded Devin just a tiny bit of Maine. While the plants and trees were wildly different, the road was narrow and wound around a lot of small bungalows. Back home, many of these would be three-season camps, not warm enough for people to use in the winter. That wouldn't be a problem here. It was more likely that you'd stay away in the summer, trying to avoid the scorching heat and humidity.

Finally, they arrived at the marina, and went in to claim their boat. They were the first of their group to arrive, and after signing all of the papers, they went aboard. It was one impressive vessel, with five bedrooms and four baths, a living area with a leather sectional big enough for all of them to sit at once, a dining table with eight chairs, and a compact kitchen with a massive refrigerator.

Sunny had the handles of her bag looped over her shoulder, and she made a bee-line for the bedroom at the bow of the boat, the big one with the king-sized bed, and dramatically tossed her bag onto it. "Dibs," she decreed, smiling contentedly. Devin whistled softly as she looked around. "I'm not gonna ask what you guys paid for this, but I know it was a lot."

"It was, but this might be the only vacation I take this year. It's worth a splurge."

"Um…" Making a show of assessing the layout, she said teasingly, "I kinda thought you'd all draw straws for who gets the nicest bedroom. I didn't know you were land-grabbers."

"We are," Sunny agreed, chuckling. "That's why I break my neck to get here early. I hate sharing a bathroom."

Devin opened the sliding glass door and stepped onto the private balcony. "We don't have to share anything. I bet there's a separate kitchen hidden behind that door."

"Closet," Sunny said. "I know the layout since we rented this exact boat last year. I got to peek into this room when Callie didn't have the door locked, guarding her fiefdom."

"Ahh. Now I know why you were driving ninety most of the way."

Sunny took her in her arms and gave her a robust hug. "I did that to keep up and not get run over. Everyone goes fifteen miles over the speed limit, which was seventy-five much of the time." She placed a soft, lingering kiss on Devin's lips. "But I'll admit that getting to choose first might have made my foot a little more leaden than normal."

"Son of a bitch!" A woman's voice called out from the center of the boat.

Sunny began to laugh. "Michele's here. I'd recognize that salty language anywhere."

By noon, everyone was aboard. Devin had never met two of the couples, but she was very comfortable with Callie and Teresa and Linda and Lauren, so she wasn't concerned that she'd feel like an outsider.

At least one member of each couple had gone to law school with Sunny, but two of them, while lawyers, didn't work in the field. But they were all professionals—professionals who Devin was sure made a *lot* of money. They just had that look about them. Excellent haircuts, tasteful gold or silver jewelry, expensive watches, name-brand golf shirts and running shoes. But the shoes didn't stay on long. Within minutes, everyone put on flip-flops or slightly more substantial sandals. Michele and her partner Gwen had taken the bedroom right next to the one Devin and Sunny had claimed, and it became clear very quickly that Michele wasn't the shy one. Nor the quiet one. While Devin was unpacking, Michele came to their door and stood there for a second, then entered and dropped to the bed.

"So...what's your story?" she asked.

Devin turned and spent a few seconds getting a good look at her before she responded. She was a large woman; tall, broad-shouldered, and sturdily built. But what caught your attention was her gaze—direct and level. She looked like she'd never backed down from a confrontation, and Devin was almost certain she was going to like her.

"What's my story about what?" she asked, turning to return to her task.

"What's the deal with you? Are you and Sunny a couple? No one can get a straight story out of her."

"Well…" Devin closed the drawer that now held her shorts and tank tops and walked back over to Michele. "I think Sunny's the best person to answer that, but I've got nothing to hide. I'm going home when I'm ready to head back to work, or when Sunny's sick of me." She smiled, trying to make it clear she was teasing a little. "Whichever comes first."

"What exactly do you do?"

Sunny came in and put her arm around Devin's shoulders in an oddly protective gesture. One she'd never used before. "If you want to chat, let's go into the living room or the top deck. But don't treat my guest like she's on trial, Michele. You're not at work."

Michele's partner Gwen poked her head in the bedroom. "Are you in trouble already?"

"Yeah," Michele said, standing and walking back towards the door. "But it wouldn't be a normal vacation if I wasn't, right?"

✦

The boat was docked on a channel at the end of the lake. If they'd wanted to, they could have hired a captain who'd take them all around, letting them relax and have someone else be in charge. But this wasn't that kind of group. It seemed like everyone wanted to pilot the boat, and Devin enjoyed sitting near the helm and watching them fight it out. It was particularly fun to watch Sunny stand her ground and make her case. She was very accommodating at home, always enthusiastically agreeing to the slightest preference Devin had. And if she ever stood up for herself with her family, Devin had yet to see it. But here, among her friends, she really tried to win the battle. At this point, Sunny and Becky, a PE teacher in the Dallas public school system, were most invested in the fight, with neither of them showing any indication they were going to give in.

"Flip a coin," Becky's partner Patty said. "We're ready to get going."

"We could do that," Sunny said slowly. "Heads!"

"Cheater," Becky groused. But she pulled a coin from her pocket and flipped it in the air. When she picked it up, she shook her head, mumbling, "I'm next," then walked away to head outside.

"Score!" Sunny's happy grin made Devin think she might be seeing the person Sunny had been when she was still in school. A woman who seemed much less weighted down by the responsibilities of her job and her family. A woman Devin would like to see more of—for Sunny's sake.

Sunny piloted the boat along the channel until they got to a wider part of the lake, which also happened to be the part packed with other boats, many of them houseboats. It reminded Devin of the interstate more than a lake, but everyone agree Devil's Cove was the place to be. Many boats were rafted up, tied together with just their bumpers keeping them from rubbing together when the wind turned them in a group.

Devin had lived on or around lakes her whole life, but she'd never seen one treated more like a parking lot than a body of water. She'd never been tailgating, not being a fan of professional sports, and not having gone to college, but she assumed this was very much like that. Jet skis prowled around constantly, mostly driven by youngish guys looking for available women, kids on inflatables floated wherever they could fit, and lots of adults lounged on floating chairs, allowing them to relax while drinking beer. A few portable sound systems competed with one another, providing ambient music for people dancing on nearly every deck. But girls probably didn't wear tiny bikinis at frosty football games, nor did guys show off their tans while cannonballing into the water, risking life and limb to impress their friends.

Her own group was a little more sedate; more of a shorts and tank tops crowd. They seemed to get as much enjoyment from watching people hop from boat to boat, singing, dancing, and acting crazy than they would have doing it themselves. But Sunny's friends could hold their own with alcohol. They had a blender going almost constantly, whipping up all kinds of frothy concoctions that didn't seem like they had liquor in them. But they definitely did, a fact Devin could attest to when she found herself laughing like a fool at the slightest joke.

Their boat was just a few yards from a group of seven powerboats rafted together, with people hopping from one boat to the next, singing off-key to the country tunes that blasted from some huge speakers one guy had fitted out on his wakeboard tower.

"If I wasn't spoken for," Gwen said, her voice low and filled with more longing than her partner probably appreciated, "I'd hop on that red boat and try to impress those two." She pointed toward a pair of women who couldn't have been out of college yet, both tan and shapely and obviously drunk. "I'd like both at once." She let out a heavy sigh. "Yet another fantasy I'll never be able to fulfill."

"You were single until you were thirty," Michele said, seemingly not bothered by her partner's wandering eye. "That was plenty of time to make all of your dreams come true."

"Yeah, but I didn't," she said, pouting a little, "and now I can't."

They were all on the top deck, a big space with a covering over the middle portion, and open skies at the bow and stern. Their lounge chairs were in the bow, and all of them had ball caps or some other form of hat on to fight the blistering sun. Michele reached over and tipped Gwen's cap back, exposing her eyes. "Permission granted," she said. "You go march over there and work your magic. I promise I won't hold it over your head if you talk them into going below and doing the nasty."

"You'd hold it over my head," Gwen said. "I know you."

"Promise." Michele stood and put her hand over her heart. "I'm promising in front of our dearest friends. No repercussions." She bowed slightly and extended her arm toward the stairs. "Be my guest. We'll watch from here and root you on."

Liquor loosened her tongue in unpredictable ways, and Devin found herself offering her opinion. "If you don't mind some advice," she said, "I'd skip the embarrassment. Even if girls like that are flirting with you—which those two are *not*, it's hard enough to get one hot girl to take off with you. Two's impossible." She lifted her glass to her lips, then realized everyone was staring at her.

"How often have you tried that?" Michele asked. "You sound like the voice of experience."

"Well..." She smiled at Sunny, who didn't smile back. "It's been a while, but..." She swallowed nervously, then tried to backtrack. "I don't act like that any more. I learned my lesson while I was still in my twenties."

"What lesson was that?" Sunny asked. She didn't look angry, just curious. But Devin was certain she'd already said too much. She just didn't have any way to get out of it in a crowd.

"Um, I learned that bars aren't the best places to find women. Even if you get lucky, it's not much fun to wind up with a woman who passes out or throws up in your car. I've experienced both," she added, trying to make Sunny smile.

"How *do* you pick up women?" Michele asked, batting her eyes in a way that made it seem she was toying with Devin. "I've been out of the game for a long time."

"The internet," Devin said, hoping they could drop this quickly.

"The what?" Sunny leaned forward and shielded her eyes from the sun. "Did you say you use the internet?"

She took in a breath and spit it out. "Um...yeah. I use a dating app."

Sunny didn't reply, but her eyebrow went up, giving Devin a suspicious look she'd never seen on her face. She didn't really want to keep talking, but thought she'd better. "I search for women in Bangor, and if I can't find any there I go to Portland." Shrugging, she said, "I'm sure not going to meet anyone in Greenville."

That seemed to satisfy Sunny, for she said, "Devin lives a couple of hours from Portland, but Bangor's not a whole lot closer. Her town's so small the bars close at ten."

"Most close at eight," Devin said, grinning. "Only one's for night-owls."

"Let's say you choose someone from Bangor," Callie said, leaning forward and speaking in a very precise manner. "Is the point to get to know women or to have sex with them?"

It was clear Callie wasn't asking in a casual way, but Devin didn't let that guide her answer. She wasn't ashamed of the way she lived, and wasn't about to lie. She just wished she hadn't started the whole thread. "Um, the point is to have sex," she said, spitting it out. "That's what I've been doing ever since I broke up with my girlfriend."

"That was when?" Callie asked. She normally didn't seem like an attorney, but this afternoon she was all business. Penetrating stare, level tone, giving nothing away.

"Um, we were together for our last two years of high school, then two years after that." Shrugging, she added, "That's been a while. She and her wife have a twelve-year-old."

"What happened?" Callie persisted. "Why'd you break up?"

"Um…" Devin looked at Sunny, hoping for a rescue, but Sunny was watching her just as carefully as every other person, waiting for an answer. "Well, in retrospect, I have to admit that Taylor didn't ask for much. Her main demand was that we live in Bangor." Devin shifted her weight, all of a sudden noticing that the chaise was pressing too hard against the backs of her thighs. "But I couldn't be happy there. I'm not cut out for a city, but Taylor wouldn't stay at my cabin for more than an occasional weekend, and that was only in the summer."

"How far is Bangor?" Michele asked.

"An hour and a half. Takes longer in the winter, of course. We get a lot of snow."

"You couldn't live halfway between your job and the town?" Michele asked, one of many unwilling to let this die.

"We could have. We *should* have. But I was naive and cocky and sure it'd be as easy to find a second girlfriend as it had been to find the first. I couldn't have guessed Taylor was the only single lesbian in the county." She let out a chuckle. "I'm sure that's not true, but sometimes it seems like it. If there are nearby lesbians looking for love, I haven't met them."

"So you broke up with her?" Sunny asked, her voice quiet and tentative.

"I didn't want to, but she wanted to buy a condo together and I wasn't willing. We fought and fought and finally I gave up and moved to my grandparents' cabin. I've been there ever since."

"Devin doesn't have running water in her cabin," Sunny said, now speaking with her normal tone. "Apparently, women aren't jumping over each other to spend the night in a cold cabin without a bathroom."

"It's not cold," Devin said, smiling at Sunny. "I've got a nice pellet stove that throws off a lot of heat." She shrugged. "But there's no bathroom, and people seem to think that's an inconvenience."

"Are you fucking nuts?" Michele asked, staring, open-mouthed.

"Probably, but I'm telling the truth. No bathroom, no running water." Shrugging, she added, "But I don't have to worry about the pipes bursting when I'm gone for a few days. I like to look at the positives."

"You're positively nuts!" Michele decided, breaking into a laugh that everyone, even Sunny, joined in.

As the sun dropped lower in the sky, a cooling wind blew across the lake. By the time Sunny went downstairs to make what would probably be their last batch of drinks before dinner, they were sitting in shade, comfortable as could be.

She'd no sooner poured the rum into the blender than Callie was at her side. Speaking softly, she said, "Devin doesn't talk like a woman who's planning on moving to Dallas. She wouldn't live in Bangor, a place so small I've never heard of it."

"It's a big town," Sunny said, somewhat defensively. "They have an airport."

Callie stood closer and let her voice drop. "I think she's going home, babe. Don't count on her."

"I'm *not* counting on her," Sunny said, quickly checking the stairs to make sure Devin didn't come down. "She's been very consistent in saying she's eventually going home." Her voice rose a little as she started to get agitated, just like she always did when she let herself think about this. "But she's driving me crazy by doing things that make it seem like she's already moved here!"

"Like what? Has she changed her address?"

"No, no, but she's got a big landscaping project lined up. I assumed she was taking things one day at a time, but she just told me she thinks she'll wait until fall to start on it. If she's planning out that far, maybe that means she's thinking of staying."

"*Talk* to her," Callie begged. "You're acting like a teenager who's afraid to let her crush know she's interested. You've got to be an adult about this."

"I should. I know I should." But she knew full well she wasn't going to. Taylor had put just a tiny bit of pressure on Devin and she'd dumped her like a hot rock. Sunny wasn't going to fall into that trap. Instead, she was going to treat her like a feral cat, continuing to put out food and stroke under her chin. That might make her so used to human contact that she'd eventually come into the house and domesticate herself.

They stayed out on the top deck to eat, with a few of them eventually going in to clean the kitchen. Devin was in charge, gently directing the other volunteers in cleaning and putting things away. Sunny approached her while she was washing the last of the pots, put her arms around her and whispered into her ear. "It's after nine. Are you going to collapse?"

"Maybe," she said, giggling when Sunny nibbled on her ear.

"Want me to take you to bed?"

"Is that okay?"

"Yeah. Finish what you're doing, and I'll meet you in our palatial suite."

Sunny brushed her teeth and washed off the sunblock, then lay on the bed, waiting for Devin. She appeared in a few minutes, lifting an eyebrow as she let her gaze roam over Sunny's body.

"I smell toothpaste," she said as she sat on the edge of the bed. "But you don't have your usual jammies on." She pulled Sunny's top up then leaned over and blew a raspberry on her bare belly. "I like your usual jammies a lot."

"I think I'll go back upstairs after I get you tucked in. I don't see these guys very often, so I want to get my money's worth."

"I don't have to go to bed. I can skip a whole night's sleep and function okay."

"It's fine," Sunny said. "I don't mind a bit." She grasped the hem of Devin's shirt and tugged on it until she'd freed it. "I'll just rub you for a while to put you to sleep, then I'll go back."

"Rub me where?" Devin asked, eyes dancing with interest.

"Wherever you want." Sunny leaned close and kissed her, getting a thrill at the thought of having sex. They'd had some form of sex almost every night, with Devin seeming to have an insatiable need for contact. That thought stuck with Sunny and she found herself asking, "How often do you have sex?"

"At home?"

"Well, yeah. I know how much you have it with me." She put her hands on Devin's shoulders and pushed her to the bed. "You're not doing it with customers at the coffee shop, are you?" She was teasing, or at least she'd been teasing when she'd started to speak. But now her racing heart mirrored her increasing anxiety. If Devin was banging every cute lesbian who came into the shop…

"I don't have the time, and I definitely don't have the interest, to be chasing women," she said, flipping Sunny over onto her back. "I've got my hands full with you." In a second, Sunny's shorts were off, then the bottoms of her swimsuit followed. Devin's warm hands started to rub her bare skin, making it pebble with goosebumps in seconds. "I love having my hands full of you."

"I love it too," Sunny sighed. "But you didn't answer my question. How often do you look for a woman to have sex with?"

Devin didn't look like she wanted to answer, but she stopped caressing Sunny's body and sat up, putting her feet back onto the floor. "Not very often. Usually two or three times a year. A little more or a little less depending on what I've got going on. Why? Is that too much?"

"Of course not. I'm just a little puzzled. You certainly have a healthy appetite. Is two or three times a year enough to satisfy it?"

"Not at all," she said, chuckling. "But it take a lot of effort, not to mention a lot of money. If I'm forced to go to Portland, I sometimes have to rent a hotel room. Plus, I have to give up a weekend of work. So I only do it when I'm about to go mad."

"No repeats? You've never met a woman you'd like to see more than once?"

"Yeah, I've done that," she said thoughtfully. "Not often now, but I tried that pretty regularly right after I broke up with Taylor." She made a sour face. "Didn't work. After you spend a little time with most women, they want to change you—just like Taylor did."

"Change you…how?"

"Oh, the usual. 'How can you live in a little cabin in the middle of nowhere? You should stay with me in Portland. There's so much more to do.' Or 'Why don't we get together every weekend?' Stuff like that."

"They were looking for a relationship," Sunny guessed.

"I suppose. But if I wanted to live in Portland, I would. And I haven't met a woman who makes me want to drive three hours and give up my best working days to see her every weekend. That'd be some woman," she said, grinning.

"I can see why they'd want more of your time," Sunny said, pulling her down so Devin's body leaned heavily against her chest. She kissed her cheeks and started to expand the territory, traveling down Devin's neck to lick her exposed collar-bones. "You're some woman," she said, sighing with longing for the closeness she craved like a drug. A drug she was sure was set to expire in the not-too-distant future.

Devin was up before the dawn, and when she crept out of their stateroom, the rest of the vessel was silent. After going up to the top deck to watch the sunrise, she reveled in the peacefulness of the crowded lake, now nearly silent. Slowly, boats started sliding past them, mostly one or two guys in a little bass boat with a small outboard engine. Devin spent a long time watching the lake wake up, then took out her phone and called Lori.

"Hey," she said, when her friend answered. "Remember that time I went with your family to Lake Winnipesaukee?"

"You mean the time you complained for a solid week that there were too many people around and too much noise?"

"Exactly," Devin said, chuckling. "Well, the lake we're on makes Winnipesaukee look like Moosehead in February. It's like an amusement park on the water."

"How much have you been whining? Is Sunny ready to tie a weight around you and toss you in?"

"I haven't whined a bit," Devin maintained. "I'm getting pretty good at going with the flow—something I needed some practice at."

"Oh, you're great at going with the flow, as long as you're in charge of the flow."

"Well, I'm not in charge, but I'm going along just fine."

"So you're liking it better?"

"I *hate* it," she said dramatically. "There are people everywhere, it's never dark, and it's never quiet. I haven't found one single place where I don't see or hear any sign of human habitation."

"Have you looked?"

"Hell, yes! Sunny keeps taking me to state parks, thinking we're way out in the middle of nowhere. But there are parking lots and bathrooms and groomed trails and discarded candy wrappers…"

"That doesn't sound too bad, Dev. Don't you ever get tired of peeing on your boots?"

"No," she said, not having to pause for a second to think that over. "I'd rather pee on my bare feet than be around other people all day long, every single day. I always knew Maine was special, but I didn't know how special it was until I got here. I would lose my friggin' mind if I had to live here, Lori."

"They have to have national parks, Dev. That state is huge! They've got to have one that you can get lost in."

"I found a couple," she admitted. "People like one in the northwest corner of the state, but I don't think Sunny wants to drive four or five hours to hike in ninety degree heat. She's odd that way."

Lori laughed at that. "You keep saying that there's nothing there for you, but you sound happy. Happier than you've been for a while."

"I am. Sunny and I get along great, and I even like her friends. So I'm getting all of my socializing in so I can be a hermit for a long while when I get back. I think I'll do that canoe trip I've been wanting to tackle. Wanna do it with me?"

"Oh, sure. I'll just lock the kids in a closet with a couple of gallons of water and an box of energy bars."

"I guess you could," Devin joked, "but I was thinking your mom might watch them."

"How long does that trip take?"

"Well, I think the whole thing, from New York to Canada is…I don't know…seven or eight hundred miles."

Lori was quiet for a minute, then she said, "I want to watch my kids grow up, you lunatic! That would take months!"

"How about just the Maine portion? That's under three hundred and fifty miles."

"You find a nice portion that won't take over two weeks and I'll do it. That means fourteen days, Devin, not sixteen or seventeen. I know how you are."

"I know you do," she said, feeling herself choke up. "And that's why I'd love to go with you. You get me, Lori. Better than anyone I've ever met."

"Then think about coming home. I miss you like crazy, girl! And the boys ask about you every single day. Send more videos, okay? They get a real thrill when you do that."

"I'll do one as soon as we hang up," she said. "You're going to think I'm at a huge marina or the world's biggest boat dealer, but this is an actual lake."

"I was out on my uncle's bass boat yesterday," Lori said. "Just Brody and me. We're trying to have one day a week where we each hang out with one kid. I think they feel more special when they get some individual time."

"I went fishing with my dad or one of my grandfathers at least once a week when I was growing up. Some of my best memories," she added. "Hey, speaking of my dad, will you call my mom if you get a minute? He left for science camp this week and I know she'll miss him."

"How long is he gone?"

"He's doing six sections, each one a week long."

"I'll call and see if she wants to come for dinner. Maybe she can be a Dev-Day substitute."

"Thanks," Devin said, misting up again. "I knew I could count on you."

If Sunny had to pick her favorite thing to do, she'd pick hanging out on the water with her friends on a hot, sunny day. She hadn't realized until now that her favorite thing could be made immeasurably better with the simple addition of a scorchingly hot woman who treated her like a princess.

There were other ways to characterize how Devin treated her, of course, especially since she'd never thought of herself as having any regal attributes. But her friends had used the term multiple times, and she couldn't really argue. Before she was thirsty, Devin jumped up to get her a drink. Moments before she felt a hunger pang, a ripe, juicy peach was dangled in front of her. Her shoulders were massaged with sunblock after every extended dip in the water, and a hat was placed on her head the moment a ray of sun hit her. But best of all, Devin's devotion gave Sunny a blessedly long weekend free of sympathetic looks whenever the topic of relationships came up.

She could tell that some, if not all of her friends were puzzled by Devin's dedication, though. They probably thought she was some sort of backwoods gigolo, intent on stealing all of Sunny's money or cheating her in some other way. But she knew better. Devin wasn't a cheat in any way. She had the makings of a nearly perfect girlfriend—who truly preferred being single. But she loved sex, she loved being close to someone she liked, and she was supremely thoughtful. It might have been smart to guard her heart more zealously, but Sunny was taking a play from Devin's book and living in the moment—a most delicious moment that she was immensely glad she'd let herself have.

The stern of the boat had a curving slide that launched you from the top deck and tossed you a few feet away from the hull. Devin had gone down the thing at least fifty times, each time swimming quickly to return to the boat, then pushing herself onto the deck with just her arms, then running up the stairs to do it over again.

Given that the rest of them slid down once, then lounged on inflatable rings while sipping frozen drinks, Devin's manic antics drew a fair amount of attention.

"Are you paying her by the trip?" Michele asked.

"She must have ADHD," Patty guessed. "Like really bad."

Callie'd been watching her the whole time. "Does she have a cocaine habit?" she finally asked. "That's not normal."

"She likes it," Sunny said, knowing that was the extent of it with Devin. If she liked something, she did it to exhaustion.

So far, Devin had tried sliding down on a plastic trash bag, with a squirt of dishwashing liquid on the fiberglass, and with her bikini bottoms jammed up between her cheeks to reduce friction. She flew down the slide again, splashed into the water close to Sunny, then her head popped up and she flung her head back to whip her hair away from her face. "Making progress," she said, grinning. "Does anyone have an Olympic caliber timing device?" She was laughing to herself as she swam back to the boat and hoisted herself up, kicking her legs like a mermaid as she swung them onto the swim platform.

Callie's tube floated close to Sunny's and she grasped the strap of her suit and pulled her close. "You don't mind that I stare at her when she does that push-up do you? I'm crazy about backs."

"I'm hoping that trick of making her suit into a thong sticks around," Sunny said thoughtfully. "If I'd known she'd wear one, I would have bought one to start with."

A frown forced Callie's brows closer together. "You buy her clothes?"

"Once in a while. She's an outdoor guide, Callie. She doesn't own anything dressy, and if I could convince her to buy anything for herself, she'd never wear it again."

"Give me a break! They have summer where she's from. I'm sure she could get some use out of a swimsuit."

"She brought two of them," Sunny said. "Both standard issue tank suits. I wanted to see more skin, so I bought her one I thought she'd look sexy in. I was right," she stressed. "Damn, look at those thighs when she pushes herself up on the deck. They're like iron."

"Can't," Callie said, her gaze locked on Devin. "I can't get past her waist."

Teresa paddled over and tugged on the little rope than dangled from Callie's float, allowing her to stay close. Then she filled her empty beer bottle with water and dumped it onto her girlfriend's head. "I can *see* you ogling Devin," she said, dipping the bottle and repeating the dousing. She turned her head to make eye contact with Sunny. "She's convinced anyone who looks like that would just lie on her back and expect you to service her in bed." She laughed as Callie grabbed her and tried to knock her off her float. "She's wrong, isn't she?" They both shrieked as they fell off their floats, then flailed around, trying to climb back aboard.

"Wrong, wrong, wrong," Sunny said. "You couldn't be more wrong. She's as generous in bed as she is the rest of the time. Sorry," she said, pausing for an instant. "Not sorry."

There was a gas barbecue grill up on the top deck, and Devin appointed herself grill cook while nearly everyone else went downstairs to either help prepare side dishes or have another drink.

The roof kept the sun off quite well, but it also trapped the smoke just enough to make it uncomfortable, but not dangerous. So Devin was a little surprised to find that Callie hadn't gone downstairs with the rest of the gang. She was sipping on a beer, and she tipped the neck of the bottle Devin's way.

"Want me to get you a fresh one?" Callie asked. "You look a little low."

"I'm good. As soon as I finish, I'm going to jump in the water again, and I don't want to be any drunker."

"You're drunk? You look stone-cold sober."

Devin waggled a hand. "I'm a long way from drunk, but I don't like to do risky things when I'm not sharp." She shrugged. "You can't spend years trying to police your clients and not realize the same rules apply to you."

Callie put her hand on Devin's shoulder and squeezed it before grabbing a plastic chair and straddling it. "I'm really sorry you had the bad luck of having Hank as a client. I know you shouldn't talk ill of the dead, but it was only a matter of time before he did something moronic."

"Thanks." She focused on the burgers and sausages that sizzled on the grill, deciding there was nothing more to say about Hank.

"But I'm glad you and Sunny have gotten close. She needs someone like you."

"Meaning?" It was clear Callie had a message to impart, and Devin wasn't in the mood to play cat-and-mouse.

Callie tipped her head back and finished her beer in a few long swallows. "Someone who doesn't make her grovel," she said, mouth pursed.

Devin thought about Callie's words while she flipped everything over. "I can't guess what that means. Who's made her grovel?"

"Everyone," she said flatly. "I've been after her for years to go to therapy and try to figure out why she accepts so little, but she won't even consider it."

Nodding, Devin said, "That wouldn't be my thing, either. I've got plenty of people to talk to. I'm not paying a stranger to listen to my secrets."

"Well, Sunny doesn't have as many. Her mom's such a narcissist she barely realizes Sunny exists, Tiffany just uses her as a babysitter, and Brittany ignores her until she needs something. Some family," she groused.

"I didn't…" Devin chewed on her lower lip for a second, torn between agreeing and refusing to engage. She quickly decided it was better to keep her mouth shut. "Sunny doesn't complain about them," she said, which was true.

"She doesn't complain about much. Probably because she doesn't think she deserves much."

Devin gave Callie a long look, having to fan the smoke away to see her clearly. Who was she referring to? Clearly not Sunny. "Um, it sounds like you're describing someone with a really shitty sense of self-esteem. That's not Sunny."

"It is," Callie said forcefully. "You just haven't known her long enough to see it. I've watched her jump through hoops for women, just to have them treat her like crap. But she takes it, and keeps trying to make them happy."

"She's not like that at all with me."

“That’s because you’re not her type.”

“I’m not? Damn,” Devin said, a little under her breath. “How does she treat women she’s into?”

Callie shook her head. “She obviously likes you, Devin, but you were thrown together in a way. If she had to pick, she’d choose her usual—an emotionally unavailable woman she chases but can’t ever catch.” Her eyes narrowed. “You’re just physically unavailable, which might be a new twist.”

“She sure doesn’t talk about Morgan as someone who treated her badly. She was crazy about her.”

“I know. I was there.” Callie stared at her until Devin made eye contact again. “I was there the whole time Morgan was jerking her around during law school, and I was the one who spent hours on the phone with her when Sunny was living down here, trying to decide if Morgan would ever be able to commit.”

“I didn’t know that,” Devin said quietly as she absently tended to her grill. “I thought they had a great relationship.”

“It had its moments,” she admitted. “But Morgan wanted to be totally in the closet with her family. I mean totally. When she finally agreed to live together, she made Sunny promise to hide all of her stuff and clear out when her family came to visit. Sunny wasn’t allowed to answer the phone, have her name on the buzzer…nothing that would let them find out. And she took that bullshit because that’s all Morgan would ever offer.”

The fire was getting the better of the burgers, and Devin removed them to a clean plate. While rearranging the sausages at the edge of the grill to allow them to cook for a while longer, she said, “Why’d she settle for so little?” She met Callie’s eyes and added, “She’s an awesome woman. Kind, thoughtful, giving, playful, supportive.” She felt her mouth quirk up in a grin. “Not to mention gorgeous.”

Callie spent a minute tapping her empty bottle onto the metal leg of the grill, rapping out a quiet tattoo. “When your dad abandons you, and your mom forces you to raise your little sisters, it’s easy to lose sight of the fact that you’re important.” She stood again and gave Devin a slap on the back. “I can see you think she is. I hope some of that gets in and she believes it too—even after you take off.”

Devin watched her leave, as puzzled as she was surprised by what Callie had said. How could anyone as bright and clever as Sunny not know how fantastic she was? When they met, if Devin had been forced to guess Sunny's biggest flaw, she would have bet money she'd be overly self-involved. But that was the furthest thing from the truth. Sunny was a giver, always trying to make sure other people were taken care of. The question that Devin had no way of answering was whether that instinct came from a not-so-healthy place.

After dinner, the whole group sat in the living area, watching a movie someone had brought. Devin sat on the far end of the "L" part of the sectional so that people who were more interested could face the screen. As she'd expected, she couldn't keep her eyes open. But Sunny was next to her, and she put her arm around Devin's shoulders and urged her head onto her chest. In seconds, the ambient sounds grew distant, then the words lost meaning and she felt herself melt into Sunny's body.

The sectional shook enough to wake Devin, and she blinked her eyes open to see that they were alone. "Did I sleep through a whole movie?" she asked, her voice soft and raspy.

"And the last innings of the Rangers game. You'd still be asleep, but I was trying to pry myself away so I could pee."

Devin flopped over in the opposite direction, letting her head land on the arm of the sofa. "I'll be here when you get back."

Sunny patted her as she got up and raced for the bathroom, and while she was gone Devin tried to wake up enough to at least walk to their bedroom. She hated to rouse herself once she was out, often finding herself fully alert and unable to return to sleep. Tonight, trying to tamp down thoughts and memories of the day didn't work, and she was sitting up running her hands through her hair to get the tangles out when Sunny returned.

"Ooo, you're awake," she said, gently sitting again and putting her hand on Devin's cheek. "Lie down and I'll rub your back."

"I'm up." She stood and started to pick up the glasses and bottles people had left on the tables. "What time is it?"

"Eleven. Everyone's up on the top deck, looking at the full moon. Want to join them?"

Devin set the glasses in the sink, turned and opened her arms. As always, Sunny stepped into her embrace and nuzzled against her shoulder, purring like a kitten.

"I love being hugged."

"We're both lucky, since I love hugging you. I'll go up if you want to, but I'd rather be alone. Is that cool?"

"Sure. Want to go to our room?"

"Uh-huh. As long as I'm up…" She let her fingers crawl up under Sunny's roomy top, caressing her bare skin. "We might as well do something fun."

"You don't have to talk me into it. Let's go." Sunny took her hand and they went down the hall to their room. After taking turns using the bath, they met in bed.

Sunny grasped her roughly and tossed Devin onto her back, a trick she loved to perform. Her legs were amazingly strong and she knew how to use them to her advantage, always surprising Devin a little when she felt herself being tossed around so easily.

"You're mine now," Sunny proclaimed, looming over her and dipping her head to kiss her soundly.

"You're not going to hear any arguments." Devin wrapped her arms around Sunny's neck and pulled her onto her body. When their bare skin touched for the first time she always got a jolt of sensation, creating a real spike in her heart rate. But tonight she wasn't able to quiet her thoughts like she usually did. There was no easy slide into a sensual cloud. Just a few nagging thoughts bugging her.

"Um, can we talk for a minute?"

Sunny dropped to her side, then lifted her head and gazed at Devin with a concerned look on her face. "What's wrong?"

"Nothing. Nothing at all." She started to stroke her back, finding that always centered her. "I was talking to Callie earlier and she said some things that surprised me."

Sunny slapped a hand over her face. "Oh, God, what did she say? I should never have left you alone with someone who's known me my whole adult life. She knows where all of the bodies are buried."

Devin pulled her hand away and placed a soft kiss to her lips. "No bodies. She just said something about you basically raising your sisters. Is that true?"

Sunny gazed at her for a long while, finally nodding. "I told you about how it was after my dad left. We talked about it right after you got here."

Devin looked into Sunny's wary eyes, searching them for information. "You told me about your dad leaving, but you didn't tell me what happened after he left."

"Isn't it obvious?"

She seemed to think it truly was, but Devin couldn't begin to guess how their lives had changed. "Not in the least. Was your mom working at the time?"

"My mom's dream was to marry a successful professional, have a few kids, then enjoy the perks of the upper middle class. She almost got there, then had the rug yanked from under her."

Devin sat up taller and leaned on an arm. "Is this okay to talk about? You don't seem very…" She didn't have a word to characterize how Sunny seemed, but she certainly didn't look like she wanted to talk.

She let out a sigh and rolled onto her back, lifting a knee and crossing the other foot over it. "You got me all charged up while I was watching you go down that slide. I've been thinking about getting you alone ever since."

"I'm wide awake now," Devin said. "We can talk a little, then use our mouths for something that'll get our heart rates pounding."

"All right." Another heavy sigh left her lips, then she gazed at Devin, waiting for a specific question.

"What did your mom do when your dad left? You said they met at work, right? So she must have had some skills."

"She was a receptionist, but most companies stopped needing receptionists by the time she was looking for work again. So she worked a bunch of shit jobs while I watched my sisters."

"Why you? *You* were young enough to have needed watching."

Well, all of our local relatives were off-limits." She thrust a thumb at her chest. "That left me."

"Huh? What do you mean your local relatives were off-limits?"

"I told you this. I'm sure I did."

"I'm sure you didn't. So tell me now."

Clearly reluctant, Sunny lay on her back and gazed up at the ceiling. "My dad's parents lived in Dallas, as did his brother. We saw them pretty often. You know...family birthdays, holidays, all of that stuff."

"Of course."

"Well," she said, now speaking quickly, "my momma blamed them or had a fight with them or something, because we didn't see them again after my daddy left."

Devin sat up like she'd been yanked by the hair. "You couldn't see your grandparents?"

"No," she said quietly. "I never saw them again. My grandmother died when I'd just starting high school, and my grandfather just lasted a year or so after she passed."

"And you didn't try to contact them?"

Shooting her an annoyed look, Sunny said, "My momma would have tanned my hide if I'd so much as considered it. I would have once I was out of the house, but they were gone by then."

"God damn," Devin said, feeling a little sick to her stomach. "You lost your dad and your grandparents on the same day."

"My uncle and aunt and two cousins too. I've never heard from any of them. I guess I should follow up, but I've kind of let it go."

This was too much to process, so Devin went back to her initial question. "So you had to watch your sisters...all the time?"

"All the time. My mom put Brittany in some crappy pre-school program, and I had to grab Tiffany and run over there the minute school was out to get them both home. Momma didn't trust me to cook, so I made sandwiches for dinner. Then I had to help Tiffany with her homework, give Brittany a bath, and make sure they were both in bed by the time Momma got home."

"You were just a kid," Devin said, with her heart clutching in sympathy.

"So?" She sounded…jaded. That was the first time Devin had heard that tone from her and it sounded so damned odd.

"So…that was pretty shitty of your mom to throw all of that onto you. Especially when she probably could have gotten some help from your grandparents if she hadn't cut them off."

"Yeah. That's all true. So what am I supposed to do? Feel sorry for myself?"

"No," Devin soothed, then corrected herself. "Yeah. Maybe you should feel sorry for yourself. You went from being a little girl to being a junior mother in a matter of days. That's just not right."

Sunny spoke again, quietly, with a faraway character to her voice. "We had to move, since Momma couldn't pay the mortgage on our house. So we had to change schools in the middle of the year. That sucked. All of my friends…gone."

"Oh, Sunny," Devin soothed, reaching out to hold her close. "That's awful. Just awful."

"It was hard for all of us. We moved to a crappy little two bedroom place in an iffy neighborhood. I guess that's all we could afford. No air conditioning," she added, like that was an afterthought.

"No air conditioning? In Dallas?"

"Nope. After a year or two we got a window unit that Momma put in her bedroom. We pretty much lived in that one room when it was hot out."

"Damn," Devin said softly. "I hope there were trees around so you could go outside and be in the shade."

"Couldn't. We had to come home the second school was out and lock ourselves in." She shrugged again. "Like I said, the neighborhood was…not kid friendly."

"And all of this happened in a matter of weeks," Devin said, her mind reeling.

"It had to have. I know kids' memories are unreliable, but I know Daddy was thrown out with no notice. Momma was always complaining that he cleaned out their checking account when he left, so she had to have started working right away." Her brow furrowed as she seemed to think about something. "I don't know if we owned the house we lived in or what, but I'm certain we left quickly. Maybe we'd just been renting and ran away from the lease."

"That's such a sad story," Devin murmured. She pulled Sunny to her again and kissed all across her face. "You must have been so confused."

"Yeah. That's a good word for it. I was confused. But so were my sisters. I at least got to have a father for a good part of my childhood. Brittany doesn't remember what our dad looked like, and God knows all of the photos were burned."

Devin had lost every bit of sexual desire that she'd had. But she didn't want to admit that Sunny's story had upset her. So she pulled her close and gently rubbed her back, waiting for a sign that she was still feeling frisky. It never came.

In a relatively short time, Sunny migrated across the bed and was now plastered to Devin's side, sound asleep. She didn't do that often, but sometimes she seemed to need the reassurance of lying close enough to feel Devin's heartbeat.

Gently, she started to stroke Sunny's head, usually able to touch her without waking her. With a soft mew, Sunny draped an arm and a leg across her body, trapping her. But this was one trap Devin didn't mind being caught in.

If only she could whisk Sunny away from all of the things that troubled her. She had an image of them living in her cabin in Maine, far from demanding relatives and a tension-laden job.

Then reality crowded out the nice thoughts, and Devin's heart started to beat faster as anxiety made her brain race as quickly as her heart.

If she couldn't go back to guiding, what could she do to earn a living? Next to nothing. There were plenty of people willing to pay for a moderately good handy-woman in Dallas, but the same wasn't true at home. There were people who had far greater skills than she did, as well as years of experience. And even if she could find some jobs, they wouldn't pay well. So she'd have to find something else. But you couldn't support a woman on what you earned cleaning motel rooms or serving meals. Especially not when most of the motels and many of the restaurants closed for a third of the year.

She tried to think of her happy place just to get rid of these distressing thoughts. But it had gotten harder and harder to conjure up images of clear, cool, running water, or the scent of the woods after a rain. It had been so long since she'd been in nature that her connection to it was fading, and that thought scared her as much as any she'd had that night. Her instinct was to get up and go outside to clear her head. But they were on a crowded boat on a crowded lake in a crowded state, and she couldn't think of a single way to achieve the zen state that used to be hers for the taking.

On Sunday morning, Sunny woke to the smell of coffee being wafted under her nose. "Want some?" Devin's soft voice tickled her ears. "If you don't, Lauren and Linda both love this bean. I could probably sell this cup for a couple of bucks."

Sunny opened her eyes, seeing Devin's devilish grin. "Ooo. Thanks for bringing the French press."

"I hated to grind the beans at home, but you have to give up some niceties to camp." She laughed. "Hard to believe I have the nerve to call this camping."

Sunny grasped the mug and took her first sip. "Mmm," she purred. "I know I should be able to tell the difference, but I wouldn't know you'd pre-ground the beans. Deee-licious."

"Becky and Patty are going to make breakfast. Want me to put in your order? You've got two choices—pancakes or eggs."

"I'm not very hungry." Sunny slid her hand across the mattress and snaked her fingers up the leg of Devin's shorts. "For breakfast." She wasn't very good at waggling her eyebrows, but she did it anyway, making Devin laugh.

"Really? I just ducked in here to get your breakfast order. Everyone will know…"

"Isn't vacation a time to do what we want when we want?" She made her eyebrows pop again. "Want to?"

Devin got to her feet and whipped off her shirt. "Always," she said, with her smile even perkier than it had been a few minutes ago. "Vacations are awesome," she added, unzipping her shorts and letting them fall to the ground. "And so are you."

◆

Sunny assured Devin that traffic going home would be bad no matter what time they left. So they stayed until the bitter end, returning the boat to the marina at six. Only Callie and Teresa were still aboard, with the others having been dropped off earlier in the day.

Callie and Sunny hugged and kissed each other's cheeks like it would be years before they'd see each other again, with Teresa rolling her eyes dramatically for Devin's benefit.

"Saturday night? Our house?" Callie asked as they broke apart.

"I think we're free," Sunny said. "I'll call you on the way into work in the morning."

Callie clapped her hand over Sunny's mouth. "Don't say that word! I'm on vacation until eight o'clock tomorrow morning and I don't want to think about that work-house until I have to."

"Love you," Sunny said, giving Callie and then Teresa another kiss. They both hugged Devin, then headed for the parking lot while she and Sunny turned in the keys and waited for one of the employees to check the craft out for damage.

They were on the road by six thirty, with Sunny's unpleasant prediction having been dead right. People had stayed on the lake until they simply had to leave, stuffing the little highway full of cars and trucks, all heading for the interstate.

"This part isn't going to be fun," Sunny said. She turned and met Devin's eyes. "But I had a great time. How about you?"

"Really great. It wasn't anything like I expected, but I truly enjoyed myself." She put her hand on Sunny's leg and gave it a squeeze. "My only regret is pushing you to talk about your family last night. Clearly, you don't like doing that, and I should have backed off."

"I didn't mind," Sunny said, giving her a puzzled look. "I've just never brought it up because I didn't think you'd be interested."

"Of course I'm interested! I want to know everything about you, Sunny. Can't you tell how much I like you?"

"Yeah," she said, keeping her eyes on the highway. "I can tell."

"I really am," Devin insisted. "I was going to ask more, but you seemed wrung out just from talking a little."

"I think I was tired from too much sun." She let out a chuckle. "Notice how I ignore the frozen margaritas as a contributing factor?"

"Now that you mention it…"

"But I'm wide awake and totally sober now, and we've got over three hours to kill. I'm happy to depress the heck out of you for the whole trip."

"Sounds fun, but lets stick to what I assume is a cheerier topic. How'd your mom get into organizing closets?"

Sunny started to laugh. "She would snap your neck with her bare hands if she heard you refer to it that way. She's a lifestyle consultant." She turned briefly so Devin could see her bright smile. "I guess she's been doing that for around ten years. While working at a ritzy department store in downtown Dallas, she got to know some of her clients. One thing led to another, and pretty soon she'd quit the store to work with a few of them."

"That's kind of amazing. She must charge a huge amount per hour to be able to trade a full time job for that."

Sunny nodded. "She charges a good amount."

Devin gave her a poke in the side. "Are you avoiding the question? Seems like it."

Sighing, Sunny said, "She charges enough to live well—if she did it full time."

"She doesn't?"

"She has three clients, Dev. I'd be surprised if she works more than ten hours a week."

"But she said…" She thought for a second. "I remember her saying she spent a full day with each of her clients."

"Uh-huh. She thinks three hours is a full day's work."

Devin knew where this was headed. "And you make up the difference."

"I have to," she said, letting out a tired-sounding sigh. "I co-signed for her mortgage, so I'm on the hook if she doesn't pay."

"You really pay the whole thing, don't you."

Sunny shifted in her seat, clearly wanting to avoid answering. But the silence continued on until she must have gotten sick of it. “Usually. She promised to pay a thousand a month, but she rarely does.”

“And you’re okay with that?”

Giving her a quick look, she said, “She’s my momma. You can’t turn your back on family.”

Devin let the topic die. While she would have given her own mom all of the money she had to her name, or a kidney for that matter, she was one hundred percent certain that her mom wouldn’t ask if she had any other options. And that made a very big difference.

Chapter Twenty

When Sunny pressed the door handle on Monday evening she heard Devin's laugh, bright and cheerful. She was definitely on the phone, speaking fairly quietly as Sunny tiptoed down the hall. It had become a kind of game to sneak up on her, made more fun because of how exasperated Devin got when she realized she'd let her guard down. But Sunny loved knowing that the guard was down, and she exploited every opportunity to expose it.

When she poked her head into the guest room, she spied Devin lying on her belly, legs bent at the knee, ankles crossed. She looked like a teenager ignoring her homework to talk to a friend, and Sunny couldn't help but linger just outside, observing her.

"It was definitely fun," she said. "I was worried I'd hate it when I saw how many boats there were, but Sunny's friends are great. Oh! The boat had a really cool slide that I went down so many times I've got friction burns on my butt." She laughed again. "I don't know how to do things half-way, Mom. What makes you think I'll learn just because I'm in a different state?"

Sunny had to reveal herself. Surprising Devin was one thing, snooping on her was another. She knocked on the door, making Devin whip her head around and squeal.

"Damn it!" She scrambled to her feet and gave Sunny a playful glower. "She snuck up on me again," she said into the phone. "Good thing I wasn't trash-talking her." A sweet smile settled onto her face. "I know I don't, Mom." Then their eyes met and she added, "Yeah, she knows that too."

That little bit of connection made Sunny's heart skip a beat. Devin was possibly the most kind-hearted woman she'd ever met, and Sunny had a feeling she got a lot of that trait from her mom.

"Yeah, I'd better. Gotta feed the landlord. Love you too. Talk to you tomorrow." She ended the call and tossed the phone onto the bed. "I'm not buying your excuse that you just walk quietly," she said, approaching Sunny with her hands snapping like lobster claws. Those claws bit at various spots on her body, making Sunny laugh like a kid.

"Please don't tickle me," she begged. "I hate it!"

"I'm not tickling you. I'm taking big, juicy bites out of you for eavesdropping." She tucked her arms around Sunny's waist and held her loosely while gazing into her eyes. "Hungry? I made a big salad with all of your favorite vegetables."

"Famished." She kissed Devin's lips, tasting oil and vinegar and Dijon mustard, her usual homemade salad dressing. "I can taste that you've already eaten."

"Five o'clock," she said, adding a sharp slap to Sunny's butt as she headed for the kitchen. "My tummy waits for no woman."

Sunny followed her, removing her dress and jewelry as she walked. "Do you talk to your mom often?"

"Yep." Devin took the salad from the refrigerator and pulled out a plate. "Just about every day."

Sunny stopped and stared at her. "Every day?"

"Uh-huh." She was carefully composing the salad so Sunny would get equal amounts of each vegetable. Meal prep was never haphazard when Devin was in charge. "I don't want to miss any news." That made her laugh, clearly teasing about how little there was to miss in her part of Maine.

"I find that fascinating." Sunny sat on a stool located on the living room side of the pass-through to the kitchen and looked approvingly at the salad. "Nice job there. Maybe you should have taken that job cleaning the restaurant. By now you'd be a chef."

"Maybe," Devin agreed, placing the salad in front of Sunny, then moving around to her side. She sat atop the other stool and crossed an ankle over her knee. Then she poked at Sunny's butt with her bare toes. "I don't think I've ever seen you sit down to dinner in just your underwear. I like it," she added, leaning over to kiss her shoulder.

"I'm still on the phone call issue. Do you talk long?"

"Usually not. But my dad's gone, and I can tell my mom's a little lonely. She doesn't mind being alone, but she needs a lot of human interaction, so I call more often and talk a little longer."

"You're a good daughter." Sunny smiled at her. "And a very good cook."

"I'm a pretty good daughter," she admitted. "But I don't call just for my mom. I miss her. I've never really been away from home, you know. This is a unique experience."

"Um…" Sunny took her fork and carefully made sure she had a sampling of snap peas and carrot and radish firmly attached. "You disappeared for a whole month not long ago."

"Oh, yeah." She nodded. "I don't count that. That's my 'getting my head on straight' time. Then I wasn't away from home so much as I was being by myself. Different thing."

Sunny caressed her cheek, smiling when Devin's eyes closed. She loved being petted as much as a very domesticated cat did. "It probably seems like the same thing to your mom. She must miss the heck out of you."

"Yeah, she does. But this has been good for me, and if there's one thing I know, it's that my mom only wants the best for me."

Sunny leaned over and nuzzled against Devin's warm body for a minute. "I hope you know how very lucky you are."

The following Sunday morning, Devin was on her belly, slithering like a snake as she tried to escape Sunny's grip. She had her by the thighs, and was pulling hard, trying to keep her right where she wanted her.

"Give me five minutes to rest," Devin begged. "Show a little mercy!"

But Sunny was insatiable this morning. Not that that was odd. Even though they had a quickie just about every night, Sundays were their time to savor each other. They got their errands done on Saturday, usually saw friends in the evening, then slept in on Sunday. That extra time in bed almost always led to a long, playful bout of sex, with Sunny often the instigator. After spending the afternoon playing in the pool, they usually went upstairs to nap, sometimes managing another roll in the hay. That schedule would have seemed insane to Devin just a few months earlier, but since she was in Dallas to make sure Sunny recuperated, her needs took precedence. To get back into work mode on Monday, Sunny needed her weekends to be super, super chill.

The phone rang, and Devin would have let it go. She knew the distinctive rings for all of the important people in Sunny's life, and Tiffany's ring exclusively signaled some favor she wanted Sunny to perform. To date, Sunny hadn't asked for anything in return from the middle sister. In Devin's view, that was no way to run a relationship, but she hadn't spoken to Sunny about it. Families were tricky things, and it was impossible for an outsider to second-guess decisions. But that didn't mean she didn't want to take the phone and throw it against the wall.

"Yeah," Sunny said, tossing her head to send her hair back over her shoulder. Damn, she looked sexy when she did that. Her hair was flat-out gorgeous, one of her best features. When she kissed her way down Devin's body, with her shoulder-length tresses tickling down her belly…

"Today? Really, Tiffany? I can't understand why you won't give me some notice."

There was not going to be any more belly tickling this morning, even though Sunny had to be throbbing. She'd spent the last half hour focused solely on Devin, so if she could give up her own satisfaction to jump to her sister's demands, she must really have felt trapped by them.

"Fine. I need a half hour to get up and take a shower." She paused, giving the wall a peevish look. "Yes, I'm still in bed. *We're* still in bed. Sundays are the only day we have to lounge around."

That was new. She never gave Tiffany any grief for her calls. Maybe she was learning to stand up for herself a little more. "All right," she sighed. "Fifteen minutes."

Devin didn't say a thing as Sunny got up and headed for the shower.

"I'm sorry about that," she called over the sound of the water starting to heat up. She poked her head back out. "Ashton will want to spend the day at the pool, but maybe we could talk him into something more interesting. He likes theme parks…"

Devin got to her feet and walked into the bath, leaning against the sink when Sunny got in the shower. "Um, it's totally cool with me if you want to spend the day with your nephew. But don't you *need* the time to relax?"

"I do." She ducked her head under the water, and Devin watched her hair change color in an instant. Now it just looked kinda mousy blonde. The magic spell had been broken. "But my sister can't leave Ashton at home by himself."

"Isn't Brittany a member of the family? Why isn't she called on for babysitting?"

"Brittany?" Sunny laughed. "God knows what she'd let him do. I wouldn't trust her with a kid for more than ten minutes."

Tiffany had a husband who had a good job. She also had a mother and in-laws, none of whom she seemed willing to call. But Devin held her tongue. This was Sunny's day off and if she wanted to spend it listening to Ashton whine…

"So? What do you think? Pool or something else?"

Now it was getting personal. "To be honest, I'm not in the mood to hang out with Ashton. Could I borrow the car? I think I'll check out those hiking paths down by the Trinity River. The ones Teresa was telling me about when we were at the lake."

Sunny rinsed off quickly, and opened the door as she hurried to dry herself. "You don't want to spend the day together?"

"Um…" It was now or never. Devin swallowed and said, "I'd love to spend the day with you, but if I'm going to be around Ashton all day I have to set some limits with him."

"Limits?"

"Yeah. Um…we have different styles when it comes to watching kids. For one thing, it makes me nervous to be in the pool with him continually going into the deep end when he doesn't know how to tread water. If he could calm down a little, I could teach him."

Frowning, Sunny said, "You can't just tell someone to not freak out, Devin. He's afraid."

"Because he doesn't know how to swim. Once he learns, he'll be calmer."

"He takes lessons…"

Devin put her hands on Sunny's shoulders and looked into her eyes. "I don't have a lot of patience with kids who aren't..." She almost said 'polite,' but walked it back. "Who aren't pretty calm."

Sunny stared at her for a few seconds. "You're saying you don't like my nephew."

"Well," she said, really trying hard to get out of the hole she'd dug for herself, "You've got to admit he doesn't like me, right?"

"You give him a hard time!"

"I guess I do. But I don't think I can stop. Kids shouldn't be allowed to think the world revolves around them."

"He's a little boy! Do you think Tiffany ought to send him to military school? Or should she toss him out on an island with a knife and a pack of matches and wish him luck? Then he can be just like you when he grows up."

Devin stared back at her for a minute, stung by what was clearly a low blow. She was just about to tell her exactly what she thought of the kid, but pulled back. Once those words were out, you couldn't retrieve them. "I'll stay if you'll let me set some reasonable limits. Final offer."

As she stalked back into the bedroom, Sunny snapped, "Rejected! And I need my car in case something happens to him."

Devin grabbed underwear, shorts, a shirt, a baseball cap and her hiking sandals and took the pile of clothes into the living room. It took her about a minute to get dressed, then she took her wallet and her phone and was gone before Sunny reappeared. That was probably a good thing. Snapping off sharp comments when your feelings were hurt never helped in the long run. A lesson Sunny obviously hadn't learned.

Devin followed her own agenda, not coming home until seven o'clock that night. The apartment was cool and quiet, so Ashton was obviously gone. She'd gone about halfway down the hall when Sunny's quiet voice said, "Devin?"

She kept walking, finding Sunny in her bedroom with the TV on low. A movie played in the background, but Sunny was lying on her side, facing the door, clearly unable to see it.

"Hi," Devin said. She was fully willing to act like they hadn't fought and just move on. Trying that out, she said, "Did you have a good day?"

Sunny shook her head, then started to cry. By the time Devin reached the bed tears were rolling down her cheeks and her shoulders were shaking. "I don't like spending time with Ashton, either. He's a huge brat, but I can't complain because I let him get away with as much as my sister does." She burrowed into Devin's lap, unable to meet her gaze. "I'm sorry I snapped at you. He'd be a much better kid if he was raised like you were."

"I wasn't put onto an island when I was young," Devin said, still wounded by the comment. "But I *was* raised to show respect for adults. That doesn't come naturally. You've got to drum that into kids."

"I know… I guess," she said. Looking up, she added, "That's not true. I don't know the first thing about how to raise a well-adjusted kid. I did a shitty job raising my sisters, and now my sister's doing a shitty job of raising her kid. That's obviously the Thompson way."

"Hey." Devin ran her fingers through Sunny's hair, trying to soothe her. "You were a kid just trying to keep your sisters from getting hit by a car or jumping out a window. You weren't their mom."

"I was all they had," she grumbled. "They were in bed most nights when Momma got home."

"That's water under the bridge now. You can't change the past, but you can try to calm Ashton down." She kept stroking her head, keeping her voice low and soft. "Kids are like dogs. They want a pack leader, and when they don't have one they get frightened and try to be in charge. That never works," she added.

"He's not my kid. How do you impose rules that a kid doesn't have to follow at home?"

"It's not easy," Devin admitted. "But he'd be happier if he learned some limits from someone. Why not make this a place where he feels safe?"

"Can we talk about this later?" She struggled to sit up, managing with a boost from Devin. "I'm starving. How about you?"

"I ate. At five," she said, smiling so Sunny would understand that she was teasing.

"Well, I had chicken bites at noon, but I need something now." She looked at the clock on the bedside table. "Want to go get ice cream?"

"Sure," Devin said, even though she'd already had a cone. Sometimes, having ice cream twice in one day was a very good idea.

Chapter Twenty-One

Sunny was clearing off her desk before heading home on a sultry Friday night. She had the shades pulled down to stop the sun from making the office too hot for the air conditioning to keep up with, but it was still hot. She wore sleeveless tops to the office in the summer, and if she could have been sure she was alone, she might have taken off her slacks. But she only had a few things to finish before she was out of there, so she tried to focus.

Her phone rang, and she answered absently. "Sunny Thompson."

"Hi, Sunny." The voice was so familiar she almost screamed. "It's Thomas Perry."

"Hi," she said, with her voice breaking. She'd met Hank's brother a few times, and it wasn't just their voices that were similar. He was also an attorney, a good one by all accounts, and he had Hank's drive and bluster.

"I'm trying to help Angelica plan for her future," he said. "Besides her personally suing the outfit who organized the trip, and the woman who let my brother drown, we've been thinking the firm should sue as well. It was a business trip, after all…"

"It was," she agreed, fighting to stay calm and organize her thoughts.

"Well, what do you say? As the surviving partner, you'd probably have to bring the suit."

"I can't do that, Thomas," she said, suddenly chilly from the sweat that had broken out on her skin. "Neither Devin nor the outfitter showed the least bit of negligence toward your brother. I understand Angelica wants to be compensated for her loss, but the firm had plenty of insurance on Hank for exactly this reason. As you said, this was a business trip, so I assume the clause that allows for a five times payout is in effect."

"My brother was a healthy, athletic, young man, Sunny. When you wind up dead, someone's at fault."

"I suppose that's true," she admitted. "And I think you know who I believe that is. Hank was warned and warned and warned again. Devin lectured us so many times we were all sick of it. But he walked across the lake despite my and Julian's begging him not to go. We begged him, Thomas. He was an adult, and he made a choice. That's *not* negligence on Devin's part."

"She wasn't there," he said, with his voice gaining some heat. "She knew he was impulsive, but she left him. *That's* negligence."

"No, that's Devin doing her job. She was finding a way to get us back without suffering too much from the storm that was coming in. There's no duty of care to be stuck to each person like a shadow. That would require three guides, none of whom ever had to dash into the woods to pee."

"Then you should have had three. Or four. I don't give a fuck how many people you had to involve, my brother shouldn't have been allowed to drown!"

"I agree he shouldn't have drown," she said quietly. "But I don't agree that it was plausible to prevent him from getting into trouble. When you're an impetuous adult, you've got to accept the risks."

"You're saying you refuse to take the lead on this. Is that right?"

"I'm saying more than that." She took a calming breath. "I'm saying that neither Devin nor Edie was negligent, and I'll do whatever I can to defend them."

"Defend *them*," he said flatly. "You won't help your own firm out, but you'll go out of your way for them."

"That's right. They did nothing wrong, and I won't support your going after them. It's not just an anonymous insurance company, Thomas. These are real people. A small businesswoman and a guide who risked her life to save Julian. And if I hadn't physically tackled her, Devin would have drown too. She was going to dive into that icy water to try to resuscitate your brother, even though she admitted the chance of his being alive were infinitesimal!"

"Why didn't you let her?" he asked, his voice breaking. "Why didn't you let her try?"

"Because Hank was dead," she said, "and I didn't want Devin to die in vain."

"You can't stop Angelica from suing as an individual," he said.

"I know that, Thomas. But I'll testify for Devin. I'll bet Julian will too."

"You'd better be prepared for a fight," he said, his voice taking on a cold edge.

"I'd rather not fight," she admitted, "but I'm perfectly willing to go to the mat on this one. Your brother was reckless, and he had an accident. No one but Hank is to blame for his decisions on that day."

"Thanks for being so understanding," he snapped. "You're all heart. I'll tell Angelica you'd be happy to have her thrown out of her house."

"The insurance policy is easily big enough to pay off that house. If she sells the firm, that'll give her a nest egg. I feel awful for her, Thomas, but ruining other peoples' lives to give her more money isn't something I can be a part of."

He slammed the phone down, making her ear ring for a few seconds. Shakily, she got to her feet and locked her door. Then she took off her slacks and stretched out on the sofa near the window. She'd be home late, but she couldn't think of driving until she cooled off—in every sense.

After a quick call to Devin to tell her to go ahead and eat, Sunny made another call, one that hit her with a slap of guilt. "Julian?" she asked when he answered his cell phone. "It's Sunny."

"Hi," he said, calm and concise as always.

"Do you have a few minutes to talk?"

"Now?"

"Yes. I'd like to come over to your apartment if you don't mind. It won't take long, but I'd like to do it in person."

"You know the address?"

"If it's the same one we have on file, yes."

"All right," he said, sounding leery. "Can you come at seven?"

"Sure," she said, hanging up. She was sitting right in front of his building, but she didn't mind waiting fifteen minutes. After turning off her car, she rolled the windows down, then eased the sunroof back to stir the limp air into some signs of life. Julian's building was a small one, just three floors, with probably no more than four apartments per floor. Sunny had learned a lot about housing from making real estate deals, and she hated the fact that developers couldn't make money on small buildings any longer. Everything had to be huge now, and she felt Dallas was suffering from that. Idly thinking of lot size and density, she snapped alert when one of her paralegals exited the building. What was Martina Rodrigues doing in Julian's building? Nodding to herself, it suddenly became clear why Julian had never brought a date to a work function. While they didn't have a prohibition against dating co-workers, he was naturally a very private guy. That wasn't a bad trait for a lawyer.

At seven, she walked over to the entry door and pressed the button under his name. After she'd climbed to the second floor, a door opened and Julian waved. He was still in his suit pants, with his tie loosened, top button undone.

"Hi," she said, pausing to see if he gave any indication he wanted to hug. He didn't, so she just walked in. "I've wanted to call a thousand times, but I…"

"You don't know what to say." He smiled. "Neither do I. That's why I left, you know. I can't stand these awkward silences."

"Then let's not have one," she said. "Mind if I sit?" His apartment was decorated very precisely, with lots of bright, primary colors. Everything was in its place, as neat as a pin.

"Please. Can I get you a drink? I just opened a bottle of wine."

"Sure," she said. She didn't comment when he brought a bottle over with more than half of it missing, and poured her a generous amount. They clinked their glasses together, but neither offered a toast. What was there to say?

"Um, I wanted to talk to you, because I wanted to hear your thoughts on Angelica suing the outfitter and Devin for negligence."

"Devin ought to sue Hank's estate," he said, his normally honey colored skin turning pink in a flash. "I've thought about it."

"You have?" She took another drink, needing the alcohol to reach her bloodstream in a hurry.

"I have," he said soberly. "I probably won't, but if I didn't think I'd be taking food out of his wife's mouth, I'd have already filed."

"You could sue the firm," she said, flinching even as she said it. "We're insured."

He shrugged. "I'm thinking about it, but I'm not sure it's worth the trouble. Why are you bringing it up at this point?"

"Because Thomas, Hank's brother, called this afternoon to ask me to sue on behalf of the firm. I refused, but that won't stop him. He's Angelica's advisor now, I suppose, and he wants cash."

"Don't we all?" he asked dryly. "I was months away from making partner, but here I am, basically starting over with a new firm. I've been set back at least two years."

"I'm sorry for that," Sunny said. "I really am."

"I hope you understand why I had to leave," he said, not meeting her eyes. "I just couldn't walk by his office every day. I would have been at the shrink three time a week." He rolled his eyes. "Once is enough."

"Are you doing okay?" she asked.

"Yeah. Pretty okay. I don't like my new firm as well, but I'm working on some interesting deals." He finally met her gaze full-on. "How about you?"

"I'm doing all right," she said.

"Do you have anyone to talk to?"

"Yeah," she said, smiling in spite of herself. "I have someone wonderful in my life." She was going to brush past the details, but she decided to be honest. "About a month after I got home, Devin came down to stay with me."

His eyes popped open and he blinked a few times. "She did?"

"Uh-huh. We both needed someone to talk to, and I think she needed to be away from Maine for a while. We're..." She shrugged. "We're involved, but I assume she'll go back. Maybe soon."

"I liked her," he said softly. "Besides the fact that she saved my life, she seemed like she'd be someone you could really rely on. I'm glad you have her."

She let out a nervous laugh. "I'm not sure I have her, but you're right. She's definitely someone I can rely on."

"I should have done more than send her a note," he said, breaking eye contact again. "But what else can you say?"

"She was touched by your note, Julian. You don't need to do another thing."

He took a breath. "So? How can I help? I can't believe you came over just to give me a status update."

"No, I'm…" She met his eyes and said, "I'd like to present a united front to Thomas. If he knows we'll both testify on Devin's behalf, he might advise Angela to just take the insurance settlement and her half of the partnership and let it go."

"She's selling?" His dark brows hiked up.

"I think so. She's got fifty-one percent, so she's in charge."

Julian leaned over and extended his hand. As they shook, he said, "I'm sure Angelica needs cash. She's never had a job, and I'm sure she doesn't want to get one. But Devin didn't do a thing wrong. I'm on your side."

"Thank you," she said, holding onto his warm hand for another few seconds. "I know it'll be hard if we have to testify, but we'll get through it."

His voice broke slightly when he said, "If I got through those minutes when I was halfway in my grave, I can get through this."

An hour later, while she was picking at the tomato, watermelon and feta cheese salad Devin had made, Sunny considered what she was going to reveal about her day. When Devin put her fingers on the back of her neck to give her a little tickle, she turned to her. "Hi," Sunny said.

"Missed you," Devin said. "Wanna talk about your day? Did something big come up?"

"A few things," she said, deciding in that moment to lie to Devin for the first time. "Nothing I can't handle."

She scooted closer and rested her head on Sunny's shoulder. "That's not surprising. You're a lot stronger than you look."

As Sunny put another bite of a perfect tomato into her mouth, she let those words roll around in her head. It was taking her some time to come into her own, but Devin was one hundred percent right. She was a hell of a lot stronger than she looked, and Thomas was going to find out just how determined she was when called upon to protect someone she cared for.

A week later, Sunny was on a call with a client when her cell phone buzzed with Devin's distinctive ring. Digging through her purse while trying to keep track of the conversation, she took a look at the screen and froze.

My grandfather had an accident. Have to go home. Five o'clock flight. Sorry I can't wait.

The call went on for another half hour, but Sunny was tempted not to bill for her time, given that her contribution had been close to nil. When it was over, she hung up and dialed Devin.

"What happened?" she asked, nearly breathless.

"It's not awful," she said, with her calm tone of voice relieving some of Sunny's anxiety. "Gramps was out fishing and hooked something big. It flipped and went in the other direction, knocking him off balance. He landed on the gunwale, breaking a pair of ribs and bruising a couple more."

"That's all?"

Devin didn't respond right away, and when she did there was more than a hint of annoyance in her tone. "Most people his age who took a fall like that would be in the hospital waiting for a hip replacement."

"He's not in the hospital?"

"His regular doctor checked him out at home. It looks like he'll be fine, but he's gonna need some help until he can drive again."

"Why can't he drive? You don't need your ribs to steer a car."

"You do when you've got a manual transmission. There's no way he can shift without pain."

Ideas for how to solve this seemingly simple problem started to zip through her head. "Your grandmother's there, right? Can't she drive him around?"

"No," Devin said slowly. "It's not obvious, but she's got macular degeneration. Gram hasn't been able to drive for a couple of years." She paused. "I'm *going*, Sunny. My family needs me."

She knew she should shut up, but Sunny couldn't stop. "You said there are guys who love to drive people around. If you can't afford that, I'll gladly help out—"

"I'm not asking for solutions. I'm going. Today."

Sunny closed her eyes and tried to think. In her soul, she was sure Devin wouldn't return, and her instinct, so fierce it roared through her body, was to hang on no matter what. "What about your job?"

"I quit."

"What?"

"I told my shift manager I needed to go, and she said if she let me take off for a family emergency, everyone would—so I quit."

"Devin! That's not like you!"

There was a significant pause. Then a quiet but steely voice responded, "You're honestly surprised that I put my family over a minimum wage job? A job I keep only because it lets me be around people for a few hours a day?"

"No, no, of course not, but quitting with no notice? It'll be hard for them to replace you." She took a breath, giving it one last try. "If you'd wait a few days…"

"I can't believe you don't know this about me, but let me make it super clear. When any member of my family needs me—I'm there."

"So they *asked* you to come?"

"I'm not sure what's going on with you, but this isn't a negotiation. Taking a fall is tough on an older person. I need to see him for myself."

"But you can't even get a flight to Bangor today. Why don't you wait un —"

"My mom's driving to Portland to pick me up," she said, cutting her off. "I'll text you when I get there." It sounded like she was just going to hang up!

"Devin!"

"I'm right here," she said, still patient, but Sunny could tell that was running thin.

"I'll miss you."

She let out a breath, like she'd just that minute stopped to consider that. "I'll miss you too," she said softly. "I'll talk to you later, okay?"

"What about your other jobs?" Sunny gritted her teeth, terrified to hear the answer.

"We'll see. I don't mean to cut you off, but I've really gotta go. I'll call you tomorrow, okay?"

"Okay." Her voice was almost a whisper. Then the line went dead. Sunny sat stock-still at her desk for a minute, then leaned back and rocked for a while, thinking. It *sounded* like Devin was coming back, or at least intended to. But being back home, surrounded by the people she loved and the places that gave her life meaning, was going to be an overwhelming temptation. One Sunny was nearly certain she'd be unable to resist.

After an hour layover in Atlanta, Devin was finally on the plane that would take her to Portland. As Sunny had so insistently suggested, she should have waited for morning, when she could have gotten a flight to Bangor. But once she'd heard about the accident, she simply had to go. A day's wait wasn't something she could tolerate.

Once the plane was in the air, she could relax a little and not worry about whether it would actually get its butt off the ground. But relaxing just let her anxiously ruminate about her grandparents. Neither was a good patient, although Gram had gotten better at complying with doctor's orders since her sight had started giving her trouble. But Gramps was independent even for a Mainer, and they were a notoriously autonomous people.

Her mind drifted to Sunny and how tone-deaf she'd been about the whole thing. For a woman who wouldn't say 'no' to the most outrageous requests from her own family, she seemed to think Devin should just throw some money at this and hope it all worked out. That would *never* happen. Jobs would come and go, but family was forever.

A flight attendant came by with a cart and Devin bought a beer, mostly for her nerves. She sat in the cramped seat, thinking about her weeks in Dallas. In some ways, it had been like the best extremely long weekend she'd ever had with a woman. During her years of hooking up simply to fulfill her physical needs, she'd only met one or two women who came close to Sunny's enthusiasm for sex, much less her talent. But it had been more than that in so many ways. Being as close as they'd been had been amazingly nice. If she could get down to see her on a monthly basis, they could make something out of this. Something long-term. Something exclusive. But you only had to be on a plane from five until midnight to realize how *very* far away Texas was.

It was truly stupid to insist on going to her cabin. They hadn't even gotten to her parents' house until two thirty in the morning. But Devin needed to sleep in her own bed, in her own cabin, on her own lake. Thank goodness her mom was such a patient person. God knew she needed to be.

A text to Edie earlier in the day had produced one of her rental canoes lying on the bank of the lake. It was an expensive one, but she knew Edie hadn't thought twice about having someone cart it across the street and leave it there. No one would steal a canoe. That just wasn't done.

All she had with her was a small backpack with some toiletries and a change of clothes. But that was all she'd need. The most important things were all inside that cabin—quiet, peace, solitude.

After flipping over the canoe, she gripped the gunwales and pushed away from the bank, then hopped in and started to paddle. *Bliss.* Within three strokes, her entire mood began to shift. By the time she'd traveled a quarter mile, she was completely tranquil—a state she honestly hadn't achieved even once since the day she'd left home.

The entire lake was hers. Quiet as a church, with only an occasional sound from some animal looking for a mate or repelling an enemy. The sound of her paddle dipping into the water, the tinkling *plink, plink, plink* as she shifted to slip it in again was more melodic than a symphony. Chills chased down her spine as a sliver of a moon glinted off the glassy surface of the best lake in the world. She was home.

Normally, Devin was up well before the dawn, always anxious to get up and out. Today, she lounged in bed, napping on and off, luxuriating in the warmth of her little spot. A memory flicked through her head, of the ways she'd sought out solitude even as a kid. Any time she could construct a makeshift fortress out of tree branches, or came upon a big cardboard box she could hide in, she was happy. Her parents still laughed about her as a toddler, crawling under the sofa in the living room and just hanging out, not even taking a toy with her. She'd simply always needed her own little place.

Surprisingly, thoughts of Sunny sharing her little space started to drift in. It made no sense at all, but Devin idly wondered how she could expand to create room for another person. It wouldn't be easy, or cheap, but she could add a second floor…

Then the impracticalities of the idea started to seep in. Sunny would have to get a job. But what could she do? The last thing Greenville needed was another attorney. But if she *could* get a job, they'd have to buy a house. Sunny wouldn't be able to live in a cabin without a bathroom for long, and they'd need a place to stay when the lake was inaccessible.

Then the dark thoughts started to seep in. Devin knew she'd have to get some kind of job as well, but there was so little to choose from. Could she stand having to drive to Bangor to work at Walmart? Sure. Most people put up with a hell of a lot worse. But how could she do that and not think about what she wanted to do. What she was *made* to do?

Unable to get her head around any of that, and determined not to let her worries ruin her day, she went to splash some cool water onto her face. After a bracing sponge bath, she put on shorts and a T-shirt, covered herself in bug repellent, then went outside to free her canoe from where she'd secured it to the porch. It took a few minutes to set up a proper tow for the canoe Edie had lent her, but she got it done, then paddled over to shore.

The loaner was heavier than it looked, but she liked the challenge of powering it over her head, then scampering across the street. She was winded when she eased it down onto the big deck, then stormed up the stairs and threw the door open. "Where's my breakfast?" she called out. "I came all the way from Dallas for a cappuccino!"

With a gleeful cry, Edie raced out, not stopping until she nearly knocked Devin to the ground.

"I'm not gonna be much help to Gramps if you break *my* ribs," she said, chuckling.

Edie gave her a playful swat, then pulled away from the hug. "I can't even tell you how much I missed you, so I won't try. I've got blueberries and blackberries from my garden. Do you want both in your yogurt?"

"I do indeed." Devin draped an arm across her shoulders as they walked to the coffee bar. "Boy, it's nice to be back home. I always knew how much I loved it here, but I couldn't have predicted how much I'd miss it. I'm a fish out of water in Dallas, Edie."

While pulling things out of the little under-counter fridge, Edie gave her that very welcome half-smile. "But something's keeping you there, and I think I know what it is." She held up her hand so it was just a few inches over her head. "She's about this high and awfully pretty."

Devin shrugged, embarrassed. "It's been really nice getting to know Sunny. She's… You know."

"Very romantic. I bet you write sonnets in your spare time."

"Nope." She sat down on a stool, waiting for Edie to work her magic with the machine. It was tough, but she'd already decided she wasn't going to instruct her in how to make designs with the foam. That was a big city affectation that Edie didn't need. "I'm just a simple girl who's better at doing things than talking about things," she said, her mouth already watering for Edie's cappuccino, even though she was certain the ones she'd learned to make were significantly better from an objective viewpoint. But her viewpoint was a long way from objective. She was as subjective as people got, and getting her coffee from someone who loved her easily outweighed a better bean or stronger steam pressure.

When Edie handed her the mug, Devin said, "We get four bucks for one of these in Dallas."

"Four?" she said, her eyes wide. "I give them away."

"That's a little crazy," Devin said, chuckling. "I know the coffee costs you a good buck." She took a sip and smiled. "Good stuff."

"You probably do better, but it's not bad."

"Past tense," Devin said. "I'm not a barista any longer. My boss said she'd have to let everyone take care of family emergencies if she let me."

Shaking her head mournfully, she said, "We've lost our way when we fire employees for caring about their families."

Edie sat on the stool next to hers and put her hand on Devin's shoulder. "Whatever you're doing, you seem great, kiddo. It's been good for you to have a woman try to civilize you. I bet you two are out doing something fun just about every night."

Devin barked out a laugh. "Far from it, actually. If anything, I'm turning her into a homebody. I buy the groceries, cook dinner for her every night, make sure she gets enough sleep, make lunch for her to take to work, run her errands…"

"Really?" Edie gave her a puzzled glance. "You used to go out for dinner every night you weren't at your mom's. Why wait to get to a big city to stay home?"

"I'm there to help, and Sunny needs some peace and quiet right now. She's lost her business partner and is doing the work of two people, Edie. I'm helping her heal by letting her relax at night."

"So…this is just doing a good deed for a friend?"

"Nah." Devin stood and gulped down the rest of her drink. "We make a great pair. I don't care for city living, but if I could get Sunny to live in Greenville, I'd be one happy cabin-dweller."

Wednesday night at the Carters'. Everything was just the way it had been, with Devin on the sofa and Caleb curled up in her lap. They were reading his favorite story, one she'd read to him at least fifty times. Brody was in Lori's lap, absently twirling his shaggy hair around a finger as he listened to his story. In the kitchen, Chris was doing the dishes, singing to himself as he worked.

If you'd have asked her when she was a young woman, Devin never would have guessed that one of the highlights of her life would be the bond she shared with her best friend's kids. She'd always liked kids well enough, but had never been around them enough to witness the quotidian tasks that let you watch and marvel at how quickly they developed and changed.

In the weeks she'd been gone, the changes had been amazing. Caleb had started to ask questions like an adult, with all of the parts of speech. No more "Go too!" Now he looked you right in the eye and said, "Can I go with you?" That was a massive change—one Lori hadn't even noticed. It was easy to miss their progress when you in the middle of it, which just underscored how much Devin was missing. And no one had to tell her that she'd never get a second chance at experiencing those milestones.

She tucked her arm around the little boy, unable to get close enough, to revel in the unmistakable scent of dirt and grass and dog that permeated an active kid by the end of the day. He'd get a bath when Chris was done, but she liked him dirty. That's when he smelled most like a kid.

Chris walked into the living room, holding a fresh beer. He just lifted an eyebrow, but Devin knew the signal. "Sure," she said. She'd have to sleep on the sofa, but that wasn't a problem. She was certainly tired enough to sleep just about anywhere. Getting only two hours of solid sleep, then cutting the grass at her grandparents' place and helping Gram weed and water her garden had drained her. Not that the work was hard. It was next to nothing compared to what she'd been doing in Dallas. But it took a lot out of her to see Gramps in pain. Not to mention how much she hated having him supervise everything from her driving to the pattern she used to cut the lawn. Normally, he was the most soft-spoken, easy-going guy you'd ever meet. But he was so damned independent he was compelled to do something—even if he could only manage criticism.

Devin had planned on staying and cooking dinner, but when her mom showed up unexpectedly and was able to take over, Devin took off. She'd had enough of her grandparents for one day, and craved her usual routine of Wednesdays with the Carters. Actually, it wasn't rare for her to spend two or even three nights with them. But Wednesdays were sacrosanct. Besides being a nice routine for her, the boys looked forward to "Dev-Day" easily as much as she did.

She could tell that Lori was slowing down, clearly trying to time the end of Brody's story with Caleb's. So she moved a little faster, even though she would have been very happy to curl up on the sofa with Caleb and hold the little guy until morning. She was so crazy about these two it was pitiful!

Too soon, she and Lori were out on the front porch, having another beer while Chris sang the kids a goodnight tune. He wasn't a fantastic singer, but he thought he was and the kids agreed. It was a nice tradition, one she was sure the boys would recall into adulthood, and it let Lori have a little time to herself each night.

"So? Did you need to come?" Lori asked.

"I think so. Gramp's going to be a handful, and it's only going to get worse as he starts to feel better. Gram's not able to stop him if he tries to get in his truck and drive, but I can—and I will."

"Well, doesn't that sound like fun?" They were sharing the swing, letting Lori lean over and bump their shoulders together.

"Nope. But I don't want my mom to have to take her vacation now. She's planning on going to visit her sister in Camden in September, and I know she's looking forward to it."

"You're a good daughter, Dev. They lucked out with you."

She laughed at that. They both knew luck had little to do with it. If you established a loving, trust-based relationship with your kids, they almost always wanted to pitch in when they were able.

"What's really going on in Dallas?" Lori asked, giving her a sidelong look. "It doesn't sound like Sunny needs you for support any more. She's doing okay, right?"

"She's doing fine." After taking another pull on her beer, she said, "I'm making good money, meeting some nice people, and getting a taste for a different place. It's been good for me."

"Uh-huh. But you could technically stay right here, now that you've had that taste."

"I guess."

"But you're not going to."

"I told Sunny I'd be back as soon as I could, and I think I should stick with that plan."

"Because…? I know you don't want to be a landscaper, so stop trying to sell me on that." Lori gave her a playful punch to the shoulder. "Business is off the charts this summer, Dev. Edie's had to push some trips to outfitters farther up the lake just to keep up. So I can't figure out why you're in Dallas when you could be doing what you love."

"Um…" She leaned over a little, upsetting the rhythmic rocking they'd been doing.

Lori put her feet on the porch and stopped it cold. "Tell me," she said, placing her warm hand on Devin's leg and giving it a shake. "You're hiding something."

She didn't want to talk. Not even to Lori. But it had been bubbling up inside of her for weeks now, and it obviously had to come out. "I'm scared," she said, her voice breaking. Angry with herself, she got up and moved away, winding up sitting on the porch, with her legs straight out in front of her, the edge of each step biting into the backs of her legs. "I can't do it again. I can't stand the thought of being responsible for people." She could feel the tears coming, the emotion burning its way up through her chest until she couldn't stop them. Leaning over, she pressed her face to her knees, then wrapped her arms around her legs and held on.

Lori was at her side, rubbing her back and murmuring soothing words, just like she did when one of the boys fell and hurt himself. It felt…better to have spit it out. It wasn't just a sour feeling she couldn't shake now that she'd shared it with someone she trusted.

"You were traumatized," Lori soothed. "It makes perfect sense that you're worried about going back to work. But you can," she stressed. "I know you, Dev. I know you all the way to the soft, gooey center you don't show many people." She insinuated her fingers between Devin's arms and her side and tickled her until she sat up and batted her hand away.

"I'm not gooey," she scoffed, unable to prevent a smile from coming to her lips. "But I can't bear the thought of having someone…a kid…an older person who's a little confused…slipping away from me. It doesn't have to be winter to lose someone. It just takes a minute of being inattentive or having your focus on the wrong thing."

"Don't you think I know that? I'm raising two little escape artists!"

Devin actually laughed at that. Caleb had figured out how to climb out of his crib months before he should have been able to. Just a couple of weeks ago, Lori had gone out at dawn to fill the bird feeders and found him on the front porch, playing with his trucks.

"You can't give them back," Devin said, one of their frequent refrains. "I loved guiding, but landscaping and handy work isn't bad." She let out a bitter laugh. "I'm making twice as much as I did here, and now that I've quit the coffee shop I'll have time for more landscaping, which pays more. I've even acclimated to where I won't drop dead from the heat—which they swear will stop soon."

"But do you like Dallas? If so, you've been hiding it pretty well."

"I hate it," she said, dropping her head and grasping her legs again. "It's fine, I guess, for a city. People are nice. Food's really good. Lots of gay people. Sometimes we hold hands in public and no one swallows their teeth. There are lots of little shady places where you can listen to music while you have a beer. And even though they don't have any wild spots, we've had some good times sitting in a park with a picnic on a cool night. But I *hate* cities. And Dallas is definitely a city."

"Greenville's too big for you," Lori said, wrapping an arm around her body and giving her a shake. "You'd be out on fifty acres in the middle of the forrest if you could afford the land."

Devin sat up and shook her head. "I don't think that's true. I like a little elbow room, but I want neighbors nearby. Just not many of them. I could be very happy on my grandparents' property."

"They've got a nice piece of land," Lori agreed. "But you're in your cabin every chance you get."

"I like being alone," she said, shrugging.

"But you're *not* alone. You're in Dallas, a city you don't like, doing a job you could do here."

She gave Lori a wolfish smile. "You've never had sex with a cheerleader."

Lori gave her an even rougher push. "I know you're a hound, but I can't believe sex with Sunny is that much better than what you've had around here."

"*That's* where you're wrong. We make magic together, Lori. And since I don't want to go back to guiding, it just makes sense to stay in Dallas for a while and get my fill."

Lori looked at her carefully, clearly not convinced. "That's what you're doing? Honestly? Just having lots of sex?" She paused. "That's what Sunny wants too?"

"Um…I'm not sure that's exactly what she wants. We haven't talked about it much, but I think she'd like a girlfriend." She swallowed around the lump in her throat. "I think she'd like me to be her girlfriend."

This time, when Lori put her arm around her shoulders, it was a gentle, supportive hug. "If you don't feel the same, you're just leading her on, Dev, and that's not right."

"But…" She sucked in a breath and forced herself to talk, even though it was harder than scaling a peak barefoot. "I don't think I can be happy going back to the way it was before."

"You can't be happy in Maine?" Lori's mouth had dropped open, and she stared at Devin like she was a stranger.

"Of course I can be happy in Maine. It's the only place I think I *can* be happy. But I don't think I can go back to hooking up with strangers."

"Why?" Lori leaned close, her eyes boring in to expose Devin's secrets.

"I'd miss Sunny," she said, dropping her head. "I know you think I'm exaggerating, but things between us are *so* good. It's taken me a long, long time to find someone I get along with this well in bed as well as out, and I hate the thought of throwing that all away before I have to."

"And when will that be? What's this big timetable that'll tell you when it's time to leave?"

Devin didn't have an answer for that. She simply looked away, refusing to even offer a guess. The truth was, she didn't have a guess, not even a wild one. And when it wasn't possible to come up with an answer, she was a firm believer in storing the question away to let it percolate. This particular question had been perking away for months, so it had to become clear soon. Well, it didn't *have* to. But if there was an answer, it would eventually come.

Chapter Twenty-Two

THE NEXT MORNING, A STREAM of air warmed her cheek. Sometimes Sunny wound up facing her in bed, so close Devin felt a part of her. She started to lean in to kiss her cheek, then heard a loud crunch. Her eyes flew open to find Caleb inches from her face, munching on some corn flakes. "You awake?" he asked, his whisper striking her as funny, given the remarkably loud crunching.

"No," she said, closing her eyes. She reached out and took the box from his hand, set it on the floor, then tucked her arm around him and pulled him onto the sofa. "I can't wake up until you give me a good, long cuddle."

Giggling, he rubbed his tousled head into the crook of her neck while she hugged him tightly. If only Sunny were here, this would be a perfect moment. Devin didn't have a doubt that Sunny would be wild about the boys, or they her. She was possibly the most lovable woman on earth, or at least among the contenders Devin had met. Caleb settled into her embrace and let out a yawn as Devin imagined Sunny lying behind her, all three of them enveloped in this perfect moment—this little bit of heaven on earth filled with unconditional love.

By the end of the week, things had settled down into a nice, predictable pattern. Devin stayed with her mom, just to be a good daughter, then went to her grandparents' house as soon as they got up. They had breakfast, then set about doing what needed to be done. After lunch, she'd drive them somewhere just to have a little variety. But by the time her mom arrived to help with dinner, Devin was ready to take off, needing a few hours to herself.

On Saturday night, she sat at a favorite local watering hole with some of her buddies. The bar wasn't much to speak of, but it was within walking distance of the spot where she stowed her canoe. Being able to have a few beers and not worry about driving was her favorite way to kick back. She'd never been too drunk to paddle, and was pretty sure she never would be, but if she was too wobbly she could always throw a couple of sleeping bags onto the floor and bunk at Edie's.

She was one of two women in this clique, made up of current and former guides, people who'd worked for Edie, and a few guys who'd just jumped in. In this crowd, she didn't usually talk all that much, since a couple of the guys were real chatterboxes. But she kept them entertained for a long time that night with tales of crowded, party-fueled lakes and apartments that looked right into office buildings. She was sure some of the guys thought she was bullshitting, but she didn't much care. Her view of Dallas was hers alone. She was sure other people would feel different if they'd spent time there.

All of the guys knew she was gay—but none of them had ever seen her with a woman. This crowd had formed after she'd broken up with Taylor, and she'd never brought one of her Portland pick-ups home.

Lucky, a guy she'd taken her first guide training course with, was sitting to her right. He'd always reminded her a little of herself, single and liking it that way. Lucky was equally quiet in a crowd, a level-headed guy who didn't have to be talking if he didn't have something to say. But they had a bond, one that allowed both of them to reveal things to each other they never would to the group.

The juke-box was blaring, but when the song finished Lucky leaned over and said, "I heard you were in Texas for…accident stuff…but it sounds more like you're there for a girl."

"Mmm…" She took a drink of her beer, thinking. "I was ready to get away for a while."

"You've been gone for months, Dev. Is this girl special?"

Her face morphed into a smile, with her body unable to resist showing the simple happiness that being with Sunny brought. "Oh, yeah. Of course. I wouldn't have stayed this long if she wasn't."

Giving her a knowing smile, he said, "But she's not special enough to make you move, right?"

"I couldn't do that," she said, not even having to think. "But if she lived here… I'd be shopping for engagement rings." She let out a laugh. "I pity the poor woman who'd have to wear a ring I'd buy."

His head tilted, making his floppy, black hair slide from behind his ear before he pushed it right back. "What's so great about her?"

"Oh, gosh." She let out a breath, thinking. "Lots of stuff. She's a lot of fun, you know? We can just be doing something simple, but it seems special when we do it together. Um, we laugh at the same stuff, and she doesn't take most things too seriously." She continued to think, letting all of their daily interactions pass through her mind. "Big one," she said, nodding, "She never pushes me to do things her way." Without noticing she'd been the only one talking, she started to get into it. "She's such a sweetheart, very giving and concerned about other people, which I love, even though her family takes advantage of her because of it. And even though we're from really different places and different kinds of families, we see things the same way." Her head nodded again. "That's rare, right?"

Lucky stuck out his lip, then shrugged. "I've never had that—"

"It's great," she said, her enthusiasm growing. "Sunny's really active and energetic and loves being outside, even though I don't think she loves the cold like I do. Um…she's got a great circle of close friends she's known for a long time." She narrowed her eyes and drew closer. "You can tell a lot about a woman by her friends, and Sunny's friends love her to death." She thought some more, finally saying, "She's just super flexible, you know? If I want to do something, she gives it a try. We even like the same foods, and she *loves* beer." Tossing her head back, she let out a laugh. "All the important stuff."

"Is she pretty?"

"I didn't say that?" she asked, eyebrows hiking up. "Hell, yes, she's pretty. I've never been more attracted to a woman, even though she looks unlike anyone I've ever been interested in." Her laugh sounded lecherous, even to her own ear. "She's hotter than hell, Lucky. And *always* ready to rock. Sunny's just about more than I can handle, and that's never happened to me before."

His grin was a little slow, the five beers he'd had taking their toll. "Then I can see why you're hanging out. You don't want to let a good one go before you have to."

She blinked at him, just that second realizing she didn't have to let go at all if she didn't want to. She was in charge here. If she wanted her, she could have Sunny. Even though those words had never been spoken, she knew they were true. After checking the time, she clapped Lucky on the back and got to her feet. "You've got a ride home, right?"

"Yeah. Bucky's driving."

She nodded and walked down the line, slapping each guy on the back, then headed for the door. It was only eight in Dallas, and she hurried down the street to get to Edie's, where the wifi signal would allow her to use the internet.

Pulling up a video conferencing app, she dialed Sunny's number. In a couple of seconds her face appeared. *Damn, she was pretty.*

"Hi, there," Sunny said. "Hold on a second. I'm at Michele and Gwen's in Austin. Let me go up to the guest room so I have some privacy."

Devin's stomach got a little queasy as the phone jerked and swayed, then Sunny sat on a chair and it stabilized. "Let me put the phone on a shelf so I don't have to hold it."

When she did that, Devin had a better view of her, now able to see all the way to her waist. "Nice blouse. Sexy."

"Oh." Sunny looked down. "Some people are over for dinner. I got dressed up."

"You look really nice." Devin found herself at a total loss. She desperately wanted to connect in some way, but had no idea how.

"Are you okay?" A sweet, caring look covered her face, the tenderness of it like a punch to the gut.

"I think so." Devin could hardly catch her breath. How had she not noticed she'd been thinking of Sunny nearly all day, every single day? When she made breakfast for her family, she thought of how she tried to sneak plain yogurt by Sunny while filling it with the blackberries she loved. When she drove Gramps to the store, she thought of being at the ridiculously expensive market by Sunny's place, cruising around the aisles trying to plan healthy meals. Even at Lori's, she'd longed for Sunny to be there so the Carters could see just how special she was. And if she'd spent any more time wishing she could show Sunny her beloved cabin, she would have blown an entire day.

"What's wrong? Is your grandfather okay?"

"Yeah, yeah. He's in pain, but he's too stoic to admit it. I think he'll be fine."

"I'm so glad," she said, smiling so sincerely that Devin almost cried. She almost cried! At a friggin' smile!

"Um, well, I don't really have much to say. I just wanted to let you know I missed you."

"You do?" Sunny moved closer to the camera, so close the lens struggled to focus, then it captured her lips, plump and moist and pink. Those same mesmerizing lips that had made Devin kiss her that first day in Dallas, even when she knew she shouldn't have.

"I really do," she said, almost choking up again. "As soon as Gramps is able to drive, I'll be back."

"You will?" Right there, in that delighted, hope-filled voice, Devin knew Sunny was hers for the asking. The words almost tumbled from her lips. But she didn't want to stumble over her thoughts out on the street in front of the outfitter. They needed to talk. To have a serious, thoughtful discussion about what they wanted, what they could have, and what they'd have to give up to get it. That couldn't happen until they were together again.

"I will," she pledged. "I can't wait to see you again."

"Oh, Devin," she said, the emotion behind that simple sigh grabbing her by the shoulders and shaking her. "I miss you," she whispered. "I think about your being at home, but in my mind everything's covered in snow. I can't see you, you know?"

"Yeah, I know. I think about you when I get up, when I'm having breakfast…" She took in a breath. "All the damn time."

"I wish I could touch you. Just for a minute. To taste how sweet your lips are." Her voice dropped, taking on a sexy timbre. "I always get chills up and down my entire body the first time we kiss…" A laugh tumbled from that luscious mouth. "I've got them now."

Devin swallowed, her legs getting a little rubbery. "Wait for me, okay?"

"Where would I go?" she asked, letting out a silly laugh.

"I don't know. Just wait. Promise."

"I will," she said, now sitting up so Devin could see her whole face again. "I'll count the days."

"Me too. Um…" She shook her head to steady her nerves and said, "I wish you were here now. I'd give anything to show you my cabin." Sucking in another breath, she added, "And I want to have you in my canoe so I can watch the moonlight shine on your hair while we paddle over there." Butterflies fluttered in her stomach from her shyness about revealing her thoughts. "Do you know that sometimes I lie in bed with you in the morning and count the minutes until the sun comes up?"

"You do?"

"Uh-huh. When those first rays touch your hair, it's…" She closed her eyes, trying to summon the image. "It's magic."

"You're so poetic," Sunny sighed.

Devin had to laugh. "I certainly am not. I just miss the hell out of you. I've got this long list of things I need to show you. Things that make me who I am. Stuff I really want you to know about me."

"We'll do that, Devin. All of it. Promise."

"Okay." She took in another shaky breath and nodded again. "Okay."

"If you want to, you could text me whenever you need some contact. I'm always glad to hear from you."

"I will," she promised. Then she let out a short laugh. "But you might regret saying that. Um, I'd better go. It looks like it's going to rain, and I want to get home before it starts."

"All right. Be safe. I worry about you on that big lake all alone."

She laughed again. "This from a woman who has a million neighbors, almost all of them driving like bats out of hell."

The trilling of a loon woke Devin and she rolled over to seek Sunny's warmth. Even a minute or two of cuddling made getting out of bed easier.

But as she woke more fully, she realized she wasn't cold. Today, the air conditioning wasn't chilling her bare skin. Then she felt Sunny's absence. Lastly, she opened her eyes to look up at the exposed beams. What had she been thinking? Loons didn't take to office buildings and high-rise apartments.

For just a second, she thought about racing over to Edie's to text her. She'd specifically said to do that when she was thinking about her. But doing that at quarter to five was just selfish. Sitting up, she let her arms dangle between her splayed legs. It was the peak of summer, she was at her favorite place in the world, a place she'd missed like crazy. Yet here she was, wishing away the most perfect time of the day longing for Sunny. This was what loving a woman did to you!

Annoyed with herself, she got up and opened the door, letting a stream of cool, fresh air into the cabin. The first rays of the sun were beginning to show on the horizon, heralding a bright new day. Damn, it would be nice to have Sunny standing next to her, nervous about what they were about to do, but willing to give it a try. Devin could just see her expression; terrified but resolved.

After taking in a deep breath of the clean, herbal scented air, she flexed her knees and leapt, diving into the deep, cold water. She let out a muted cry as she blew a stream of bubbles out, but once the shock was over she decided it wasn't all that bad. Definitely over sixty-five. About normal for the first days of August. As she kicked hard to surface, she laughed at herself. A smarter woman would have tested the temperature *before* diving in.

The lake was as smooth as silk, with only a few wood ducks breaking the glassy surface. Not a single boat, no lights on in any of the nearby homes. That thought made her laugh too. Nearby wasn't actually very close.

Just for fun, she decided to swim for a while. But first she had to pee. It always took a few seconds for her bladder to release, since it definitely liked the water to be warmer. It finally complied, and she stayed in the warm spot and tread water for a minute. You could tell a lot about the wind and the flow of the water by seeing how quickly the heat dissipated, and given her warm spot lasted for a while the water was kind of lazy this morning.

She liked to swim quietly at dawn to avoid disturbing any wildlife, so she stayed low in the water and did a slow breaststroke, arms and legs submerged. It took a while to reach a little cove she liked, then she slowed down and dampened her movements as she got close. The sun had broken, now looming just over the trees. When she shielded her eyes, she saw him, a big buck dipping his head into the cool water. Catching sight of a moose at this part of the lake was a pretty rare occurrence and she did the minimum to stay afloat, wanting to keep him in her sights as long as possible. Sunny would have loved this so much! If Devin hadn't been trying to be stealthy, she would have slapped herself. She couldn't view the whole world through Sunny's eyes. That would take the sparkle off every great experience.

The moose lifted his massive head and stared right at her. They were conspicuously solitary creatures, coming together only to mate. She'd never seen one that appreciated being looked at, but this one didn't leave as quickly as most. He shook himself, with his narrow, bony shoulders hunching, and continued to look her over. Their eyes were locked on each other, sharing this moment in time. Two solitary creatures, each acknowledging the other.

Then he shook his great head, grumbled a huffing sound, turned and ambled away to tick another day off his life clock, moseying around in the woods.

That struck her right in the solar plexus. She'd always identified with moose, admiring their solitary nature. But that wasn't really who she was. She wanted love. She wanted closeness. She wanted intimacy. But she'd given up all of the good things you got from a relationship just to escape the few bad ones. But with Sunny the good outnumbered the bad so heavily it didn't seem like a sacrifice to be tied down. *Tied down.* She said the words to herself a few times, testing them out. Being tied down by Sunny sounded pretty nice. Really nice, as a matter of fact. She started to swim back, now moving quickly since every creature was awake and looking for the first meal of the day. She stopped mid-stroke and bobbed in the water. Being with Sunny was definitely worth a huge sacrifice, but living in Dallas might be more than she could stomach.

What then?

⁂

They hadn't been church-goers when Devin was growing up, but in the last few years her mom had started going to a service in Sangerville. It wasn't like any church Devin had ever heard of, since they didn't spend much time talking about God or Jesus, but she kind of liked it. And she definitely liked hanging out with her mom on a Sunday morning.

The only summer clothes she had at the cabin were shorts and T-shirts, but the place was pretty casual, and they drew so few people she was confident they'd let her in if she'd been wearing a string bikini.

Her mom's little SUV was parked in front of the church, and she could feel herself smile just seeing the car. The congregation shared the building with the original inhabitants, a Presbyterian church that had been there for over a hundred years, but this group definitely didn't need the whole place. Instead of using the regular pews, they set a bunch of chairs in a circle, more like a support group meeting than a service.

When she tossed the main door open, all ten of the congregants looked toward her, with her mom beaming a smile that melted her heart. How could you beat the feeling you got when your mom looked like you'd made her day just by walking into a room? You couldn't.

By the time she reached the group, her mom had moved across the circle to a pair of empty chairs. Then Devin was wrapped in a hug, and her racing mind and vague sense of unease floated away. They'd figure this out. She and her mom made a very good team.

⁂

It was after nine when the service ended, and Devin was so hungry she'd been ready to chew on the handouts. Instead of driving home, they went to a little cafe in town, where she ordered a breakfast big enough to last until dinner.

"What have you been up to this morning?" Peggy asked. "I know you didn't roll out of bed at seven thirty."

"Seven thirty? I don't have the flu," she said, chuckling. "No, I got up around five and went swimming. Saw a moose," she added. "A big buck. He looked me right in the eye from about ten yards out. Big guy. Five or six years old."

"Ooo, too bad you couldn't get a picture."

"It's up here," she said, tapping her temple. "And I won't need electricity to pull it up any time I like."

"What else is up in that head? It's not like you to drive over to Sangerville to sit in church on a perfectly beautiful summer morning."

"Can't a woman just want to see her mom?"

"Sure. But you could have come by the house once you'd exhausted yourself doing something you actually wanted to do." She took a sip of her coffee, giving Devin a knowing smile. "Something's up."

"Could I hide stuff from you when I was little? 'Cause I sure can't now."

"Not much. You've always been pretty transparent. It's the eyes." She reached across the table and touched the skin just in front of Devin's temple. "They're very clear windows to your soul. They always have been."

Devin looked down, unsure how to start. "Um, I've been telling myself I'm just…" She shrugged, not used to talking about sex with her mom. "That Sunny and I are just, you know, having fun together."

"Uh-huh," she said, clearly trying not to smile. "You're enjoying each other's company."

Devin nodded, appreciating that her mom was just as uncomfortable as she was talking about it. "But I miss her," she said. "I miss her a lot."

"And that surprises you?"

"Yeah." She nodded more forcefully this time. "I dislike Dallas so much that I thought I'd be in heaven to be home. But…I miss her," she said, knowing she was just repeating herself. "I'm not getting the same kind of pleasure I usually get from doing things like paddling to my cabin or going for swim. I want to be doing those things with *her*." Her lips were pursed together as she thought for a second. "I had no idea that would happen."

"Do you think you're falling in love, honey?"

"I must be. I mean, yeah, I think I am."

A big smile covered her mom's face. "That's fantastic! Sunny seems like a very good person, and I can tell how happy you are with her."

"But not in Dallas," Devin said, getting to the heart of the matter. "I can't see myself living there, Mom. Not for any woman."

"Well, that's not great. If she's willing, I suppose she could get a job somewhere around here…"

"Where? Bangor? Portland? You know how I feel about living in a city. Just because they're smaller than Dallas doesn't mean I'd like them any more."

Peggy reached across the table and gripped Devin's hand firmly. "If you're not willing to make sacrifices, maybe it's not love."

"But I think it is!" She was so jacked-up she didn't see the server arrive, carrying her breakfast on three separate plates. "Sorry," she said, moving her coffee and water so there was room. Then her mom's orange juice was placed on the little remaining space.

"I ate before church," Peggy said.

"I would have, but as the whole world knows, I don't have a kitchen," Devin grumbled, while slathering cream cheese on a bagel. "Sunny would go crazy living in my cabin."

"You could live with us…"

"If I'm going to live in a regular house, I want to be close to work—" She dropped the bagel and let her head droop at the same time. "I don't think I can go back," she said, her voice a harsh whisper.

"What? Not go back?" Peggy gripped her hand again. "What brought that on?"

"I'm worried about losing another client." Her eyes shifted up. "I couldn't take that, Mom. I swear I couldn't." She swallowed and got the last bit out. "I'm afraid."

They didn't settle anything, but Devin felt better for having talked it out. They met back at her grandparents' house, where they worked with her grandmother to tend the garden. She got along pretty well with her vision problem, and was still able to plant and weed and harvest. But she needed a sure hand to help her move around the raised beds that Devin had built for her almost ten years earlier.

Peggy had given her a quick summary of Devin's problem, and now the three of them kicked it around. It was kind of weird, talking to your mom and grandmother about your love life, but they were equally level-headed women, neither of whom cared what sex or race the person you loved was. But you'd better not bring home a jerk. They'd set you straight in a second!

"I'm not sure you can work this out," her grandmother said, after offering up some completely unacceptable options. "It would be one thing if you didn't need much money, but if this poor girl's supporting both her mother and her sister…"

"I think she likes being a lawyer, Gran, something we don't need. Edie's lawyer's a good one, but he and his wife had to set up an accounting practice just to stay afloat. There's not enough legal work here to keep him going."

"I'm not sure what to tell you, honey." She latched onto Devin with her pale blue eyes and added a warning. "But do this girl a favor and don't tell her how you feel until you're sure you're willing to do whatever it takes to stay together. Getting her hopes up and then coming home alone isn't right."

Devin nodded. Her grandmother was one hundred percent right. She had to know exactly what she was willing to give up for Sunny before they went further. That meant being as meticulous about this as she'd been about planning a trip. The stakes were just as high.

Devin drove back to her parents' house, then waited impatiently for her mom, who needed to stop at the store. The dogs were happy to see her, and they all played together in the unmowed acreage next to the house. She liked the long, drying grass as much as the dogs did, with all of them hoping for an animal of some sort to run by. The dogs were a little long in the tooth, but they seemed five years younger when they took off after a mole or a chipmunk, loping along like puppies until they gave up without shame.

Finally, her mom pulled in and Devin went out to help her bring the groceries into the house. "What's all of this?" she asked, seeing four bags full of food. "I'm not going to eat as big a dinner as my breakfast."

"I'm making your dad's new favorite salad, so I bought a watermelon."

"Dad? He's coming home?"

Peggy laughed. "Six weeks passed pretty slowly for me. It seems like he's been gone for ten." She gazed at Devin for a second. "You honestly didn't know he was coming home today?"

"You kept saying he'd be home soon, but I thought you meant in a couple of weeks."

"Honey, that's why I tried to talk you out of coming home. He doesn't start school for another month, and he's really looking forward to hanging out with Dad. You know how they like to go down to the diner in the morning and gossip until the lunch crowd shows up."

"So I can go back to Dallas?"

"As soon as you like." She gripped Devin's ear and pulled her close, then gave her cheek a kiss. "I have a feeling that's going to be *really* soon."

The next morning, Devin, her dad and her grandfather all piled in her car to take her to the airport. The airfare was shockingly high, but she wasn't about to wait for a week to save a couple of hundred dollars—possibly the first time in her life she'd been such a spendthrift.

For all of them to fit, she had to squish herself into the backseat, which was meant for a bag of groceries or a child still in diapers. But only her mom had a car with a real backseat, and she needed it for work.

So they rumbled along the narrow, curvy road, with Devin continually bumping her head on the roof.

"How are you doing back there, Buddy?" her dad asked.

"Hanging in. This isn't much different from the airplane, so I'm getting some practice in."

"Buddy's got a girl," her dad said, making her reach forward to give him a shot to the arm.

"I assumed so. Falling for a girl's the only thing I could think of that would keep you away from home so long."

"I'm definitely falling," she admitted, "but I'm not sure this is all going to work out. Dad's jumping the gun a little."

"You won't know if it works until you look back and see how many years have passed," her grandfather said, looking thoughtful. "I hope you luck out like your dad and I have. We got the best of the bunch, didn't we, Mark?"

"We did, Harvey. We really did."

A flash of a memory hit her. Just a year or two ago, she'd slipped into her parents' house, unannounced, on an afternoon in June. Just before she called out a greeting, she poked her head into the den to find her parents dancing together while some sappy song played in the background.

She'd been transfixed, unable to look away. While her parents were always openly affectionate, this was more than that. Her father's eyes were closed, with his head resting against her mother's, while holding her close. As the song ended, he'd turned his head to plant a scorcher on her mom's lips, nearly making Devin cry out in shock. As she silently backed out of the house, it dawned on her that it was their anniversary, a day they usually observed simply by having a special dessert. It had never occurred to her that they probably added a little horizontal fun to the celebration, but she was actually thrilled that they did—once she'd settled her nerves. If she and Sunny could have the same kind of long-lasting chemistry as her parents' did, they'd both be very happy women.

Sunny had been running around the office like a madwoman. Despite having a pretty good substitute for Julian, no one was doing Hank's job, and she couldn't think of hiring another lawyer without telling him or her that the partnership was probably going to be sold soon.

She'd heard nothing from Angelica for weeks, and had decided to let sleeping dogs lie. That might not have been wise, but she had so little influence over the woman that it hardly mattered. She'd do what she wanted in terms of the partnership, and Sunny would have to go along. That's what you signed on for when you settled for less than fifty percent of a partnership.

It was after six, the time of day she could nibble away at her inbox. Despite missing the heck out of Devin, she had to admit she got more work done when she was gone. Not having to get home for dinner gave her an extra couple of hours to work—exchanging a clean in-box for a case of indigestion from having a burrito or a pizza delivered.

Her cell rang and she felt her shoulders rise and fall in dismay. Was that the reaction most people had when their mother called? She hoped not.

"Hi, Momma," she said, putting her on speaker. "What's up?"

"I've been stood up. I had plans to go out to dinner with my friend Candace, but she had to cancel at the last minute. I hate to have wasted all of the time I put in this afternoon trying to look good. If you left right now, you could pick me up and we could still make a seven o'clock reservation. What do you say? I know you haven't eaten."

Sunny took a look at the computer screen. One hundred and twenty seven new e-mails. If she spent two hours plowing through them she might have a better sense of any landmines that could explode in the morning.

"Come on, now. I haven't seen you in weeks. Your Latin lover isn't there, right? Tiffany said she had to go back to…wherever she's from."

"She's not Latina," Sunny said, sighing. "She just tans easily."

"Well, you should dig into her ancestry. White people don't turn that color."

"Momma, I know this might surprise you, but Devin wouldn't be more or less appealing if she were Latina, but she's not. Can we drop it, please?"

"It's dropped. So? When can you be here?"

It had become abundantly clear that her mom didn't care for Devin, but the side benefit to that was that she didn't call as often. That meant that Sunny hadn't seen her in a month, a very long time given their usual schedule. Going out tonight might satisfy her for another month, which would be kind of awesome. "All right. But I can't stay out late. I've got to get in here by seven tomorrow morning so I can wade through my emails."

"I thought you went to the gym in the morning."

"I try to, but things have been crazy."

"You're not getting any younger, Sunny. I was thrilled to see that you'd dropped the weight you put on last winter, but that gets harder to do with every year."

"I'm sure that's true," she said, distracted by shutting down her computer.

"With your build, an extra pound does you no favors, but an extra five will give you more chins than the Chinese phone book."

The woman had the ability to guilt-trip you for not seeing her, then slap you sharply while dropping little racist bombs—all in less than minute! "Then maybe I should skip dinner," she said, just to get her own little dig in.

"Nonsense. You know you'll just go home and eat ice cream or something awful. Pick me up in forty-five minutes, and we'll have a sensible meal. Just keep your hands off the dinner rolls. Carbohydrates aren't your friends."

"Got it. I'll be there soon. Really looking forward to it!" she lied.

Sunny was tempted to grab a dinner roll, slather on all of the attendant golf ball-shaped butter, and shove it into her mouth in one huge bite. The image of her cheeks stuffed full, with butter oozing out of her mouth was strangely satisfying, but she behaved and shunned the delicious-looking things while they wafted their mouth-wateringly yeasty scent right at her. It just didn't provide any lasting joy to taunt her mother, who had the ability to out-taunt the best in the business. It was like picking a fistfight with Mike Tyson in his prime. You might get a moment's pleasure at having the guts to challenge him, but you'd be unconscious a second later, unable to enjoy the Pyrrhic victory.

"I've been thinking about selling my apartment," Winona said. "With mortgage rates so low, I think this is the perfect time to buy a three-bedroom. What do you say?"

"Bad idea," Sunny said, already seeing dollar signs flashing in her eyes. "Rates are low, but prices are strong. You'd have to pay over a hundred thousand dollars more to get a comparable place with an extra bedroom. A place you'd want to live, that is," she added, not mentioning that her mother required an address close to the most exclusive neighborhoods in the Metroplex.

"With rates low, that'd only be a few hundred more a month. It couldn't hurt to look."

Even though she tried to act like she was speculating, Sunny knew she'd already found the place she wanted. Her mother never proposed something she hadn't thoroughly thought through.

"If you can afford more, take a look. But I'm already stretched thin," Sunny said. "I can't chip in any more. Truly."

"But you've got a roommate now. How much is Devin paying you?"

"She buys the groceries. That's plenty."

"Not the way she puts food away! I've seen grown men eat less than she does." She leaned so close Sunny could smell her perfume. Her voice was low, but firm. "You can't let people take advantage of you like that. She should pay her fair share." A devilishly sweet smile appeared. "Then you'd have plenty of cash to help me get a decent place to live."

Sometimes, Sunny was honestly stunned at the words that came out of her mother's mouth. How did someone have the unmitigated gall to demand you charge your…whatever Devin was…rent so you could throw your money away on a more expensive condo that was nothing but an unreasonable luxury?

"I can't do it, Momma. Sorry, but I can't."

A cold, flinty expression cover her mother's face. "I think you've forgotten how I sacrificed for you girls. How I went from being a full-time mother with a very decent home to slaving away in a department store six nights a week, only to come home to a dumpy little place in a bad neighborhood."

"I haven't forgotten," Sunny said quietly, staring at the white linen tablecloth. "I was there too."

"You were a child," Winona hissed. "You weren't the one forced to find a job and struggle to pay the bills. If I could capture all of the tears I shed those first years after that louse of a father of yours left us, I could have filled the gulf. The pressure to keep the wolf from our door nearly drove me mad!"

Every time Sunny allowed herself to think of how her mother's life had been turned upside down in a single day, she almost cried. As bad as it had been for her and her sisters, her momma had it worse. She'd been abandoned, betrayed by a man she'd trusted enough to have three kids with. A man she'd been sure she'd spend the rest of her life with.

Sunny sank down in her cushioned chair, a little sick to her stomach. "I know it was hard for you, Momma."

"Hard doesn't begin to cut it," she whispered harshly. "But I lifted myself out of that pit, and now I deserve a little respect."

"I *do* respect you. I just can't afford to take on any more debt. I know you think I make a huge salary, but that's just not true. With Hank gone…"

"We'll talk about this later," Winona said, shutting the conversation down as their server appeared, bearing their entrees. "But it's time for you to take another look at your budget. A few hundred dollars a month couldn't possibly make a dent in a big time lawyer's salary."

Devin didn't arrive until seven, having fought through the rain-choked highways in a cab to finally reach the building. She was a nervous wreck at the thought of seeing Sunny, having spent the whole flight coming up with a plan for how to stay as close as they'd been without clearly stating her feelings. Her grandma had been one hundred percent right. If she wasn't certain she was willing to make any necessary sacrifice, it was unkind to open up yet.

Her heart fell when she opened the door to a cool, quiet, dim room. She tossed the curtains open, seeing the reflection of the setting sun in the glass-walled building across the street. Just a week away had made it seem strange again. As far from nature as it was possible to be.

Now that she was in the apartment, doing this as a surprise seemed kind of stupid. But she didn't want to call Sunny now and announce she was home. If she was at work this late, she needed to be.

Even though she'd done nothing more than sit all day, Devin felt grimy from the journey. So she took a long shower, feeling a little revitalized by the time she'd dried off and put on her favorite bedtime attire—a tank top and roomy boxers. As usual, she was working on a book, and she sat on the sofa and let the conditioned air blow over her. A breeze off the lake would have been so much nicer…

Devin dropped the book and reminded herself that focusing on what she missed wasn't a good practice. The only way to be truly happy was to enjoy the moment she was in. She shifted her body to face Sunny's entertainment center, letting her eyes roam over the photos resting on the shelves, focusing on the one where a joyful looking Sunny was leaping into the air in her cheerleader's uniform. It didn't matter that a bunch of office workers were a few feet behind her. Sunny would be home soon, and that's the moment Devin was ready to savor.

Devin had chosen one of her favorite books, a door-stopper about a sexy surgeon and a relatively straight woman who was having a baby. She'd read it many times, but it was a great book for a trip since it took a full day to plow through. It was super satisfying to reread a favorite book, even though she knew every scene by heart. She slapped the book closed at ten o'clock, misty-eyed and content, then spent a little while daydreaming about the happy couple, imagining the life they'd be able to fashion with their new baby.

Then, drained from travel, she got up and wrote a note that she left on the sofa, with the light of a table lamp shining on it. Sunny would definitely see it when she turned off the light, even if it didn't hit her that a light shouldn't have been on.

Just as she passed the front door, a key slid in the lock and she turned. Then Sunny was right in front of her, wearing a surprised smile with a big dose of delight thrown in. Instead of her usual business suit, she wore a summery print shift that hugged her body, along with bone-colored sandals with heels that lifted her almost to Devin's height.

A burst of energy zipped through Devin's body, all traces of fatigue gone in a heartbeat. Her arms were around Sunny before she knew she'd moved, then fingers slid through her hair as she was held in place for a hot, hungry kiss.

One of them started to move down the hallway, although she couldn't have said who set them in motion. They were like a human bumper-car, tapping against one wall only to bounce off the other as they made slow progress, kissing feverishly as they moved. After a short pause by the door to the guest room, they kept going, finally reaching Sunny's unmade bed, where Devin gasped as all of the air was knocked from her lungs. Sunny rubbed against her from lips to toes, covering her body with her delicious warmth.

Devin flipped her over, hovering above her for a second, desperately needing to look into her beautiful eyes and just take her in. "I love you," she said, with the words leaping from her mouth without thought or permission. "I had to rush back to tell you that."

Sunny's hands cupped her face, dark blue eyes searching hers for a few uncomfortable seconds. What if she didn't feel the same? Then their lips met and merged again, as they shared sweet, sexy kisses. Finally, Sunny stopped for air and looked up at Devin, breathing heavily. "I love you, too. I *love* you," she repeated, like she had to make sure Devin understood how sincere her feelings were.

"I was tired a minute ago," Devin said, beaming a big grin. "And it's past my bedtime…" She made a show of looking at the clock. "But I think we should stay up late and make up for lost time."

"Like I'd let you sleep!" Sunny laughed hard, showing her perfect teeth, looking as happy as Devin had ever seen her. This was all she wanted—to make Sunny this happy every single day.

After rolling onto her side, Sunny stood and tried to unzip her dress. But Devin was on her feet in a second. "Let me," she said, taking a nibble from her delectable neck. Goosebumps chased down Sunny's arms as she stood there patiently, tilting her head to allow her hair to curl around a shoulder now bared as Devin slipped the dress down her arms. So sexy!

"I missed you so much," Devin murmured as her arms slid around Sunny's body from behind, clutching her close. "Sometimes I don't step back and see what's really going on. There's no way it should have surprised me when I realized I loved you." She turned her, then leaned in to let their foreheads touch gently. "But it did."

"I thought it was just me," Sunny said. "But you touched me like a lover."

"Sometimes I have to be hit over the head before I realize what I'm doing."

"I really love what you're doing now," she purred.

Sunny laced her hands behind Devin's neck, allowing her unfettered access to her body. Having now seen most of her underwear, Devin knew she had some ordinary sports bras that she wore to the gym. But all of the things she wore to the office were super sexy—which, now that she thought about it, was kinda weird. Her thumbs rubbed over the hardening nipples, then she bent and licked a wet stripe up her neck, just to taste her skin. "Why do you wear such pretty stuff to the office? Are you having an affair with one of your law clerks?"

"I don't have any law clerks," she said, chuckling. "And, no, I'm not. I just like to feel a little sexy in a non-sexy place. It's slightly subversive," she added. "My quiet rebellion against the monotony of the office."

"I have never, ever slept with anyone who wore sexy undies." Devin let her fingers drop to tease all along the tops of her lacy bikinis. "I didn't know what I was missing."

"Keep that up," Sunny murmured. Devin kept teasing that tiny bit of skin, then Sunny laughed and said, "I meant keep not sleeping with other women who wear sexy underwear."

"Not a chance." Devin hooked her fingers inside the fabric, then bent to ease them down and peer up at Sunny from below, a really nice perspective. "I'm going to be wrapped around you every minute you're not at work, so I won't have time."

"Do you honestly think you can be happy here?" Sunny asked, her expression showing a little anxiety.

Devin stood and took Sunny in her arms to hold her tenderly. "My grandmother told me to keep my trap shut until I was sure I could give up Maine to be with you." She blinked slowly, realizing that might have been a good idea. "But I couldn't. I saw you and had to tell you."

"I'm glad you did. Really glad," she added, hugging her tightly.

"I *think* I can give up Maine, but I'm not sure. I guess we have to—"

Sunny's fingers pressed her lips closed. "Later. We'll figure things out as we go along. Isn't that what you like to do?"

"Yeah, but this is different. We have to—"

Again, Sunny stopped her. "It's late. Why don't we stop worrying about *how* we'll make this work and just start making it work." A big, sexy grin made her eyes twinkle. "I know one way to start."

Without a word, Devin wrapped her arms around her and jerked to the side, where they fell onto the bed together, both laughing. "Is this how you want to start?" she asked, trying to look innocent.

"Just like this," Sunny said, purring like a tiger as her hands started to roam. "With my mouth and my hands and my body all over yours."

"No objections." She let out a laugh. "That's how lawyers talk, but that's just about the only term I know. I'll have to learn more over time."

"I like that thought," Sunny said. "Time. With you."

"I didn't tell you this, but that was my grandfather's contribution to our situation. He said we'd only know if we'd been in a successful relationship when we look back over the years." She flipped Sunny onto her back again and started to kiss her in earnest. "I want to look back with you," she said, when she lifted her head to breathe. "I love everything about you," she added, rising up on her forearms to gaze into Sunny's eyes.

"I'll do everything in my power to make you happy, Devin. Anything," she whispered, her voice breaking.

"I'm already happy. You just have to be yourself. Just be you."

"I'll be me—but better. How's that?"

"Too much. Just you is perfect. Now why don't you lie back and stop worrying? I can tell you're already overthinking this. Chill," she soothed, easing the lines from Sunny's forehead. "We're already good. We'll just keep going." She started to kiss down the center of her body, focusing her attentions on her belly, a reliably ticklish spot. "That's what I'm going to do right now. Just keep going," she said, looking up to lock her gaze on Sunny's grin.

"No tickling," she warned, pinching Devin's cheek.

"Then I'll just skip over this part and get to the good stuff." She grasped one of Sunny's thighs and slung it over her shoulder, letting her nuzzle close. "My favorite place in Dallas," she sighed.

"Touch me," Sunny whispered. "Let me feel your kisses."

Devin didn't reply with words. They'd spoken all they needed to for one night. All they had to do now was enjoy being together, and she was fully ready to start.

CHAPTER TWENTY-THREE

SUNNY STRETCHED AND SHIVERED AS she tried to maneuver around in bed to stop the alarm from bleating. It was ice cold in the bedroom, and she hated to take even a hand from under the comforter. But the noise was too annoying to ignore and she stuck a hand out to silence it. With an unhappy sigh, she flopped over onto Devin's side of the bed, finding it cold. But then a sense memory of their night flooded her and she felt a smile grow. They were in love!

Ignoring the chill, she got up and raced for the bathroom. She'd had to pee for hours, but couldn't make herself wake up enough to manage it. As soon as she finished, she was so cold she had to get into the shower just to get her blood flowing. After entering the enclosure, she turned the temperature up as high as it would go. By the time she could dial it back and start to wash, a sweet-faced woman pressed her lips to the glass. Sunny matched her, sharing a quasi-kiss. "Still love me?" she asked.

The door opened and her big mug was held close to her face. On the side of the burnt orange ceramic, alongside the longhorn logo, Devin had used some of Sunny's lipstick to draw a big heart with their initials inside. "I'm not very flighty," she said, chuckling. "When I make up my mind, it tends to stay made up."

Sunny tried to lean forward to get a real kiss, but she couldn't reach Devin without getting her wet. "Can you wait for me to finish? I have to kiss you goodbye."

"Where am I going?" she asked as she closed the door.

"Damn! I forgot you're not my barista any more. What are you going to do all day?"

"I wrote to my clients to tell them I was back, so I'm ready to get busy with the ones who've stuck with me. I think I'll put my flyer up at all of the local stores again. That worked fine last time, so it should work again."

"You're happy doing yard work?"

"Happy enough to keep doing it. But I'm going to try to find more handy-woman jobs. The grass has to slow down in the winter, and I don't think anyone's going to need snow removal."

"Not often," Sunny agreed. She cracked the door open and pressed her lips into the cold air. "Kiss?"

"Any time you want one." Devin's warm lips touched hers for just a moment, but it was enough. The smallest amount of contact gave Sunny a burst of feeling that would easily power her through her day.

"Mind if I drive you to work?" Devin asked. "It's supposed to be over a hundred today, and riding the bike to Plano to cut a lawn doesn't sound like a heck of a lot of fun."

"Any time you want it."

"I've got an ulterior motive," Devin admitted. "If I come to pick you up, you'll feel too guilty to let me sit in the parking lot for long."

"Any chance of taking me to the gym after work? I didn't go once last week."

"Every chance. I'll tag along if you can have a guest. It's about time I visited a gym," she said thoughtfully as Sunny stared at her departing form.

Devin had never been to a gym?

They were on the road so early that traffic wasn't bad at all. When it was like this, Devin kind of liked driving. But riding the bike was more fun. Probably more dangerous, too, but you couldn't have everything. Sunny looked perfectly content to be sitting in the passenger seat, paging through something on her phone. This probably wasn't the time to bring up a sensitive topic, but they didn't have enough free time to let things come up naturally.

"Um, wanna talk about the fact that we slept in your bedroom last night?" she asked, realizing that was probably too abrupt an approach when Sunny's head whipped around and she stared at her. "Sorry," Devin winced. "We just don't have a lot of time to talk, so I thought I'd just…"

"It's all right." Sunny nodded to herself, then took in a deep breath. "Well, I started to lead you into the guest room, but I had files piled all over the bed." She reached over and gave Devin a pat on the leg. "Didn't know you were coming."

"Right. I saw them this morning. But we could have put them on the floor."

"And ruin such a dramatic seduction?" She laughed at the description. "Of course we could have, but it hit me last night that it's silly to act like I have a one bedroom condo. I set my room up just the way I want it, and it's dumb to let it sit there, unused." When she turned her head to gaze at Devin for a second there was a hint of sadness in her expression, but nothing heart-wrenching. "Morgan never even saw that room decorated, Devin. It's not a shrine. Her life was cut short, but mine wasn't. Acting like she lives there doesn't do a thing for her, and it makes me sad." She added a more enthusiastic pat to Devin's thigh. "If I had time, I'd sell the place and find something that fits me—and you, better."

"Can you afford ten acres in downtown Dallas?" Devin asked, trying to keep a straight face.

"Probably not," she said, chuckling. "But we could afford a real house. A bungalow like my sister has would be ideal. Then you could be *my* handy-woman. I've always wanted one," she added, batting her eyes.

"We'll see. Let's wait until the statute of limitations is up. If Angelica sues me, you won't want to own anything together 'cause someone will show up with a warrant and snatch my half away."

That evening, Devin tried to keep her focus sharp while she drove, but Sunny looked so cute she had a hard time managing. For a snack before exercising, Devin had brought her a container with grapes and chunks of pineapple over a scoop of cottage cheese. It soon became crystal clear Sunny didn't like cottage cheese. She simply wasn't going to say so. Several times, Devin had caught her surreptitiously trying to clean a pineapple chunk before she popped it into her mouth, without much luck.

"I can tell how much you're enjoying that," Devin said. "Have you always loved cottage cheese?"

"It's good," she said, clearly lying. "Really good."

"So what do we do at this gym? Climb ropes? Run sprints?"

Sunny poked her in the ribs. “I can’t tell if you’re being serious. Have you honestly never worked out at a gym?”

“Honestly. Why go to a gym when you can be outside?”

“Mmm. Mostly because it’s seven o’clock at night and still ninety-two degrees.”

“I can’t argue with the facts. But personally I’d find a cool lake and swim for exercise.”

Sunny patted her on the leg, clearly trying to placate her. “As soon as you find a cool lake, we’ll do that.”

“No need. I know you like your gym, so we’ll give it a go.” She tapped the container with her finger. “Spoon some of that cottage cheese into my mouth. No sense in wasting it.”

The gym looked more like the headquarters of a good-sized corporation than a place to run around. They stood in front of the main building for a few seconds, with Devin ogling it. Three stories tall, glowing like a million lights had been flicked on, it was the most impressive building she’d ever been on the verge of entering. Other gym-related buildings were spread out over many acres, with enough parking for all of the cars in Piscataquis County. “Holy moly!” Devin breathed. “This is a gym? The one at home used to be an ice cream parlor that went belly-up. I took a look inside when they were fitting it out, and all they had were a few benches and a rack full of iron.”

“This is a nice one,” Sunny admitted, smiling demurely. “I’m picky about things like this. I want to make sure I work out in a clean, well-maintained spot.”

“They’d better have a big cleaning staff,” Devin said, shaking her head in amazement. “This place is monstrous!”

The lobby was amazing. The locker room was amazing. The class rooms were amazing. And when they got to the particular room Sunny was looking for, not only the instructor, but the bodies of nearly every woman and man in it were amazing. It seemed like a breed of super-humans had been created in a lab to live in this hive of activity. “All of this to avoid going outside,” Devin murmured to herself.

"People love working out in groups," Sunny whispered. "They get motivated when they have a schedule and a leader." She approached a tall blonde woman who looked like muscle covered in tanned skin and said, "I brought a friend, Sonya. We'll stay in front so she sees your cues."

"Glad to have you," the woman said, taking Devin's hand and squeezing it in an iron grip until the bones ached. "Just watch me carefully. I always call out the next sequence before it's time to move on." She clapped her hard on the back, rattling her brain. "You'll do fine."

People were limbering up, going through their own programs to get ready. It was chilly inside despite the shattering heat, so Sunny wore a thin track suit. But before she started to warm up she unzipped the jacket, revealing a bright pink and orange print sports bra. Then she dropped her pants, leaving only black, skin-tight boy-shorts. If they'd been at home, Devin would have teased her about wearing so little and revealing so much skin. But she wouldn't think of embarrassing her in public, so she just took it all in. Every luscious inch.

As they both limbered up, Devin couldn't ignore the other women who made up seventy-five percent of the class. Most of them looked darned good, and were dressed awfully nicely, like they were modeling workout clothes. But even though a lot of them were more her type, at least the type of woman she *used* to find attractive, they didn't do a thing for her now. Since she'd been with a woman with some meat on her bones, she'd clearly gotten over her interest in girls without curves.

Sunny went over to a rack and picked up very light weights for them to use. "I think you'll be able to handle these," she said, smirking. "I've seen what you can do to a helpless pile of firewood."

Sonya put on some ear-shattering hip-hop music and started to call out instructions, slowly showing them how to perform a jab, a hook, an upper-cut, and a body shot, as well as duck to avoid being hit—all in unison. It was like your first day at boxing camp, but Devin didn't have any trouble following along. Mirrors covered every wall, and she thought she looked like she belonged, even though she wasn't wearing a super-fashionable outfit. But her sports bra and running shorts showed off her abs, which she had to admit were as tight as anyone's.

Then they started to add their legs, doing kicks in every direction legs could go. Sonya was so encouraging it was almost laughable, but she really did seem to care that people kept up and challenged themselves.

Devin was still keeping pace and feeling good. She had the time to look to her left and see Sunny's skin start to turn pink, just like it did when they were really going at it. That screwed her up and she started to let her concentration lag, beginning to think about making love the second they got home. When she tried to get back into formation the music had not only changed, someone must have speeded it up! Soon Sonya was calling out the moves in rapid succession, doubling them up. "Gimme ten quick jabs," she'd yell over the music, "then duck twice and let me see eight strong karate kicks. Eight! Seven…"

Devin had to use every bit of concentration she could summon to keep up, but she couldn't *quite* manage. As soon as she was throwing a proper hook, everyone else was onto body shots. Fists were flying, legs were kicking, all accompanied by quiet grunts that people obviously couldn't mute. Then sweat started flying. The woman on her right had long, straight hair that was drenched, and every time she kicked out to the right she'd snap her head to the left, letting a fine spray hit Devin in the face. Sunny might think she had a clean gym, but her classmates were throwing all kinds of yucky stuff around!

Sneaking a look at the clock, Devin saw they had another half hour to go. The clock must have stopped, since they'd clearly been going for over an hour already. Then they picked up the weights and really got moving. Sunny was working like a demon, face as red as her hair, her entire body flushed. Now they worked in some dance moves, and Devin could see that her new girlfriend had them down! She'd never really thought about what you had to do to be a cheerleader, but it only made sense that you could dance your ass off. Sunny's hips swayed and dipped, distracting Devin so thoroughly she was tripping over her own feet. Thankfully, they moved back to the boxing moves, concentrating on their arms for so long her own felt like cooked noodles. Finally, blessedly, the music slowed again, and they started to cool down, doing all sorts of stretches. After the music ended,

Devin crumbled to the floor, spread out like she'd been run over by a steamroller.

"Gonna die," she moaned.

Sunny leaned over her, with some fat beads of sweat dropping onto Devin's chest. "I thought you were in shape," she teased.

"Not. Not. Not in shape. If this is shape—I'm not in it."

It was really nice to see that Devin's pride wasn't hurt. She was puzzled, Sunny was sure of that. But she didn't try to defend herself or explain away her inability to keep up. Since she swore she wasn't sure her arms could hold the wheel, Sunny had to drive home. "Want to go back tomorrow?" she teased. "I usually do a spin class that really kicks my butt, but there wasn't space for us tonight."

"Only if there's a section for seniors or people recovering from serious injuries." She gave Sunny a seriously puzzled look. "They have a place big enough to ride bikes?"

"Exercise bikes. They're like racing bikes, but they don't have a front wheel. The class is *intense*."

"No can do," she said, holding up her hands. "It'll take me days to recover from this. No way I could do a repeat."

"Oh, sure you could." Sunny reached over and patted her leg. She hadn't thought to tell her to bring a set of dry clothing, and now the poor thing was in barely more than her underwear, dripping wet, trying to adjust the air conditioning so she didn't freeze.

"That's where you're wrong. Those flesh covered robots might be able to do that every day, but I'm a real human."

"I'm sure I'd be crying if I tried to keep up with you when you're working. It's just what you're used to."

"I will *never* get used to that. Amnesty International ought to put a stop to that nonsense!"

"Now you see why I can wrap my legs around you and flip you," Sunny said, reaching over to poke her a couple of times.

"You're strong enough to flip me right through the windows if I don't hold onto something. At least I know why now. I think I'm going to install some kind of straps to the bed so I'm not found in the street."

"Aww…" Sunny grinned at her when she had a second to face Devin. "It makes me feel good to have you acknowledge that I can kick some butt when I have to."

"A whole lot of butt. Is some of that from being a cheerleader?"

"I guess. I took years of gymnastics and tumbling and all kinds of stuff."

"Huh." Devin was quiet for a few seconds, then said, "How did you get away from babysitting to do any of that?"

"Oh. I didn't start until I was almost in high school. I had a PE teacher at school who thought I had promise, and she talked my mom into letting me take a class. I took to it like a duck to water, but I had a growth spurt and it became clear I couldn't stick with gymnastics. That's when I switched to cheerleader training. We *love* cheerleaders in Texas. Love, love, love."

"And your mom was cool with that?"

"Yeah," she said, thinking of how encouraging her mom had been. "I think she considered cheerleading the height of accomplishment for a girl. When I made my high school team, I'm sure she was more proud of me than when I got a scholarship to UT law."

"Mmm. My parents would have loved for me to get a scholarship to college, but I wouldn't have gone, so I guess it hardly matters."

"You're as smart as a whip, Devin." She gave her a slap to the leg. "And if your parents were any prouder of you, it'd be illegal."

"They like me pretty well," she admitted, chuckling softly. "Who watched your sisters when you were gone?"

"When I became a gym rat, Tiffany had to take over. I think she still resents me for that."

"Wasn't all of that expensive?"

"Uh-huh. But they kept a couple of spaces for poor kids. Then, when I got older, I helped out with the younger kids. Kind of a work/study thing." She met Devin's eyes for a second. "That kept me out of the house even more, making Tiffany take over all of my old jobs. She wasn't happy about that."

"Now she's getting paybacks," Devin said. "That's why she never gives you notice about babysitting."

Sunny thought about that for the rest of the ride. She'd never seen it that way, but it made perfect sense. Tiffany was trying to even the score, maybe subconsciously, but that didn't make it any less irritating.

The next morning, Devin had a very pleasant bike ride to get to her job, installing a ceiling fan in Highland Park. The heat and humidity had finally broken. It wasn't even seventy-five degrees when she left the house at nine, a development she was nearly giddy about.

She had her headphones on, although she was careful to make sure one side was off her ear to allow her to hear traffic. Stopping for a second, she dialed Lori and waited for her to answer. "Bad time?" she asked.

"Good time. I just dropped the boys at my mom's. I'm headed home to actually clean my house, which looks like a toy store exploded. What's up with you?"

"Went to Sunny's gym yesterday. I took some pictures that I'm going to send when I have wifi. You would not believe this place, Lori. It was a friggin' palace!"

"Nicer than the Piscataquis Y?"

"Oh, damn, I forgot about the Y. That's a nice one," Devin said. "I went to a birthday party there once." She shook her head, snapping out of the memory. "Um, I can't really explain what Sunny's gym was like. This happens all the time," she admitted. "This stuff is so different from what we're used to, it's like I'm in a different country—or planet."

"I thought you'd have settled in by now, Dev. Especially since you're committed to being in a relationship. You're a very adaptable person."

"I am? How do you think?"

"Well, you went from your parents' regular house to living in an apartment with Taylor, then to your cabin. You seemed happy in all of those places, and they were all really different."

"No. No. They were slightly different. This is massively different." She steered around a pothole, then yanked the handlebars sharply to the left when a guy tossed his door open without looking. "I didn't call to complain. I just…" She let out a sigh. "Sometimes I feel like I don't have anyone to talk to. Sunny doesn't understand why I miss Maine so much, and you don't understand why I dislike Dallas. Neither of you really understands the other place enough to know what I'm talking about. You know?"

"You know I'll listen, even if I can't exactly empathize, right?"

"I do. Sunny would too. But I'm kind of afraid to tell her how much I hate it here. She'll think that means I'm not happy with her, and that's just not true."

"Even though I want you back, you know I'm happy you found her, don't you?"

"Yeah. I know you want me to be happy."

"Absolutely true. So you think she's the one who can handle you?"

"Yeah. I mean, as much as I can know. My grandpa says you don't know until you look back and see all of the years behind you, but I don't think I agree with that. Even though Taylor and I didn't last, the years we had together were damned good. That relationship wasn't a failure in my book."

"Your mom ran into her the other day. She said Taylor was astounded to hear you'd moved to Dallas for a woman."

"Jesus," Devin sighed. "Of course she would be! I wouldn't even live in a condo in Bangor for her."

"Maybe you love Sunny more, huh?"

"I do, Lori, but I don't want Taylor to know that. My mom should have just said I was good and left it at that."

"You know one of the main things I like about you?" Lori asked, throwing Devin for a loop.

"Um, I could guess, but the list is so long—"

"Uh-huh," Lori said talking over her. "Besides your humility, I like that you still care about Taylor's feelings, even though it's been like sixteen years since you broke up. I really like that you don't blame her for the breakup, either. That's rare."

"Shouldn't be. If you really love someone, you give them at least a little piece of your heart. That stays," she insisted. "Sunny's the same way, you know. She talks about the woman she loved like she was perfect, even though her best friend assures me she wasn't."

"That's good to hear. If I ever meet this fantastic woman, I bet I'll like her."

"You will. Both things," Devin added. "You'll meet her and you'll like her. I was hoping that we'd be able to go home for my birthday, but she can't take off until the law firm stuff is settled."

"Want me to come down there?"

"Yes," Devin said before the sentence was finished. "But why don't you wait until things slow down for Chris? You could come down for a couple of weeks during mud season."

"Sold," Lori said. "I'll start saving right now so we can swing it."

"Um, speaking of sold, it looks like Hank's wife has found a buyer. Did you know they have brokers for selling law firms?"

"How would I know that?"

Devin laughed. "Just what I said. Anyway, there's a bigger firm that probably wants to buy them. Sunny's going to meet with them and see how that goes."

"She might go to work for them?"

"I guess. She's been pretty vague about it all, but I guess that's because she doesn't know what's going to happen either. We're kind of up in the air about everything."

"Well, you'll know soon. I just hope they make her an offer that she likes, or they pay so much that she can retire. Then you can come home and buy one of those big houses on the lake. The ones that have plumbing."

"Ha! She said she'll be lucky to get back what she put in, whatever that means. I got the distinct impression she'll need to find another job to keep the money train rolling."

On a cool, drizzly Saturday morning, Sunny cuddled up to Devin's side, loving the way their bodies always seemed to drift together sometime before dawn. "You awake, baby?" she asked, keeping her voice as soft as she could make it.

"Mmm-hmm." She turned, revealing a perky smile and bright eyes that had clearly been open for a while. "Just waiting for you."

Sunny snuggled closer, then started to run her fingers over Devin's belly. That part was always super warm, and sometimes ticklish. "Would you mind spending the day with Ashton?"

"Really?" Devin's eyebrow rose. "When did the phone ring?"

"It didn't. I was going to call Tiffany today and ask if we could see him tomorrow." She smiled at the surprised look on Devin's face. "Yes, I want to actually schedule some time with my nephew. I'm going to ask if we can pick him up at ten."

"We're picking him up?"

"Uh-huh. Then I'll have some control over when we drop him off," she said, smiling brighter at the delighted look Devin was giving her.

"Awesome," Devin said. "Really awesome."

Sunny started to pat and rub her belly again, saying, "I'm going to try to be firm with my sister. I'd like to see Ashton, but on my terms. From now on, I'm not going to answer my phone if she calls at the crack of dawn." She let out a laugh. "You might actually have to wrestle the phone from me, but I swear I'm going to try."

"She won't give up easily," Devin said. "People tend to push harder when you take something away from them."

"Then I'll have to push back." She nodded forcefully. "I'm not a pushover at work. It's silly to be one at home."

Devin slid out of bed, lifted her arms and stretched. "If you can try to change, I'll try to change. I promise I'll give the kid a break."

"I was thinking it might be good practice to set some boundaries." She pulled the covers over her head, then slowly peeked out from them. "I can't believe I even said that!"

Devin sat on the bed, her eyes bright with interest. "If you really want to do that, let's decide on what they should be."

"Really? That's what you do? I thought you had to come up with them as situations developed."

"Well, that's kind of true," she allowed, "but you can have some guidelines you agree to. Like…"

"Like having to go to his favorite restaurant and order the same thing he does?"

Devin shrugged. "I think he wants to have control in any way he can get it. Going to his favorite place is fine. But I'm never going to order those damn chicken bites," she said, chuckling. "I love chicken, but there isn't a part that's called a bite. I don't care if you go along with him, but I'd appreciate it if you don't try to talk me into it just to keep the peace. Deal?"

Sunny extended her hand, and they shook. "I guess the good news is that since it's too cold to swim, we won't have the fight over when to leave the pool."

"There will be something else," Devin said. "Let's just agree that we'll let him make as many choices as we can, but once we've made a decision about something—we won't back down because he whines."

"I'll give it a try," Sunny promised. "Let's try to think of something to do that'll tire him out."

"You've come to the expert," Devin said, clearly pleased to have a role. "I can tire a kid out better than anyone in Texas."

The next afternoon, Sunny stood at the base of a old grain silo, watching Devin patiently instruct Ashton in the art of rock climbing. She hadn't even been aware that people had repurposed some old grain silos for this kind of thing, but Devin had gotten online and found a few options guaranteed to tire a boy out. They'd let Ashton choose, and Devin had been obviously pleased he'd picked her favorite. They'd only been there a short time, but the kid was already not loving it, mainly because it wasn't coming to him easily. He got frustrated so fast it was actually kind of pathetic, but Sunny tried to have some sympathy for him. That had been Devin's big contribution. To let her see that Ashton hadn't been a jerk from birth. He was simply crying out for order, for rules, for attention, and he'd learned whining was the best way to get that.

They both looked awfully cute, with helmets and climbing harnesses strapped tight. But Devin looked cuter. Her shorts had ridden way up because of the harness, exposing the fantastic muscles in her thighs, one of Sunny's favorite parts of her.

Devin grasped the rope with one hand, turned to make sure Sunny held the line, and jumped onto the first toe holds to showed Ashton how to climb just a couple of feet. "Want to try again?" she asked.

"No." He glared at her. "It's too hard."

"Not really," she said. She turned back to the wall and started to climb, keeping going until Sunny was looking at the soles of her shoes.

"You're too high!" Sunny insisted.

"Funny." Devin gave her a grin, turned back and raced up the wall like a chimp, reaching the top in what seemed like seconds. "Helloooo down there," she called, before rappelling down the wall, bouncing down the vertical surface like it was made out of rubber. When her feet hit the ground, she turned to Ashton, who was too surprised to snap off a complaint. "Wanna do that?"

"I can't," he said, with his voice taking on that awful whiny tone he'd perfected.

"Nobody can at first. You've got to learn the technique, then practice." Shrugging, she said, "We're out in the middle of nowhere, and there's nothing else to do around here, so…" She looked up to the top. "I could go up a few more times, but it might be more fun if you tried."

"Help me," he said, meeting her gaze for possibly the first time. "Don't let me fall."

"You won't fall," she promised. "You'll lose your footing. Everyone does. But your harness will keep you up. I guarantee that."

He gave her a suspicious look, then faced the wall and put his foot on the first toe hold, no more than a foot from the base. When he turned to Devin, she moved over to help with the rope. "We've got you," she said soberly. "Your aunt and I won't let you fall. Promise."

He took in a deep breath, and pulled his skinny little body up, managing to balance for a second. "Good job," Devin said. "Now put your left foot on the purple block. Good. Now your right hand on the green one. Almost got it… Nice!"

Sunny shifted her gaze to see the excited look on Devin's face. She was going to teach this kid to climb. No doubt about that. There was also no doubt that Sunny loved this patient, thoughtful woman with every bit of her heart.

⌖

So far, fall had been pretty iffy in terms of weather. Devin worked up to twelve hours a day when the sun was out, but she'd lost a lot of time to rain. Those days seemed to frustrate her, even though they usually meant Sunny got something time-consuming and delicious for dinner. If Devin wasn't working outside, she couldn't stand to be lazy inside.

They didn't often eat in front of the TV, but Sunny could see that Devin wasn't in the mood to talk on this chilly, rainy evening. After finding a nature documentary on Arcadia National Park in Maine, Sunny carried her plate over and sat in her usual spot on the left side of the sofa.

Devin sat next to her, with her attention locked in within two seconds. All you had to do was show her plants or animals or geological formations she wasn't familiar with and she was yours.

After a while, Sunny looked to her right to see that Devin had barely touched her food.

"Not hungry?" Sunny asked.

"Huh?" She turned, briefly, then went right back to the program. "Yeah, I'm hungry, I guess. This is just so interesting." She took another bite, then Sunny saw her fork descend to her plate and remain there. Devin clearly preferred eating earlier in the day, but she'd let her favorite dining time slip later and later, claiming she enjoyed eating with Sunny. But she usually picked at her meal, making Sunny guess she nibbled a lot as she cooked.

They'd tuned in while the program was in progress, and after a half hour the closing credits started to roll. "Can you see if that's going to be shown again?" Devin asked. "We missed an awful lot."

Sunny took the remote and quizzed her smart TV, finding it had just been a random re-run. "Maybe I can buy it for you."

"All right," Devin said immediately, a very rare response for her. "I'd love that."

After getting up to get her phone, Sunny came back and searched for a DVD or a place to stream the documentary. While looking, she said, "I'm surprised you've not been to Arcadia. It's nearly in your backyard."

"I was there. Once," she said glumly. "I did a training course not far from there and spent a day looking around. That show just made it look so beautiful," she said wistfully. "Nature porn."

As the words left her lips, Sunny regretted them. But they were out before she had time to stop herself. "You'd go back in a minute, wouldn't you."

"A second," Devin said. Then she clapped her mouth shut and looked away.

Now that the topic was out in the open, she couldn't just ignore it—as much as she wanted to. Sunny scooted over and put her arm around Devin's shoulders, pulling her close. "Is there anything you like about Dallas?"

Devin turned slowly, blinked a couple of times and said, "You're here."

"Jesus," Sunny whispered. "There's nothing?"

She looked like she was trying hard to come up with something. "I like your friends," she said with confidence. "We always have a good time with them. And it's nice to go out for a good meal without driving forever. Um… The state fair was pretty awesome," she said, smiling brightly. "I had no idea you could deep fry almost anything on earth."

"Devin," Sunny soothed. "That's not enough."

"It has to be. We don't have any options."

She started to get up, but Sunny grasped the pocket of her jeans and held her in place. "Is there anything I can do to make it better? You know I'd do anything in the world to make you happy."

Devin shrugged, looking like she'd thought this through many times. "You could work less. We usually only see each other for two hours a night during the week. That's…not great."

"I don't think I can do that, honey. As it is, I'm barely getting by. Before you came, I was at work until eight most nights, and I always worked on Saturday."

"Um, going hiking on the weekends would help. There has to be someplace we could be alone, isn't there?"

"I'm sure there is," she said, even though she wasn't very sure of that at all. The kind of solitude Devin needed was hard to find.

"Maybe I should try to find a job that gives me more human interaction. I like fixing things, but I'm alone most of the time." She let out a small smile. "I love being really alone, but I'm not crazy about being lonely, which I kind of am. Some days I don't talk to anyone but you."

For reasons she couldn't fathom, it took until that minute for the enormity of Devin's sacrifice to hit Sunny. She'd given up family, friends, community, weather, her cabin, a job she adored, and her beloved Maine—just for Sunny. In return she got—Sunny. Nothing else. Nothing she would have chosen.

All of the things that Sunny enjoyed about Dallas; the warm, dry weather, having close friends nearby, her spiffy gym, great restaurants serving her favorite Tex-Mex dishes, every kind of pastime that a big city could offer—meant almost nothing to Devin. While she liked some of them, Sunny was sure of that, they weren't things she'd choose—and that was huge.

The lump in her throat was almost too big to speak around, but she got the words out. "Maybe we have to live apart."

"What?" Devin leapt to her feet and towered over her, clearly stunned.

Sunny stood and put her hands on Devin's waist, feeling her tremble. "Not break up. Just—live apart."

"You'd want that?" She'd grown pale in a second, so pale she looked ill.

"Of course not, but I want you to be happy. Whatever it takes, Devin, I have to be sure you're happy."

"I'm happy with you," she said, the look in her eyes so tender it was heartbreaking. "When I was home, the place didn't have the same pop it used to. I still loved it, but it wasn't right." She put her hand on Sunny's cheek and caressed it. "You weren't there."

"How about this," Sunny said, thinking quickly. "I get four weeks vacation. If you went back, I could use that time to visit you for a week every quarter. "

"A month? That's all we'd have?"

"No, no, we'd…" Sunny thought hard. "You make most of your money in the summer and the winter, right?"

"Yeah. Spring's slim pickings, and fall's only good sporadically."

"So you could live here during the spring and fall. Those are the best times here anyway."

She certainly didn't look happy, but there was a little glint of hope in her eyes. "If we were together for six months a year, would that be enough to make you happy?"

"No," Sunny whispered, before breaking down in tears, clinging to Devin like a lifeline. "I love being with you, Dev. Coming home to you is the highlight of every day." She got hold of herself and tried to act like an adult. "But six months is a whole lot better than nothing. I could live with that," she said, with much more confidence than she possessed. "I'm sure I could."

Devin gently flicked the tears from her cheeks, then held her face in her hands and gazed into her eyes for a few seconds. "That's not good enough. I couldn't be happy in Maine if I knew you were unhappy in Dallas." She wrapped her arms around Sunny and held her tight. "We'll tinker with the way we've got things set up now. I swear I have nothing against Dallas as a city—except that it's a city. If we got rid of ninety percent of the people, and ninety nine percent of the buildings—I'd love it here."

"That's not going to happen, sweetheart. I think you'd better give some thought to my offer. You deserve to be happy, and if we each get a good portion of what we want—that might be all we can manage."

"Not yet," Devin said, dismissing the idea out of hand. "We'll talk about it again in a year or two. Until then, I'll start mulling over how to get a real job. One I can get some satisfaction from. That'll help."

"Any ideas?" Sunny asked.

"Not really." She shrugged, then headed for the kitchen to neaten up. "I don't think Dallas is the ideal place for a woman who knows an awful lot about winter camping." She turned and gave Sunny a sad smile. "But I'll figure something out. Love conquers all, right?"

Devin had been a little mopey all week, while insisting she was fine. Sunny realized that was getting to be pretty common occurrence. It didn't seem like she was in a bad mood, but she had less and less to say. She seemed to be turning inward and brooding over her own thoughts, something she hadn't done before.

On a whim, Sunny searched the web, looking for someplace rustic, and not too far away, that they could go for a weekend trip. She found a spot, one she was sure would perk Devin right up, but they were closing soon for the winter so she had to book at once. Reaching Devin on her cell phone, she said, "Hey, could you take Friday off? I found a weekend getaway I'm sure we'd like, but I've got to pull the trigger today."

"Sure. I could do that. But I'll have to work late today and tomorrow. Is that cool?"

"It is. I'll work late too. Meet you in bed at nine?"

Devin laughed. "It's getting like that, isn't it?"

"Not if we can help it. Get your schedule in order, 'cause I'm taking you to a place I am one hundred percent certain you're going to like."

"Sounds better than good. See you tonight. Oh! Do I need to buy anything for this trip?"

"Not a thing. It's all inclusive."

"Um…" Devin cleared her throat. "If it's one of those beach things with a thousand other people where you play volleyball in the pool and drink Jello shots…"

"Devin," Sunny said, chuckling. "We've met. This is the opposite of that. Promise."

Chapter Twenty-Four

Sunny seemed to get a lot of pleasure out of having little secrets, so Devin didn't press her on the specifics of their destination. But when they got on a plane headed for Montrose, Colorado, she perked up. They had mountains in Colorado, and not many people liked mountains more than she did.

As the plane began to descend, Devin got as close to the window as she could, marveling at the peaks, some already dusted with snow, even early in October. "My God," she whispered. Turning to Sunny, she said, "Do you think Maine looks like this from the air? I wasn't by a window either time I flew during the day."

"I don't think so. The Rockies are pretty darned high."

"I like high," she heard herself say, sounding so wistful she had to laugh at herself. "I think I'm part mountain goat."

"You're going to get to test those legs this weekend," Sunny said, slapping her lightly on the thigh. "Hope you're up to it."

After an annoyingly long drive in an airport van, they finally reached their destination, Telluride. The driver had given it away the moment they'd gotten into the van, but that didn't spoil the surprise. Devin knew Telluride was a ski resort, but she also knew there wasn't any significant snow yet. That meant they were going to get to hike—one of her very favorite things. Her expectations were minimal. All she hoped for was a place to sleep—bed, tent, or bunkhouse, and a few meals, the simpler the better. Since they hadn't brought any camping gear they clearly weren't going to cook on the trail. But that was cool. The hiking was the draw.

After dropping off the other passengers near town, a ridiculously cute spot that looked like an updated Victorian era mining outpost, the driver began to thread his way up the mountain passes, with Devin so itching to get out and experience the beauty that she considered running alongside. Finally, after an hour and a half, they slowly approached an unpaved, rutted road. A very nicely carved wooden sign said they'd arrived at Bighorn Gap. Devin beamed a grin at Sunny. "I'm already happy. I'd empty my savings account to see a bighorn up close."

Sunny grasped her hand and gave it a squeeze. "This is going to be great!"

After a bumpy ride, they turned to approach a rustic building that must have been a hotel. Devin wasn't an expert, but she guessed it contained around fifteen rooms, at most. That wasn't too bad, especially since everyone would be doing something different—she hoped. Hiking with thirty other people wasn't her idea of fun.

After Sunny settled up with the driver, an energetic young guy came racing out of the building. "Good morning," he said, full of sunshine. "Checking in?"

"We are," Sunny said. "Thompson."

"I'm Chad," he said, shaking Sunny's hand. "We're very glad to have you, Ms. Thompson." He had a tablet computer with him, and he found her name in a second. "Let me load your things in a golf cart, and we'll be off."

Devin cocked her head, but let him put their bags on the back of a very snazzy cart, then she and Sunny got aboard.

"You haven't stayed with us before, have you?" Chad asked.

"We haven't," Sunny said. "But when I read about your facilities, I knew we had to come."

"Your timing was perfect. You just made it under the wire." He showed a bright smile. "It's been getting into the low forties at night, but you'll be warm."

Now even more confused, Devin had to concentrate on holding herself into the cart as Chad took the turns along the asphalt path as quickly as he possibly could.

When they rounded a bend, Devin heard, then sniffed, then saw, a rushing river. It wasn't terribly wide, but it was really moving along. "The trout have been going crazy this week," Chad said. "Do you fish?"

"Do I fish?" Devin said, about to drool. "Do you have gear I can use? I've got nothing."

“You’re all set,” he said, full of confidence. “Everything you need is in your tent.”

“Tent?” She jerked upright. “We’re camping?”

“We’re glamping,” Sunny said, chuckling. “Glamorous camping, which is more my style than yours.”

“It’s not too glamorous,” Chad insisted, clearly sensing Devin’s more rustic sensibilities. “It’s…well, you’ll see.” In another moment, Devin did see. Four big canvas tents sat about ten yards from one another, all surprisingly close to the river. They looked like the kind of tents someone would build if they’d been nomads, but had decided to give a permanent home a try. In other words, a very nice, very large tent, just short of a small, free-standing house.

“I’ve never seen anything like this,” Devin marveled. “How do you keep them from being swept away when the river rises?”

“We haven’t had any trouble. They’re up higher than they seem. All of those plants in front there cover up the base.”

“Oh! I hadn’t noticed the steps to get inside.”

“Just three,” Chad said. “But that allows us to hide all of the plumbing.”

“Plumbing,” Devin said, laughing a little when her eyes met Sunny’s. “What will they think of next?”

Chad gave them such an extensive tour of their tent that Devin was afraid he was going to waste the rest of the day. But he finally went to the screened-in porch and tossed the door open to leave. “One last thing. Would you like to walk over to the dining room for lunch, or have it delivered?”

“Delivered,” Devin said, not even giving Sunny the option. “Can we do that for dinner too?”

“You can.” He crooked a finger and Devin joined him at the door. “See that fire pit? If you’d like, one of our cooks will grill a steak or a nice piece of fish for you right there. You can eat under the stars.”

“With all of the other people?”

“Only with your fellow tent mates. But my guess is that you’ll be the only ones choosing that option. Like I said, it’s been chilly.”

"I'm from Maine," Devin said. "I don't even dig my gloves out of the closet until it's freezing. We'd love to eat outside."

"Two votes?" Chad asked, poking his head back inside.

"Anything she wants is perfectly fine with me," Sunny said.

Chad paused in the doorway for a moment, then showed a grin. "Are you honeymooners?"

"Not yet," Devin said, beaming a smile at Sunny, who was blushing, "but after this surprise, I'm ready to propose."

They sat in the roomy Adirondack chairs that circled the fire pit to eat their lunch, just ten yards from the melodious river that had definitely captivated Devin.

"I hate to drop this on you so suddenly," she said, staring at the rushing water, "but I'm staying. Right here. You'll call my parents, won't you? I'll miss you all, but this is the spot I was meant to live in."

Sunny reached over and grabbed her hand. "I knew you'd be crazy about this place. I've been looking at the website twenty times a day, knowing you'd love the heck out of it."

She saw Devin's chin lift, then watched her gaze travel along the mountain peaks that stretched out as far as the eye could see. "Gorgeous mountains, a trout stream, and a huge tent with a great bed and a six foot long tub. Oh! And a guy who's going to cook for us over an open fire. I understand if you have to go back, but I can't. Just pay for my lodging every month, okay?"

"They have guides around here," Sunny said. "I checked. Only for fishing, but…"

"Think they need a real estate lawyer?"

"Probably not. Telluride's pretty small."

"Denver?"

"It's six or seven hours away. Longer in the winter, I'd guess."

A devilish smile made her lips quirk up. "You can visit me on the weekends."

"I'm going to have to find one hell of a job to pay for an apartment in Denver, full-time residency for you here, and my dependents back in

Dallas." She got up and went to sit on Devin's lap, then leaned in and kissed her soundly. "But to see that smile on your face is worth whatever I have to do."

Devin patted her butt as she got up. "After lunch, how about a thigh-busting ride up that hill Chad suggested? Our mountain bikes look really nice."

"You're on. Bring a rope in case you have to drag me along."

Laughing, Devin said, "I've seen those thighs in action, both at home and at the gym. You could dust me if you wanted to."

Sunny had packed for Devin, just to keep their destination a surprise, and she'd done a perfect job. Now Devin had on a new set of long underwear, a wool sweater, and her wind-stopping shell. Sunny, of course, had on her full length down coat, the one she'd worn on the fateful ice-fishing trip. Even though it brought back some awful memories, Devin was determined to disconnect it from that time and just look at it as the coat that allowed Sunny to agree to eat dinner outside when it was only forty-five degrees.

They were, in fact, the only people who'd chosen to dine al fresco, making it even cooler in Devin's eyes. Once their food had been cooked, their personal chef had packed all of his tools and supplies up, loaded everything into his golf cart, and taken off, leaving them to eat in peace. He'd made sure they had a full bottle of wine, of course, along with more food than they could eat in two days.

Devin looked up, completely pleased to not be able to see a single light flicker anywhere around them. Sunny assured her that tourism would pick up as soon as the ski runs were operating, but Devin wouldn't be around to see that. She could luxuriate in the belief that all of this land, hundreds of thousands of acres of it—was untouched by man.

Sunny's fork made a clinking noise when she speared a bite of fish, and Devin studied her in the flickering firelight. She was eating like she was in a contest of some sort, clearly wanting to get the fish and the vegetables into her mouth while they were still warm. But Devin didn't care if hers was ice cold. She hadn't felt so good since she'd been back in her cabin in

August. Looking at the rushing water, she had to admit that she preferred a good river even to her precious lake. This little spot truly might be the most perfect place in the world for her to live. But they were only going to get two nights to indulge in that fantasy. She had to soak up every bit of this beauty while she had it in her hands.

◈

Sunny flew upright, flicking the water off her face. *What in the hell?*

Devin's demonic laugh snapped her into reality. Sunny turned to find her standing there grinning, wearing waders that went all the way up to her armpits. A rod and reel were in one hand, and the strap for a creel was over her shoulder. In the other hand was a steaming cup of coffee, which she handed to Sunny. "I promise there's no river water in it, but it's not as good as I make at home."

"What's in there?" Sunny asked, pointing at the basket.

Devin rested her rod on the bed, then tipped the creel over and opened it.

"Fish!" Sunny squealed.

"Yep. Nice ones. I'm going to walk up to the lodge and give them to the cooks. Do you like trout for breakfast?"

"Is that a joke?" Sunny eyed her suspiciously.

"I guess that's a 'no.' Well, I'll be up at the lodge having the breakfast I caught. Come up when you're ready." She leaned over and kissed her. "Be ready fast. I can't wait to start hiking."

Sunny watched her go, so enormously relieved to see how happy she was that she didn't even mind that she'd had drips of ice cold water tossed onto her face to wake her up. Well, she minded a little, but darned little.

◈

On Sunday afternoon, Devin pressed her face up to the window, looking down until they climbed to a height that obscured her vision. "I wanna stay," she pouted. "I could learn those rivers and be a great fly-fishing guide. Think I could earn enough to support us and your dependents?"

"I looked at what those guides charge. We'd have to struggle to afford a cabin without plumbing—and you don't have any grandparents in Colorado who'd give us one."

"Isn't that always the way?" Devin asked, slumping down in her seat. "You find you're perfectly suited to live in Paris or Malibu or Portofino… but you can't pay the rent."

"Life is tough," Sunny agreed. "But it's so much nicer when you have someone next to you who makes a less-than-ideal place pretty ideal."

"I've got that," Devin said, smiling so sweetly that Sunny had to lean forward and give her a chaste kiss.

"So do I. And my girlfriend makes me as happy as I ever thought I'd be."

"Even when she drags you a heck of a lot farther than you wanted to hike?"

"I loved it," Sunny said. "Actually, I was honored that you let me tag along. I truly meant it when I suggested you go off alone this morning."

Devin leaned over and spoke into Sunny's ear, tickling it with her breath. "Want to know a secret?"

"Sure."

"I've discovered I like being alone in the woods—with you." She sat back against her chair, with a self-satisfied grin on her face.

"Really? You honestly didn't need to be alone?" She started to laugh. "I was going to send you here all by yourself, but the price was for two people. There was no way I was going to pay for two and only send one."

"If you're ever tempted to send me somewhere alone—resist the urge." She smiled as she placed her hand atop Sunny's. "Unless you need to get away from me for a while."

"That's not going to happen, Dev," she said, smiling at the expression that now seemed much more like it had a few months ago—content and tranquil. "We're a matched set."

On the first Saturday after Thanksgiving, Devin lay on her back, with Sunny snuggled up next to her. They always lazed about in bed on the weekends, even though Devin's natural instincts were to get up with the dawn and see what was going on out in the world. But there wasn't much natural world around her, and she'd come to really enjoy exploring Sunny instead of a forest.

She was still only half awake, with Sunny even less so, and they both started when the phone rang. It was the shrill ring Sunny had assigned to her sister, and they both stared at the device as it shimmied on the bedside table. "Gonna get that?" Devin asked, not at all sure Sunny could resist.

"Nope." She reached over and hit the "decline" button, then burrowed into Devin's body with a sigh.

"Proud of you," Devin whispered.

"That's only step one," Sunny murmured. "Stay tuned for the next act."

After they'd had breakfast and a lazy return to bed, Devin got up to shower. "Got any errands to run?" she asked as she stretched.

"Just one." She picked up her phone and dialed a number, meeting Devin's gaze as she said, "Hi, Tiffany. Yeah, I did get your message. Sorry I couldn't watch Ashton today. Uh-huh. No, I'm fine. Uh-huh. I've started turning my phone off when we're in bed. Uh-huh," she said, rolling her eyes dramatically. "I guess that could happen, but there aren't many emergencies that can't wait until we wake up." She started to say something, but waited for a few seconds. "Uh-huh. Listen. I'd like to talk to you about something. Can I take you out for coffee? Yeah. Today would be good. No, no, I can't do that. I only have an hour." She nodded. "Sounds great. I'll be there by ten." She hung up and smirked at Devin. "Want to come with me?"

"I do not!" she said, laughing as she leapt for Sunny and wrestled her into a tight hold. Her lips were right by Sunny's ear, and she whispered, "But when you come home, I'll give you a treat. Actually, I'll give you treats until you beg for mercy."

Sunny was purring with pleasure. She snuggled even closer and said, "I'm kind of scared to talk to her, but kind of turned on. I hope that's from thinking about making love to you again."

Devin didn't reply, thinking Sunny was probably getting a little charge from finally taking the wheel. But she'd let her figure that out for herself. That was part of the fun of learning to stand up for yourself.

There was an industrial-chic espresso place not far from Tiffany's home, and they agreed to meet there to prevent Ashton from tagging along. Sunny had already received her order, and was sitting on a stool in the window, watching her sister walk across the parking lot. She had to admit they looked a lot alike, especially when they were casually dressed, but Tiffany always looked like she dressed to attract men, something Sunny had never been good at, much less interested in.

Even on a Saturday morning it looked like she'd spent time putting herself together. Her hair looked perfect, and her clothing had been tailored to hug her snugly. Comfort was never on the agenda for Tiffany. As she walked in front of the window, Sunny could see she'd put on eye makeup, and had just the right amount of lipstick for a weekend morning.

Waving when Tiffany saw her, Sunny stayed where she was, guarding the empty stool next to her. When Tiffany had gotten her coffee, black, two packets of Splenda, she sat down and peered at Sunny for a moment. "Are you sure you're all right? You're not sick or anything, are you?"

"I'm fine," she insisted. "I just wanted to have a talk."

"About?"

"Things in general." She took a sip of her cappuccino, still unable to find one as good as the ones Devin used to make for her, and spit it out. "I want to spend more time with Ashton," she said, watching Tiffany's eyes grow wide.

"Great! How about tomorrow?"

"No, tomorrow's not good," she said, even though they had no plans. "How about next Sunday? We could pick him up around nine or ten."

"Mmm, that's late for us. We like to tee off by eight, before it gets hot."

"Mmm. Makes sense." She took a breath. "Maybe you could find a babysitter to watch Ashton until ten."

"A babysitter?" Tiffany's eyebrow rose as she tilted her chin down, looking at Sunny like a teacher disappointed in your test score. "When you're going to pick him up anyway?"

"Well, I can't think of a better way to make sure we both get what we need. You want to leave your house by seven thirty, and I don't want to leave mine until nine thirty." She didn't add another word, having decided to wait Tiffany out.

"Then come earlier," she said, clearly confused by this change in her normally compliant sister.

"Go later," Sunny said. "Or take him with you for the first two hours. I'll happily pick him up when you make the turn. He could take a few shots to start developing a love for the game."

"He's too young," she said dismissively. "He doesn't have the patience to be quiet or wait his turn."

"Um, when you do think he's going to get that?" Sunny asked, trying to be subtle, but acknowledging she'd failed when Tiffany fixed her with a scowl.

"I don't need parenting advice," she snapped.

"I apologize," Sunny said, gripping her sister's arm briefly. "I wouldn't like someone telling me how to raise my kid, either. I'm just suggesting that this might be a good time to get him interested. I know the game means a lot to you."

"I don't care about golf," she said, with a dismissive flick of her wrist. "But Eric loves it *so* much. With him being gone every other weekend, a round of golf gives us a chance to spend a few hours alone. Ashton would…" She caught herself and tried again. "He honestly hasn't expressed an interest."

"Got it," Sunny said. "So? Do you want us to pick him up next week?"

"Yes, I do," she said, with her voice growing a little strident. "At *eight*."

Sunny was not going to get into a power play. She stood up, then leaned in and kissed her sister on the forehead. "I love you. And I love Ashton. Spending one or two Sundays with him a month would be great for me. But I need extra sleep on the weekends. If you want me to pick him up on Sunday, I'd love to. At *ten*."

She gave her shoulder a squeeze, and headed for the door, with Tiffany calling out, "We're not done here!" But Sunny was completely done. She'd set the first boundary with her sister, and was tingling with pleasure. The only thing that would make her feel even better was the pleasure she was sure awaited her when she got home.

By the beginning of December, Sunny had the firm running like it had before Hank's death. She hadn't been able to cut back on her hours to any great extent, but she was no longer afraid to turn on her computer in the morning.

Early on an Monday, she was zipping through her emails, trying to clear her in-box before the new batch started to roll in. When her phone rang, she picked it up.

"Sunny Thompson."

"Sunny? It's Angelica."

She'd picked up her coffee mug, but lowered it back to the desk slowly, as alert as a guard dog. "Hi. What's new?" *Oh, that was a dumb thing to say.*

"Well, I've had some really good discussions with Hamilton and Foster. You know them, right?"

"Sure. Of course. They're a good firm. Well respected."

"Yeah. They seem like it. They made an offer, Sunny, and Thomas and I think we should take it."

"All right," Sunny said. "Are you just letting me know? I mean, the decision is yours, Angelica."

"Oh, I know that. Mainly, I wanted to let you know that Mike Hamilton said they wanted to talk to you about joining them. I think he'd like some continuity."

"I'd be happy to talk to him. Thanks for letting me know."

"No problem. I hope you land somewhere nice, Sunny. Hank would have wanted you to do well."

"Thanks," she said, tears coming to her eyes. "I know he would have wanted the same for you. He always spoke well of you, Angelica. Always."

She could hear her sniffling, than Angelica said, "He could be a big pain in the rear in public, but he was as sweet as sugar when we were alone. I miss him like crazy."

"I know you do. But hang in there. I can tell you from experience that you can love again. If you're open to it, love can find you."

"Thomas told me it's found you," she said quietly.

Oh, shit! She should have realized they'd start snooping around on Devin. They'd want to know all of her weak points if they were preparing to sue. "Yes, it has. But I swear my feelings for Devin are completely separate from my belief she wasn't negligent."

"You can't separate things like that, Sunny. If you're in love with her, you're going to defend her."

"I do love her," Sunny said, "and I'll defend her with everything I have."

"I'm not sure what I'm going to do," she said sounding thoughtful. "Thomas really wants me to sue, but I haven't made up my mind. If you're going to fight me, it might go to trial, and I don't know if I can handle that."

"I wish there was a way for you to have enough money to live the life you expected, Angelica, but—"

"A few million from Devin's insurance company would help."

"I checked on that," Sunny said. "Edie only carries a million dollar policy. If you won more than that, she'd have to sell her business. Maybe her home. And Devin makes very little money, so I'm sure her pockets aren't very deep. Is it fair to slap them with a huge judgment they'd never be able to pay?"

"Is it fair that my husband's dead?"

Sunny took a breath. "It's terribly unfair, Angelica. *Terribly*. But does that inequity entitle you to financially destroy two other peoples' futures?"

"No one's going to come out of this in better shape than when they went in, Sunny. That little bonding trip was the stupidest idea you guys ever had, and someone should have to pay."

Sunny didn't correct her. It would have been cruel at this point to tell the truth. The trip had been *all* Hank's idea, and the more she and Julian had complained, the more he'd dug his heels in. That was Hank. He might have been as sweet as sugar when he was at home, but at the office he was the very definition of "pain in the rear."

Devin had gotten home late, and only had time to make a vegetable salad for Sunny's meal. She'd eaten the majority of her own dinner as she'd peeled and sliced away, finding that she liked eating like a toddler, taking a bite or two every couple of minutes.

She'd just started to plate a large portion, along with a tiny one for herself when she heard Sunny's key in the lock.

"Don't kick me to the curb," she called out, "but we're stuck with salads again. I got roped into putting up twenty strings of Christmas lights and —" Devin snapped her mouth closed when she saw the look on Sunny's face. "What's wrong?" She dropped the dish towel she'd had in her hand and moved around the island to get closer.

"Does my expression always give everything away?" she asked, revealing a wan smile.

"No, but it does today. What's wrong?"

Sunny squeezed her shoulder, then walked over to the sofa, where she dropped her briefcase and nearly fell to the seat, displaying none of her natural poise. "Angelica sold the firm. All gone," she added, sighing.

"Oh, shit!" Devin climbed over her legs to sit next to her, searching her face. "Are you upset?"

She turned and let a half smile crook her lips. "A little. Hank and I built that place up from a three person office to a nice firm. We grew every year, and probably would have added two attorneys this year. But now—it's gone."

"And she didn't even ask if you approved? That's harsh, Sunny. Really harsh."

"She informed me this morning. Then I spoke to one of the name partners on the phone. He wanted me to meet with him to see if I wanted to move over there, but I turned him down. If I'm not in charge, I'd rather move on."

"Just like that?" Devin blinked in confusion. "You said there would have to be a transition."

"There will be. We're going to move clients over starting in two weeks, then I'll go over there for a while to make sure the new people assigned to each client understand what's going on. If all goes according to plan, I'll be out of there by early in the new year."

"Will you have time to find a new job while you're doing that?"

"Well, they're going to give me a month's salary as a bonus for helping with the transition." She shrugged. "That's not much of a severance package, but they didn't have to offer me anything. Next time I enter into a partnership, I'm going to include a big, juicy, golden parachute for myself."

Devin had no idea what a golden parachute was, but half of the legal terms Sunny used went over her head. "Is that what you'll do? Start another firm?"

"I have no idea," she said, sticking her feet out and lacing her hands behind her head. "I'm not even going to think about looking for work until I've wrapped up this transition. I need a break."

Devin tucked an arm around her and held her close, relieved when Sunny let herself be embraced. "You'll figure out what you want. I have confidence in you."

"Thanks," she said, cuddling up like a puppy. "I guess I should tell you the bad news, huh?"

"Bad news?" She felt her body stiffen. "Given that you were talking to Angelica…"

"Yeah." Sunny lifted her head and looked into Devin's eyes. "She's being pressured to sue you, but she hasn't made up her mind."

Devin felt her eyes close, and she sat there quietly for a few seconds. "What's your instinct?"

"I honestly can't guess. If I were going to sue someone, I'd start the ball rolling as soon as possible. The fact that it's been nine months and she's still waffling…"

"Damn," Devin murmured. "I'm worried about myself. Obviously. But I'm more worried about Edie. She's got a business and a nice house and they own some rental cabins. She could lose everything, Sunny."

"Let's hope for the best, okay? Maybe Angelica will back off."

"Maybe," Devin said, musing that if Angelica had even a little bit of her husband's personality, backing off wasn't in the cards.

◆

It was still early, not even nine, but Sunny looked a little pale. Devin got up, then reached down and took her hand, pulling on it steadily. "Time for bed."

"So soon? Now that you don't go to work at dawn, we could stay up until ten, couldn't we?"

"You look like you're fading. I think all of this stuff with the new firm upset you."

Sunny allowed herself to be hauled to her feet, then tucked her arm around Devin's waist as they started for the bedroom. "I guess it has," she admitted, "but I'm not as upset about losing the firm as I thought I'd be."

"No?"

"Not really. I'm ready to let the firm be in the past. Now I'm concerned about my future. I didn't earn a fantastic salary, but I had control over what I earned, you know? I won't have that if I work for another firm as a hired hand."

Devin gave her a sidelong look. "I don't think I get your point."

"Well, Hank and I had control over expenses. Obviously we had some level of control over bringing in new clients and hiring new associates. The choices were ours, and the draw we took reflected that. As an associate, I'll just get a salary. If they want to dump more work on me, I won't get a raise. Someone else's decisions will affect my work life, but not my income."

They'd reached the guest room, where Devin usually peeled off to brush her teeth and get ready for bed. But she kept going, guiding Sunny into her bath. Devin sat on the edge of the counter and said, "We've never had this talk, but maybe we should. I don't want to pry, but you can go for a while without a salary, right?"

Sunny started to put a stripe of paste onto her toothbrush, her focus more locked-in than it had to be for such a simple task. "Define 'while.'"

"I don't know. I have no idea how long it might take to find a job you'll like. Do you?"

She shrugged. "It can definitely take a while. It all depends."

Devin waited patiently for Sunny to finish brushing, then said, "You didn't answer my question. Do you have a good cushion?"

"Good?" She started to take her sweatshirt off, then picked up the pajamas she'd left in the bathroom that morning and slipped the top on. "If I'm off more than a month, I'll have to dip into my retirement fund."

Leaping to her feet, Devin nearly shouted, "That can't be true!"

Even though it wasn't funny at all, Sunny let out a chuckle. "It certainly can be. I've got a huge overhead, honey. I don't live paycheck to paycheck, but I'm not far from there."

"*I* don't live paycheck to paycheck, and there are months I don't make a thousand dollars!"

"What are your fixed expenses?" Sunny asked, raising an eyebrow.

"Fixed? Three hundred."

Not replying immediately, Sunny finished dressing and went into the bedroom. "My fixed expenses are a few times higher, Dev. My real estate empire, health insurance for my mom, my car, the health club..." She trailed off as she started to pull down the sheet and blanket. "Add in all of the restaurant meals, lunches at work, haircuts, gas, clothing, dry cleaning, house cleaning... It adds up."

"What's your monthly budget?"

Sunny neatly stacked the decorative pillows onto a chair. "I don't really have one. I spend what I have to and save whatever's left."

"I'm not saying we have to do things my way," Devin said, trying to keep the frustration from her voice, "but that's a crazy way to run your life."

Sunny looked up sharply. "Crazy?"

"Crazy," Devin insisted. "You don't spend until you're broke. You set a budget and stick to it. We need to do that, Sunny. Now."

Sunny pulled the bedspread off and started to fold it. She didn't look at Devin, but even without seeing her face Devin knew she was angry. "I've never asked you to bail me out, and we don't share finances. That means I've never done anything to hurt your credit score. So how do you think you have the right to tell me how to handle *my* finances?"

"Oh, shit." Devin sat on the bed and let her head drop until she held it in her hands. "I'm so sorry," she said softly. "I was so surprised, I jumped in like you'd done something dangerous while we were camping." She looked up and their eyes met. "I really am sorry. You don't have to structure your finances like I do mine."

"But you think I should," Sunny said, sitting next to her.

"Well," she said, taking in a breath, "I'm careful with my money, and I've got a good amount of savings, given my income. So, yeah, I think my way is the right way."

"I've *never* had to follow a budget. I've always made enough to cover everything."

"It's not too late to start," Devin said, hoping Sunny gave in without a fight.

"How would I start?"

Relief flooded Devin when she realized she'd hooked her. Once she was curious, she was ready to jump in. "We sit down with all of your bills and figure out exactly how much money you have to earn to handle your obligations. Then we see how much is left and decide how to allocate it." She met her eyes again and gentled her voice. "Once we have a budget, I'll know how much I have to contribute. I've been sponging off you for long enough."

"You don't sponge. You pay for all of our groceries, you do all of the cooking, and you'd clean the house if I'd let you. That's huge."

"Not if we don't know what our budget is. I have a feeling my contribution's going to have to rise—a lot."

Saturday was a rainy, windy, gloomy mess of a day, and the state of Sunny's desk echoed it. Her statements and bills were spread all over it and the bed, and Devin seemed more alarmed with every revelation.

They now had a list of all fixed expenses, and a much longer list of Sunny's discretionary spending. It wasn't pretty. Actually, it was damned ugly.

Devin paced around the room, looking worried but really cute with a pencil stuck behind her ear. "First question," she said, still pacing. "Is there something wrong with your sister?"

"Wrong?"

"Does she have mental problems? Or some physical limitations not obvious to a casual visitor?"

"What do you mean? Brittany's fine."

"Then why are you paying for her?" Devin stopped and struck a pose, hands on hips, legs spread.

"She's…" Sunny shrugged. "She's never really gotten on her feet. When her last boyfriend threw her out of their apartment, I helped her buy a house so she had some stability."

"You didn't *help* her," Devin said. "You bought it for her, and now you're paying all of the bills."

"I have to. It'd go into foreclosure if I didn't."

Devin stared at her for a second, then started to pace again. "Your mom's in good health?"

"She's fine. She complains about every ache and pain, but she's never had anything seriously wrong with her."

"Then she needs to work more hours. You can't afford to pay her mortgage and her real estate taxes and fill her cupboards with everything from nail polish to Scotch, Sunny. You don't have the money to do that."

"But I do! I've been doing it for years."

Devin sorted through the statements, finally coming up with the one she wanted. She thrust it in front of Sunny's face. "Read the balance."

"Ninety five hundred and forty dollars."

Shaking it in the air, Devin said, "You have less than ten thousand dollars in savings. I don't mean to be rude, but that's insane! I've got four times that, and I make less than fifteen percent of what you do."

"You have fewer expenses," Sunny explained once again. "I can't get out of these debts, so I have to find a job that pays more."

"That's not the answer," she said, her voice low and firm. "If you ask me, you should sell all three of your real estate holdings. You and I should live somewhere cheaper and closer to your office, and Brittany should move in with your mother if she can't make it on her own. If you forced that option on her, I have a feeling she'd refuse and figure something out. Same for your mom. One day she's going to *need* for you to pay for her and you're not going to be able to because you're broke!"

"I'm not broke," she said dismissively. "I've got money in my retirement account."

"Not nearly enough. You should have four times that amount. But you took a big withdrawal to buy your mom's condo. And another one for God knows what." She stared so intently that Sunny gave up the info.

"I took money out for Brittany's house, too. Putting down twenty-five percent made the monthly payments much more affordable."

Devin slapped herself in the head a few times, as frustrated as Sunny had ever seen her. "You can't do that," she said, almost whining. "Retirement funds have to be allowed to grow. They're untouchable."

"Well, there's no way I'm going to convince my mom to move, unless it's to a bigger condo. She's been on me to upgrade for months."

Devin grasped her by the arms and held her still. When she spoke, she was calm and cool, but her words were harsh. "The money you spend on your mom and your sister is optional. You've chosen to keep them dependent on you, but you don't have to keep going. You can let them test their wings. I'll bet they can both fly if they have to."

Sunny stared at her, realizing Devin had no earthly idea what she was talking about. It was easy to say what you should and shouldn't pay for when it wasn't your family. But when it was, you were stuck. Completely and irretrievably stuck.

The new year was only a few days old when Devin picked up her phone early one morning, saw the caller ID, and said, "Cold enough for you?"

Edie laughed. "Not nearly. But that snow we got last week looks like it's going to make a good base. We got five more inches last night, and I'm finally going to start arranging for some trips."

"Awesome! I know things have been slow so far."

"Fishing's been good, so I'm not complaining. So? What do you say? I've got a couple who got engaged when you took them out five years ago. They want to celebrate by going snowshoeing again, and they want you to take them. Three days, anywhere you want."

"I don't have any plans to come back," Devin said, feeling like a knife pierced her heart every time she said that. "Sunny's about to start looking for a new job."

"In Dallas?"

"Maybe Austin," she said, able to summon some enthusiasm about that. "We went there for Thanksgiving and Christmas, and I liked it a lot. It's homier than Dallas, even though it's still huge. Sunny prefers it, too."

"What about you, honey? Are you getting what you need?"

To make sure Sunny didn't hear her, she went into the guest bedroom and pushed the door mostly closed. "I'm fine, Edie. I'm still doing some landscaping and a lot of handy-woman stuff. We're trying to figure out how I can get some more wilderness trips in but…" She wasn't about to explain that they were trying hard to live on a very lean budget and simply didn't have the money to travel. "It's tough," she finished.

"I've never met a person who needed alone time as much as you, Dev. Well, other than Jasper Stoneham."

"He was crazy as a loon! Actually, he talked to loons, and he believed they talked back."

"Maybe they did. He was awfully good with birds. They say he went through a twenty-five pound bag of feed a week, just from the birds who ate out of his hand."

"I don't talk to birds," Devin scoffed. "I just like to be alone. That's when I have time to think."

"So what do you do when you *don't* have time to think?"

"You just miss it," she said, with a wave of sadness threatening to knock her off her feet. "You just miss the hell out of it, Edie."

After catching up on all of the people they knew in common, Devin hung up and went into the kitchen to make Sunny's lunch. Now that they were following a strict budget, they ate every meal at home. The fancy grocery store was off the table, too. Now they went out to a big box store on Saturday and loaded up. Sunny probably wouldn't have chosen to have the same protein three or four times in a week, but when chicken thighs were on sale, they ate chicken thighs until they went through a family pack.

Devin had just finished cutting up carrot sticks and radishes for Sunny's mid-day snack when she looked up to find her staring at her.

"I heard you on the phone," she said. "Was that Edie?"

"Yeah. You can choose between leftover meatloaf or Texas chili. What'll it be?"

"It's not *Texas* chili," Sunny chided. "It's just chili. That'll be fine. I've only had it once this week." She walked over and stood next to Devin. "What did Edie want?"

"Not much."

"Sounded like she was offering you a trip." Sunny took a carrot stick and started to munch on it.

"Uh-huh. I turned it down. I don't think the clients would like the snowshoeing we have around here."

"Devin," Sunny said, turning her and holding onto her hips. "Do you want to go home and work for a while? I know you missed seeing your family at Christmas. Why not go and stay for a few weeks? You can do a few trips and get some alone time."

"No thanks," she said. "I'm out of the guide business."

"What?" Sunny touched her chin, making her lift her head so their eyes met. "Since when?"

"Since March," she said, pulling away so she didn't have to look into Sunny's probing gaze. "You were there."

"Wait. Wait." She grasped her and turned her again. "You're saying you wouldn't lead a trip even if you were home?"

"I've given it up."

"Devin!" Sunny wrapped her arms around her and hugged her tightly. "You've never said that! You've never even implied that. What's going on?"

She hadn't brought up her feelings in nine months, and she didn't want to bring them up now, but they were always honest with each other. That was the foundation of their relationship, and she couldn't ignore one of their bedrocks.

"I'm afraid," she said, forcing herself to look into Sunny's eyes to check them for any signs of disappointment. "I've never run away from a fear, but this one has me by the throat."

"Oh, sweetheart," she soothed, while clutching her close. "Why didn't you tell me?"

"It doesn't matter. We live in Texas. Guiding was my old life." She lifted her arms and put them around Sunny's shoulders, feeling more in control when she was the hugger rather than the huggee. "My new life is with you, being a handy-woman."

"I thought you were going to find something you liked better." She tilted her chin to be able to kiss along Devin's jaw.

"I've found a few things, but none of them pay better than what I'm doing. I might just hire a couple of people and start a little business. There's a lot of demand out there."

Sunny gazed into her eyes and blinked, looking like she was holding back tears. "You've given up so much for me, and all you have to show for it are awesome thighs from riding a bike all over the Metroplex."

"Not true." Devin shifted to be able to reach her mouth, then they kissed for a long while, enjoying the closeness at the beginning of the day. "I spend every night with the woman I love. I was tired of being a moose—just socializing when I wanted to mate. This is what I want, Sunny. I'm happy with you."

"I know that," Sunny said softly. "But are you happy enough?"

A week later, Sunny came into the house at five, an unreasonably early hour. Under one arm she held a bottle of wine, and under the other she'd stuffed a fat file folder. When she dropped her bulging briefcase, she let out a sigh. "Finished," she said. "Perry Thompson, LLP is history."

Devin took everything from her and placed it on a chair. She grasped Sunny around the waist and lifted her, leaning back until Sunny's feet were off the ground, then kissed her as her feet kicked out impotently.

"Well!" she said, when Devin placed her back on the ground. "I had no idea you could pick me up."

“Says the woman who could bench press me with her thighs.” Walking over to the wine, she picked it up and read the label. “Champagne.” Nodding, she added, “Did this eat up all of your mad money for the week, you unrepentant spendthrift?”

“It was a gift,” she said, snatching it and taking it into the kitchen to put it in the refrigerator. “I had a late lunch with Callie, then took off.”

“You left work that early?”

“I left as soon as they handed me my bonus,” she said, chuckling. “But I told them they could call any time and I’d answer questions gratis. They seemed happy.”

Devin went into the kitchen to start dinner. “That was nice of Callie to commemorate your firm’s closing.”

“Yeah,” Sunny said. She sat on the stool at the passthrough and smiled. “Maybe I’ll take it with me and we can have it on our first night at your cabin. Kind of romantic, huh?”

“My what?” Devin could feel the blood drain from her face.

“Your cabin. We’ll be in Bangor tomorrow afternoon by two, and Chris is going to come pick us up. I figured we’d stay the night at your parents’, then go into Greenville on Friday. That’s when we’re picking up our clients,” she added. “When we get back on Sunday, we’ll finally get to go to your cabin, as long as the lake is frozen, which Chris swears it is.” She clapped her hands together. “We’re all set.”

Knees wobbly, Devin moved over to sit next to her. She stared at Sunny for a long time, then said, “Could you repeat all of that? I must be having some sort of hallucination.”

Sunny grasped her face in her hands and kissed her soundly. “We’re going to do that trip, Dev. I’m not going to let something like this hang over your head. You’re going to get rid of these bad feelings.”

“It doesn’t *matter*,” she insisted. “We live in Dallas, and we’re planning on staying here. The fact that I can’t take strangers ice fishing has no meaning!”

Sunny was still holding her, and they locked eyes as she began to nod. “It matters a lot. You can’t let this color the way you feel about yourself.

We're going to Maine, and we're staying until you get your confidence back."

"What if I…can't?" she asked, shame filling her.

Gripping her shoulders tightly, Sunny gave her a shake. "You're the bravest woman I've ever met. You'll get over this in no time. But if it takes a while—I've got the time to spend. I'm officially unemployed."

Chapter Twenty-Five

It was amazingly cold when Devin stepped out of her parents' house on Friday morning. She'd gone out while Sunny was still getting ready, just to scrape the snow off the windshield and get the heater going.

Her dad came out a minute later, in his shirt-sleeves. "Need a hand?"

"It's freezing out here! Go put your coat on."

He laughed and stuck his hands in his pockets, watching her work. "I never thought I'd see the day you complained about twenty-five degrees, Buddy. Texas has turned you into an orchid."

"Twenty-five?" she squeaked. "I thought it was five—at the most!"

"Nope. It's balmy." He moved to her side and took the scraper from her hand. "How are you going to handle sleeping outside for two nights? Is Sunny going to have to knock the icicles off you?"

"I thought I'd be doing that for her," she admitted. "Gosh, I thought a two-person team would be enough. I was going to keep her warm, while she tended to my fragile psyche. Maybe we need a third to keep us both from freezing."

"Hey," he said, wrapping an arm around her as he finished and tossed the scraper into the back of her car. "You don't have a fragile psyche. You went through something horrible, Buddy, and it's going to take some time to get your confidence back. But you will."

It felt so good to be enfolded under his protective arm, like she was a nestling seeking the protective shelter of her parent. She'd never thought of herself and her dad as birds, but it was a nice image. She could see them as a pair of snowy owls, sitting on a high branch, ignoring the snow and the bracing wind as they surveyed the forrest.

"Remember when you fell into the lake when you were little?"

"I told Sunny about that," she said, laughing. "She said she'd never have gone near water again, but I told her that's not an option up here. You've got to go right back out, trying to make yourself believe you've had your dip and won't have another."

He pulled away to stare at her for a few moments, his smile growing. "That's how you remember that?"

"Yeah. Why?"

"You wouldn't go near the water for the rest of the winter! And the next year, you wouldn't step foot on that ice until it was thick enough to support trucks. You were terrified!"

"But I got over it," she insisted, trying to defend her reputation as a true Mainer.

"You sure did." He hugged her again, keeping her pressed tightly to his side. "You were a tough kid, and now you're a tough woman. Eventually, you got back on that ice—with a little more respect for it than you'd had before. And that's exactly what you're going to do now."

Edie caught sight of Devin and ran for her, covering the twenty feet between the register and the front door in mere seconds. "What a sight for sore eyes," she said, holding Devin in a bearhug until she struggled to free herself.

"I'm not alone," she said, her voice muffled by Edie's fluffy sweater. "Be polite."

"It's very good to see you again, Sunny," Edie said, after somewhat reluctantly letting Devin go.

They shook hands, with Sunny commenting, "Doesn't anyone know it's cold out? Your hands are hot!"

"Does she really think this is cold?" Edie asked Devin. "I saw a guy pumping gas in shorts yesterday."

"I'm afraid she'll turn into a popsicle out in the woods. When we go back to Texas she might melt into a puddle at the airport."

Edie took a look at the clock above the door. "Your clients will be here in fifteen minutes, and I know you want to check your gear. You'd better get a move on."

"Fifteen minutes?" Devin's eyes nearly popped from her head. "You said they wanted to get going at nine!"

"I lied," Edie said, clearly unrepentant. "I didn't want you to drag Sunny over here at the crack of dawn. Fifteen minutes is plenty of time to check out the bindings on some snow shoes."

"Everyone wants to control me," Devin grumbled, heading for a door with a sign that said, "Employees Only."

"I don't try to control her," Sunny said quietly, making Edie chuckle. "She always seems like she knows exactly what to do."

"How are you going to handle this?" Edie asked. "Are you going to say you're Dev's guest? Or do you want the clients to think you're a guide, too?"

"If they're sentient, they'll know I'm not. We thought we'd tell the truth—up to a point. I'll say I'm a friend from out of town, tagging along to help out. We won't add that it's Devin's confidence that needs a boost."

Edie moved to get closer to Sunny and speak softly. "Even if she never works for me again, I can't bear to see her walk away because she's afraid. She's one of the best I've worked with, Sunny, and, believe me, a lot of fine guides have walked through those doors. Devin's a natural."

"In almost everything," Sunny agreed. She gave Edie's arm a squeeze and went into the storeroom to find Devin moving equipment around.

"Hey," she said when Devin looked up, clearly nervous.

"Can you shake those sleeping bags out and make sure they're clean? Some of the guides don't check the equipment out properly when they return it." Her voice sounded tight, and was pitched a little higher than normal.

Sunny began to work, taking a look at the gear at Devin's feet. "You're going to carry all of that?"

"I thought I would." She had a vaguely insolent expression on her face, like she was daring Sunny to contradict her. She picked up a length of braided rope and looped it into a neat bundle, then lay it on top of the length of rope that was already on the floor. She had six pairs of ski poles gathered for four people, along with five pairs of snow shoes and spare parts to repair everything. Of course, she needed a pretty big tool kit to handle all of that work, and Sunny was expecting to find a power drill and a generator. But she wasn't about to make fun of Devin's preparation. Something caught her eye, and she bent to pick it up.

"Is this the beacon you used when you went on your little hike?" She always referred to Devin's month in the wilderness that way, rather than the more appropriate term—falling off the face of the earth.

"Yeah. I was thinking about buying another one…" The first glint of indecisiveness flashed across her face and Sunny went over to her. She was about to hug her, but got the unspoken message this wasn't the time.

"Do they wear out that quickly?"

"No. It should last for years and years."

"Um, wasn't it expensive?"

"Uh-huh," she said, bending to start putting all of the gear onto her handy sled, just like the one she'd taken on the fateful trip.

"You never carried one before, Dev. Having one is probably enough, okay?"

She looked up and Sunny saw how massively nervous she was.

"It will be fine," Sunny said, keeping her voice soft and sure. "Promise. The weather's great, no storms in the forecast, there's snow on the ground, and your clients are a known commodity. This is the best scenario you could hope for to get your feet wet."

"More socks!" She ran out to the display and picked up four pair, not bothering to pay for them or mention them to Edie. Knowing Devin, she just wanted them as insurance. Insurance Sunny prayed they wouldn't need.

That night, they lay in their tiny tent, sleeping bags zipped together. Their faces were just inches from each other, and Sunny could still smell the pasta with spicy arrabbiata sauce on Devin's breath, even though they'd just brushed their teeth. But it was a nice smell, reminding her of how charming Devin had been during dinner. When she was "on," she spoke a lot more than normal, laughed a little louder, and acted very much like she was in charge. That was a nice combination, but Sunny liked the quieter, more laid-back Devin just as well. They were both precious.

"You know," she said quietly. "We haven't failed to get after it many nights since we've been together. Are we honestly going to skip two in a row?"

A sly smile settled onto Devin's pretty lips. "If you're in the mood, I'll get right on it, but we've gotta be super quiet. The last thing you want to hear your guide doing is having sex."

"No, the last thing you want to hear is her peeing on your tent." Sunny laughed at the puzzled look on Devin's face. "I was trying to think of something weird that you'd never want to hear. How'd I do?"

"Not bad." Devin put her hand on Sunny's hip and pulled her closer. Now she had the slightly devilish grin she often got when she wanted to start things off. "So?" They kissed, gently, for a long time, with Devin pulling her closer and closer. When she spoke, they were pressed firmly against each other, with Sunny able to feel Devin's lungs expand when she took a breath. "Keep going?"

"I want to, but I don't want to have to be quiet." Sunny pulled her hand from the warmth of their sleeping bag and tugged on Devin's nose. "Even though you're as quiet as a mouse, I don't want to have to think about Bill and Mandy hearing us."

"Good," Devin said, giving her another long kiss. When they broke apart, she said, "I like to concentrate exclusively on you, not other people."

"We're in agreement." Sunny turned onto her side and let Devin spoon up against her. "I love having you hold me. When I've had a bad day, knowing you're there makes all of the little aggravations just fade away."

"Did you have aggravations today?"

She sounded a little unsure of herself, and Sunny craned her neck to see her face. "None. I hope you didn't, either."

"It was a good day," Devin said, smiling contentedly. "I was afraid of going, but I love being out so much that Mother Nature kinda made up for my nerves. It was a very good day," she added, "and a lot of that was because you were here."

"We make a good team, baby. And we get to do this all over again tomorrow."

"Yeah," Devin said, her warm breath tickling the back of Sunny's neck. "Can't wait."

Sunny stood on wobbly feet, trying to find her balance while holding onto Devin's gloved hands. "I don't want you to skate backwards," Sunny said. "It's dark out and you could easily miss something."

"I won't miss anything," Devin said, a smirk firmly attached to her mouth. "But just so you don't worry, I'll be right next to you, going in the proper direction. I just want to make sure you're comfortable before we start."

"These don't feel much like inline skates." The blades actually felt as thin as a sheet of paper. "Are you sure the motion's the same?"

"I've never been on inline skates," Devin said, chuckling.

Sunny slapped at her, nearly falling onto her butt when she did. "You lied to me!"

"I did not! I didn't say I knew they were similar from personal experience. My friends who've done both say they're the same when you're just moving around kinda slowly."

"That's what we're doing? Moving around slowly?" She nodded her head toward the dark shape in the water that seemed very far away. "Slowly will get us to your cabin?"

Devin did a neat little turn, stood right next to Sunny, then grasped her hand. "We'll start slow, then speed up when you get your sea legs. Which you will. Quickly."

"You're so sure of yourself," Sunny said, laughing along with her. "But I'm the one who's going to struggle to stay upright."

They started at a snail's pace, but within three strides Sunny was smiling. "You weren't lying even a little bit. This is very much like inline skating."

"I don't lie to you, partner." She beamed a smile that the rising moon caught with its mellow light. "I never knew that taking a trip with a partner would be so awesome. Thanks for pushing me."

"You're welcome. We all need a little push once in a while." She took in a deep breath of the stunningly crisp, clean, pine-scented air. "If I'd known how much fun it was to lead a trip, I might have become a Maine guide—Texas division." She laughed at the way that had come out. "Not that I led in any way, but I was paying rapt attention to how you did things. I let myself view the whole trip through your eyes."

"It was good all around. Good clients, good weather, good snow." She turned her head and let out a breath, leaving a little cloud of vapor in her wake. "But I'm still very skittish about being with a more demanding crowd. Or worse weather. Or…something bad." Sunny could see her shiver, even through three layers of clothing. "There are so many bad things out there that can happen."

"And so many wonderful things that it's worth whatever time we have to invest to get you comfortable again, honey. There's no rush."

Sunny held onto the railing and pulled herself up the stairs, jiggling the door latch while Devin laughed at her antics. "Give me a second. I do lock it, you know."

"So all of the thieving ice skaters stay out?"

Devin moved to stand beside her in front of the door. "There are lots of people out here in the winter. I doubt anyone has ever tried to get in, but I don't want some kids to trash the place on a dare." She had to play with the key for a minute, but it finally seated itself and the door opened. Devin took in a deep breath, loving the smell of her little hideaway. Whatever mustiness it had during the summer had gone by now, and the place mostly smelled like the pellets for her stove. Delightful.

"It's adorable!" Sunny cooed. "Seriously, Dev." She dropped to her butt and unlaced her skates, then moved inside so Devin could do the same. "I thought it would be freezing cold since no one's been here, but it's not at all."

"That's because I put a lot of money and time into winterizing it." She'd gotten her skates off and had brought both pair inside so they'd dry out. After pulling her little flashlight from her pocket, she moved the beam across the single room. "Hold on and I'll light a lantern." She got one going, then stripped off her coat. "When I fire up the pellet stove, you'll be toasty warm." She filled and lit it while Sunny was wandering around the small space, touching everything.

"This is very much like you," she said, the fondness in her voice unmistakable. "Neat, clean, and orderly. Kind of like Edie's storeroom, but I think you have more gear."

"No I don't," she said, laughing a little. "Well, maybe I'm close. I allow myself to spend twenty-five percent of my discretionary money on gear. I'm always saving for something I don't really need."

"Even though it's a little overstuffed, I see your personality in your cute little decorating touches."

"This is still my grandparents' place, so some of the stuff is theirs." The space was already starting to warm, and she removed her sweater, leaving her long underwear top on. "Let's see," she said, "what all did I do to put my mark on the old place?" Moving across the room, she tapped on the glass. "New double pane windows. They only had windows on the sides, but I added the one in the back. In the summer, I can leave the door open and have flow-through ventilation."

"Good idea. You have screens, right?"

"Given that I don't want to be picked up and carried off by mosquitos, I sure do." Tapping her foot on the floor, she said, "I took up the whole floor, added sub flooring and insulation, then put it back down. Took me forever to mark every board so I could put every one back into the right spot, but you can't get this kind of old-growth wood anymore. It was worth the trouble."

"It looks great," Sunny said as she doffed her coat and moved around the bed to put her arms around Devin. "And it's cozy. Just the place to snuggle up next to you and make up for lost time."

Devin laughed at the expression on her face. Kind of a mix between sexy and playful. Really nice.

"Hey, wanna do something cool?"

"Sure. I love doing cool things."

"Put your coat back on. You'll need it." Devin went to the door and said, "Give me a minute to clear the snow off the porch." Then she got busy, using an old broom she kept on the deck for this exact purpose. It didn't take long, since the snow hadn't melted much and was still pretty light. She popped back in and grabbed a plastic tarp and took the down comforter off her bed. "One more second." It took a little longer than that, but not long at all. Then she went back in, put her coat on, and took Sunny's hand. Once they were outside she said, "Until you took me to that damn mountain river, this was my favorite place on the planet." She sat down and leaned against the wall, able to stick her legs straight out on the deep, covered porch. "Come on," she said, patting the now-cushioned floor. "You're in my inner sanctum. No one but my family has ever been out here with me."

Sunny gracefully folded her legs under her and cozied up to Devin's side.

"In the summer, we have big chairs out here, but we store them at my grandparents' house in the winter." Laughing, she said, "Don't even ask what a ridiculous job it is to get them to shore in my canoe. But my grandpa built them himself, and he's very protective of his creations."

"This is…perfect," Sunny said, with a serene smile on her pretty face. "I feel like I can see to the ends of the earth."

"Just a few miles," Devin said, "but it does seem endless, doesn't it? Not to mention what it looks like when you tilt your head back."

They both did, in unison, then let out soft sighs. "Unbelievably gorgeous," Sunny said. "Oh! A shooting star!"

"We'll see them every few minutes, but given that was the first one we've seen together, I think we should make a wish." She grasped Sunny's hand and closed her eyes. "Ready?"

"Ready."

Then warm lips touched her own and Devin opened her eyes to see Sunny's surprisingly dark lashes. "Did you make a wish?"

"I did. And I already got it." She wrapped her arms around Devin and hugged her tightly. "How about you?"

"Gotta keep them secret. They won't come true if you talk about 'em."

Sunny stuck her lower lip out for a second. "But I made it clear you were my wish. Can I make another one?"

"Normally, no," she said thoughtfully. "But I'll make an exception since you're new around here."

Smiling, Sunny closed her eyes tightly and kept them that way for a minute. "Got it. And I really, really hope this one comes true."

"There's another one," Devin said, pointing. "I'll wish for the same thing again, since I really want mine to come true, too." She closed her eyes and took in a breath, then let it out slowly. "I think that should do it. We're good to go."

"We're very good," Sunny agreed. "Very, very good." She wrapped her arm around Devin and they sat there in the nearly still night, listening to the whistling of the gentle breeze through the trees. "Actually, this might be the best I've ever been."

On Wednesday evening, they rushed a couple of day-hikers back to Edie's, then got into Devin's car and drove for a surprisingly long time.

"Does Lori live in Canada?" Sunny asked.

"Not quite, but she's twenty miles closer to it than I am. We're by the southern part of the lake, and she's near the middle."

"I don't have a good sense for what that means."

"Well, we could get there pretty fast if the lake was ice free and we had a fast boat, but it's not and we don't. Chris wanted land, so they had to be pretty far from town to afford a nice parcel."

"Is that what you'd like? I mean, when we retire here."

Devin's face lit up in a nanosecond. "We're going to retire here?"

"Of course! I'm going to save some money, and we'll retire the first moment I can afford to."

"Cool," she said, still grinning. "Well, there's a part of me that wants to live remote, but it's also nice to just visit remote spots. Being out in the middle of nowhere drives Lori crazy sometimes, and we're more alike than different."

"I bet it's Chris who wanted to live away from people."

"Correct. And he usually gets his way. But Lori's not generally unhappy out here. It's just when they're snowed in that she hates it."

"Interesting. I'd think people out here would have snow blowers."

"Uh-huh," Devin said, a sly smile covering her face. "Most do."

Finally, they pulled off onto what was clearly an unpaved road. Even with the blanket of snow, it was a little like going over a thousand sets of railroad tracks. "Kind of rough," Sunny said. "How long is their driveway?"

"Not very. But we're a mile away from it. I guess this is a county road, but they don't plow it."

"How do they get out?" Sunny asked, alarmed.

"Chris has a plow on his big 4x4, but if he's out on a trip…"

"No wonder it drives Lori crazy out here!"

"With two little boys, who've both been to the ER more than once. She's been begging me to buy a big-ass truck, and I try to convince myself she just thinks it'd be safer for me, but I think it's really so I can come bail her butt out when she's stuck."

"I know what Lori means to you," Sunny said softly. "You'd dig her out by hand if she needed you."

"I sure would," Devin said, tearing up. "She's the sister I would have chosen if I'd gotten the chance."

They passed turnoffs to a few homes on the drive, small places tucked in amid the trees, all of them in need of paint or other repairs. If Sunny had to guess, she would have said these were older people who'd had decent jobs but hadn't saved enough to provide for a very plush retirement. People who simply couldn't afford the upkeep required to keep a house looking sharp. They reached the end of the road, with a sign warning drivers to turn around. But Devin turned into a drive Sunny hadn't even seen, and crawled down a short, relatively steep incline. This house was clearly not owned by older people. Children's drawings were affixed to the windows, some plastic trucks and boats lay in the snow by the front door, and a kid's sled rested against the clapboard siding. Before they'd knocked on the front door, someone flung it open and two rambunctious little guys flew out, neither wearing a coat.

Devin bent and swooped the smaller boy into her arms, and he burrowed his face into her neck, the way Sunny often did. Clearly, she had a very compelling pull, but Sunny was surprised to see little boys so drawn to her, given how standoffish Ashton was—and vice versa.

The little guy was about three, and his brother looked up at Devin with what was clearly disappointment. She saw it as well, bent again and grabbed him in her other arm, grunting from the effort. "You're so big I can hardly get an arm around you!" Turning with her burden, she said, "Caleb is in my right and Brody's in my left. Guys, this is Sunny."

"Good to meet you," Sunny said, taking her glove off and shaking each little hand.

"Hi," Brody said, but his little brother turned and nuzzled harder against Devin.

Sunny patted his back and said quietly, "I don't blame you for not letting go of her. She hugs great, doesn't she?"

Devin rolled her eyes, but Caleb peeked out timidly and gave Sunny a curious look.

"You're gonna like her," Devin said, addressing both boys. "She's a lot of fun."

"How much of my heat are you going to let fly out of this house?" a male voice boomed.

Smiling, Devin stepped inside and settled both boys onto the floor. "Tell me how much you missed me," she said before being picked up like a child by Chris. Sunny hadn't focused on him on the day he'd come to save them from the lodge, but now she took him in. He was a big, tall, muscular guy with dark hair, an even darker beard, and twinkling brown eyes. But his most distinctive feature was that he was clearly crazy for Devin.

"I missed you a ton," he agreed, then put her down even though he looked like he could have tossed her over his shoulder and gone on a twenty mile hike. "Chris Carter," he said, extending his hand to Sunny.

She shook it, mentally comparing his grip to that of a gentle bear. His big paw bore deep, wide calluses, but he grasped her hand almost delicately.

"Sunny Thompson. It's very nice to meet you all, even though Devin talks about you so much I feel like we've known each other forever."

"We will," he said, showing his teeth when he smiled. "Lori!" he called out. "Come be sociable."

"You're supposed to be helping," she yelled back. "I can't do all the work and be sociable at the same time."

Devin smiled at Sunny. "She's a very gracious host. Spends all her time watching shows on how to throw elegant dinner parties."

As Devin spoke, a tall, trim, outdoorsy-looking woman walked into the room, wearing a red and blue plaid flannel shirt, jeans and work boots. She had some of the same hearty affect that Devin gave off, but she was actually a little gayer looking. She grabbed Devin from behind and hugged her until she grunted, then made eye contact with Sunny from over Devin's shoulder. "Sorry, but I'm not letting go. I claimed her years and years ago, and I've got dibs."

"I'm happy to share," Sunny said. She put her hand out and they shook, while Lori's arms were still loosely holding Devin.

"I know everything about you, Sunny," Lori said. "If I talk to Dev for a half hour, twenty-eight minutes are about you."

"That can't be true, since she tells me every little detail about all y'all after you speak."

Lori planted a big, noisy kiss to Devin's cheek. "Maybe we talk for more than a half hour. You know how chatty she is."

"Oh, that's her," Sunny agreed, laughing. "Never shuts up."

While Devin and Chris stayed in the living room to play with the boys, Sunny stood in the spacious kitchen and tried not to suck too badly at helping. "I'm good at setting the table," she offered weakly. "Devin does all the cooking."

"She likes to," Lori said, chuckling. "Probably because she's never had to. It's impossible to get her mom to give up her domain." She pointed to the cabinet behind Sunny's head. "Plates are in there. Use plastic for the boys." She started to drain some pasta, commenting, "Neither Chris nor I really like cooking, so we trade off. Whoever cooks gets to sit down while the other one cleans up."

"Devin cleans up too," Sunny admitted. "Come to think of it…" A burst of anxiety hit her, and she steadied herself by grabbing onto the counter. "She does everything! How in the hell did that happen?"

Lori gave her a warm smile. "You don't have to worry about her. I'd hate to meet the woman who could boss her around if she didn't want to be."

"Oh, I don't do—"

"I'm teasing you. I know you don't take advantage of her. Or at least I know she doesn't feel like you do. Either way, she's happy."

"That's so weird," Sunny said, still not able to get her mind around their patterns. "I've always been the one to make sure things were running smoothly. But Devin stepped in like I'd hired her to manage the place!"

"That's her to a T. If you have everything under control, she can relax and go along with the program. But if her dinner isn't on the table when she's hungry—she's taking over."

"I've let this get completely out of hand! She takes care of me like it's her top priority, but I haven't been doing the same for her."

Lori had obviously reached a stage of the dinner prep that allowed for a break. She jumped onto the counter and let her feet dangle for a second before she started to softly kick the lower cabinet. "Would you like to know why Dev's not living in Bangor, parenting a kid?"

"Huh?" Sunny stared at her, mouth agape.

"You know about Taylor. But I bet you don't know the real reason Devin took off."

Sunny was across the room in a split second, ready to grasp Lori by the shoulders and shake her. "Tell me!"

After chuckling at Sunny's outburst for a second, Lori grew thoughtful. "Both Dev and Taylor were very nurturing people, but Taylor was more forceful about it. After a while, I think Dev started to feel that Taylor was controlling her more than caring for her. She *hates* that."

"What did she do? Tell me exactly, so I don't do it."

"Devin's happy," Lori said, with her smile growing. "I promise you that."

"Tell me anyway. You can't be too careful."

"Okay. For one, Taylor didn't like her being a guide. She was always trying to get her to turn down longer, more dangerous trips. She hated when she went off on her own, too." Shrugging, she said, "All of the stuff you kind of unconsciously do when you love someone. But she also cooked, cleaned, and ran their errands. There was nothing for Dev to do and I think she started to feel like she was still living with her mom. She has to feel like she's needed to be happy."

"So it wasn't living in a city? She's been very clear that was their only problem."

"Have you ever been to Bangor?" Lori asked, with a wry grin.

"Briefly. Just to go to the airport."

"Well," she said, sliding off the counter to give Sunny a pat on the back, "it's no Dallas. Dev doesn't like cities, but she'll put up with living in one to be with someone she loves. If I were you, I wouldn't change a thing. Whatever you're doing is working."

Their social obligations had them at Devin's parents' house the next night, their first chance to have a relaxing dinner together.

As soon as they walked in, Sunny felt the warmth of the family extend to her. Both Peggy and Mark acted like she'd been part of the group for years, showing her the kind of familiarity she usually only experienced with close friends.

Peggy had only been home from work a short time, and she was clearly running a little late. Some of the food was still sitting in grocery bags, and she was just starting to peel an onion when the three women went into the kitchen.

"We're having dinner *tonight*?" Devin asked, hands on her hips, looking like a supervisor trying to spur her workers into stepping it up.

"If you'll take over here, I can start browning the meat," Peggy said. "I need onions diced, carrots peeled and chopped, and pearl onions blanched and peeled. Are you up to it?"

Devin turned to Sunny and smiled. "I get to cook. Take a picture, because this might never happen again."

"That's about all I can do in a kitchen," Sunny said.

"Your mom says you're a good eater," Devin reminded her, heading to the sink to wash her hands.

"That's not a compliment, Dev."

Looking up, Devin said, "It's not?"

"No, honey. That just means she thinks I'm fat."

"Fat," Devin grumbled, turning back to her task. "Stupidest thing I've ever heard."

"You can keep us company, honey," Peggy said, "or go talk to Mark. He's allergic to kitchens."

"I'll do that," she said, after taking a snap of Devin wielding a knife, with both dogs sitting at her feet, clearly waiting for something to fall in their direction.

Mark was sitting in an easy chair in the den, with the local newspaper in his hands, a cable news show on television. "Hey there," he said, looking up when Sunny entered. "Are you here to help me figure out the state of the world?"

Sunny sat in the matching chair next to him. "I guess I can try. What's the latest?"

"A few tidbits about the galaxy," he said, rolling his eyes. "Not enough information to really let you understand anything, of course." He turned the sound down when they went to the next story, harping about the dysfunction in Washington. "I always hold out hope that one of my kids will mention some science news they've seen on TV or read about." He paused for a second and smiled. "I've been waiting for years."

"What are they most interested in?"

"Mmm, the usual. Anything about extraterrestrials, anything about sex, and some of them are concerned about climate change." His expression grew thoughtful. "Those are mostly the kids who hunt or fish. They see how conditions are changing and it worries some of them."

"I've never given any serious thought to aliens coming to earth," she said. "Maybe that's more of a guy thing."

"Maybe," he allowed. A little smile appeared, very similar to one Devin showed once in a while. "I was thinking about you, well about Buddy just the other day when one of my kids said it was obvious there was no intelligent life in the universe because we haven't been visited. That's nonsense, of course."

Sunny's eyes grew wide, but she tried not to show her surprise. If Mark believed aliens walked among us…

"I tried to explain to this kid that he was looking at it with too narrow a perspective. The earth is hundreds of millions of years old, but humans have only been around for the blink of an eye. For all we know, some of the building blocks of life came from another planet."

"I guess that's possible," she said, not having much knowledge or interest in human origins to keep up her end of a conversation. "How did that make you think of Devin?" While she found his use of the term "buddy" for her ridiculously cute, she didn't want to use it herself.

"Oh, right. Well, I was trying to get this kid to think about the big picture. About how many things have to happen simultaneously to have alien visitors. You have to have two civilizations both at a similar development, at least one with beings that have the ability to travel a great distance, with an atmosphere that can support a being that developed in a very different place." He laughed a little. "I could go on for a long time, but my thought was that's what happened with you and Buddy."

"It is?"

"Yeah, in a way." His smile grew, exposing a pair of dimples that made him even more handsome. "It's taken Buddy a long time to get to a place where she's able to accommodate an alien visitor."

"I'm an alien?" she said, chuckling.

"You're a human she's not related to," he said. "I'm not sure why, but Buddy's not been good at letting women inside." His gaze locked on Sunny, making her feel like she was under a microscope. "I'm not sure if you've changed her, or she was just ready for you. But she is," he said, smiling again. "She really is." His voice lowered and he took a quick look toward the kitchen, obviously trying to make sure they were alone. "Given that I married the first woman I ever seriously dated, I was a little jealous for the first few years she was running through women, but then I started to worry about her. I didn't want her to wind up alone once she got to the point where she couldn't just bat her eyes at a girl and have her climb into her lap."

"I think she could keep that up for a long time if she wanted to," Sunny admitted, starting to chuckle. "Some of my best friends would snatch her away from me if they had a chance!"

"We don't talk about this in any depth," he said, "but I've gotten the impression she's been getting tired of the game. I think your planets have aligned at the perfect time, Sunny, and I want you to know Peggy and I couldn't be happier for you both. You've picked a good one. I promise you that."

"There isn't a doubt in my mind that's true," she said, deeply touched at his sincerity. "I'm pretty happy with her whole little solar system, too."

"Who's got a solar system?" Devin asked, somehow managing to appear without a sound.

"Long story," Sunny said, reaching up to take her hand. Devin plopped down onto her lap, being very playful. Taking her lead, Sunny wrapped her arms around her and gave her a squeeze. "But you're my north star."

Devin sat at dinner, meeting her father's gaze. They discretely rolled their eyes in sequence, but she knew he was just as interested in the conversation as she was. Neither of them had anything to contribute to it, but it was very cool to watch her two favorite women really get into a topic.

"So you traveled with the team to football games?" Peggy asked.

"Uh-huh," Sunny said, with her accent growing the longer she talked about being a cheerleader. "Our traveling squad was smaller than we had at home, but I got to travel to three or four games a year. And we all got to go to bowl games my last two years," she added. "Those were a very big deal."

"How did you do all of that and keep your grades up?"

"It wasn't easy," she said. "I had to learn how to manage my time pretty efficiently. Strength training, Pilates, cardio, and a couple hours of practice nearly every day. It's supposed to look like effortless fun, but it's hard work!"

"You should see her in the gym, Mom," Devin said, giving Sunny a fond grin. "She put me to shame when I tagged along one night."

"I wish I had the room to put in a little gym," Peggy said. "I stay fit by walking the dogs, but I don't do any strength training."

"You can come by the high school," Mark said. "Coach Gibbons would be happy to have you."

She gave him a look. "I'm not going to work out with a bunch of sixteen year old boys, Mark. I'd feel like an idiot!"

"Maybe we can work something out," Sunny said. "Even though I'm sure I'll stay active while we're here, if I don't work on my strength, I'll start to lose it."

Devin opened her mouth, ready to tease that Sunny was so strong it was sometimes like being on a bucking bronco, but she thought that might be a little much for her parents to hear. There were a lot of things that it was best to never, ever think about, and the ways your daughter and her partner had sex were high on that list.

The weather turned warmer after they'd been in Maine for a week, melting much of the snow and making the ice near the bank of the lake sketchy enough for Devin to declare they were house-bound until it firmed up again.

Even though Devin was crazy about her family, she seemed to have a low tolerance for staying with any branch more than a day or two. So after they'd spent one night with her parents, then her maternal grandparents, they headed for her paternal grandparents' after finishing up a very unsuccessful snowmobile trip.

She was in a cranky mood, and spent much of the thirty mile drive complaining about their clients, a pair of young guys who'd stiffed her out of a tip, even after Edie had refunded their money.

"It's not the money," she repeated, grumbling. "It's insisting that we go out, then complaining that conditions were bad. *I* told them it was bad. *Edie* told them it was bad. But they're the experts. Jerks."

"Well, they drove down from Quebec. I guess they decided it was worth a try."

"Worth my time?" Devin shot Sunny a perturbed look, a rarity for her. "Edie will try to pay me, but I wouldn't think of taking it. So we wasted a whole afternoon and a quarter tank of gas for jack shit."

Sunny placed her hand over Devin's and felt the small muscles move under the skin when she shifted the car. "Is something wrong, honey? I can count on one hand the number of times you've lost your temper over something like this."

Her mouth was set in a firm line, and she shook her head. But after another minute passed she said, "I get grouchy when I'm homeless."

Sunny gripped her hand briefly. "That makes perfect sense. I hope you're not moving around for me. I like hanging out with your parents."

She shrugged, looking uncharacteristically juvenile. "I do too, but it's different now that we're together. I'm used to stretching out with you, which we can't do in that little bed." She turned briefly to reveal a slow smile. "Among other things."

"We got after it just last night!"

"I know, but we didn't let go. We were super quiet, not to mention quick. Just the idea of my grandparents hearing us is enough to make me self-conscious."

"Am I getting in your way?" Sunny asked gently. "If you'd rather be alone for a while…"

"No!" she said forcefully. "I love having you with me. It's just that my routine's messed up. Before, I'd stay with Lori a lot, but I can't do that with you."

"Because…?"

"We're not going to share the sofa, Sunny. Or have six of us fighting for the only bathroom." She let out a sigh. "I lived like a vagabond before, but that doesn't work now."

"But you're sure you want me to stay?"

"Positive," Devin said, giving her a warm, bright smile. "As soon as it gets really cold, I'll be happy again."

Sunny gave her a pinch. "That makes one of us, you little polar bear."

Sunny seemed a little antsy as they got closer to town, but Devin chalked that up to being nervous about meeting this set of grandparents. "They'll like you," she teased, making Sunny slap her hand over her face.

"I'm so transparent!" She was quiet for a second. "Are you sure?"

"Positive. They're both laid-back and easy to get along with. Plus, my grandma treats me like I'm still a baby, so you'll get a kick out of that."

"Where have they been?"

"Jackman. It's a little town in the western mountains. My grandpa's best friend moved out there a long time ago and they visit each other for weeks at a time."

"That's cool. Is it a nice town?"

"Well, they call it the Switzerland of Maine, but I kinda think the person who coined that term had never been to Switzerland." She laughed a little. "I haven't either, but I've watched ski races held there. Those are *mountains*. Compared to Switzerland, we've got big hills."

"Don't complain about your hills. They're still much bigger than anything you'll find around Dallas."

"I've noticed," Devin said, as she pulled onto the road that led to her grandparents', smiling when Sunny tugged the visor down and fussed with her hair. "You look fantastic," Devin said. "Isn't my opinion the one that matters?"

"No! You have to say I look nice. I've got to work it to impress your grandparents."

As soon as Devin pulled into the drive, her grandfather was on the porch, his arms stretched out wide for a hug. Playing along, she took off running, acting like she was going to leap into his arms. But a startled cry from Sunny stopped her cold.

"I wasn't going to actually do it," Devin said, laughing.

"She had to stop that when she was ten," her grandfather said. "She would have sent me to the hospital." He wrapped Devin in a tender hug, softly saying, "We've missed you an awful lot."

"Is that Mittens?" her grandmother's voice asked. Then the door swung open and she was nearly smothered. "You're skin and bones," she insisted, patting all over Devin's body.

"I'm the same as always," she said, wriggling out of her grandmother's grip to introduce Sunny—whose eyebrows had hiked up an inch.

"Mittens?" she asked, clearly trying not to laugh.

"My grandparents, Bernard and Therese," Devin said. She put her arm around Sunny's shoulders. "And this is Sunny."

"It's very good to meet you," Therese said, shaking Sunny's hand like it was a pump she was trying to get water out of. "Even though Mittens has told us all about you, we've been dying to actually meet."

"Mittens?" Sunny said one more time.

Therese pulled Devin close and kissed both of her cheeks. "When this one was a toddler, we couldn't keep her in the house during the winter. She ran right out the door every time it opened, so I taught her that she couldn't go out unless she was dressed properly." She laughed, and Devin laughed along with her. Her grandma was such a jolly soul that you simply had to. "As soon as she heard the door crack open, she'd run to me with her little hands in the air, saying, 'Mittens?'"

"I was a polar bear cub then," Devin said. "Winter's always been my favorite season."

"That's just about the cutest thing I've ever heard," Sunny said, entering the house, with Devin pretty sure the nickname wasn't going to go unused.

They sat around the dining room table, talking, until Devin could see her grandfather trying to hide his yawns. So she sent them off to bed and started to clean the kitchen while Sunny attempted to get the always balky internet to work on her phone.

"I can help," she said, clearly distracted.

"I've got it. I can see you're itching to connect to the outside world."

"I've got…" She trailed off, engrossed. After a minute, she looked up and said, "I need my laptop. I'll be back."

Devin watched her go, a little puzzled. Now that Sunny wasn't working, she'd seemed to consciously take a vacation from the tyranny of the little device, but something had obviously caught, and held, her attention.

A while later, Devin climbed the stairs to their bedroom. Her grandparents had moved to the guest room on the first floor a few years earlier, which allowed her and Sunny some privacy, which she couldn't wait to enjoy.

When she entered the room, Sunny was sitting on the bed, typing furiously. She didn't look up or even flinch when Devin crossed the room, but her head snapped up when Devin perched on the edge of the bed.

"Did you tiptoe in?"

"Nope. You were engrossed."

"Still am. Give me a minute, okay?"

"Yep." After brushing her teeth and changing into her pajamas—a long-sleeved t-shirt and an old pair of long underwear bottoms, Devin went back into the room to watch Sunny type a few final dramatic keystrokes.

"Sent," she said, then closed the machine. A small smile settled on her face. "That's the first time I've done any lawyering in over a week."

"Ahh." Devin pulled the covers down and slipped into bed. "Helping out the guys who bought your firm?"

"I was marking up the release that Angelica wants me to sign before she cashes me out. Hank's brother must have drafted it, since it was one hundred percent in her favor." She laughed a little, clearly not bothered by that. "It was actually pretty standard. I could have signed it as is, but I'm temperamentally unable to put my name on anything I haven't fussed with."

"And then you'll get your share?"

"Uh-huh. She's going to wire it to me. I'll probably have it by the end of the week." She stood up and started to undress, moving quicker than normal since the house was much colder than she was used to. She jumped into her pajamas, flannel ones, then went to brush her teeth. When she returned, she sat by Devin and took her hand.

"This is the biggest chunk of money I'm ever going to get—the equivalent of two year's salary. I want you to know that I'm going to make sure it doesn't slip through my fingers."

Devin just nodded, not entirely sure what that meant to Sunny.

"No splurges," she promised. "No expensive vacations. No fancy cars. I promise you that every dime I spend is going to go toward something that lasts."

"Like putting it into a bank?" Devin sat up enough to kiss her. "Banks last a long time."

"I'll keep it safe," she promised. "I think I have a higher capacity for risk than you do, but I won't speculate with it."

"Want my advice?"

"Of course, honey."

Devin gave her another kiss, then pulled her down so they were lying next to one another. Leaning close, she whispered into her ear, "Don't spend a single, solitary dime."

Chapter Twenty-Six

On Friday afternoon, after a much more successful snowmobile excursion, they dropped their clients off at Edie's. Devin started to put the coveralls and boots the guys had worn away while Sunny went over to get a cup of coffee and check her mail.

The temperatures had plummeted the past few nights, firming up the ice that Sunny suspected hadn't been very weak to start with. But Devin was understandably skittish about ice safety, and Sunny expected she'd stay that way for the rest of her life. Luckily, they were now able to go back to the cabin, but that meant she had to use Edie's wifi signal before they took off. She assumed she'd eventually break herself of the habit of checking in every day, but for now she was still tethered to voice mail, texts, and email.

Devin meandered over once she was finished. "Wanna go crazy and go out for a burger and a beer? We haven't had a meal in a restaurant since we've been here."

"I'm rich," Sunny said, turning her phone around so Devin could see the very large number that was now reflected in her bank account. "We can afford dessert, too."

"Our clients gave me a twenty dollar tip," Devin said, giving her a wry smile. "When that's spent, we'll go home."

It was just four o'clock, but Sunny didn't think it was possible to be too early for Devin to have dinner. They zipped up and walked over to a bar, not a restaurant at all in Sunny's estimation. But the bartender, a guy stuck with the name Badger, ducked under the pass and came to the door to give Devin a burly hug, and that made up for the lack of ambiance. In Sunny's opinion, people who'd missed Devin were good people.

They didn't sit at the bar, as she'd expected they would. Instead, they took a little table for two that was right in front of a window, letting them watch the darkening skies and the occasional truck rumble by.

Devin suggested burgers, and after she went to the bar to order, she returned with two beers. "All the way from Portland," she said as she set them on the table. "English brown ale. I think you'll like it."

Sunny took a sip, and nodded. "It's good. Smooth. It doesn't have much of a bite."

"No, it doesn't." She gave her a lecherous smile. "But I do, and I'm gonna show it to you when we get back to the cabin. I've missed being all alone with you."

"Same here. Even though I like every member of your family, you're my favorite."

Devin seemed perfectly content, smiling as she took off her jacket and rocked back in her chair. Knowing her, she'd be happy to just sit there, not needing to talk. But Sunny wasn't wired that way, and she tossed a small grenade out, watching for Devin's reaction.

"Want to talk about money?"

Devin's eyes grew wide. "Do we need to?"

"I think we do." Sunny took a big sip of her beer, letting its chocolaty taste warm her all the way down. "I've been thinking about money a lot, given that I'm only going to get a paycheck for a few more weeks."

"Yeah," Devin said, no longer rocking in her chair. Her attention was locked in, with her barely blinking.

"After tomorrow, you don't have any trips scheduled until next Friday. Would you mind if I dashed home for a few days?"

"For…?"

"A couple of things. A guy I went to school with wants to talk with me about joining his firm."

"But I thought you didn't want to work for anyone."

"I probably don't, but I like this guy and he hinted that he's amenable to partnering up."

"In Dallas?"

"Austin," she said, "which makes the prospect even more attractive." Before Devin jumped in with more questions, she added, "So I want to talk to Adam, but I also need to meet with my financial advisor."

Devin's eyebrows shot up. "*You* have a financial advisor?"

"Nice expression," Sunny said, giving her a pat on the cheek. "You look like I just told you I had the Easter Bunny locked up in a closet."

"The Easter Bunny might be a better financial advisor than whoever told you it was okay to pull money out of your 401-K."

"Hey, just because I do dumb things doesn't mean I've been advised to do them. I promise my advisor has a good head on her shoulders. And this time, I'm going to listen to her."

"You're not going to do anything speculative with the money you got from the sale, are you?"

"Devin," she soothed, "I must not have made myself clear. That money's our security. I promise I won't run through it."

"But if you're not working—"

"I know, honey, but I promise you I'm going to figure things out. I know it won't be easy, but I'm going to take charge. It's about damn time."

When Sunny got off the plane on Sunday afternoon, she started to smile the moment she saw a blonde head wedged in among the scrum of limo drivers at baggage claim. By the time she'd snaked through the crowd, Callie was there, holding her arms wide for a hug.

"How can I miss you so bad in such a short amount of time?" she asked as she squeezed Sunny hard. Pulling away, she placed her hands on Sunny's shoulders and gazed into her eyes for a few moments. "I know exactly why. We don't talk on the phone for an hour every day. You've gotta install a satellite receiver if you're going to be out in the wilderness for long, girl. Not being able to talk to you for days at a time has me on my last *nerve*."

"Me too," Sunny sighed, nuzzling against her oldest friend. "As much as I love Devin, she'll never know me like you do."

"Same goes for Teresa, but I'd never admit that to her." She put her arm around Sunny as they turned for the parking lot. "Some things are best not said aloud."

They got into Callie's modest sedan, and headed for Sunny's condo. "My appointment's at five," she said. "Simone and I are going to have drinks while we talk. Want to join us?"

"I don't think so. But the minute you're finished, hop in your car and come to our house for dinner. I've got to make sure Simone's as tough on you as she needs to be."

"She's very competent," Sunny said, finding it odd that she had to defend her advisor to both her best friend and her partner. Maybe that would change if she actually started listening.

◆

It was almost seven o'clock when Sunny walked out of the hotel bar, heading into the teeth of a brisk, cold breeze. But she had her down coat on, and was toasty warm. Though her body was shaking, she couldn't blame the weather. Anyone who said Simone wasn't tough didn't know her at all. With laser-like precision, she'd whipped along the line items on Sunny's budget, cutting many, reducing some, and handing the paper back with red cross-outs defacing it. Following even half of Simone's recommendations would be hard. Doing all of them? Impossible.

◆

Callie allowed her to have a drink and nibble on some crudités before she began to question her. "So?" she said, "what's the verdict?"

"Worse than I thought," Sunny admitted. "She wants me to sell both my apartment and my car."

"Agreed," Callie said, with a grin beginning to show.

"No questions? The woman basically told me to upend my whole life!"

"Your apartment's too expensive," Callie said. "And your car's ridiculous. No one needs to spend the kind of money you do on that crazy thing."

Deflated, Sunny picked up a carrot and took a bite. "Are you going to help me unwind? The car's leased, you know."

"I will hook you up, girlfriend," she said, clearly excited. "Both of those millstones are about to take leave of your neck."

◆

The next afternoon, Sunny spent an hour dusting the apartment, having suspended her cleaning service during her absence. It was amazing how insidious dust was in Dallas, given they had relatively heavy clay soil. But it was able to get through or under or over any kind of barrier to settle on every surface. At six, Callie arrived, just as perky as could be. Sunny never knew her friend would get so much pleasure out of someone else not spending money, but it was clear she did.

"How did you get a real estate agent to show up on such short notice?" Sunny asked as she took her coat and hung it up.

"We're friends. I'm sure you've met Eleanor before, even though you don't remember her. She used to be with Elena Fernandez. You know, the cute gynecologist."

"Oh, I remember her," Sunny said. "She was a doll."

"Well, Eleanor was the one you didn't notice when the two of them walked into a room. You'll like Eleanor. She's good at her job, and I know she'll work hard for you."

"She'd better. Now that this ball is rolling, I want action."

"What did Devin say about all of this?"

"I can't talk to her," Sunny said, almost whining. "She and her best friend took her two little boys on a camping trip."

"It's January!"

"Her friend is easily as crazy as Devin is, with neither of them having any idea it's too cold for camping. I'm just thanking the sweet lord that I'm not there, or I'd be right out in the cold with them. I'm crazy too, but only about Devin."

At six thirty, the doorman called up and Sunny went to open the door. When a mildly attractive woman strode down the hall, she recalled meeting her years earlier. "Hi, Eleanor," Sunny said. "I'm glad you could make it."

"Good to see you again," Eleanor said. She entered, then gave Callie a hug and a kiss. "Is this the apartment we spoke about?" she asked, turning in a circle.

"This is it," Sunny said, taking over. "And I'd like to sell it as quickly as possible."

At ten o'clock the next morning, Sunny gave her car a fond pat on the butt as a guy drove it into the garage of a huge dealership. Callie had arranged for the whole deal, using her brother-in-law's cousin, the general manager, to make it happen fast.

"Well, that just knocked seven hundred bucks a month off my back," Sunny said. "If I can get rid of the condo as quickly as the car, this is going to be a very productive few days."

Callie put an arm around her shoulders as they returned to her car. "What's next on your list?"

"I guess I'll head over to my gym. After I work out, I'll go talk to the people in the membership office. I think I can go on hiatus for up to six months before they cut me."

Callie looked at her for a few seconds before saying quietly, "I hate to think of your being gone for six months."

"I don't think I will be," Sunny said. "Devin's been doing very, very well. As soon as she's able to lead a trip on her own, I'm going to get back to lawyering."

"Your interview with Adam is tomorrow?"

"Uh-huh. We're meeting for dinner." She let out a laugh. "I think that means he's too busy to squeeze me in during the day. But first, I've got to have lunch with Momma. This time I'm going to make it clear that she's not getting a bigger condo, no matter how much she begs."

Callie opened her mouth, then shut it quickly. Even though she hadn't spoken, Sunny knew exactly what she would have said—and she absolutely didn't want to hear it.

Once Callie had left to go back to work, Sunny spent a while packing up a few boxes of her most prized possessions, planning on leaving them at Callie's house. Then she slipped into a dress and put on an appropriate amount of makeup for lunch at the most elegant spot in Dallas. While she knew Devin would disapprove of blowing a wad of cash on a meal, she had an ulterior motive. Her mom was always well-behaved in public, and the spot she'd picked was the current spot Dallas's classiest women frequented—her mom's target audience for her business.

An hour later, they were shown to a cozy booth, with the deep purple suede fabric tickling the backs of Sunny's legs as she scooted across it. The hostess left them with menus and a wine list, then slid away.

"I've been after you to come here ever since it opened," Winona said. "What's the occasion? On a Tuesday, no less."

Sunny took a long look at her mom as she smoothed the gleaming white linen napkin across her lap. Without a doubt she was as happy as a clam, not having any idea that the back of a shovel was metaphorically aimed at her head. For that matter, she hadn't known that Sunny had been gone, giving an additional clue to the strength of their bond.

"I wanted to talk over some things with you, Momma, and I thought this would be a good spot. Might as well go out with a bang, as you always say."

"Go out?" she said, raising an eyebrow.

The sommelier arrived, glanced at the unopened wine list, and said, "Would you like some assistance picking out a wine?"

"I'd like a Gibson. Very dry. Two onions," Winona said. She batted her eyes at him. "You can manage that, can't you, sweetheart?"

"I certainly can. For you?" he asked, gazing at Sunny.

"I'll have sparkling water," she said, even though she craved a drink so badly she could taste one. But she needed to have all of her wits about her, even though her hands were already shaking.

"What did you mean, 'go out,'" Winona asked again, never one to miss a clue. "Who's going out?"

"Just an expression," Sunny said. "But I suppose you could take it literally." She sucked in a deep breath and gripped the edge of the table to hide her trembling hands. "I'm not going to be looking for work for a while, Momma. We're going to be in Maine."

"Maine?" Her mouth dropped open just a tiny amount. "It's almost February. Didn't you learn your lesson the last time?"

"Not really," she said. "I already knew it wasn't a good idea to ignore the advice of an expert. It was poor Hank who didn't listen."

A server came over with their drinks, and she took a gulp of her water while her mother watched her warily. "Having Hank drown was very hard on Devin. She hasn't been able to even think about going back to work, and it's a job she truly loves. So we're going to stay in Maine until she gets her confidence back."

Frowning, Winona said, "Why do you have to be there? You must think your dream job is just going to fall into your lap the minute you're ready for it, but that's not how things go, Sunny. You've got to put your nose to the grindstone and hunt a job down—*now*."

"I'm not going to do that," she said, with what felt like rocks rolling around in her jittery stomach. "I haven't made this clear before, but Devin and I are in love, Momma. She's my partner now, and her getting her confidence back is more important than my job. When she's feeling better, I'll start looking…somewhere."

"That might not be Dallas?" *Ooo, she wasn't happy about that.*

"It might not be. We both like Austin, so that's a possibility. Devin definitely prefers it."

"So Devin's in charge now. Is that what you're trying to say?"

"No," Sunny said. "Not at all. Neither one of us is in charge. We're partners. We make decisions together."

"Well, *your* vote is to stay in Dallas. She can figure something out once you're settled. Brittney said she was a whiz at getting her TV working again. I'm sure the cable company's always hiring."

"Maybe we'd better order," Sunny said, hoping for a break to stop her from saying something harsh.

Her mother picked up her menu and started to peruse it, saying, "I don't know what diet you've been on, but you should stick to it this time. This is the first time in years you actually have a jawline." She took another long look at Sunny, as if she'd just sat down. "You don't look like a raccoon any more, either. Those dark circles you had under your eyes are finally gone." She let out a heavy breath. "I fail to see the pull, but at least you're trying to keep yourself looking good for your little girl scout."

Hard to believe anyone could offer a compliment that was more of an insult than that, but her mother truly had a gift.

After ordering, Sunny got down to business. Every part of her wanted to delay, to hope for a better time, but there wasn't one. It was now or never.

"Momma, I've been looking at my life from every angle since Hank died. Now that I'm out of the partnership, I have the chance to make sure my next step is the perfect one for me."

"It's the perfect time to start earning some real money is what time it is. These are your prime earning years, Sunny. If you get left behind now..."

Sticking to the script, she said, "That's not how I look at it any more. These are my prime *living* years."

"What in the name of Jesus is that supposed to mean?"

"Just what I said. In the past, I put making money and having nice things at the top of the pyramid. But now I've realized the things I bought weren't making me happy, so I've changed my priorities."

"Of course the things you bought didn't make you happy," she said dismissively. "You never made enough to have *truly* nice things. You have a sad little apartment, no weekend place, and you couldn't have gotten into a decent country club if you'd slept with the membership director. If you saw the homes my clients live in..." She sighed, looking a little dreamy. "You'd see what real money can buy."

"Then why do you say they're neurotic messes who spend all of their money on therapy?"

"They might be neurotic, but they're perfectly happy," she sniffed. "And I help make sure they stay that way. When I accompanied Lorna's family to Aspen for Christmas, she told me how jealous her friends were that they didn't have someone like me. That's what money does for you. It lets you buy people who'll take away all of your stress."

"Well," she said, taking another gulp of water, "we'll never have that kind of money, and that's fine with me. We've got each other."

"Fine. Go live in a tent with your little girl scout. I'm finished living in a tiny place. I need some room, and it's time to get it done."

"No, it's not," she said quietly. "Actually, it's time for you to contact some of Lorna's friends." She closed her eyes halfway, like that would protect her from the fiery glare she knew would come her way. "You're going to need more money to afford your *current* lifestyle, Momma, because after March, I'm going to have to cut back."

As Winona's mouth opened, their server returned with their appetizers. As soon as he bustled away, a harsh whisper stung Sunny's ears. "What in tarnation are you talking about?"

"No matter where I work, I'm not going to put in sixty hours a week again. I'm going to cut back in order to make sure that Devin and I have time together."

"That's your business," she snapped. "Cut back all you want, but don't think you're going to start with me."

"I'm not starting with you. I'm cutting my expenses across the board to make sure we have money in the bank for emergencies, as well as retirement. I'm simply not going to be able to help you or Brittney in the same way I have been."

From under the table, a hand gripped her arm and squeezed it so tightly her fingers started to tingle when the blood supply was cut off. "The hell you say," Winona whispered. "Don't you even think of getting chintzy with me. After all I've done for you? All of the heartache I've suffered?"

For a change, Sunny didn't let her hog the martyr spotlight. "You're not the only one who's suffered, Momma. I've had my share of pain," she said, knowing she could dissolve into a puddle of tears just thinking of the losses she'd experienced. "Daddy didn't just leave you. He left us, too."

"He was a no-good, lying, cheating, shiftless bum," she snapped. "We were all better off without him."

"You chose to cut him out of your life, but we didn't." She leaned close and said the words she'd thought a thousand times but had never uttered. "If you hadn't be so dang awful to him, he might have kept in touch with us. And I know Granny and Grandad wouldn't have fallen off the face of the earth if you hadn't pushed them away. That was your doing."

With her face turning a vivid shade of pink, Winona got up with an amazing amount of composure, picked up her purse, and glided toward the front door. Sunny turned to watch her leave, sliding right by the hostess, ignoring whatever words the woman offered.

Numb, she sat there for the longest time, feeling like she couldn't remain upright. But slowly, by focusing on Devin and the life they would build together, she felt her spine stiffen. She had a goal now, and a partner who would have her back, come hell or high water. The only way to earn loyalty was to return it as well as she could. This time, that meant standing up to her mother for the first time in her life. With a sigh, she realized it wasn't going to be the last.

Sunny wasn't in the mood to talk, but she kept up her half of the conversation with the driver. Telling the guy she'd just sold her car had been a mistake. He was now hungry for information about how she planned on getting around town, offering his card if she wanted to work out some sort of off-the-books arrangement to use him as her personal cab.

She was so preoccupied by his near-badgering that she didn't see her mother standing by the building's entry until she'd thrown the door open and had one foot on the pavement. If she'd been more aware, she would have dived for the floor and told the driver to step on it.

It was hard to believe, but she and her mom had never had a significant fight. Lots and lots of small skirmishes, many instances of sharp words, and, she was embarrassed to admit, many occasions of pure snark on her part. But they'd never had a fight that lasted for more than one or two sentences. That was solely because she'd never had the nerve to stand up for herself. It was easier to just agree to whatever demands her mom made, and hope the next claim didn't come too soon.

This time it was different. She'd known this wouldn't go down well, but she honestly hadn't been able to predict what her mother's next move would be. Having her show up at the apartment hadn't even been on her list of possibilities, but here she was, looking like she was seriously contemplating filicide.

"I assume you want to come upstairs?" Sunny said, not bothering with a greeting.

"It took you long enough to get here. Why were you in a car? Did you get a DUI?"

"I did not," Sunny said. They started for the lobby, and she decided to get the next bit of news out of the way while security cameras were trained on them. "I sold my car." She swallowed nervously, then spit the rest out. "My apartment's going next."

Her mother's jawline got rock hard, but she didn't say a word while they were in the lobby. As soon as they were on the elevator, her voice rose to a dramatic pitch. "I don't know who you think you're messing with, missy, but I'm not about to let you stash your cash somewhere. I don't know what kind of bullshit you're cooking up, but I'm not eating it."

Sunny tilted her head to point her gaze at the camera. "The doorman can turn a microphone on if he thinks there's trouble in here. You might want to keep your voice down."

Like someone had stuffed a sock into her mouth, Winona didn't say another word until they were in the apartment. As the door closed, she marched over to the TV and switched it on, cranking up the volume. Then, when she was sure no strangers could hear her, she jumped right back into her rant.

"What's really going on? Are you hiding your money so that greedy bitch can't get her hands on it?"

It took Sunny a second to realize she meant Angelica. "I told you the truth, Momma. I'm going to live more simply. I'm not hiding anything, especially money."

Winona's face was flushed, and beads of sweat carved a couple of stripes through her foundation. "I need at *least* two thousand a month," she seethed. "I don't care how you get it, but I need it."

"No." Sunny didn't feel a tenth of the bravery she was trying to display, but she knew she couldn't crack now. Numbers raced through her mind, with that big, fat balance in her bank account continuing to float to the top. She could write a check for twenty-four thousand dollars and barely miss it. That would get her mother off her back for a full year. But instead of caving in, she calmly and cooly said, "I'll pay your mortgage and real estate taxes for February, but that's it. I'm not working, and I refuse to dig into my savings."

Like someone had come in and physically drained the anger from her, Winona dropped heavily onto the sofa, looking up at Sunny with a truly pathetic expression on her face. She didn't look like the formidable, frightening force that Sunny had cowered from as a child and tried to avoid as an adult. She simply looked like a woman about to turn sixty, who was seeing her nice, upper-middle-class lifestyle teeter on the brink of annihilation.

"What do you want?" she asked, clearly about to cry. "Do you want me to beg?"

Sunny stepped back in horror as her mother dropped to her knees and clasped her hands together. "I'll beg. I'll grovel if I have to. But don't turn your back on me. Please!"

Sunny stood there, frozen. Indecision, doubt, and disgust all congealed to make the butterflies in her stomach multiply tenfold. How could you watch the woman who gave birth to you pleading for mercy? The numbers continued to dance in her head. Devin wouldn't like it, but she wouldn't complain if Sunny gave her every dime she'd asked for. The words were on the tip of her tongue. All she had to do was agree and this would all pass.

But then she thought of Devin. A woman who'd worked hard and spent modestly her whole life. A woman who'd earned far less than Sunny, yet had more in savings. It wasn't that Devin didn't want nice things. She was simply mature enough to only buy the things she could reasonably afford. How was it fair to chip away at their windfall just to keep her mother in an apartment she refused to pay for—even though she could?

Sunny walked over to sit on the sofa, looking into her mother's eyes. She'd paled beneath her foundation, and her body trembled roughly. Winona was a sad sight, with all of her poise and nearly regal bearing having disappeared. It took a moment, but Sunny thought of her role in this craziness, and how she'd help build up these lofty expectations. That let her gain a little sympathy not just for her mother, but for her sister, too. She took a breath and said, "The last thing I want is for you to beg, Momma. I know it's going to be hard for you to adapt, so instead of a month, I'll cover the next two months for both you and Brittany."

"It's time for Brittany to stand on her own two lazy feet," Winona said. "Just add what you've been giving her to my pile."

"Two months," Sunny repeated. "You're both going to have to work harder or live with less." Shakily, she got up and went to the guest bedroom where she kept her checks. It took a second to dig them out, since she'd reordered things when they'd worked on their budget. *Budget.* Money was the root of all evil, wasn't it? If only she could throw a load of it at her mother this would all… Like a bolt, she was struck with a truth she must have been blind not to have seen before. This wasn't about money. It had never been about money!

Her mother had never been a very warm or loving presence, but she'd been…content before the divorce. But from that day on, she'd become not just embittered, but resentful. All this time, Sunny had assumed that resentment had been directed at just one person. But it hadn't! It was so powerful it had hit nearly everyone, but it had been centered on her. She couldn't even guess if her mother resented having kids at all, or just hated having to support them on her own, but she…did…not…want…them. None of them.

Once Sunny had started to make some money, Winona had attached herself like a leach, but even then they didn't have a true relationship. They hadn't spent a holiday together since…she couldn't even recall the last one. Winona had pitted her children against each other, continually making Sunny, and to some extent, Tiffany, responsible for things far too adult for them to handle competently. It had been impossible for Sunny to be an authority figure to a sister just fifteen months younger. They were all kids who were just bungling through life, but Winona poked at Tiffany in particular, stirring up resentment whenever Sunny had dropped the ball.

She was sick with disgust, with rage at the injustices she'd been forced to suffer. And now she was supposed to throw *more* money at her. For what? Just so she could demand still more? For a moment, she teetered on the edge of marching into the living room and throwing her mother out on her ear. But she'd agreed to pay her off, and she hated going back on her word. Checks in hand, she went to the kitchen counter to fill one out, with her hand shaking hard. From the corner of her eye she saw her mother get to her feet and straighten her clothing.

Sunny turned and extended the check, which was snatched before she could blink. Then her mother composed her expression, ran a trembling hand through her hair, and walked straight for the door.

A soft creak was the only sound as the door opened, then closed with a muted click. Stumbling, Sunny made it to the sofa and collapsed onto it, with her blouse sticking to her sweaty back, and her legs rubbery. With a stab of clarity, she decided that she would likely never see her mother again. Her gut ached with shame when she realized that was the way she preferred it.

Sitting on the sofa for the longest time, not flinching until the lights in the office building next door caught her attention, she labored to compose herself, then got up and called Callie.

"Hi," she said when her friend answered. "Will you come over?"

"What's wrong?" Callie asked, her voice immediately filled with worry.

"I think I've become an orphan—even though both of my parents are alive and well."

Hours later, they waited for Teresa to drive over to pick Callie up. With her bare foot, Sunny pushed empty beer bottles across her coffee table, counting, "Nine, ten…" Then she let out a muted laugh. "Oops! Where'd those shot glasses come from? Which one of us got the whiskey out?"

"You," Callie said. She wore the slacks to a chalk colored pantsuit, jacket abandoned, blue striped blouse untucked, shoes off. Her slacks were a wrinkled mess, and her hair looked like she'd just woken up. But she was smiling, and had her arm around Sunny's shoulders as they slumped against each other. "You got me stinkin' drunk, but I'm so proud of you I don't even care that I'm gonna get lectured all the way home."

"You're proud of me?" Sunny asked, closing one eye to be able to focus.

"Damn proud of you." Her hand absently patted Sunny's head, but she didn't hit her target very precisely, mostly glancing off the sofa. "What you did took guts. Lots of guts."

"Nah." She rested her bottle on her belly, just then realizing she had on a dress that had climbed so high only her underwear was underneath her. While trying to lift her hips to tug on the fabric, she nearly spilled her beer. Holding on tight, she let the dress issue fade. "I almost gave in, you know. But then I thought of Devin."

"I'm so glad she's not afraid to tell you what's what," Callie said, grinning slowly.

"She doesn't. Not really." She sighed, almost able to see her lover's sweet face. "I honestly just want her to be proud of me. She's sooo brave, Callie. I want to be like her when I grow up."

Callie's phone rang and she glanced at it, then started the difficult process of getting up. She made it, but not before she fell to her knees and had to start afresh. "Time for me to face the music," she said, trying to put one foot in front of the other. When she reached the door, she turned and started to laugh. "Why can I see your underpants?"

"Got a dress around here somewhere," she said, letting her head fall to the back of the sofa. "Can't find it."

"Love you," Callie said, tugging hard on the door handle before clearly realizing she had to push it. "I'm good," she called out, waving.

Sunny waved back, then started to close her eyes. For just a moment she wondered why there was a long wool coat and a black briefcase hanging on her coat rack. Then she closed her eyes, almost, but not quiet able to ignore the insistent knock on the front door.

With a throbbing headache, Sunny sat at her kitchen island the next morning, sipping on a cup of coffee that turned her stomach. But she needed the caffeine, so she soldiered on, getting it down so she could make her next call. After dialing her sister, she waited for a second, then heard her voice. "Sunny?"

"Yep."

"Are you back?"

"Just for a couple of days. How about lunch? Can you get away?"

"Lunch?" Tiffany was clearly puzzled, justifiably so since they never spent time together socially. "Today?"

"Yeah. I'd really appreciate it if you can squeeze me in. I'm going back tomorrow, so this is the only time I can spare."

"Um, okay. What time?"

"Whatever's good for you."

"How about eleven? I know that's early…"

"No problem. I've got a lethal hangover, so I'm not going to be able to eat anyway. I just want to see you."

"Hangover?" she asked tentatively.

"Don't ask."

"Meet me at that organic juice place by my office. You can have something healthy. Do you know where I mean?"

"I do. See you then."

Tiffany looked very polished and professional when she walked into the bright juice bar with the big splashes of citrus colors on the walls. In Sunny's mind, Tiffany was still about ten years old, unhappy to be taking orders from her older sister, undermining her in any way her devious little mind could conjure up. Besides being patently untrue, that wasn't the right way to think about her. Tiffany had a pathological need to hold onto her husband, and she'd dedicated her life to making sure she wasn't left high and dry like their mother had been. When Sunny thought about it that way, she could manage some sympathy for her, an emotion more helpful than the deep sense of dread she normally felt when Tiffany's face showed up on her phone.

Sunny stood and they exchanged quick hugs. "Buy you some juice?" Sunny asked. "The Immune System Booster isn't bad."

"I usually just get a wheatgrass," she said, taking her wallet from her designer purse to head over to the counter. Sunny gave herself a pep talk, forbidding herself from barfing when she had to watch her sister drinking grass.

Vivid green slurry in hand, Tiffany sat next to Sunny in front of the window. "Everything all right?" she asked tentatively.

"No, but things are heading in the right direction." She took a sip of her drink, feeling like the acid from the orange juice might eat right through her stomach lining. "I had lunch with Momma yesterday," she said, thinking of the right way to frame their meeting. "She's been after me to buy her a bigger condo, and I wanted to tell her that wasn't going to happen."

"Oh, God," Tiffany said, twitching her head to make her bright red hair slide behind her shoulder. "That means she's coming for me next."

"Do you…" Sunny blinked in surprise. "Do you give her money?"

"Of course! Anything to get her off my back." Tiffany gripped her arm, giving it a tight squeeze. "But I can't cover a new condo, Sunny." She lowered her voice, even though they were the only people in the shop. "I have to sneak the money out of a separate account I keep. If Eric knew how much I gave her..." She rolled her eyes dramatically. "He would literally kill me."

Sunny hoped *that* wasn't true, but she couldn't let Tiffany's choices influence her own. "I'm cutting her off, Tiff."

The hand on her arm tightened until Sunny's arm tingled. "You can't!"

"I already did, and I'm not going to change my mind. I'm going to pay her and Brittany's bills for two more months, then I'm out."

"You pay Brittany's bills?" Her face whitened. "I'm paying for her car!"

"I pay her mortgage and her health insurance," Sunny said. "Sometimes her utilities."

"Fuck!" Tiffany let her head drop to the counter. "What am I going to do?" she moaned.

"Maybe you two have enough to support two additional adults, but if you don't, I'd urge you to do what I'm doing. Cut them off and refuse to give in." She swallowed when her gut felt like it might revolt, took a breath and added, "If you do that, you'll get a good sense of how Momma feels about you. Be prepared."

Tiffany covered her face with her hands, then let two fingers splay apart to reveal a single eye. "What did she say?"

"I don't remember most of it. She just yelled for a while, then she got on her knees and begged. Literally begged."

Her hands dropped to the counter as her mouth opened. "Momma begged?"

"She did. While crying," she added. "I thought my heart was going to burst right through my chest. But then I let myself think about how my money goes her way, but nothing comes back my way. You know?"

"She calls less when you pay," Tiffany said miserably.

"That's usually true, but I decided that wasn't a big enough return on my investment. I figure I've paid back all of the money she's spent on me at least six times over. Given our relationship seems to be mostly about money, I can walk away without feeling too guilty."

"I don't think I can do that," Tiffany said. "She scares the crap out of me."

"It's like ripping off a bandage, Tiff. It hurts like hell, but then it's gone."

"But she needs the money, Sunny. She swears she does."

Sunny shook her head slowly. "She *wants* the money. There's a difference. At some point, she probably will need our help. When she's unable to work, or if she's ill, I'll gladly help her out. But now? Both she and Brittany are lying around goofing off while we support them. What sense does that make?"

"None," she admitted, "but I don't think I can stop."

Sunny patted her shoulder as she got up. "If you want some emotional support, just call. But if it's easier to keep paying, god knows I understand."

"Where are you off to?"

"Austin. I've got a dinner meeting with a guy who might want to partner with me."

"Mmm," she said, frowning. "Ashton won't like it if you're so far away. He keeps talking about going rock climbing with you guys."

"They offer climbing lessons at a lot of places, Tiff. I think he'd like doing something with kids his own age."

"I'm sure he would, but who's got the time?" she asked, slugging down her wheatgrass as she picked up her purse and followed Sunny out the door.

CHAPTER TWENTY-SEVEN

ON THURSDAY NIGHT, SUNNY PULLED the down comforter up to her nose, waiting for Devin to get into bed. Just four nights of being away had honestly been too much. She laughed at herself, as devoted to this woman as she thought it possible to be, all in less than a year.

Devin finished brushing her teeth, opened the front door to spit onto the snow, then raced the few steps to the bed, slipping in and wrapping Sunny in a robust hug.

"Having Caleb in my sleeping bag was tough," Devin said. "He fidgets all night long, and I always worry he's gonna pee." She patted Sunny's face. "You're a big improvement."

"Nice to know my role," Sunny said, chuckling.

"He kept me warm, but I've decided I prefer sleeping with a woman who makes me tingle all over when she lies next to me." She nuzzled against Sunny's neck. "Like you do."

"I missed you like crazy," Sunny said. "It was especially hard not to be able to talk to you at night. I'd look at the 'locate a friend' app and see a little pin by Edie's, but it always said, 'previous location.' It couldn't find you."

"But you knew I was here, just waiting for you."

"Well, you might have been just about anywhere, but you're not the type to wander off."

"I am definitely not the type for that." She slipped her arms around Sunny's body and effortlessly pulled her atop her own. "I'm more the type to be slavishly devoted to you. And…" She added, grinning sexily, "to save up four days of unbridled passion to rock your world. Ready?"

Sometimes Devin really delivered on that promise, but Sunny could see she was teasing tonight. While she had no doubt they'd make love, she could see that Devin wasn't in the right frame of mind just yet.

"I'll always be ready for you, baby. But I should tell you a little more about my trip."

Devin shifted her hips, depositing Sunny onto her side. "I tried to pull information out of you on the whole ride home."

"The roads were icy. I wanted you to concentrate."

"I tried again at dinner, but you wanted to know all about the camping trip." She playfully tugged on Sunny's ear. "You had a job interview that you haven't mentioned!"

"Got time now?"

"I can work you in." She batted her eyes. "Start your story the minute I dropped you off at the airport on Sunday. Anything that happened between then and right this minute is of supreme interest."

"A lot of things happened," Sunny said, realizing the four days had felt significantly longer. "But now that it's over, I think I've got a little perspective."

"Perspective? You got that from your financial advisor?"

She brushed her fingers across Devin's forehead, easing away the lines that had formed. "Yeah. Perspective. Starting now, my expenses are going to be in line with my income." She got a zing of satisfaction when she saw Devin's eyes widen.

"You don't have any income!"

Sunny stroked Devin's downy cheek, watching her beautiful pale eyes sparkle from the fire that burned in the stove. "I know that. But I've been fighting making the cuts that make sense, trying to find a way to do what's right for me, while not feeling like a shit for turning my back on my family."

Devin nodded slowly, still cautious.

"It took a while to face the fact that it simply isn't possible to do what's right for me…for us while not upsetting my mom and my sister."

Devin started to speak, but Sunny wasn't finished. "I decided that guilt wasn't a good enough reason to keep things the way they were." She nodded, finally feeling at peace with her decision. "On Tuesday afternoon, I took my mom to lunch and told her that I wasn't able to help her out any more." She swallowed, still able to make her stomach flip at the thought of the last look she'd shared with her mother. "I'm not going to change my mind, even though I think Momma's cut ties with me."

Devin's mouth was open, and she seemed unable to get a single word out.

"It hurts like hell, Dev, but it dawned on me that she doesn't care for me at all—not really." She swallowed around the lump in her throat, just seeing the sympathy in Devin's eyes making her well up. "I don't know if she loved us before my daddy left, but since then she's treated all three of us like hell. If I hadn't had a little spare money, I'm sure I'd have heard from her as little as Brittany does."

"Why didn't you tell me?" she murmured, letting her hand caress Sunny's face with the most delicate of touches. "I hate to think of you doing that alone. I could have been there for you, baby. I *should* have been."

Nodding, Sunny said, "I know you would have been. And maybe I made a mistake. But this felt like something I had to do for myself—by myself. It was a test, Dev, and I'm so damn proud of myself for fucking acing it."

Devin's arms slipped around her body, pulling her in for a long, tender hug. "I'm so sorry she hurt you. Want to talk about it more?"

"Not really. It confirmed my suspicions, the ones that have kept me from doing this years ago. In my heart I knew she needed my money more than a relationship with me, but I didn't want to be right about that."

"Maybe you're not," Devin said, pulling away to offer the most hope-filled expression Sunny had ever seen. "It's possible she's just angry that you changed the rules. Maybe she'll surprise you."

"I don't think so. But I'm sure she'll contact me again. There's no way she's going to let her meal-ticket go without a bigger fight."

"If that's how she views you, she doesn't deserve your time, much less your money," Devin said, her gaze having turned fierce.

"My momma isn't a good person," Sunny admitted. "I can try to convince myself that's not so, but it's the God's honest truth. It's going to hurt—it already does—but it's just stupid to keep this sham of a relationship going. If she wants to change how we interact, I'll gladly give it another try. If not—we're done."

"I can't..." Devin bit at her lip, clearly about to lose it. "I can't imagine how it must hurt."

"You'll never have to, baby. You've been given the gift of loving, caring parents. They'd sprout wings and fly before they'd turn their backs on you."

"I'm so lucky," she whispered, letting her gaze slip away from Sunny's face. "It's just not fair."

"No, it's not. But life isn't fair. You got the parental jackpot, and I got zilch."

"My parents will always be there for you, too," Devin insisted. "I promise you that."

"I'm not worried about that, Dev. I'm really not."

"How about Brittney? Did that go better?"

Sunny laughed. "I don't know if that child's really easy going or just clueless, but she just shrugged. She's dating some guy now, and she seems to think he'll start paying for her. She seemed...resigned. Like a woman who's been getting a government check she knows doesn't belong to her."

"Wow," Devin said. "You've had quite the exciting few days!"

"I didn't finish my list," Sunny said, laughing to herself when Devin's eyes locked on her again. "I'm getting rid of the car and the apartment, too."

"What?" she said, her voice a whisper. "How?"

"Callie found a good real estate agent, and she came over and took a look at the place. Eleanor's sure it'll show well, and the market's strong. With rates as good as they are, it should move. I'm even willing to sell it furnished if that will help."

"Sunny! You've made a lifetime of changes in a few days!"

"Not a lifetime. These were all things that I knew I should do, but haven't had the courage to pull off. Being with you has helped me see the light." She scooted closer and spoke quietly, nearly whispering into Devin's ear. "I'm going to be free—for the first time in my life. I'm never going to allow stuff to own me again. I'm never going to work my butt off just so I can afford an expensive apartment in the trendiest neighborhood, or a luxury SUV, or a health club nice enough for a queen. That stuff wasn't making me happy, and the pressure to afford it all was killing me." She took in a breath. "But the most important thing is that I will never again give my money to people who take me for granted. You don't get a free hand out just because we're related."

This time when Devin wrapped her in her arms, she was deadly serious. Her hug nearly pressed all of the air from Sunny's lungs, but she relished the sensation. Even though Devin hadn't said the words, Sunny knew she'd earned something precious—Devin's respect.

Chapter Twenty-Eight

The next morning, Sunny woke to a pair of blue eyes staring at her from mere inches away. "That freaks me out," she grumbled, turning over.

"It freaks me out to have you go on a job interview you didn't even mention! I've been staring at you for an hour, trying to wake you up with the intensity of my curiosity."

"You're a funny one," Sunny said, sliding out of bed and starting to get dressed. Getting ready to go to the outfitter's to pee wasn't something you could dawdle around about. Devin did the same, with her eyes still locked on Sunny.

While sitting on the top step to put her skates on, Sunny said, "I had a good conversation with Adam."

Devin stepped over her to lace up while standing on her skates, a feat Sunny couldn't imagine. "Got any more?" she asked, obviously starting to get irritated.

"Give me a second. I can't think and lace up at the same time."

In a flash, Devin had swatted her hands away and was handling the job herself. "Talk."

"All right," Sunny said, laughing at her partner's tenacity. Then it hit her that Devin was probably freaked out that she might have accepted a job. "We just talked for a while," she said, taking Devin's hand when she held it out to help Sunny stand. "Nothing much happened, honey, that's why I didn't bring it up the second I saw you." She squeezed her hand as they started to skate. "Then you pounced on me last night before I'd told you everything."

"You pounced on me," she said, giving Sunny's hand a squeeze. "I was lying there, minding my own business when you rolled on top of me and started kissing my lips off."

"Still there," she teased, using her gloved hand to tap somewhere near Devin's mouth. "I promise I'll let you know whenever something important comes up. Right away," she stressed.

"That's it? You don't expect follow up from this guy?"

"No, there might be follow up," she allowed. "He's a good guy, whom I'm pretty sure I'd mesh with. His practice has grown to the point where he's got to expand or start turning away business, which no one wants to do. But I told him I'd only be interested in being equal partners, and that took him by surprise." She smiled at Devin's still-nervous look. "Not a good surprise. I think he hoped I was looking to be a hired hand. Maybe a junior partner."

"You're no one's junior," Devin scoffed. "You could run the biggest firm in the country."

Sunny smiled at her, touched by her crazy talk. It didn't matter that Devin was dead wrong about that. The fact that she believed it was the cool part.

As January moved into February, their social circle got a little wider. Most of their leisure time was spent with Devin's parents, grandparents and the Carters. But she seemed to know just about everyone around greater Moosehead, and was invited to each gathering large enough to merit a celebration. Most were low-key birthday parties where they brought their own beer and a hot dish to share, but one Sunday morning Devin announced they'd been summoned to brunch, then she spent a long time going through her things, fussily picking out the nicest sweater and slacks that Sunny had yet seen her wear. They drove over an hour, with Sunny gasping in amazement when Devin pulled up in front of a glorious Victorian home, beautifully restored.

"You know the people who own this?" she said, mouth hanging open.

"I've got some classy friends. And all of them are going to be here today, so knock yourself out."

They got out of the car and walked up the sidewalk, which didn't have a flake of snow on it, even though they'd gotten a pretty good dusting the night before. "Very neat people," Sunny said. "Thoughtful, too."

"It's heated. Turn toward the sun and you can see a little steam coming off it."

"Heated?"

"I told you, these are my classy friends." She gave Sunny a very enigmatic smile as she pressed the bell. Strains of some classical tune Sunny knew she should be able to name sounded out, then a smiling, handsome man opened the door. His after-shave filled the doorway, then he gave Devin a very fond smile and pulled her into a hug. "You little devil! Going and getting a woman without telling a soul." He released her, then grasped Sunny's hand. "Nathan and I have been dying to meet you, Sunny. Come in, come in," he urged. "We'll all starting with mimosas. Is that good for you?"

"Absolutely," she said, entering the sunny enclosed porch that was decorated like a Ralph Lauren catalog.

"I guess I should introduce you properly," Devin said. She put her arm around the man, who was probably a little older than they were, but was doing everything possible not to look it. "Andy's a plastic surgeon at the hospital where my mom works. When I came out to my parents, my mom made me go talk to him." She laughed. "I'm still not sure why. I guess because you were the only gay person anyone in my family knew."

Andy grinned at her. "I've known Peggy for…oh, God, can it be thirty years?"

"I think it can," Devin said. "But you've only known me for twenty. That sounds better, doesn't it?"

"It sure does. Nathan!" he called. "The girls are here!" He guided them into the formal entryway, which was also filled with a thousand small things to make it look casual, which it very much was not. There were many voices coming from the room to the right, and soon they were being introduced to six other gay men.

"I wish I could say we all live close by," Andy said, "but we don't. Michael and Bill's primary home's in Boston, Tom and Sam's is in Portland and Mike and Rich live full-time in Bangor. The rest of us all have weekend houses somewhere around here."

Another man, equally fastidious, but showing a little more wear and tear on his face, came out of the kitchen, carrying two glasses. "Mimosas for the ladies," he said dramatically. He handed one to Devin, saying, "Yours has a half ounce of champagne. I know how you are."

Devin kissed his cheek. "Nathan, meet my girlfriend. The utterly fantastic Sunny Thompson."

"It is *so* good to meet you," he said. "We never thought we'd get this one to settle down with a nice girl."

"She's really nice," Devin said, grinning. "Smart, too. Sunny's a lawyer."

"In Texas," she said. "If you need to buy real estate in Dallas, I'm your girl."

"Real estate?" Nathan said, perking up.

"Don't get him started," Andy warned. "He'll have you in the corner, talking shop all afternoon."

"Nathan's the number one real estate agent in the area," Devin said. "I think that means he sold two houses last year."

He slapped at her hand like a teacher would. "If I told you how much I sold in Portland last year, you'd faint. I only dabble up here."

"If you want a face lift, a house decorated, a product advertised, a merger or an acquisition, or another house decorated, these guys can fix you right up," Devin said. "But not one of them has ever been out with me on a trip."

"It's enough for us to have such a cute little butch in our group," Nathan said, giving her a hug. "We get a jolt of testosterone just being around you."

"I should be insulted by that," Devin said, laughing, "but I guess you insulted yourselves more."

"Pay no attention to him," Andy said. "Let's go start on the canapés Mike and Rich's houseboy made. They're divine."

Sunny followed the group into the dining room, thinking, *Houseboy?*

On the way home, Devin drove into the teeth of a storm that had come upon them with no warning. "It's gonna take a while to get home," she said, her attention locked onto the road.

"That's okay. We can talk about brunch. I swear, Devin, I couldn't have been more surprised to see who you hang out with. Those guys were stunningly rich!"

"Only some of them. But they're all fun, aren't they? I think they regard me as a mascot or something. Their Christmas party is awesome, as you'd expect."

"I love discovering these little things about you. You keep me guessing."

"That's my goal," Devin said. "You can give me a progress report any time you like, but I have a feeling I'm going to exceed expectations."

Despite knowing many people who hunted, Sunny had never given any thought to what it actually felt like to participate in the sport. In fact, she still wasn't on board with calling it that, since she was almost certain the animals hadn't penciled their names onto the sign-up sheet. But on a devilishly cold, snowy, windy day in early February, she found out what all of the hubbub was about.

Devin had agreed to help out her friend Lucky, since he had a group of five who wanted to hunt raccoons.

Just that afternoon, Sunny had learned that you needed dogs to hunt raccoons. Not many dogs. Just one or two with good instincts. Lucky had two, a pair of tall, rangy hounds who seemed like they'd been snorting coke when they ran around Edie's parking lot, the meet-up spot for the trip.

Lucky was a handsome devil, who also seemed gentle and emotionally open if the lasting hug he gave Devin was any indication. But when he turned to greet Sunny, she saw a fire in his eyes that took her right back to college, when guys telegraphed their interest within three seconds of meeting a girl. She was certain this guy knew she was already spoken for, but he sure looked like he wanted to cut her from the herd and ride off together. Given that Devin didn't seem to notice, it was possible that Sunny was reading him wrong. But she tucked her hand around Devin's arm and possessively pulled her close while he gave them their marching orders.

"If I could get all of these guys in my truck, I'd be able to go alone," he said. "This bunch will be easy to keep track of. One of them's recovering from knee replacement, one had a heart attack last year, and two have never hunted."

"That makes four," Devin said, her warm breath forming tiny clouds as she spoke. "You said you've got five."

"The last guy, Daniel, is the one who set the trip up. Seems decent." He shrugged, with his rising shoulders barely visible through his insulated coveralls. "He loves hunting and he wants to show his friends it can be fun even in the winter."

"So…" Devin gave him a narrow-eyed look. "You want theme park hunting?"

"Yeah," he agreed. "They want to be outside and have a hunting experience, but they can't walk far or fast."

"Or shoot well," Devin added.

"Daniel says he's been taking them to a shooting range," he said, not looking convinced that would help.

"Have they pre-paid?" Devin asked.

"Yep."

"Then let's get this show on the road," she said. "I guess they'll want to sit around a fire. Want me to be in charge of that?"

"That'd be great."

"Want to cook on it?"

"Sure." He stuffed his gloveless hands into the slash pockets of his coveralls. "But I didn't buy any food."

"Front me," Devin said, sticking out her hand.

Somewhat reluctantly, Lucky pulled out his wallet and handed her a few bills. "Get fish," he said. "Then we don't need knives."

"Got it. I'll buy everything I'd need for a friggin barbecue." As she started to walk to her car, she said, "I've taken more daring trips with Girl Scouts."

"Girl Scouts are in better shape," Lucky called after her.

Sunny and Devin kept one dog between them on the trip up, with three mostly silent guys in the backseat. While Sunny had always believed she was a dog lover, she was now quite sure she wasn't a hunting-dog lover. At least not this particular hunting dog, Honker, who was fidgety, anxious, and very easy to startle.

Given how much preparation they'd had to do, it seemed silly to drive less than a half hour away for the big expedition, but they arrived at their campsite at three o'clock in the afternoon, reaching it via snowmobile, with each truck having towed two of the machines.

It was frankly weird to ride along on a snowmobile while the dogs loped beside them, sniffing the snow like it held the secrets to the universe, but that was obviously the only way to get everyone to the site without stressing any of the less able guys.

They weren't going to stay overnight, so their on-site preparations were few. Devin had strapped her sled to the back of their snowmobile, and she pulled out all sorts of things Sunny was sure she never normally carried. After donning her snowshoes and using them to tamp down a big circular spot in the snow, she gathered some green sticks and placed them on the packed ground. By the time she was ready, what little sun there had been was well behind the trees, with dusk falling like a stone.

Devin was ready to fight the darkness, though. Atop her neatly laid out sticks, she set out a fire pan and built a small blaze using split hardwood she'd taken from the pile behind Edie's. Once it was throwing off some much-needed warmth, they all sat around the fire, talking. Not talking much, but it still could have been considered a conversation—about hunting.

It was getting dark when Devin got up to start the dinner preparations. Hoping to dash away from the group to pee, Sunny caught Devin's eye and pointed to a stand of trees that was already in deep shadow. She took the time to put on a pair of snowshoes, her memory of sinking into hip-deep snow serving to remind her to be prepared. In the blink of an eye, Devin was rushing to put on her own shoes. "I can go alone," Sunny said quietly, aware that the campfire conversation had stopped the moment she'd gotten up. Devin didn't speak her reply, but her slow head shake showed she wasn't willing to negotiate. Resigned, Sunny followed along, letting Devin choose the place, which was, of course, not the one she would have picked.

At the cabin, Sunny had been practicing with the little rubber funnel-like thing that allowed a woman to pee standing up. She'd successfully managed to use it from the doorway, but Devin hadn't been wild about her peeing on the porch, so she now used it only while camping.

Regretfully, having the device didn't make the endeavor a slam-dunk. You still had to get past a lot of clothes, and women's long underwear didn't have a fly. Finally, she had her pants down, funnel ready for use. "Can you aim that flashlight somewhere else, honey? I know we share a lot, but…"

"Sorry," she said, chuckling. "I should have known better. I'd never be able to go if there was a bright light on me."

While trying to convince her bladder to cooperate, Sunny said, "You know, this whole day has been a revelation. I had no idea you could leave for a hunting trip at one o'clock in the afternoon. I was sure it was a pre-dawn activity."

"Not when you're looking for something that's mostly active at night. I doubt these guys are excited about hunting for raccoon, but there isn't much in season right now. You've gotta take what you can get."

"I'm trying to figure out how we're going to hunt and not kill each other. Traipsing around in the dark with loaded guns sounds like a surefire way to wind up in the hospital." She waited a beat, then added, "Especially when they're not agile or experienced."

"I'm going to lecture them through dinner," Devin said, looking a little ghostly as her flashlight now illuminated only parts of her face. "I promise it's much safer than you'd think."

"Wouldn't take much!" Sunny said, yelping when she pressed a bit of snow between her legs to rinse off. No matter how often she did that, she'd never, ever get used to it.

After the logs had burned to carbon, Devin replaced them with charcoal, then got the cooking fire going. The fish she steamed in foil was surprisingly good, even though it had come from the grocery store rather than the lake. Then the guys began to relax, opening up a six-pack as they started to talk a little more freely. Devin didn't seem concerned, which Sunny found more than strange. The guys were clearly large enough to metabolize a single beer, but it was weird to see Devin allow them to drink before handling guns. Devin and Lucky didn't drink, of course, and Sunny wasn't about to have a cold beer when it was eighteen degrees out.

Lucky had been very chill the whole day, but he finally got up and started to organize what Sunny assumed was the main event. He secured GPS tracking collars around the dogs' necks, then he let them smell something that must have been a dead-ringer for a raccoon, making them whine and jump and yodel. Finally, he let them both off the leash, and they took off like shots into the pitch black night. No one else moved to follow, and Sunny's staring at the side of Devin's face didn't seem to catch her attention.

This was hunting? Letting dogs run around while they sat in the frigid cold, talking about some of the most boring stuff in the world? Devin looked perfectly content, but that wasn't odd. She could easily go for a night without saying a peep, but she was clearly interested in rifles and scopes and weapon mounted tactical flashlights, if her now-animated voice was any indication. But Sunny would have paid a good buck to have access to her phone, which she hadn't brought—even if all she could do was play solitaire.

Slowly, apparently the way he did everything, Lucky pulled out a little device and blew into it, creating some god-awful squawking noise. That made the dogs bark and growl even more energetically, as they raced around the woods, with Lucky leisurely watching their progress on his GPS.

The dogs had been gone what seemed like an awfully long time before there was another flurry of activity, this one a little more dramatic than the last, maybe because Devin got involved. She was always hopping around like she had ants in her pants, making even a routine task have more weight. She'd delivered a sober, lengthy lecture during dinner, and now she handed rifles to the two guys who didn't have their own weapons, while the other guys got theirs out and laid them across their legs when they sat down again. That was it! Sunny supposed they were making some progress toward actually shooting something, but it was scant!

It took another good while before Lucky jumped to his feet, showing some excitement. “They’ve got one,” he announced, his hearing more precise than Sunny’s, who couldn’t detect a bit of difference between these growls and the ones the dogs had been making all along.

Everyone stood, strapped on snowshoes, then followed Lucky, with Devin taking up the rear. Each of them had headlamps on, with their combined candlepower illuminating their path well enough that Sunny felt safe tromping through fresh powder on a pitch black night. But she was still skittish about the weapons, even though the guys were following Devin’s gun safety lecture to a “T”.

The dogs’ calls grew louder and louder, and finally the group got near, finding the dogs leaping at a sturdy tree, about to go mad with their drive to kill. Sunny shivered at the blood-lust they revealed, but they shut up in a split second when Lucky tossed a couple of chunks of raw meat to them. Before Sunny could blink, they lay down and started to gnaw at their food, completely unconcerned with the raccoon they’d just lost their shit over.

A tall, stocky guy named Daniel had arranged for the trip, and the group agreed he’d get the first shot. He had another flashlight, this one attached to his rifle. The beam carefully tracked the branches of the tree, then it hit a pair of yellow eyes. Sunny almost cried out, but she managed to hold it together, flinching when a single shot rang out through the forrest, and a quiet “thump” resulted in the first kill of the night. Her beam caught the blood stain that started to spread and she thought she might be sick. Then Devin’s hand was on her shoulder, gently turning her while whispering, “We can move away now, okay?”

“Yeah,” she said, tasting bile at the back of her throat.

They only walked a few paces, with the other guys doing something with the carcass. Out of earshot of the others, Devin said, “If you’d rather, you can just stay at the campsite when we find the next one.”

“There’s going to be more?” Sunny asked, stunned.

“Yeah,” she said, clearly keeping it simple.

The other guys were ready to head back then, but before she started to walk Sunny said, "Damn good idea. I think I've learned hunting's not my sport."

⌖

They'd been so busy since she'd returned from Texas that they hadn't had a full evening with Devin's parents. But on the Monday after their raccoon hunting trip they drove to the Savary's for dinner. When they arrived, Peggy was fresh in the door from work, looking a little harried. "I normally take the dogs out to stretch their legs, but I don't think I'll have time," she said, still in a pair of maroon scrubs. "You girls don't mind just having a roasted chicken, do you? I think I've got Brussels sprouts, and beets, and… I could make some mashed potatoes. " She was sending off some nervous energy, and Sunny realized that walking the dogs was probably her way of transitioning from a busy work day to her more relaxed self.

Sunny put the wine they'd brought into the refrigerator, saying, "Why don't we let Devin make dinner? I'd love to go out for a walk with you, Peggy."

Clearly caught off guard, Peggy said, "Have Devin make dinner?"

"She cooks for me every night in Dallas." Reaching over to pull Devin's sweater up, she gave her a pat. "She's back at her normal weight, so she must be doing something right."

"Hey!"

Sunny hugged her briefly. "You're a wonderful cook. So why don't you get moving? Your mom needs some transition time."

"I do?"

Devin moved over to the oven and turned it on. "I promise I know how to roast a chicken, Mom. Go stretch your legs."

Suspiciously, Peggy said, "But do you know how to roast beets? I put them—"

"In a foil packet in a hot oven, with some olive oil and salt and pepper. I swear I can cook," she insisted.

Mark came wandering in, and draped his arm around Devin. "What's going on?"

"I'm going to cook dinner," she said.

"Can you?"

"*Yes*," she insisted, clearly frustrated. "I'm never allowed to, but I know how."

"Then get to it," he said, chuckling. "I thought you could only cook over an open fire."

"Not to make an obvious point, Dad, but if you can cook on an open fire, an oven's pretty easy."

Mark turned to his wife, still smiling. "I think our baby's growing up, Peg. Let's give her a shot. If she screws it up too badly, we'll go out for burgers."

Rolling her eyes, Peggy shrugged back into her coat. "I can't stand here and do nothing, so let's go poochies!" The dogs raced to her, both sitting down awaiting their leashes. "Don't burn the house down," Peggy said, laughing softly as she opened the back door, pulled along by the dogs.

Sunny put her coat and gloves on, and slipped one of the leashes from Peggy's hand. "I love being out for an evening walk," she said, taking a deep breath of the clean, crisp air, lightly flavored with woodsmoke. "I never did this in Dallas."

"Really?" Peggy turned to look at her. "Devin wasn't dragging you outside every two minutes?"

They started down the long drive to the road. It hadn't been plowed, but the tracks from Mark's tires were wide enough to navigate comfortably. "No, not really. She recognized I was beat after a long day. She adapted to my schedule within a day, Peggy. Then she spent every moment trying to make me feel like myself again." She put a hand on her shoulder. "You and Mark have raised a wonderful woman."

They'd reached the road, which had been plowed so many times it was packed hard all the way across. You just had to make sure not to get too near the edge, since that wasn't necessarily as firm as the middle. You wouldn't hurt yourself if the edge collapsed, but you'd wind up in a snow bank you might need a hand to get out of.

Peggy grinned at her brightly, saying, "I'll easily agree my girl's pretty fantastic, but I think she's just naturally sweet. I can't take credit for her good nature."

"I just hope I'm helping her like she helped me. I can't tell how much progress she's making."

"Mmm. I can't either," she said soberly. "I was hoping you'd have some clues."

"She seems happy," Sunny said. "Which is great, of course, but I can't tell if she's getting her confidence back. I'm not even sure how I'll know."

"How has it been going out with her?"

Sunny waggled her hand. "Good and bad, depending on the day. We went on a ridiculous hunting trip on Saturday afternoon that I pretty much hated. Devin would never agree, but I just slowed her down and gave her another person to worry about. The poor woman was trying to cook dinner, but she wasn't able to relax enough to let me go pee on my own. She watches me like a hawk."

"Well, she sings your praises every time we talk. I got the impression you were helping a lot."

"She's just being nice." Rocky, the younger dog, started to race ahead, and Sunny slowed him down by pulling hard on his lead. "I'm not Devin," she called out, laughing. "I can't run in the dark on a road I'm unfamiliar with."

"I love this," Peggy said, her smile visible in the half moon light. "I usually cut the walk short because I'm racing to get home and get dinner started, but you were right. I really need some time to transition."

"Couldn't Mark…?" She snapped her mouth shut, sure Peggy didn't need any advice on how to run her life.

Scoffing, Peggy said, "He'd eat a bowl of cereal if he were in charge of dinner. I don't think either of us planned this, but we have a very traditional marriage. I do the women's work, and he does the men's work. It's silly," she admitted, "since he gets home at least an hour before I do, but it's what we fell into."

"Relationships just sort of…happen," Sunny agreed. "But I want to make sure Devin and I get started off on the right foot. I want her to rely on me like I do on her. I'd feel a lot better if I was adding something right now. At best, I'm companionship."

"That's what she needs," Peggy said. "She just needs another set of eyes until she's confident again."

"I guess."

"Um, what then? Can you see yourself doing this for long?"

"Do I want to be a Maine guide?" She let out a laugh. "I'd be an awful one. Thankfully, I'm pretty happy being a lawyer."

"Do you miss it?"

"A little," Sunny said as she concentrated on staying on the tamped down snow on the road. "But I've been feeling so guilty about *not* missing my family that I haven't thought much about work."

"I wish things were better for you," Peggy said, which Sunny found to be a lovely response. No solutions, no dismissal of her feelings, just a wish that Sunny felt better.

"I do too. The lawyer I interviewed with when I was in Texas has been asking around about me," she said. "He called some of the people I've worked with and they immediately called to tell me."

"Is that a job you'd like?"

"Maybe. I like that it's in Austin, for sure, but I'm not sure if that's because I prefer Austin or I just don't want to be too close to my family." She sighed, her guilt pressing down on her. "I'm hurt by how my mom treated me, but I'm angry with myself for how I've ignored my nephew. I've got to start calling him more often."

"How old is he?"

"He's nine now. That's old enough to guilt-trip me for being gone."

"You said he's an only child, right?"

"Uh-huh. And I was just about the only person who played with him." She shrugged. "My sister really wanted a baby, but Ashton's simply not her priority—her husband is."

"That's just about impossible to make up for," Peggy said, putting the situation into a neat little box. No matter how many times Sunny let Ashton play in the pool, or took him out for chicken bites, she'd never be able to make up for his parents not being over the moon about him. That was a psychic scar he'd carry with him for a long, long time.

Chapter Twenty-Nine

THE NEXT AFTERNOON, THEY WERE at Edie's, waiting for a mom and two small kids up from Boston to see moose. You had to let your clients set the schedule, but it annoyed the hell out of Devin to start off on a trip doomed to failure. No matter how often Edie stressed to clients that moose were almost exclusively visible early in the morning and at dusk, some people didn't want to get going early enough or stay late enough to see a damn thing.

Sunny seemed to actually like driving around for hours, wasting gas for no reason at all. Actually, it was kind of fun to watch her nearly turned around in the passenger's seat, chatting away at the clients, making them believe they just had to keep their eyes peeled, and they'd get lucky. If the kids were little enough, she'd guarantee they'd see one, then, when they'd struck out, make Devin pull her sweater aside to show them her tattoo. As of yet, none of the kids had been disappointed enough to slug her.

Devin looked up when she heard Sunny's phone ring, then watched the color drain from her face as she extracted the device from her pocket and say, "Hello?"

Alert at a tiger, Devin watched every flickering muscle, hearing her say, "Yes, she is here. Do you want to talk to her? All right." Then she handed the phone over, saying only, "It's Angelica."

Devin hadn't known her hands could get sweaty in the space of two seconds, but they definitely could. She wiped one on her jeans, then gripped the phone and held it to her ear, while walking toward the office to have some privacy. "Hello?"

"Devin?"

"Yes. Hi, Angelica."

"I guess I should have taken your number," she said, a surprisingly lighthearted tone to her voice. "But I figured Sunny would know how to reach you."

"Yeah, she does." That was a dumb thing to say, but she was stumped. Why would Angelica call after all this time?

"You're probably wondering why I'm calling…"

"I assume you had a question. No?"

"No. I think I know everything I need to know." She took in an audible breath. "Hank's family isn't happy with me, but I've decided not to sue you."

Devin gasped in response, realizing Sunny was behind her when a pair of arms tucked around her waist. "Obviously I'm glad, but…"

"I talked to Julian. Really talked to him. His lawyer warned him not to, but he kind of goes his own way."

"He seemed like that," Devin agreed.

"So, I asked him every question I could think of. We were on the phone…I don't know. Two hours?"

"That's a lot of questions," Devin said.

"Yes, I had a lot of questions. Anyway," she said, sighing again. "He convinced me that you would have had to be within a foot of Hank to get him to stay off that ice. I…I didn't realize that Julian had tried to stop him. Did you know that?"

"I didn't read the police report," she admitted, "but Sunny said they'd both begged him not to go."

"Julian did more," Angelica said. "He got in front of him and tried to block him. But Hank couldn't stand to have anyone in his way. It's like he never got past being a defensive lineman. When someone was in front of him, he couldn't resist knocking them aside. That made him a good lawyer, but… Well, you know the rest. Did you know we went up there?"

"You went up where…?"

"To where Hank died," she said. "Thomas and his parents and me. During the summer. I think we were in the right spot. A guy took us out in a fishing boat."

"I had no idea," Devin said. She gripped Sunny's hands for a moment, then peeled away to sit on the edge of Edie's desk. "Did that… Are you glad you went?"

“Uh-huh. Pretty glad. I mean, I pictured it in my head, and I saw some pictures, but I needed to see it for myself. It didn’t look like a place that would pull you in and kill you,” she added quietly.

“It’s different in the winter,” Devin said. “Really different.” She cleared her throat and continued, “I know this is too late to matter, but Edie’s no longer going to book trips on the lake unless the people have experience. If you don’t know anyone who’s fallen in, it’s too easy to dismiss how dangerous it is.”

“Maybe I’ll come see it during the winter. I don’t know why I want to, but I think about it all the time.”

“I’ll take you,” Devin said, moments before regretting the words. “I mean… Not this year. But when I’m feeling more confident.”

“This has taken a lot out of you hasn’t it?” Angelica said, with the empathy in her voice making Devin want to break down in tears.

“It’s been hard,” she admitted, “but I didn’t love Hank. What I feel is nothing compared to what you’ve been through.”

“I guess,” she agreed, “but I’ve been going to grief counseling. They say it affects people in lots of different ways. At least that’s what I’m finding out. One of the people in my support group only witnessed an auto accident, and she’s a total mess.” She let out a wicked-sounding laugh. “We’re not supposed to talk about each other, but you don’t know her, so what could it hurt?”

“It couldn’t hurt a thing,” Devin said. “I’m sure you’re right about grief,” she said, looking at Sunny. “We all deal with it in different ways. But we’ve all got to face it, I suppose.”

“My counselor says if you don’t deal with it, it deals with you. I think she’s right about that.”

“It sounds like you’re doing pretty well,” Devin said. “I’m really glad to hear that.”

“I moved back home,” she said. “Sold the house and rented an apartment on the gulf just a short drive from where I grew up. I’m thinking about selling real estate. My parents own an agency, you know.”

“No, I didn’t know that,” Devin said. “I bet you’d be good at it.”

"I guess we'll see. Can I talk to Sunny for a minute? I want to hear how she's doing, but I wanted to get my news out before I lost my nerve."

"Yeah, of course," Devin said. "Thanks for calling, Angelica. You just let me know if you ever want to come up during the winter. You can call Sunny. Wherever she is, I'll be close." She handed the phone to Sunny, clapped her on the back, and went to find Edie. As relived as Devin was, Edie would top that tenfold.

That night, Devin, Sunny, Edie and her husband Mike all sat around a table at a surprisingly refined local place. It wasn't fancy by any means, but they had tablecloths and servers, a change of pace from having the cook run out with your order when he had a free minute.

Edie had invited them, and Sunny had assumed that Devin would be in the mood to, if not celebrate, at least to share their relief. But it had taken a little work to even talk her into accepting the invitation, and wrangling her into a good mood wasn't possible.

They were sharing a bottle of wine, and Sunny tried to hide her laugh when she caught sight of Devin trying to look like she enjoyed it. She was a very good sport in almost all situations, but her expression always gave her away. At least to Sunny. That must have been what happened when you studied a woman like an archeological dig.

After the server had taken their orders, Edie held up her glass and said, "I'm pretty sure none of us feels like clicking our heels for joy, but I know we're all relieved to not have the threat of a lawsuit hanging over our heads."

"Count me in," Devin said, touching the edge of her glass to Edie's. "Relief is all I can manage, but I've got a lot of it." She started to take a drink, but stopped with the glass halfway to her mouth. "To Hank," she said quietly. "May he rest in peace." Then her hand started to shake, and she set the glass onto the table, pushed her chair away and raced for the front door.

Sunny sat there for a second, frozen with indecision. "Should I take her coat to her? She'll freeze out there."

"Give her a minute," Edie advised. She quickly drained her glass, then reached over and grasped Devin's, taking what could only be called a gulp from it before putting the glass down in front of herself. "I don't know what I was thinking trying to get her to socialize tonight. She no more wanted to go out than she wanted this wine."

"It's hard to tell sometimes," Sunny said. "Usually, she perks up when she's around people who understand. But sometimes she lets her guard down, and then..." She let out a sigh, feeling frustrated and powerless. "I was right there with her, but I know we've never felt the same way about the situation. I don't think she'll ever get over blaming herself."

"She didn't do a thing wrong," Edie grumbled. "Not one single thing."

"You know I agree with you, but that doesn't matter. She holds herself to a higher standard, Edie, and that's what she didn't meet." She blew out a breath, slipped her coat on, then picked up Devin's jacket. "Be back in a minute."

Devin was right outside, shivering, with her arms wrapped around her waist. She looked up, revealing the same expression a cornered cat would have—surprise coupled with an intense desire to run. Usually, Sunny would have let her go, but tonight she pulled her into a hug and wrapped her own coat around Devin's body, pulling her in like a child. In seconds, she seemed to lose all of her strength, draping herself against Sunny, who struggled to keep her feet under her.

Devin sobbed piteously, letting out far more emotion than she ever had before. But they didn't exchange a word, neither having any that would make the pain go away. All they could do was hold each other and hope it got easier over time. Sunny was sure it would—for her. But she wasn't at all sure that was true for her precious Devin. Her gentle heart might have been scarred beyond repair.

She'd managed to eat her dinner, but the stilted, uncomfortable meal seemed to go on forever. Once they were back in the cabin, Devin couldn't relax. She felt like she'd rubbed herself with poison ivy, with every part of her itching and uncomfortable. Sunny was watching her like a hawk, even though she was trying not to look like she was. After just a few minutes,

Devin couldn't take it any more. She got up and grabbed her coat, then a balaclava and her down mittens. Sunny watched her move around the room, but didn't question her.

When Devin got to the door, she said, "I need to get a little exercise, okay?"

Thankfully, Sunny simply nodded. "Whatever you need, honey."

What a relief! She didn't have to explain or reassure her or justify why she needed to blow off some steam. The understanding in Sunny's eyes was the nicest gift she could have given.

"I love you," Devin said, her voice breaking. "I'll be gone a while, okay?"

"Less than a month?" Sunny said, smiling a little at their long-standing joke.

"Maybe a couple of hours. If that's okay."

Sunny had been sitting on the bed, still dressed, but with her coat off. She got up and stood right in front of Devin, not touching her. Then her eyes moved across Devin's face for a few seconds, silently searching for something. "Here's how this is going to work," Sunny said. A hand moved to rest on Devin's shoulder. "You're in charge of you. When you need to do something, do it. You've never wandered away just for laughs, since you're a very connected, very thoughtful woman. So when you need alone time, take it—even if you think I won't like it. I'll do the same, okay?"

Devin nodded, afraid she'd start crying again.

"We're here to support and love each other, baby. Sometimes that means we have to be a little selfish."

"Okay," she said, unable to look into Sunny's caring eyes. "Love you."

"I love you too." She pursed her lips together, like she had to stop herself from saying anything else. Devin was certain she wanted to remind her to be careful, and she greatly appreciated that Sunny knew her well enough to know that was a given. Then she went to the small table where Devin kept her electronics, picked up the beacon and handed it to her without comment.

"Thanks." Devin dipped her head, embarrassed to have forgotten to take it. "Go to bed if you're tired. I'll be fine."

"I know you will," Sunny said, then gave her lips a sweet brush with her own. "Not a doubt in my mind."

When she pushed it, Devin could skate fast. She'd timed herself at twenty-five miles per hour once, but she couldn't keep that up for long. Tonight, she settled into a moderate, but still taxing pace, closer to fifteen, and let the rhythmic push of her skates against the smooth ice lull her into a trance-like state. That was the key to feeling better—to move but not think. Thinking was what got her into trouble.

When she was in a maudlin mood, she could see the terror on Julian's face, hear Sunny's wail, and feel her own heart race like a locomotive. There was no way to resolve those feelings. All she could do was try to break through them, and the only way she knew to do that was by immersing herself in nature. It sucked that Sunny was probably worried sick, but what she'd said had been absolutely true. They each had to take care of themselves to have a good relationship. And having a supportive, loving relationship was her main goal at this point in her life.

Consciously turning off those thoughts, she focused on the sounds her skates made. *Skritch, skritch, skritch.* The noise carried across the lake, nearly the only sound the puzzled animals had to worry about as they looked out of their dens and nests, trying to figure out what the humans were up to on this cold, clear night.

It was all Sunny could do to not lace up her skates and try to follow Devin. But she'd never be able to catch her, not to mention the certainty of undoing all of the good she'd done by simply letting her go. She knew she'd handled that well. Seeing the relief in Devin's pale eyes made that clear. But not being able to follow, or even call anyone for reassurance made the night a very tough one. But that's what love sometimes was—having to accept some anxiety so your partner could work out her problems on her own. It sucked, but the reward made the pain worth it in the end. She just wished the end of this particular bout of pain came soon.

Just before midnight, Sunny heard the thump of skates climbing the stairs. Jumping out of bed, she opened the door, finding Devin, with her balaclava caked with little balls of ice around the openings for her nose and mouth. She whipped it off and entered, then dropped to the floor to remove her skates. "Made it," she said, standing again to take off her jacket.

Sunny helped her get the rest of her clothes off, all of them soggy. Devin's whole body was pink from exertion, glowing with sweat. Sunny took a hand towel and blotted her dry, with Devin compliantly raising her arms so all of her moist skin was accessible. Then she went to the built-in cabinet under the window and found a T-shirt and boxers, obviously too hot for her normal winter sleepwear. They got into bed without another word, then Sunny settled against Devin's side when she lifted her arm in invitation, her body still radiating heat. Even though they didn't speak, Sunny knew she was better. She just gave off a calmer, more peaceful affect, one Sunny was very, very glad to see return. In just a few minutes she could feel herself drift off, reassured that her very warm, much more content partner was right where she belonged—at her side.

It seemed like only a short time had passed, but Sunny's eyes blinked open when Devin started to creep out of bed. "Is it time to get up?"

"It's six," Devin said quietly. "Stay in bed if you want. I'll run over to Edie's and see if any trips have come in."

"I'll get up." Sunny sat and tried to get her eyes to open.

Devin urged her to curl up on her side, then she sat back down and pulled Sunny into her lap. Fingers trailed through her hair as Devin gently said, "We don't have to talk about last night, do we?"

"Not if you don't want to," Sunny said, yawning.

"Good. 'Cause I don't. But I know you'd listen if I did."

The fingers running through her hair would put her to sleep in seconds if she didn't fight it. She decided not to fight it. "Bring me a cup of coffee, okay?"

"You got it," Devin whispered, leaning over to kiss her cheek. "Be back soon." Then she playfully tugged on Sunny's ear. "You can pee on my porch if you need to."

"Love you," Sunny said, feeling that pleasant fog that meant sleep was just a heartbeat away.

Devin crept back into the cabin after having a leisurely breakfast with Edie. They didn't talk about the night before, but she was sure Edie was relieved to have a normal conversation, lighthearted and easy.

"Hey," Sunny said, sounding slightly more awake. She sat up and ran her fingers through her hair, then went to splash some cold water on her face, something she hated to do. Devin watched her, kind of enjoying the girlish squeal she always let out.

After putting a fleece over her pajamas, she sat on the bed and extended her hand, smiling when Devin placed the cup of coffee in it.

Sunny took a few sips, then said, "Any interest in talking about last night?"

"Mmm, there's not much to say, honey."

"There is," she said, gazing into Devin's eyes. "Do you think you might like to talk to a therapist? I know you don't like the idea, but carrying guilt around like this just isn't good for you."

"I don't feel guilty any more," she said, a little puzzled. "I told you that months ago."

"But…" Sunny stared at her, unblinking. "Why were you so upset last night?"

"I'm sad," she said, feeling the sorrow in the pit of her stomach every time she had to talk about it. "A guy that was so vibrant, so full of life just…disappeared." She snapped her fingers. "He was gone in an instant. Every part of him, every bit of his potential, the kids he might have had, the good times he would have enjoyed. All gone." She sat down next to Sunny and pulled her knees up to her chest, hugging them tight to warm herself. But the coldness she felt wasn't from the weather. It was from the loss. "I think about Angelica all the time. What must it have been like to have gotten that phone call?"

"It was horrible," Sunny said, with her chin starting to quiver. "I'm the one who made it. And I got one just like it when Morgan died, but mine was from a stranger."

"I'm so sorry," Devin said, grabbing her and holding her in her arms. "You know better than anyone what it was like."

Sunny burrowed into her embrace, not speaking for a few minutes. "I haven't let myself grieve," she said. "I've been so protective of you and so worried about the threat of a lawsuit that I haven't just let myself sit with my feelings. But I need to," she said softly. "Hank was a good guy—most of the time. He was kind of like a brother to me. A guy you fought with, who teased you, a guy who'd throw you under the bus to avoid getting in trouble. But he was also protective of me and remarkably understanding when Morgan died. I miss him," she said, starting to cry.

Devin held her in her arms, soothing a hand across her hair. They'd get through this. They just needed to talk about it a little more. A prospect she really hated, but one that probably couldn't be avoided.

On Friday evening, Sunny and Peggy were out for their walk, just the two of them letting the dogs set the pace. Devin expressed no interest in joining them, which had puzzled Sunny at first. It had taken her a couple of weeks to realize Devin was simply allowing Sunny time to get to know her mom. That was Devin-style thoughtfulness. She never made a big deal out of things. She just saw a way to accomplish something, then either stepped in or stepped out of the way so it could happen on its own.

"Did Dev tell you my big news?" Sunny asked.

"I've heard no news at all, other than the fact that you've been a great help on those moose safaris she hates so much."

"She's telling the truth there," Sunny agreed. "I'm actually performing a necessary task when we waste a few hours of people's money." She let out a laugh. "If it's a trip for small kids or elderly people, I'm holding my own. But my *big* news is that I sold my apartment. Furnished. I don't even have to go to Dallas to pack up my personal things. And if I didn't know this before, I know it now. Having a few good friends sure does make your life easier."

"That's wonderful!" Peggy said, showing a big grin. "But…" Her expression turned sober. "What does that mean for the future?"

"It's still up in the air. The guy I interviewed with is close to offering me a partnership. Or he thinks we're getting married," she added, chuckling. "I've talked to him every day for the last week."

"And if he makes an offer, you'll take it?"

"No," she said, shaking her head so firmly her stocking cap almost came off. "I've made it clear that I'm not ready to get back to work yet. It seems the more I hesitate, the more he wants me."

"He sounds straight," Peggy said, chuckling.

"Yeah, he is. I've told him all about Devin, and I've made it clear I've got to have her vote before I can join him."

"How would that work?" Peggy asked. "Do you have to buy in?"

"Oh, yeah. It'll take all of the money I get from the sale of my apartment, and I'm making substantially more than I thought I would, since they're kicking in for the furniture. It's a lot of money."

"So…" She pulled on Rocky, who was, as usual, trying to run ahead. "If Devin agrees, you'll leave right away?"

"I don't think so," Sunny said, having given this more hours of thought than she could count. "I don't think Devin's quite ready. But she's close, Peggy. I see her out with clients and I can tell she's almost forgetting how easy it is to have something terrible happen. She'll get there, but until she does—we're staying right here."

Chapter Thirty

LATE ON THE FOLLOWING SATURDAY morning, Devin sat at the coffee bar, sipping a cocoa. She'd been staring at Edie for a couple of minutes, but her boss was really good at ignoring things she didn't want to see. Sunny had been chatting with Edie, and she walked over and threaded her fingers through Devin's hair to ruffle it a little. "Why are you giving Edie such a dirty look?"

"Not like she'll pay attention to it," she grumbled. "I'm just pissed she gave Chris that ice-fishing trip. She told me all she had was this bullshit snowmobiling, but he hasn't had to take anyone out on the putt-putts since I've been back." She took another sip of her cocoa, but it wasn't cheering her up like it usually did. "She's treating me like she did when I was brand new and she didn't think I could handle the tough stuff."

"The hunting trip was tough…"

"No, it wasn't," she said, mildly annoyed. "And she didn't book that, anyway. That was Lucky's gig."

"Oh, right," Sunny said, nodding. "Well, you haven't told her how long you're staying, honey. Chris works for three different outfitters. She's probably giving him the better jobs to keep him busy so he doesn't wander off."

"You think so?"

"Maybe. Why don't you ask her, rather than scowl at her?"

Devin started to get up, then dropped back onto her stool. "I'm still stuck with this trip today. I'll talk to her this afternoon, when I'm not so grouchy."

Sunny was still playing with her hair. That usually felt good enough to relax her, but it wasn't working today.

"Why do you hate the snowmobile trips so much?"

She looked up. "You don't?"

"I kind of like them. People are usually really excited about going, and that's contagious. And I love getting out on the lake and really letting it go. I love speed."

"I guess," she said, not agreeing, but not wanting to be a grouch. "It helps that I don't have a governor on my throttle."

"The other machines do?"

"Of course. I have to be able to go faster than they do. Some of those people would take off and I'd never see them again."

"I thought you were just cooler," Sunny said, laughing. "I thought your machine was so intimidated by you that it did whatever you told it to do."

The bell over the door gave off its musical jangle and Devin looked up. A middle-aged guy entered, followed by two high-school aged boys. *Ugh.* Her least favorite kinds of clients. The kids were always reckless, and the parent usually made her the bad guy, implying that he'd let the kids do whatever dumb thing they wanted if the mean lady hadn't stopped them. But she was stuck, so she got up and went over to greet the group, Sunny at her side.

Devin might not have liked this kind of trip, but Sunny thought they were great. They were easy, there wasn't a lot of instruction involved, the people were usually excited about going, and she and Devin were home in their cozy bed by dark. She would have done one of these every day if she'd been in charge.

It didn't hurt that a lot of people wanted to leave at noon, a very civilized time that allowed an opportunity to lure Devin back to bed after they'd skated to Edie's for a trip to the bathroom and a bite of breakfast. Once she got back to civilization, she planned on individually thanking each of the tiles in her shower, but so far the absence of running water hadn't been too much of a pain.

This parent, a divorced dad from Portland, was named Joel. The boys lived with their mom in Camden, and spent every other weekend with their dad. Joel was about her and Devin's age, with Ethan having turned sixteen the day before, his younger brother Seth nearly fourteen. They seemed like well-mannered kids, but they didn't pay much attention to

Devin's patient safety instructions. Like most kids that age, they preferred goofing around and messing with each other whenever they could get away with it.

But Joel was right on top of them, watching them carefully, correcting every little thing they did. He had his work cut out for him. At that age, boys were hormone-charged balls of energy, and all you could do was be patient until they grew up a little.

Joel decided he'd ride alone, leaving Ethan and Seth to share a machine. Sunny could tell that wasn't Devin's ideal set-up just from the expression on her face, but Joel knew his kids a lot better than she did, and he pushed his point, with Devin giving in without too much of an argument. Ethan lorded his advanced age over his younger brother, reveling in that fact that Edie allowed sixteen-year-olds to drive. Seth wasn't happy about that, but Sunny assumed he'd get his older brother back by giving him a shot to the kidneys every once in a while.

The family wanted the usual three hour tour, and they set off on their well-practiced route, Sunny in the lead, Devin at the back. Sunny was sure this was part of the reason Devin was bored by snowmobile trips. She'd been taking people on this exact route for fifteen years, chosen because it was safe, and scenic, and took exactly three hours if you stopped to take a peek at each of the overlooks. Practicality and efficiency ruled in the tour business.

Every few minutes, Sunny could hear Joel yelling, but she couldn't her the actual words he was saying. Devin's voice rang out once in a while, launching into her, "I've got this under control," spiel, the one she used to reassure her clients they could relax and let her run the show.

They'd been out for about an hour, and the weather was turning. Big, dark clouds covered the western skies, promising to drop a load of snow on them at any minute. But what the clients didn't know was that they were going in a fairly tight circle, never straying too far from home base. If things got bad, they could cut back across the lake and return in forty-five minutes, even at the furthest point of the tour.

Sunny pulled up at the first overlook, a pretty spot that let them look over a logging road to get a good view of a valley. It was probably even prettier in the summer, when you could see the contours of the hills better. But it was still nice when covered in snow, and she turned off her machine, waiting for Ethan. He got close, then hit the accelerator hard, making the machine fly over a log to land, nose down, in the deep snow. He was plastered against the windscreen, with Seth scrunched up against him, barely able to get his hands free to beat him on the back, yelling, "You stupid jerk! You could have killed me. *Dad!*"

Joel roared up, leapt off his machine in an instant, then gently and not so gently pulled his boys off. By the time Devin parked, Joel had them over in the trees, lecturing them sternly.

"Fuck," Devin grumbled. "Edie's going to throw a fit if we have to tow this thing out of here."

Sunny stared at the machine, perched at a very odd angle. "No tricks up your sleeve?"

"None. Brute strength is the only option."

Once the family returned, with the boys properly and thoroughly chided, Devin, Joel and Ethan used their collective strength to tip the machine back, while Seth sat on it to help redistribute the weight. Sunny basically stayed out of the way, but cheered them on while squirming around, mimicking their efforts.

It took longer than Sunny thought it would, given that she was certain Devin could move mountains, but they finally pushed the machine back over the log to flop noisily on the tamped snow. Devin jumped on it and got it going again, then took off without a word, obviously testing it for safety. When she returned, she met Joel's eyes and said, "These things are tougher than they look. It's fine."

"Are you sure?" This guy was clearly a worrywart.

"Positive."

He started to say something, but Sunny cut in. "I'll trade," she said. "I'm certain my machine's fine."

He looked at her for a few seconds, then nodded. "Normally I wouldn't let you do that, but their mother will kill me if something happens because they were on a damaged machine."

"I'm sure this one's fine," she said, patting the seat of the leaping snowmobile, "but you need to be confident when your kids are involved."

Devin gave her a sour look at her offer, but she expected that. If given a choice, she knew Devin would let the kids walk back for being reckless, but they had to keep the customers satisfied—even when they'd created their own problems.

The stop had taken much longer than they usually allowed, so they got back on and started to ride again. This was Sunny's favorite part of the trip, when they rode along a nice path on the edge of a ravine. At the bottom of the steep drop-off, a beautiful little babbling brook ran pure and true even in this cold. Devin had explained why that happened, but Sunny'd already forgotten. She just thought it was cool.

She was still in the front, and she'd adjusted her rear-view mirrors so she could keep her eye on the rest of their pack. Once again, Joel kept yelling, noticing everything his boys did, even though they weren't doing much from Sunny's perspective. Devin kept shouting up to Joel, who was now riding directly behind Sunny. She could hear Devin's voice saying the same thing over and over. "Everything's fine," she yelled. "The boys are doing great. Just watch where you're going!"

Joel's nitpicking had to be driving Devin nuts. He'd been easier to manage when he'd been behind the kids. Now that he was in front, he kept standing up and turning around, never a good idea. Sunny was about to stop and reorder them when Joel's machine began to drift to the left. Then it picked up speed when he must have accidentally hit the accelerator rather than the brake. Like a shot, he plunged down the small hill to hit a tree stump right at the edge of the drop off. Screams rang out through the forest as the machine stopped its forward momentum while the back fishtailed, then settled.

Sunny stopped and raced for him, unable to find a clear path. The trees were skinny and closely spaced, making her have to bob and weave to get near. Devin didn't bother with those niceties. She gunned her machine and raced through the woods, knocking over saplings, clipping low-lying branches and bottoming out hard when she flew over a bump. Then she was off the machine, running the rest of the way, dropping to her butt to slide down the last steep drop off.

Sunny had been going as fast as she could, but she was still twenty feet away when Devin braced herself, took the coiled rope she'd obviously carried with her, and tossed the looped end to Joel. "Slip that under your arms," she called out, a model of calm. "I've got you."

Finally getting close, Sunny let out a startled gasp when she saw just how precarious the situation was. The machine was mostly on solid ground, but the tail end was definitely not. There was nothing below it but a killing fall.

"Sunny," Devin said as she hurriedly wrapped the rope around her waist twice, "make sure the boys stay calm."

Sunny had no idea how to do that. The kids were up on the trail, both crying, with Seth pleading for Devin to save his dad. Sunny started for them, but stopped when she heard the creak of shifting snow behind her.

"Falling," Joel screamed, then the entire edge of the cliff cracked and broke away. Devin flung herself to the right as the machine started to free-fall, then was yanked off her feet like a doll. She slammed into a big tree as the snowmobile began to tumble down the ravine, thumping along until it crashed noisily, seconds later. Joel dangled over the precipice, trying to cry out but unable to. The rope was so tight around his chest it probably kept him from taking a full breath.

Sunny was on Devin in what seemed like slow motion, but was probably just tenths of a second. She appeared dazed for a few rapid beats of Sunny's heart, then she shook her head and gasped out, "Get the boys."

"Get down here!" Sunny yelled and both of the kids stopped howling and started to move.

Sunny yanked furiously at the rope that bound Devin to the tree, but it was as tight as a wire. Devin's beautiful face was bloody and scratched, with her left eye swelling so rapidly it had nearly swollen shut in a few beats of Sunny's pounding heart.

The boys slipped recklessly down the hill, banging into a few trees as they tumbled, then they were next to Devin, both of them clearly terrified.

Devin gave Sunny a look that begged, "Don't screw up!" then said, "You have to pull your dad up. He'll be really, really heavy, but together you can do it."

Sunny started to edge over to the spot, but Devin gasped out, "Get on your belly. Spread your weight out."

Dropping to her knees, and then her belly, Sunny crawled to the edge, seeing the terror in Joel's face as he dangled. She tried to get her hands under the rope to pull, but the force had dug it into the earth, having cut through the snow like a hot knife. "I don't know what to do!"

"Back here," Devin said. Sunny ran to her, with her heart thumping so hard it was tough to hear. "I can loosen it. When it starts to go, wrap it around your hands and dig your heels in. Grab onto whatever you have to, but hold on." Then she started to turn, grimacing as she unwound the rope she'd looped around her waist. As she got free, the rope began to grow slack, then Joel cried out again as he dropped a few inches, his body now scraping along the side of the ravine.

Devin was in charge again, quickly wrapping the tail end of the rope around each hand, one foot pushed against a tree to stop herself from sliding. "He's too heavy to pull. We're going to have to let him go—gently."

"No!" Sunny cried. "We can get him! We have to!"

"We aren't strong enough to pull him up without his help, and he can't help when the rope's around him like that," Devin said, showing not a flicker of emotion. "The face of the ravine isn't too steep. He won't tumble."

"We're going to let you down, Joel," she called out. "We won't let you fall, but you're going to slide a little. We've got you," she added, emanating confidence. "I promise you that."

As soon as she'd finished speaking, she intentionally let herself slide down the hill, slamming into another tree that stopped her progress. The rope groaned and Sunny watched, terrified, as Joel banged against the wall, landing against a deep pile of snow. He kicked his feet, trying hard to get some purchase, then one foot caught, with the other right behind. He was stable enough to ease the rope a little, gasping, "I couldn't breathe!"

"Stay right there," Devin yelled. "We're going to pull you up, but I need more rope." She tied the free end to a tree, then raced for her snowmobile, grabbed a few things and was back in a flash, looking more and more like she'd been on the losing end of a really bad bar fight as her face continued to bruise. Taking another length of rope, she made a loop in one end and tossed it down to Joel. "Put this one around your hips," she said, then she tied the free end to a sturdy tree.

"All right, guys," she said, addressing the boys. "Grab a stick and twist it into the rope like this." She picked up a sturdy stick and broke it over her knee. Then she threaded the rope around it and twisted it tightly. "That'll give you something to hold onto. We're gonna pull your dad up."

They stumbled around in the snow, finally finding sticks that were strong enough to use. Then all four of them got them threaded along the rope and started to pull with all of their might, Sunny and Seth on one rope, Devin and Ethan on the other. Grunting from the effort, they began to make some progress, inching him up a little at a time until Joel was at the edge. He must not have been hurt badly, since he grabbed onto a sapling large enough to help him hang on while they tightened their grip.

That helped a lot, and with another few hearty, backbreaking pulls, Joel flopped onto the compacted snow, panting from exhaustion laced with panic.

The boys started for him, but Devin grabbed Ethan's coat and tucked an arm around Seth's waist, holding them tight. "I'm not sure the ground's stable. Let him crawl up to us."

He did, slowly. Then he fell, face first, into the pure, white snow. Both boys grabbed him and turned him over, where he lay, staring up at the sky for a few seconds. "I thought I was dead," he said, sounding completely amazed that he wasn't.

His boys pulled him into an upright position, then tried to help him to his feet. "Ribs," he gasped as they pulled.

"Give him a minute," Devin said. She got down on her knees right in front of him. "How are you?"

"Better than you," he said, eyes wide. "What happened?"

"A tree mugged me. I'll explain when we're having a cup of hot cocoa at the outfitter. We just have to decide how we're getting there. I can call for an evacuation team, but it'll take a while."

"I think I can make it," he said. He rolled over and got to his knees, then stood with his boys' help. "I'm sore, but I don't think anything's broken." He looked down at the gash in the earth where his snowmobile had gone over. "I'm going to need a ride."

"Let me get my machine out and you can ride with me," Devin said. With her hand on Joel's shoulder, she spoke slowly and clearly. "It's going to take you a few minutes to get your bearings. There's no need to rush. Got it?"

"Yeah," he said, looking a little pale. The adrenaline was probably fading, letting his mind start to replay the last few minutes.

"Why don't you sit down," Devin said. "Your coveralls will keep you dry."

He didn't put up a fight, probably too weak to argue.

Then Devin met Sunny's eyes and said, "Give me a hand?"

They had to climb back up at an angle, moving from tree to tree, pulling themselves along. When they were out of earshot of the others, Devin said, "Are you all right?"

"Are you?" Sunny asked, having to fight the need to wrap her arms around Devin and hold her. She dug her boots hard into the snow to get up close so she could take a better look and winced at the bruised, bloody skin that had been perfectly smooth just an hour before.

"I'll be fine," Devin said, reaching up to touch her eye. "Just don't arrange for any formal portraits for a while." She smiled crookedly, with her swollen lip preventing it from traveling all the way across. "You didn't answer my question. Are you okay? I know that had to bring back some awful memories."

"If you're okay, I am too," Sunny said. "I just can't wait to get out of here. I've never wanted to leave a place as much as I do right now."

Devin gave her a long, sympathetic look, with the impact of it striking Sunny right in the heart. What a stupid thing to say. The way they'd felt after Hank had drown had been much, much worse. This accident was going to have a happy ending. For all of them.

They'd had to spend an hour with a deputy, a guy Devin knew from around, to make the accident report, with a volunteer paramedic poking around on Joel while they talked. Devin refused his offer to take a look at her, knowing she was just bruised and scraped up. Edie's husband arrived and he drove Joel and the boys back to their motel, with Edie following along in her own car to bring Mike back. That finally gave Devin a minute alone with Sunny. But she no sooner had her arms around her than the front door opened and her parents rushed in.

"Oh, my God," her mother cried when she got a good look at her. "Why aren't you at the hospital?"

"I'm fine," Devin said, but her mom nearly pushed Sunny out of the way to get to her and put her hands on her face. "How do you know you haven't lost vision in this eye?" she asked, tilting her head towards the light.

"I'm fine," Devin insisted. "I smacked my face against a tree, but I didn't scratch the eye."

"What happened, Buddy?" her dad asked, putting an arm around her shoulders.

She looked at him, trying to open the swollen eye to no avail. "We had a rough afternoon." She took in a breath and finally let some of the emotion out that had been building for the last hour. "But I'm back, god damn it. I am *back*."

Devin desperately wanted to go back to the cabin, but she allowed her mom to win this argument. She and Sunny were in her childhood bedroom, getting ready for bed. Other than two beers, she hadn't taken anything for her aches and pains, but she'd dutifully kept a cold can of beer on her eye while they'd had dinner at her favorite tavern.

Sunny reached down and pulled Devin's sweater over her head, then tugged at the long underwear top. As she got it off she gasped, then her cool fingers gently touched what Devin assumed were rope burns.

"Jesus!" she whispered. "Doesn't this hurt?"

"Hell, yes," Devin said, chuckling. "I'm a human being, aren't I?"

"Honey, we should have gone to the emergency care place. You're covered in bruises and cuts and burns!"

"I'm not paying a lot of money for someone to tell me I'm bruised, Sunny. I know my body. Believe me, this doesn't hurt anything like a broken rib—which I've had. I'm just sore."

"And strangely happy," Sunny said, cupping her cheek. "I'm bruised, too, but emotionally. I keep thinking of Hank. Kind of reliving it, I guess. But you seem perfectly fine."

Devin nodded, then moved as quickly as she could to take the rest of her clothes off. She went to her dresser and pulled out an old sweatshirt, deciding her stiff muscles would feel better if she was extra warm. Then she hopped in and waited for Sunny to join her.

Once they were on their sides, facing each other, she said, "You lost someone you cared for when Hank died. While it devastated me to feel like I contributed to a man's death, it was losing my nerve that's been with me every single day since it happened." She put her hand on Sunny's face, unable to stop smiling. "But today, when I had to act—it was still there. I haven't lost my nerve. I did what I had to do, and I saved that dope's life." She let out a short laugh. "I know I shouldn't think of him that way, but if he'd kept his ass in the seat and let me do my job we would have been home hours ago. And I wouldn't have looked like a tomcat after a fight."

"I'm sorry you got so banged up," Sunny said, delicately kissing each of Devin's many scratches and scrapes. "I feel a little guilty about this, but I'm glad Joel was a dope." She placed a very gentle kiss to Devin's swollen lips. "If that gave you back your confidence, it was worth it."

Grinning, Devin ran a finger over Sunny's lips. "You *should* feel guilty about that. Joel's gonna have nightmares about that fall for years. And the boys will probably never go near snow or snowmobiles or cliffs or ravines or trees for the rest of their lives!" She laughed softly. "On the other hand, they all needed to learn to listen to instructions and follow them. If today didn't convince them of that, they're hopeless." She put an arm around Sunny and hugged her as well as she could. "I'm confident I can prepare properly, think quickly, and not freeze. So as soon as you want to go back to Texas, I'm ready to leave."

"I'm on vacation," Sunny said, smiling. "My apartment's in contract, and I'm not going to be paying for anything other than health insurance starting next month. I'm in no rush."

Devin nodded. "I can understand not wanting to leave Maine when it's at its most glorious. But when the snow's gone and you're in muck up to your shins, you're going to yearn for some wide open, arid space."

"Then we'll find some. Until then, I'm ready to lead another snowmobile trip."

"Listen to this," Devin teased, poking all around her ticklish waist. "Now you're leading trips. Before I know it, you're going to be taking classes to get certified."

"One guide in the family is plenty. Maybe I can qualify as a guide assistant."

Devin scooted a little closer, just so she didn't have to stretch and make her body ache more than it already did. "You're overqualified for that," she said, tilting her head to kiss her soundly. "You are already Maine's number one assistant guide."

Chapter Thirty-One

When Sunny woke on the last Monday in February, she stretched and yawned for a few seconds, then rolled over and let Devin take her in her arms. When they didn't have a reason to rush, they snuggled against each other for a while, neither speaking until they'd woken more fully. Not many things felt better than lying in a chilly cabin, with her head on Devin's chest, her strong heartbeat sounding unusually loud in the otherwise silent cabin. When Devin woke enough to start to run her fingers through Sunny's hair, she stretched again and spoke. "Do we have any trips scheduled this week, honey?"

"Not until the weekend. Why?"

Sliding her hand up under Devin's thermal shirt, Sunny let her fingers dance over the silky skin. "Want to go camping?"

"Really?" Devin asked, her voice filled with excitement.

"I would love to get away with my favorite guide. Just the two of us."

"I'm on it," she said, jumping to her feet. "I'll get my notes and pick the perfect spot." She had a notebook in her hands before Sunny could blink. "Do you mind if we have to drive for a while to get there?"

"I don't mind if we drive to Nova Scotia. Pick whatever works, baby, and wake me up when you're ready to go."

After breakfast, they loaded up Devin's car and drove for a couple of hours, mostly watching the road instead of talking. The view was kind of odd from Sunny's perspective. Not long after they'd arrived in Maine, she'd decided it was much nicer to look at trees than the vast tracks of plains you saw when driving for a few hours outside of Dallas. But she hadn't realized how remarkably monotonous the view could become. They'd been in every direction from Greenville, but each view was about the same. Tall, dark green pine trees, many of them so perfectly spaced they were as orderly as Christmas tree farms, with blankets of snow on their faces. The trees were atop a uniform bed of pure white snow, with that tableaux rarely broken. Of course you'd come to a town every now and again, but they were all small, very small, with a little main drag containing two or three stores, a post office, and a church. Other than that, it was you, the snow, and the pine trees. But even though it was boring in a way, it was so pretty, so verdant, that she'd grown to love it. Like the Dutch must have felt about rows of uniform tulips, Mainers must have loved the pines that hugged every state road she'd been on. And while she couldn't call herself a Mainer, it helped when you understood what the locals loved about a place.

Once they'd arrived at the parking area for a state park they hadn't yet traveled to, Devin stopped the car, hopped out and started to organize their stuff. She hadn't brought her little sled this time. They were each going to carry their own stuff, or most of their own stuff. Sunny had a feeling her partner would keep more than her share. But she liked the thought of Devin treating her more like an equal. Sunny could see her share a little more of the responsibilities on every one of their trips, and that gave her a flicker of pride.

They were going to start off snowshoeing, then switch to skis if the conditions were right. Devin carefully wrapped some adjustable straps around two pairs of skis and slung them over her shoulder like she was carrying a giant quiver.

"Is that comfortable?" Sunny asked.

"Yep."

"Are we going someplace special?"

"Kinda." She revealed a charming grin. "When you're with me every place we go is special."

Sunny poked her in the ribs. "Details, please."

"Well, if I were alone, I'd just ski. But the first part of this trek is hilly, and there aren't any groomed trails. I could lead and have you follow the trail I cut, but I'm not sure you're confident enough on your skis to keep up. So...we've got both."

"Sure this is what you want to do?"

"Who picked the route?" she asked, winking as she turned and started to walk, ignoring the groomed trail to head off for parts unknown.

◆

Devin had been right on about the climb. Sunny might have been able to do it, but she also might have slid right back down five or six times. Another year of practice would help a lot, something she was already planning. Given how Devin loved winter, Sunny had made a vow to herself that they'd spend most of her vacation time in Maine, letting Devin fill herself with the snow and the cold and the silence—along with generous helpings of family and friends. It wouldn't be ideal, but four weeks of that would definitely make a dent.

After they'd bushwhacked their way through the trees to reach a crest, Sunny moved into the fading light of the afternoon sun and gazed across a gorgeous valley, tiny hills and snow-covered streams and ponds as far as the eye could see. "This is magical," she whispered, sure they were in a sacred space.

Devin put an arm around her shoulders and gave her a quick smile. Then she faced the valley as they stood there to watch the sun begin to set on their magical little spot—perhaps the only people with that view at that exact moment. This was precisely what she'd come to love about Maine. The easy accessibility of a deep, peaceful solitude, one they could relish together.

◆

Two hours later, their camp was organized, they'd had a surprisingly spicy Mexican-inspired instant meal, and their campfire was burning hot. Given Devin religiously followed the *Leave No Trace* camping dogma, they'd used a fire ring that a previous camper had cleared of snow. Sunny silently thanked him because if there hadn't been a permanent spot designated for fire, Devin wouldn't have created one herself. She truly believed the only way to treat the land was to leave the lightest imprint of her visit as possible.

They needed every bit of heat they could get, given the temperature was near zero. They had a tarp on the snow, their pads and sleeping bags placed upon it to give them a nice, warm cushion. They stretched out in front of the fire, cuddling. Every few minutes they'd turn over, so both sides of their bodies stayed toasty. But having Devin behind her took care of that pretty well, fire or no fire.

They were facing the blaze now, and Devin's soft voice barely reached Sunny's ears through her wool hat. "Do you ever miss work?"

"Miss it?"

"Uh-huh. You worked so hard to get where you are in your field. I'd think you'd miss some parts of it by now." She let out a laugh. "I have no idea what you do, so I can't guess which parts you like best."

"You know what I do," Sunny said. She turned and faced Devin, then tried to pinch her cheeks, doing a clumsy job with mittens. "I talk on the phone a lot, I review a million documents, I negotiate, I try to reason people out of doing stupid things… Lawyer stuff."

"Okay. Do you miss lawyer stuff?"

"Sure. It's my profession, Dev. I wouldn't say it's a calling, but I was drawn to it from the first."

"How come?" she asked, clearly interested.

"Um, I guess because I have a facility for it. I love negotiating, and I love getting the best deal possible for my clients. Is it always fun? No way. But it challenges me, and I like that."

"What else?"

"Mmm, you get a certain amount of respect when people find out you're a lawyer, and that's kind of cool. The money's nice, too."

"I can see that," Devin said, rubbing her cold nose against Sunny's. "I've never gotten used to having much money, but I can understand you'd want to keep the tap running once you got it started."

"Um, I told you I'd let you know when I had news," Sunny said, bracing herself a little. "Well, Adam and I talked turkey yesterday." Devin's eyes grew bigger as Sunny spoke. "He's willing to make me an equal partner, but it'll take all of the money I get from the sale of my condo, plus a little more."

"I don't know what that means," Devin said, no longer smiling. She pulled away and sat up, then adjusted her hat to make sure her ears were covered. "Why do you have to spend all of your money?"

“That’s the way it’s done, honey. You buy into a partnership, then you split the profits.” She tried to amp up her excitement, knowing Devin would share it if she could sell it properly. “Last year, Adam netted almost three times what I drew with Hank. We’d have to split that, of course, but I’d still be making really good money. I could buy a condo close to the office, so we could get by with one car.” She smiled. “And since we’d be set financially, you could take it slow and concentrate on finding a way to get your needs met.”

Devin put on a smile that looked a little forced, but she lay back down and wrapped Sunny in a hug, murmuring, “All I want is for you to be happy. Deeply happy. Wherever and whatever that is, I’m all in.”

“I know that.” Sunny looked into her eyes, shining brightly in the orange light of the flickering flames. “There’s nothing I’m more sure of.” Sunny grasped her face and kissed her gently, then more forcefully. Being outside, all alone, with just the stars watching over them, raised her temperature—fast.

Devin returned her kisses, making them hotter by the second. Then Sunny was on her back, with Devin hovering over her, kissing her senseless. “Let’s go,” Devin said, her voice rough with desire.

“The fire…”

“I’ll put it out later. Right now, I’ve got to get my hands on you.”

She was so damn good at making Sunny feel like the hottest woman on the planet, such an extravagant gift that she’d never be able to show her appreciation. They scampered to their feet and carried their gear back to the campsite, with Devin giving her a hand to drop to the tent floor and take her boots off. Then Devin got her own off and put both pair in the zipper pocket on the outside of the tent, safe from animals seeking shelter in a warm, moist, temporary home.

They stripped off their coats, then got the pads and the bags down and zipped together. Then they climbed into the biggish bag, immediately cuddling close.

“I’ve never made love outside in the winter,” Devin said. “But I think we’d better get our hands warm first or we’ll hit the roof when we touch each other.”

"You haven't had sex outside?" She poked her gently in the chest. "The queen of winter hasn't done her favorite thing?"

"Nope. My only chance would have been with Taylor, and she wouldn't camp when it was this cold. Some Mainer," she added, scoffing. "She wasn't tough like you."

"I'm tougher than I thought," Sunny agreed. She wrapped her arms around Devin's neck and pulled her down for kiss after kiss, finally coming up for air to gaze into her eyes for a long time. "We both are."

Devin was curled up in a ball, obviously trying to stay warm in the very cold night, while Sunny wrestled with her mind, which was so unsettled she couldn't begin to turn it off. When that was true even after a very spirited romp in their sleeping bags, Sunny knew she had to focus on her feelings, troubling though they were.

What she sensed she needed, but couldn't get, was some kind of absolution for even considering tearing Devin away from the place she loved so much.

In some ways, it seemed crazy to even think about moving to Austin. So far, they'd had a great time in Maine. And Sunny's enjoyment hadn't simply been from watching Devin suffusing her senses in her snowy wonderland. Sunny had enjoyed it too. Loved it, really. But wasn't there a difference between having a great vacation and making that vacation into a life? Something kept niggling at Sunny's brain, telling her this couldn't last. All vacations came to an end, then you had to get on with earning your living.

Essentially, the problem was that this *was* Devin's life; skiing, fishing, hunting, hiking, riding snowmobiles, dogsledding. All of that was in her DNA, and making a little money while sharing her passion with others was simply the price she had to pay to live a modern life. That was a mindset Sunny didn't share in the least. While it was fun to camp and hike, it was a treat. She got *satisfaction* from negotiating, from putting deals together, from interacting with clients, and juggling a lot of balls in the air. While a vacation from that was awfully nice, she was starting to long to return to her normal—her profession.

She'd known this before, but was now being starkly reminded of a fact. When you were part of a couple, you had to learn how to make joint decisions. Unfortunately, it turned out that Devin did this by refusing to push her own agenda. She simply refused. Over time, Sunny was determined to nudge her to be more of an advocate for herself. But there wasn't time for that now. Sunny was going to have to make the call, and she truly, deeply, hated that prospect. She would have to decide whether to go back to the life she'd earned through years of schooling and hard work, or chuck it all to earn basically nothing as a sidekick. A sidekick to the most wonderful guide Maine had ever seen, but a sidekick nonetheless. One of them wasn't going to get her heart's desire.

They were lying in bed at Devin's paternal grandparents' home, trying to decide what to do all day. They'd had a few warm days, along with a couple of inches of rain, rendering their options few. Sunny was beginning to see what Devin meant when she said shoulder seasons could be tough. You could bundle up and spend the day outside, but there wasn't enough quality snow for winter sports, and yanking your boots out of gloppy mud made hiking or even walking more of a challenge than the benefit it provided.

Devin's phone buzzed and she reached across Sunny's body to check the text. "Mmm," she said, making a soft sound. "Lucky."

"Lucky what?"

"Lucky, my buddy. Hunting," she added, keeping it brief. "I know you don't want to go, but I hate to leave him in the lurch. He's got two guys and two kids ready to leave, and his usual helper didn't show."

"How long?"

"Just overnight." She sat up and ran her hands through her hair, with it settling pretty neatly. "Mind?"

"You're pretty terse today," Sunny said, sliding her hand up the long-sleeved T-shirt to scratch Devin's back.

"Yup," she said, chuckling softly as she moved around to have Sunny's fingernails reach different spots.

"Do you want to go?"

"Uh-huh. I like kids."

"Then go." Sunny gave her a gentle push, watching as Devin started to put it into gear by pulling her shirt over her head. Her tattoo caught Sunny's attention, and she sat up as well, grasping Devin around the waist as she dipped her head to lick all around the outline. "When you come home, I'll show you how much I've missed you…and moosie."

Devin turned to give her a surprisingly sexy smile. "I could blow ten minutes…"

Sunny slid out of bed, bending over to place a delicate kiss upon a rock-hard nipple. "Good. I'll use that time making your breakfast. Get a move on." She reached over to tweak the other nipple, saying, "No one can accuse you of being hard to arouse."

"And no one can accuse you of being into quickies," Devin called out as she marched toward the bathroom.

"All true," Sunny agreed. "Ten minutes is only long enough to whet my appetite for you, which I promise will be ready and waiting when you return."

A few minutes later, Devin took the wrapped egg and cheese on toast and put it into the slash pocket of her jacket. She held Sunny in her arms for a long minute, giving her a very appreciative, very loving look. "Thanks for letting me go," she said. "Will you go stay with my parents?"

"Don't know. I'll see what your grandparents are up to. Maybe I'll hang out here."

"Love that," Devin said, lowering her head to offer a gentle kiss. "Love you, too."

"Get going, sweetheart. Lucky's waiting."

"I'll have my beacon," she said. "I'll ping you when we make camp."

Sunny wrapped her in a hug, noisily kissed her cheeks, then planted a long kiss to her lips. As they broke apart, she heard Devin's grandmother enter the room.

"Oh, I remember those days," Therese said, letting out a laugh. "Over fifty years ago, but I still miss them."

Devin released her hold, and dashed over to kiss her grandmother on the cheek. "Gotta go," she said, heading for the door. "Take care of Sunny for me." Then she was gone, out of the house and racing down the driveway.

"The child never learned to walk," Therese said, clucking her tongue. "She went from crawling to running in a single afternoon. Where's she off to?"

Sunny took a cup from the cabinet and poured Therese a cup of coffee. "She's filling in for a guide who didn't show up. I'm actually not sure where she's going, but she's taking some guys and their kids on an overnight hunting trip."

Therese accepted the cup with a smile, then sat at the table to add enough milk to lighten the color to a pale tan. "What's on your schedule for today?" A soft laugh bubbled up. "Now that you've dodged that bullet."

"Oh, god, I hate hunting," Sunny agreed, chuckling along with her. "I've never been so bored." As she walked to the stove, she patted Therese on the shoulder. "Can I make breakfast for you and Bernard?"

"He's been gone for an hour," she said, cocking her head at Sunny. "Do you think we lie around in bed all day?"

Sunny took a glance at the clock, seeing it was just six fifteen, then registered that Therese was fully dressed for the day, hair neatly arranged, with just a touch of lipstick applied. "I don't think any member of Devin's family does that," she admitted. "I've got my work cut out for me to get on your schedule."

After putting a couple of slices of bread in the toaster, Sunny leaned against the counter to wait for it. "I don't have anything planned for the day. Can I help you do anything?"

"You can," Therese said, patting the seat next to her. "You can sit right down here and tell me if I should book a flight to Dallas."

"Dallas?"

"Or Austin, if that's where you end up. I'm not going to let months go by again if my Mittens is down in Texas. Bernard and I are going to take advantage of the fact that we're still able to travel, so you'd better have a guest room ready."

Sunny didn't reply for a minute, focusing on buttering her toast to keep herself from crying. The love these people had for Devin caught her by surprise every once in a while, making her both enormously pleased and stunningly envious. She sat down and took a bite, chewing carefully. "Um, I'm still not sure what I'm going to do," she admitted. "Devin's left the decision up to me, which I pretty much hate."

"Mmm, she would," Therese said, nodding as she took a tiny sip of her coffee.

"But why? This affects her much more than me. There's nothing she truly likes about Dallas, Therese, and Austin won't be much better. I'd prefer it if she'd just tell me she wanted to stay. Then I could figure out if my need to go is greater than her need to stay."

"Do you love your home the way Devin does?" Therese asked. Her pale eyes scanned Sunny, then locked onto her, unblinking.

"No," she admitted. "Not the way she does. I could list all of the things I like, which are many, but the only thing about home that I truly love are my friends. I'd miss them desperately if I left."

"Oh, don't give short shrift to that," Therese said. "Nothing makes up for missing the people who mean the most to you."

"Like you did when Devin was in Texas," Sunny said softly.

She nodded a couple of times, gazing down at the table. "When Mittens was gone," she said, taking in a sharp breath, "it felt like the center of our lives was missing." She reached over and grasped Sunny's hand. "But I'm so proud of her for going, and even prouder of her for being willing to go back." She bit at her lips for just a second, with her composure slipping. "But sometimes I wish she was a little more selfish." A few tears started to roll down her soft, pale cheeks. "I'm so glad she's found you, but I don't want her to leave. I…I think I got all of the family's allotment for selfishness…" she muttered, clearly angry with herself as she wiped at her eyes. "Please don't tell Mittens I made a fool out of myself."

Sunny scooted her chair over and put her arms around the woman, giving her a gentle hug. The arms that encircled her were thin, the hug almost tentative, but it was one of the nicest Sunny could recall receiving. In less than a year, she'd been fully accepted, and lovingly welcomed into this incredibly close family. And she was going to wrench Devin away from this for a…job? Was she out of her damn mind?

There were closer places to find a reliable wi-fi signal, but Edie's was the one Sunny liked the best. After borrowing Therese's car, she made the drive, promising to pick up some pecans for a pie. Once at Edie's, which she now considered her office, she could chat with the employees for a bit, then sit by the coffee bar and catch up on her email. When she needed privacy, like she did today, she went into the storeroom to use the phone. That's why she found herself pacing around amidst boxes of swimsuits, shorts, T-shirts and running shoes as she made call after call.

The most vital was to Nathan, Greenville's star real estate salesman. After talking to him at length, Sunny had enough information, and enough assurances to make the next call. She actually had a lot of damn nerve to even broach the question, but she found herself speaking to Julian, saying, "Have you ever considered relocating to Austin?"

Devin followed Lucky into Edie's parking lot the next afternoon. It took a few minutes for everyone to unload their gear and settle up, but she was more than happy to see the wad of twenties one of the guys pressed into her hand. She'd gotten along well with the whole group, but she wasn't surprised to get her tip from a fairly flirty guy named Dan. As the group waved goodbye and got into their own car, Devin turned her back and spread the cash out for Lucky to see. "I got a hundred," she said.

"A hundred!" Shaking his head, Lucky revealed the two twenties he'd been given. "I should have been a girl," he grumbled.

"I'm splitting with you," she said. "I shouldn't get more because they liked my butt." Laughing a little, she added, "I'm glad Sunny wasn't there. Dan was checking me out like he hadn't seen a woman in ten years."

"I didn't notice," he said, tugging on one of her twenties. "You keep eighty. You spent a lot more time with the kids."

"Don't mind if I do," she agreed. "This is a damn good tip. I think I'll splurge and take my girlfriend out for a burger."

"Big spender," he said, chuckling. "I can see why she's not in a rush to go back to Dallas."

Her phone chirped, and Devin pulled it from her pocket to see a text from Sunny. "Ha! She's right next door." Devin put her arm around Lucky's waist and gave him a hug. "I'd invite you to join us, but I want her all to myself. Thanks for the trip," she added. "Call any time."

Then she started to cross the parking lot, lowering the zipper on her jacket to take a sniff. Not *terrible*, but she was a long way from fresh. She'd brushed her teeth after breakfast, but that was it. With luck, Sunny would want to shower together for a welcome home.

After pushing the door to the local bar open, Devin spied Sunny sitting at a table by the kitchen, with Badger sitting across from her. He had help on the weekends, but during slow times he was the bartender, the cook, and the busboy. "Aren't you supposed to be working?" Devin asked, tugging his stocking cap down over his eyes.

"No customers except Sunny, and she's already eaten."

Devin grasped his arm and pulled him to his feet. "Then you can cook for me. Double cheeseburger, please, and don't be stingy with the fries."

"Everybody thinks they know how to run my business," Badger grumbled, giving Devin a good-natured smile.

She sat down on the chair he'd relinquished, then leaned all the way over to place a gentle kiss on Sunny's lips. "I was just telling Lucky I wanted to take you to dinner. Little did I know you'd take yourself."

"Hadn't planned on it," she said, her voice a little less crisp than normal. "Your grandfather wanted something from the hardware store, so I rode into town with him. I figured you'd want to go back to your parents' tonight, so rather than make you go all the way out to your grandparents' house to pick me up, I decided to wait here for you."

"How long…I mean how many beers have you been waiting?"

"Three," Sunny said, holding up the proper number of fingers. "I'm a little buzzed."

"I'd try to catch up, but I'll have to drive us home. Kinda unfair," she said, tugging on Sunny's nose. "I'm the one who had to sleep on the rocky ground last night." She picked up Sunny's glass and drained the last ounce of her beer. "But I'm not going to complain. I like that you're willing to come in here and chat with Badger."

"I like him," Sunny said. "Now that everyone knows I'm a lawyer, I get to give free legal advice to every third person. Badger would not believe that I don't know diddly-squat about patent law, so I hope he seeks additional help before he tries to patent his raccoon-proof trash cans."

"Diddly-squat," Devin said, chuckling. "I like the things that come out of your mouth when you've had a few drinks."

"Take me home and I'll show you a few more things I know you like," she said, amping up her sexy voice in a playful manner.

"Gotta eat first," Devin decided. "I'll need my strength."

"Hmm…" Sunny looked up and nodded when Badger held up a beer glass. "What should we do to pass the time? I know," she said, grinning like a kid. "I'll tell you about the conversation I had with Adam today. Interested?"

"Desperately," Devin said, her stomach flying to her throat in two beats of her heart.

"Well," Sunny said, drawing out the word, then smiling at Badger as he set another draft onto the table.

Devin grabbed the beer and took a healthy slug. She had so much adrenaline going through her veins that her body wouldn't even register a little alcohol.

"It's all right," Sunny said quietly, reaching over to grasp Devin's hand. "I turned down the job."

"You did?" Her mouth was as dry as dust, but she got out another few words. "What does that mean?"

Sunny took a sip of her beer, obviously still in a playful mood. "It means my vacation continues."

"But why?" Devin asked, getting to the heart of the matter.

"Mmm, I've got a lot of reasons, but the biggest one is that I didn't feel right having to use all of the proceeds of my condo to buy in. That just seemed like too large an investment."

"But you'd make that back, right? I mean, your salary would be higher as a partner than if you were just an employee."

"It would," Sunny agreed, "but it would take a number of years to equalize. And if we decided we didn't like Austin…" She shrugged. "It was just too big a risk, especially since I promised I'd be much more careful with my money." She gripped Devin's hand tenderly. "I take every promise I make to you very seriously."

"Was Adam upset? I know I would be if you'd turned me down."

"Well, he wasn't interested in me like you are," Sunny teased, "but to make up for breaking his heart, I introduced him to someone who he actually might like better than me."

"Who?"

"Julian," she said, smiling like the Cheshire Cat. "Julian's not very happy at his current firm, and Adam really didn't want an equal partner. So I suggested he consider Julian as a junior. That would give Julian a salary bump, while letting Adam keep a little more for himself."

"That's so cool!"

"They haven't even met, but if it all works out, it would be good for both of them. I think Adam would really like Julian. Hank and I sure did."

"You're a nice person," Devin said, so mesmerized by the warmth of Sunny's eyes that she didn't even notice when Badger stood by the table, bearing her burger.

"Look alive," he said, sliding it in front of her. "Get your head in the game, Dev."

"It's dinner, not a competition," she said. "But thank you. Looks great." The second Badger was gone, she grasped Sunny's hand again. "Now what?"

"Now...you eat," she said, taking another drink. "When you're finished, we go home and I scrub you clean then make you see stars. I can, you know," she said, batting her eyes.

"About work," Devin said, starting to load her burger up with condiments. "What are you going to do about work?"

"Not sure. But I've got some ideas. I've got to let a few things percolate. No rush."

"You don't have a salary coming in," Devin reminded her.

"I'm aware. I also don't have many bills." She swiped a fry, and blew on it before popping it into her mouth. "Put your sweet little mind at ease, Devin. We'll sort this all out soon enough."

The second Sunday of March was remarkably warm, not to mention bright and clear. The glorious day reminded Sunny of just how long they'd been in Maine, with spring clearly bearing down on them.

Devin had recently surprised her by presenting her with a pair of muck boots, shin high and very well insulated, and she wriggled her toes as she drove, warm and dry and ready for anything that mud season could throw at her.

Devin had been hinting with some frequency that the slow season was upon them, and now would be the ideal time to return to Texas, if they were going. But Sunny had resolutely ignored the hints, unwilling to make any plans until she had everything in order.

As much as she missed her friends, Texas was slowly beginning to seem like a place Sunny had visited—but had no deep connection to. That was a very strange sensation, but it had been building and building as she'd changed her perspective. She was a fifth generation Texan, but her connection to the place was suddenly as fragile as a spider's web.

She snuck a look at Devin, sitting in the passenger seat of the car. Atop her shirt she wore only her wind-stopping shell, looking perfectly warm even though it was barely above freezing. But she believed anything above thirty-two degrees was the dividing line between winter coat and spring coat, and Sunny was sure she couldn't change her. Not that she wanted to. Devin was just about perfect exactly as she was.

They'd been driving for a half hour, heading north along the west side of the lake, with Sunny following the directions she'd written down. She'd always used her phone for directions at home, but service was too spotty up here to be reliable, so she'd learned to write things down just to be safe.

She rounded a gentle curve, then slowed down and checked the numbers on the mailboxes by the road, not exactly sure how much farther she had to go. Then she spotted the rusty mailbox and turned into a short drive, seeing a big, white BMW SUV parked in front.

"Isn't that Nathan's car?" Devin asked.

Sunny rolled her eyes. You couldn't keep any kind of secret from her. She was just too damn sharp. "Maybe," Sunny said, content to tease her if she couldn't surprise her.

"Unless he left Andy and lost everything in the divorce, this isn't his place."

Sunny took another look at the little bungalow, slightly hurt by Devin's dismissal of it. While it was true that it was in rough shape, Sunny saw nothing but potential. Only a thousand square feet, with just one outdated bath and an even more outdated kitchen, the little house sat on two full acres of prime lakefront. That was the draw in her view.

"This might not be his cup of tea," Sunny said, "but I think it could be ours."

Devin turned and stared at her, not speaking.

"Let's take a look," Sunny said. "Then we can talk."

Slowly, Devin opened her door and got out, still staring warily at Sunny. Nathan opened the front door as they approached and gave them both hugs and kisses. "I can't believe I'm showing a house in this kind of shape, but I think the land is worth twice what they're asking." He seemed contemplative as he turned his head and surveyed the sad-looking little home. "If I had this piece of property, I'd knock down this abomination and put a big, rough-hewn log home on it. Real Montana kind of rugged. I might even buy a cowboy hat," he decided.

"You'd look nice in one," Sunny said, having to take up the slack for Devin, who seemed too puzzled and confused to even make conversation. "It'd be nice if we had that kind of money, but the house isn't the focus right now. We're looking for the largest piece of lakefront land we can afford."

"We are?" Devin said, her voice squeaking.

"Oh, God, I hope I didn't sound like the pompous prick I can be," Nathan said. "I get carried away easily, Sunny. You know I think this is a great piece of property for you two."

She touched his arm reassuringly. "I don't take offense. If I had a lot of money, God knows I'd spend it. But Devin and I both agree that we have to own our home, we can't let it own us." She smiled at Devin who was starting to come out of her shock. "We've chosen to go small and cheap."

"I think you've hit that right on the button here," he said, checking his big, gold watch. "But don't get too comfortable with not having much money. As soon as you get licensed in Maine, you're going to be a very busy woman."

"You're getting licensed—"

Nathan interrupted. "I'm sorry to be so abrupt, but I've got to show another place this afternoon. One of the islands is up for sale and I've got a big fish I'm trying to reel in."

"No problem at all," Sunny said. "We'll just make sure the door's locked when we leave."

He kissed them both, saying, "Have fun, lovebirds. Take all the time you want, and call me later to let me know what you decide."

Then he was gone, leaving them alone in the small, dark house. Devin stepped forward and took Sunny's hands. "Is there something you'd like to tell me?"

"Uh-huh." She nodded, smiling at the adorably expectant expression on Devin's face. "I want to become a Mainer. I know I'll never be a *true* Mainer, but I'll do my best to be an excellent transplant."

Devin slipped her arms around her waist and hugged her tightly. "You want to stay?" she whispered, her voice catching.

"I want to stay," Sunny said, one hundred percent sure. "Our time here has passed in a minute, Dev, and every day has been a vacation." She pulled away and ran her fingertips lightly across Devin's soft cheek. "A vacation with the woman I'll always love."

"But this is so different, Sunny. It'll be such a big change—"

"Almost like the change you made when you went to Dallas for me. But there's one big difference."

"What's that?" she asked, blinking her eyes slowly.

"I love Maine." She took Devin by the shoulders and gave her a gentle shake. "I *love* it here, sweetheart. I truly do. And no matter how much you've tried, you'll never love Texas. It's just not in your blood."

"But you haven't been here in May. The flies can drive you stark-raving mad! And the mosquitos are awful in the summer. You won't like that at all, Sunny. And I know you don't want to go on hunting trips. They can be miserable. Getting up before dawn to sit in a blind waiting—"

"Shh," Sunny soothed. "I'm a lawyer, honey, not a guide. I'll go on a trip with you every once in a while, but only for fun."

"Really?" she said, with just a hint of disappointment in her voice.

"Really, Dev. We need to each do what we're good at, and for me, that's real estate law. Nathan's sure he can keep me busy, but if he can't, I'll figure out some other way to exercise my lawyering instincts."

"There's not enough business around here," Devin said, her voice filled with anxiety. "I don't think Nathan sold three houses last year."

"He sells plenty in Portland," Sunny said. "I'll have to drive over there once or twice a week, but you've got to go where the work is."

"And that will make you happy?" Devin asked, her excitement clearly building again. "You're sure?"

"So long as I can visit Dallas a few times a year, I'm dead sure. I want to live here, Dev. With you. I want this to be our home."

Devin wrapped her in a crushing hug, with Sunny able to feel tears on her cheek as their bodies molded together. "I'm so happy," she whispered, "even if we have to live in this awful piece of crap."

"Oh, it's bad," Sunny agreed, wiping her own tears away. "But I brought your dad out the other day, and he said it had good bones. It just needs a lot of updating."

Devin released her to stare, open-mouthed. "You brought my dad out?"

"Your mom and your grams too. Separate trips." She smirked at the look on Devin's face. "Every once in a while, when I say I need to go use the internet to have a long Skype call, I'm lying."

"I can't believe…" She slowly let her gaze travel around the house, then murmured, "This is going to need a lot more than upgrading."

"But it's *cheap*. It's been on the market for over a year and no one's even looked at it in six months. Nathan said the seller would take much less than asking just to get rid of it."

Once again, Devin looked around suspiciously, clearly trying to picture the dark, cramped rooms in another layout.

"We can afford it, Dev. I can pay cash for it as well as the upgrades. And when we're all done, we'll have enough in savings to cover our fixed expenses for a few years. *Years*. I ran the numbers twice."

"Our own house," Devin said, nodding as she meandered around the small rooms. "Could we tear out these walls and make this one big space?"

"That's what your dad thought we should do. He's very excited about helping out. He says he'll see how our remodeling goes, then he'll think about doing the addition your mom wants."

"Oh, yeah, that'll happen," Devin said, laughing a little. "He's all talk, but my grandfathers actually follow through with their projects. With their help, we could get this sorted out by the time winter comes." She grasped Sunny's hands again, beaming. "Are we gonna do this?"

"I think we should. It's a great piece of land, and we're only about twenty minutes away from Chris and Lori." She let out a short laugh. "They drove over last night and took a family vote. It was unanimous, honey. The Carter's think it's the perfect spot."

With her grin growing, Devin said, "You know where the perfect spot is?"

Sunny could see this one coming from a mile away, but she loved the predictability of it. "Where?"

Devin wrapped her in a fierce hug and gave her a tender, lingering kiss, pressing their lips together until they had to break apart to breathe. Those pale, mesmerizing eyes locked onto Sunny as Devin spoke softly and confidently. "The most perfect spot on this earth is wherever you are—as long as I'm right next to you."

EPILOGUE

ON THE FIFTEENTH OF AUGUST, Sunny woke in Devin's childhood bed, groggily slapping her hand behind her to confirm she was alone. Idly, she wondered how she always knew that Devin had already snuck out, but whatever method she unconsciously used, she was rarely wrong.

There was a little noise coming from the kitchen, and some nice breakfasty scents wafting down the hall, so she got up and put on shorts and a T-shirt, then pulled her hair back into a pony tail. She was going to have to get it cut, but wouldn't chance it to the local hair salon. Once the summer rush was over, they were going to spend two or three weeks in Dallas, wearing out their welcome by crashing with each set of her friends. Then Sunny could visit all of her professionals—from dentist to stylist. Devin would make fun of her, but she could live with that. She *couldn't* live with a bad haircut.

Spent plates sat in front of Mark and Peggy, both of them reading. No Devin, but the dogs both got up to offer a hello.

Sunny squatted down to let them lick her neck, looking up when Mark said, "You just missed her."

"Missed her?" She scrambled to get up, leaving a pair of disappointed pups whining for more love. "Devin left?"

"Just a minute ago," Mark said. "She said you were sleeping so soundly she couldn't bear to wake you."

"But she couldn't bear to wait, either," Peggy remarked, standing to walk over to the counter to pour a fresh cup of coffee and hand it to Sunny. "I told her to either wait or wake you, but you know how she is."

"My friends are here!" It wasn't easy, but she tried to hide how utterly pissed off she was. Their cell phones didn't work out here, so she had no way of catching her antsy lover before she got all the way home.

"I know," Peggy soothed, giving her a one-armed hug. "She had a list of things she wanted to do before they were up, so I said I'd take you home."

"She drives me crazy," Sunny pouted, sitting down to drink her coffee. "Waiting is absolute torture for her, but she won't wake me up!"

Chuckling, Mark said, "You've got to give her points for thoughtfulness. But then you have to take points away for impatience. I guess it's a wash."

"Oh, she's nearly perfect and she knows it," she said, unable to stop herself from smiling. "Insufferably perfect."

"I can take you right now," Peggy said.

"You don't have anything on your schedule?"

"Oh, a few things, but I can get to them later. I'm going to take Mom for a manicure, but that's not until eight."

Sunny checked the clock, seeing it was only six thirty. "I don't want you to drive all the way to our place, only to have to go nearly that far to pick up your mom." She was easily as anxious as Devin was to get home, but she just couldn't ask Peggy to drive all over creation to satisfy her whims. "I'll go with you, then you can run me home. My friends will probably still be asleep, anyway. They're running on central time."

"Are you sure, honey? You know I don't mind."

"I'm positive." She leaned over and clapped her hands together, with both dogs jumping to their feet and running over to her. "That gives us time for a walk, fellas. Let me put some bug spray on, and we'll go work some energy off."

"She means anger," Mark said, his dry sense of humor always making Sunny laugh.

"True," she said, giving his hair a playful ruffle. "Devin's a lucky girl in that I mostly complain to the trees, rather than her face."

"Peggy? Is that something you'd like to—"

His comment was cut off by a hand clapped firmly over his mouth. Then Peggy leaned close and kissed his cheek, saying, "It's too late to change me, honey. And trying will only get you into trouble."

As long as they were at the salon, Sunny got her nails done as well. She'd let them go, rarely wearing polish now, but her friends were all buffed and pampered, so she splurged.

Once they were back on the road, Peggy said, "How does it feel to have your first house guests?"

"Good," Sunny said, turning to smile. "Really good. I kind of wish we'd made the house three bedrooms, but I had to stick to my promise. 'No bigger than we absolutely need.'" She chuckled softly. "Me and my big mouth."

"I didn't hear you girls come in last night. Were you up late?"

"Pretty late. I borrowed Edie's big SUV, then drove to Portland to pick everyone up. After we got home, we sat around and ate the delicious snacks your daughter prepared, and had a few drinks. Well, I had a few drinks. Devin was the designated driver."

"Maybe that's why she was up with the chickens," Peggy said. "Let her drink tonight and she might stay in bed like a normal person."

"I hate to point out the obvious," Sunny joked, "but Devin's a long, long way from normal."

When Sunny flung open the door to their cozy home, she expected to find everyone lingering over coffee in their spacious, sparkling new, eat-in kitchen. But the place was silent, with not a dish in sight, nor a crumb on the table. Devin's car was parked in its usual spot, though, so they couldn't be far. Before taking off to find the group, she needed to pee, then realized their bedroom door was closed. Cracking it open, she spied Gwen, still in bed. The door made a muted squeak, and Gwen rolled over and grunted, "That woman of yours is crazy."

"No argument," Sunny said, entering to perch on the side of the bed. She put her hand on Gwen's warm back and gave it a scratch. "Any idea where my crazy woman is?"

"Now? Hard to tell. They left ages ago."

"For…?"

"Something about making us Mainers. I said I was perfectly happy remaining a Texan, so I stayed in bed."

"Making you Mainers?" Sunny stared at her, waiting for more.

"She said she wanted to paddle out to an island to watch the sun rise."

"*Our* island? That takes an hour, and that's if Devin's really cranking it."

"No, not yours." Gwen sat up and gave her disheveled hair a little order. "She said yours was too far. Is there a closer one?"

"There are a few. Did she say how long a trip it was?"

Scratching her head in confusion, Gwen said, "Not sure. I guess we'll find out when they get back."

"No way," she said, jumping up to head for the bathroom. She found her sunblock and started to apply it, grumbling. "Why can't she just sit still for two minutes? Is that too much to ask?"

"I think so," Gwen said, laughing to herself as she flopped down and closed her eyes again. "She's a live-wire."

"Oh, shit," Sunny said. "She had to take both kayaks. I can't follow."

"She borrowed one from somebody," Gwen said. "She left one in case I changed my mind." Laughing, she said, "She doesn't know me very well yet."

It was going to be a warm day, so Sunny put her swimsuit on under her tank top and quick-dry shorts, then added a cap to keep the sun from her eyes. She had a few guesses about which island Devin would pick, and she started off for the first, the closest of the bunch. Steady, quick strokes got her there in twenty minutes, but there was no sign of the group. So she kept going, making sure to follow all of the paddling tips Devin had given her. It had taken a while to learn to use the big muscles in her torso, rather than the smaller ones in her arms, but paddling properly made you go much faster, and kept you going much longer.

She almost passed by the second island, but a sole figure sitting on the dock made her turn and pick up the pace. Michele was sitting there, leaning back on her arms, head tilted up to let the sun's morning rays warm it.

"What in the world are you doing here alone?" Sunny called out as she swung by.

"I was dumb enough to kayak out here, but I'm not dumb enough to paddleboard to the next island."

"Paddleboard?"

"Yeah. Callie and Teresa were up for it, but I wasn't about to fall into this freezing lake."

"Where's your kayak?"

"Around the other side. Devin left a paddleboard for you in case you came out. She said you never let a challenge pass you by."

"Challenge?" She tilted her hat back and stared at Michele. "What do you mean by that?"

"She said something about not believing any of us could pass the hearty Mainer endurance test. I told her she could kiss my butt, and waved goodbye. When I'm damn good and ready, I'll go back and have a second breakfast. Kayaking is hard work!"

"I'll kill her," Sunny growled, starting to paddle around the island to find her board. "What in the hell is wrong with that woman?"

"I don't know," Michele said, lying down on the dock to sun herself like a lazy cat. "But there might be some kind of pill she can take for it. You ought to check that out."

It took a few minutes, but Sunny got the paddleboard into the water, then slid onto it from the dock and tested her balance while holding onto Michele's hand. She'd gotten pretty darned good at paddling, but she had to admit the first few strokes always had her knees quaking in fear. If she'd been doing this in Texas it wouldn't have been anything to worry about. But here, where the water was still an ice cold sixty-seven, she truly hated to take a tumble. Devin laughed her ass off whenever Sunny slipped, but it had already been determined that she was part polar bear, a trait Sunny didn't share.

"I'm off," she said, bending her knees to take a strong stroke. "If those nincompoops come back while I'm out looking for them, tell Devin she'd better come find me if she knows what's good for her."

"Will do. But knowing her, she'll have everyone taking dives off a cliff by now."

"Thankfully," Sunny said dramatically, "there aren't any cliffs close to the lake. At least there had better not be."

Over the summer, they'd borrowed paddleboards from some of their neighbors, people from bigger cities who used their cabins only in the summer. Almost everyone had every kind of toy, from power boats to tiny little one-person sailboats. Sunny had always considered herself to be pretty ballsy, but Devin had her beat. She'd saunter over to introduce herself to each family after they'd made their initial appearance of the summer, carrying a six pack of beer or something she'd baked, and return with an open invitation to borrow their stuff, enormously pleased with herself. Of course, the neighbor got a pretty good deal in the bargain, since Devin could be counted on to do nearly everything from repair a small appliance to help put in a new dock—free of charge.

Still, Sunny had no idea how she'd gotten four paddleboards onto the little island where she'd left Michele. But by now she'd learned that Devin worked in mysterious ways.

The bright sun shone over the tops of the tallest trees, but there was such a nice, cool breeze Sunny was able to paddle hard without getting too hot. When she and Devin went out together, Devin would dive into the water at some point, but Sunny had never joined her. Her years of working out in the Texas heat had given her a much greater tolerance for warmth than Devin would ever have.

Still, even though she wasn't overheated, once the sun was right in her face she began to sweat. But she kept up a quick pace, determined to ace Devin's insane hearty Mainer endurance bullshit test. After twenty minutes of all-out effort, she reached the most likely island, one where some of Devin's grandparents' friends had a nice cabin. As she got close, she spotted Teresa lounging in a hammock hanging between two spindly pine trees that somehow clung to the rocky ground.

"Jesus H. Christ!" Sunny yelped, so frustrated she was ready to curse a blue streak. "Where is that woman?"

"By now?" Lazily, Teresa took a peek at her watch. "If Callie hasn't died of exposure, they're at your island. If she has, I hope the last words in her head were the ones I spoke to her. 'I told you so, dummy.'"

As Sunny got close, she saw three paddleboards propped up against the porch. "They swam?"

"Uh-huh. You know Callie can't refuse a challenge. I think Devin hinting that Texans weren't as tough as Mainers got under her skin. She's a dang fool," she added, putting on an accent she didn't usually use.

"Screw it," Sunny declared, too tired to continue. "I'm going to wait right here for them. I don't need to win the 'who's dumbest' test."

"Plenty of room," Teresa said, tossing her legs onto the ground and patting the space beside her. "Devin was sure you'd happily jump in and swim over, but Callie told her there was no way you'd do it. It's nice to know that Devin's still got her work cut out for her to know you as well as Callie does."

The island had a tiny bit of sandy beach, and Sunny paddled right onto it, before jumping off to land in about a foot of icy cold water. "Shit!" she cried before running up to Teresa.

"Have a seat," Teresa said, scooting over a little more. "We'll just sit here and watch the world go by until those lunatics swim back. Hearty Mainers," she scoffed.

Sunny was just about to sit down when she said, "Did Devin really say I'd jump right in?"

"Yeah," she said, chuckling. "She said you're as close to a native Mainer as anyone she's ever met." Her grin grew brighter when she added, "I think that means you've lost every ounce of sense you've ever had."

"Oh, crap," Sunny sighed, knowing she had to do something she really didn't want to do. "Every morning that we're at the cabin she dives in and swims for ten or fifteen minutes, but I've never joined her."

"Why would you?" Teresa asked. "No one wants to swim in water this cold."

"Devin does," Sunny said, shrugging. "She swears it clears your mind and boosts your mood."

"Your mood's fine. No one's going to think less of you for not jumping into an ice cold lake." She blinked her big, brown eyes a few times, then said, "Devin won't, will she?"

"No. Definitely not," Sunny said with certainty. "She never pushes me to do anything." Turning to gaze at the glassy water, she let out a heavy sigh. "I've put it off all summer, but I know she'd love it if I'd go with her—

even once." She whipped off her tank top, then her shorts. Sharing a smile with Teresa, she said, "Being in love makes you do the dumbest stuff!" Then she took a running start, pulled her knees up to her chest and leapt in. It felt like someone had hit her right in the chest with a roundhouse punch. As she expelled air from her lungs and started to rise, the numbing cold hit her, and she heard the high-pitched squeal that she had no control over.

As her head broke through the water, she yelled, "Stupid! I am a stupid, stupid woman!"

"Get going if you're going," Teresa said, laughing her butt off. "Want me to paddle over with you? I'd hate to have you freeze halfway there."

"I'm fine," Sunny said, beginning to warm up faster than she thought she would. "But keep your paddle close by in case I start to scream."

Teresa jumped up and grabbed her paddle, then pushed Sunny's board deeper into the water and struggled to get her balance, holding the paddle up like she was on a high-wire. "I'm right behind you," she called out.

"I'm fine," Sunny insisted.

"And I'm right behind you," Teresa repeated. "Get going!"

Before she'd gotten into gymnastics, swimming had been Sunny's favorite sport, and she'd gotten into it again in the last month, sticking to the shallower, warmer lakes which everyone called ponds. How a body of water a hundred feet deep could be called a pond was a mystery to her, but she supposed everything seemed like a pond when compared to Moosehead's depth of over two hundred and fifty feet.

It was about a quarter mile to the cabin, a distance she regularly completed in the ponds. But it seemed farther today, probably because the water was four or five degrees colder than she was used to. Five degrees didn't seem like much on land, but those few degrees really got your attention in the water.

Teresa was paddling slowly behind her, really taking it easy. But Sunny knew her friend could step on the gas if need be, and she had to admit it was a relief to know she was back there—just in case.

It took a few minutes to get into a good, steady rhythm, but Sunny finally got comfortable. Then it was just concentrating on her stroke and fighting to keep it smooth. The sun was behind her now, and a slight tailwind made the effort a little easier. Eventually, she spied Devin's island, sitting atop the lake proudly. Despite her labors, she felt herself smile like she always did when she first spotted it. Any place that meant a lot to Devin made her smile, and her little cabin meant more to her than Sunny could fathom. Devin's willingness to move to a normal house just showed in the most crystalline fashion how deep her commitment to their relationship was, and Sunny paid her back by going out to the cabin at least twice a week. Giving up a toilet and running water was a small price to pay to keep a contented smile on that sweet face.

As Sunny grew closer to land, she saw someone outside, finally able to pick out Callie's fair hair. Her heart started to beat faster when it hit her that Devin might have gone off to do something even dumber! She kicked it into gear to sprint that last fifty yards, panting from the effort when she grabbed onto the tiny dock and pulled herself up. "Where is she?" Sunny gasped, certain she'd reached the end of her journey. If Devin had set off for another endurance test, she was on her own.

"Waiting for you," Callie said, giving her a sly, enigmatic smile.

"Waiting for me?" A big, sun-warmed towel settled around her shoulders. Then Teresa paddled up alongside and accepted a hand from Callie to pull her onto the rocky land. She was smiling just as cryptically, puzzling the hell out of Sunny.

"Why's she inside?"

Both of her friends shrugged, clearly struggling not to laugh. "Search me," Callie said. "I guess she prefers being inside on a nice August morning."

"That's crazy. Devin never wants to be inside." She clambered along the rocks to reach the steps. As she flung the door open, she nearly barreled into Devin, who stood in the middle of the room, holding a big bunch of flowers. Sunny had helped out in the garden enough to recognize the plants from Devin's grandmother's yard, the pristine white, yellow and purple flowers looking particularly vivid in the filtered light that shone in the cabin.

Devin's hair was still wet, but her clothing was bone dry—a pale blue chambray shirt and navy shorts that showed off her tanned skin and made her eyes as blue as the summer sky. A smile that made her look both excited and shy had Sunny so flummoxed she couldn't even form a question. But she didn't have to come up with a single word, since Devin had obviously prepared herself perfectly for this moment.

She took a step forward, standing so close they nearly touched. "You know what I'd like?" she asked, with a little grin beginning to show.

"Um…no."

Devin leaned closer, with her smile growing. "I'd like to pull you into the center of my life, along with all of the people who mean so much to me. I want you to join my family, Sunny."

"Oh, Devin," she said, tears already beginning to form.

"And I want to join yours. I'll do my best to work my way into your group. To have your friends think of me as one of their own." She held out the bouquet, the blooms so fresh and fragrant they were intoxicating. "You know how much my gram hates to cut her flowers, but she wrapped this bunch up just for you."

"You're going to make me cry," Sunny said, wiping her eyes with the edge of the towel.

"I don't want you to cry." Devin wrapped Sunny in a tender embrace. "I just want you to say 'yes.'" She pulled back and smiled broadly. "Will you marry me?"

"Yes," Sunny said, her voice quaking with emotion. "Nothing would make me happier."

In a flash, she was enveloped by Devin's body, then she felt her world shift slightly, winding up tilted at an angle, gazing up into clear blue eyes while being supported by the strongest, surest arms she'd ever hoped to feel. Their lips met gently, then with more purpose as she felt Devin's heart opening up to her. A few warm tears touched her cheeks, and when she opened her eyes, Devin's beautiful eyes overflowed with emotion. "I love you with all my heart," she whispered, smoothly placing Sunny back on her feet.

Something cool and heavy was placed in Sunny's hand and she looked down to see a piece of stone, light gray with a darker streak running through it.

"On my very first solo camping trip," Devin said quietly, "I found this."

"What…?"

"It's a hand ax," she said. "I know it's really old, but I can't even guess its age. I should have taken it somewhere to have an expert check it out, but I was worried they'd find it was valuable and want to keep it." She shrugged, looking a little embarrassed. "It meant too much to me to risk that."

"Tell me why," Sunny said, seeing that Devin had more to say.

"Um…" A small furrow formed near her brow. "I'd just turned thirteen, and I'd started to guess that I was gay."

"Ooo," Sunny whispered, gently touching her cheek. "Were you upset?"

"No, but I felt like I really had to think about it, you know? Before I told my parents, I mean."

"And you think best when you're alone."

"Yeah." She grinned, probably looking like she had when she was just a girl. "My mom didn't want me to go, but I needed to be alone to think this through. On my second day, I started to dig a latrine and hit this." She wrapped her hand around Sunny's and hefted the object in their joined grip. "I made up this whole story about a native girl who was out on her own, trying to figure out her life." Her smile grew a little when she said, "I'm sure it was all fantasy, but it made me feel really connected to this tool." She closed Sunny's fingers around it and said softly, "It's the most precious thing I own, and I want you to have it now." She sniffled a little and added, "That was the day I decided I was gay. The day I knew I'd always love women." She leaned close and whispered, "Even in my wildest childhood dreams, I never guessed I'd find someone like you."

"God, I love you," Sunny managed, barely able to speak.

Devin tipped her head back and howled like a wolf, laughing as she did. The door opened and both Callie and Teresa flew in, their arms wrapping around her and Devin in a fervent hug.

"Congratulations!" Callie kissed Sunny's cheeks so hard she made a loud "smack." Then Teresa did the same before kissing Devin with equal vigor.

"We have to go tell your family!" Sunny wrapped her arms around Devin and held on tightly. "I can't wait!"

"Don't have to," she said, with a smug smile making her even more irresistible. She went to the door, with Sunny following. Devin jogged over to the dock and waved her arms, then a pontoon boat puttered into view, filled with all of Devin's family, the Carters, and Gwen and Michele, who were obviously part of this devious plan. "Get ready for the world's best engagement party," Devin crowed, clearly proud of herself.

Sunny looked into Devin's eyes as her arms gently wrapped around her body. "How did you work all of this out?"

"With a lot of help," she admitted, laughing. "When you went to the airport yesterday, Chris and my dad and I got it all organized. But that wasn't the hard part," she said, shaking her head. "Trying to talk your friends into helping out was like pulling teeth. To do the swim, I had to promise Callie we'd name our first child after her—boy or girl."

"Um, Devin," Sunny said, staring hard, "we're not having children."

"I know. But if you accidentally get pregnant, we've got to name the baby after Callie."

Blinking in confusion, Sunny said, "Are you sure your father's a science teacher? I think you missed some basic facts of reproduction."

"I did not," she said, suddenly serious. She took in a breath, her expression so guileless that Sunny was taken aback. "When I was a little girl, my parents told me that when two people love each other very much, they touch each other in a special way. Every once in a while, through nothing but their bodies and their love, they create a baby." Her head tilted a little, and she locked those gorgeous blue eyes on Sunny. "What did I miss?"

"Not a darned thing," Sunny murmured, with her heart thrumming with love for the tender, innocent woman she held in her arms. "You've got every bit of that right. In fact, if we had a little privacy, I'd be touching you in a very special way right this moment."

Devin's grin was so attractive, Sunny longed for a little privacy. Just a few moments alone to show Devin what was in her heart. Then, without stopping to censor herself, she turned her wish into reality. Despite the hum of a motor swiftly approaching, and her closest friends standing just a few feet away, Sunny threw her arms around Devin and gave her a sizzling kiss, locking their lips together until she finally heard the faint sounds of people cheering through her love-filled haze. "And they lived happily ever after," she promised, taking Devin's hand to leap into the arms of their family—a delightful melange of every person who loved them without reservation—and would continue to for all of the days of their lives.

The End

By Susan X Meagher

Novels

Arbor Vitae
All That Matters
Cherry Grove
Girl Meets Girl
The Lies That Bind
The Legacy
Doublecrossed
Smooth Sailing
How To Wrangle a Woman
Almost Heaven
The Crush
The Reunion
Inside Out
Out of Whack
Homecoming
The Right Time
Summer of Love
Chef's Special
Fame
Vacationland

Serial Novel

I Found My Heart In San Francisco

Awakenings: Book One
Beginnings: Book Two
Coalescence: Book Three
Disclosures: Book Four
Entwined: Book Five
Fidelity: Book Six
Getaway: Book Seven
Honesty: Book Eight
Intentions: Book Nine
Journeys: Book Ten
Karma: Book Eleven
Lifeline: Book Twelve
Monogamy: Book Thirteen
Nurture: Book Fourteen
Osmosis: Book Fifteen
Paradigm: Book Sixteen
Quandary: Book Seventeen
Renewal: Book Eighteen
Synchronicity: Book Nineteen
Trust: Book Twenty
United: Book Twenty-One

Anthologies

Undercover Tales
Outsiders

You can contact Susan at Susan@briskpress.com

Information about all of Susan's books can be found at www.susanxmeagher.com or www.briskpress.com

To receive notification of new titles, send an email to newsletters@briskpress.com

facebook.com/susanxmeagher

twitter.com/susanx